EVERYTHING WENT SILENT.

George's smile froze as his eyes fixed on something over Ellie's shoulder. Puzzled, she started to turn, but an arm looping around her neck stopped her midmotion. Something pressed against her temple, and she could feel the metal, hard and cold, even through her knit hat.

"You move, and she's dead," a voice rasped in her ear.

George's hands raised to shoulder level. His gaze was fixed on the gun, and his expression was so cold that he didn't even look like himself.

"Don't you try anything, either, pretty girl." The man's voice changed when he talked to her, syrupy and sickening. "If you don't make a fuss, then no one gets hurt. And if you do…"

He didn't need to finish the rest.

Published by Sourcebooks Casablanca, an imprint of Sourcebooks, Inc.
P.O. Box 4410, Naperville, Illinois 60567-4410
(630) 961-3900
Fax: (630) 961-2168
www.sourcebooks.com

GONE
TOO DEEP

KATIE
RUGGLE

Published by Sourcebooks Casablanca, an imprint of Sourcebooks, Inc.
P.O. Box 4410, Naperville, Illinois 60567-4410
(630) 961-3900
Fax: (630) 961-2168
www.sourcebooks.com

Printed and bound in the United States of America.
LSC 10 9 8 7 6 5

To the brave and dedicated people who make up the Hartsel Colorado Fire Department. I know I should've dedicated the firefighter book to you, but I had to do the siblings first, or I would've never heard the end of it. Just kidding, sibs (sort of).

Chapter 1

ELLIE ALMOST DIDN'T TAKE THE CALL. IF HER DATE hadn't been so completely, utterly, and excruciatingly boring, she would've let it go to voice mail. But thanks to Dylan's never-ending monologue about his triathlon training, she seized the opportunity to escape when her phone made her tiny purse vibrate under her hand. Ellie didn't care who it was—a reminder from her dentist would have been better than listening to Dylan talk about how brick workouts affected his lower GI tract.

"Please excuse me," she interrupted with an apologetic smile as she pulled the phone from her purse. "I have to take this."

Sliding off her barstool, she booked it as fast as her stilettos would take her toward the ladies' room. On the way, she tapped the screen to accept the call.

"Hello?" She fully expected it to be a telemarketer, since she didn't recognize the number. The seven-one-nine area code covered a big chunk of South-Central Colorado.

"Eleanor?" a male voice asked.

"This is she." Definitely a telemarketer. No one who knew her well called her by her full name. It was worth listening to this guy's sales pitch, though, just to get away from the brain-sucking boredom that was her date.

"Eleanor."

The voice sounded familiar. She frowned, trying to place how she knew the caller as she ducked into the bathroom. It was empty and blessedly quiet compared to the loud music and chatter filling the main part of the club. "Yes?"

"Just…just wanted to say sorry to you, baby."

As recognition hit, Ellie's fingers went numb, and she almost dropped the phone. When she tried to speak, only a faint wheeze emerged from her throat.

"They're coming for me," he continued, his words fast and urgent. "I've managed to get away from them so far, but I wanted… I wanted to tell you, just in case. I'm sorry. Sorry, sorry, sorry."

"Dad?" she finally managed to squeeze out of lungs compressed with shock.

"Yeah, baby girl. It's me. I haven't… I haven't been a good dad. I know that. I know. But I wanted to say I'm sorry. I love you, baby. I've always loved you, but things are just not right…not right in my head. If I could've been a better dad, I would have. I would."

Her knees felt wobbly, and she slid her back down the wall until she was sitting on the floor. "I know, Dad." Her voice shook as badly as her knees. "I know you can't help how you are. I love you, too."

"They're trying to kill me, baby. Trying to keep me quiet. I can't, I can't… *He*'s trying to keep me quiet. I'm going to hide, though. I'll do my best to stay alive. I want… I want to try again with you, try to be better this time. Will you…would that be okay?"

"Yeah, Dad." Tipping her head back against the wall, Ellie closed her eyes. "That would be great."

"Good. Good." His words slowed for just an instant before the anxious patter started again. "I'm going to Grandpa's cabin. I took you there that one summer, do you remember? The cabin? We had fun, didn't we? You had fun?"

"I remember." Her voice broke on the last word. "We did have fun." She'd been ten, and they'd had a great time—at least until Baxter had had an episode and barricaded them both inside the cabin. Getting them out had required the efforts of a SWAT team and several law enforcement agencies. That had been Ellie's last unsupervised visit with her father.

"No one else knows about it. I should be...should stay hidden. They won't find me there. As soon as it's safe, I'll come find you, okay? We'll try again. I'll be a better dad this time. I promise. Promise, promise."

The alarm bells going off in her head finally penetrated her shock and sadness, and she sat up straight. "I believe you, Dad. Why don't you come to me right away? You don't need to go to the cabin." The thought of her mentally ill and obviously unmedicated father wandering alone in the wilderness was terrifying. "I can pick you up. Where are you?"

"At Gray Goose's house. They killed him, baby girl. Chopped off his head and dumped him in the reservoir. They'll kill me, too, if I don't hide. Need to hide. Can't die, can't die. If I die, I'll never get to try again with you, baby, and I know I can do better. I'll do better."

"I know you will, Dad, but you don't have to hide. I'll come get you. I'll keep you safe, okay? They won't be able to get you if you're with me. What's the address?"

"No, no, no. Don't come to Simpson, baby. They can't get you. Not you, not you. Stay away from them. They'll kill you, too. Not you, not my baby girl." He grew more and more agitated with each word.

"Dad, it's okay. They won't get me." The monsters in Baxter's head only tormented him. "I'm safe. I need to get you safe, too."

"I'm going to the cabin. I'll hide there. You stay away. You stay away, baby. You need to stay far away."

"Dad…" Her phone gave the double beep of a lost signal. "Dad!"

She fumbled to call the number, but it immediately went to an automated message telling her that the voice mail was full. A sob caught her by surprise, and she pressed a hand over her mouth as if to physically hold it back.

The restroom door swung open, and a pair of laughing women walked inside. When they saw her, their smiles immediately died.

"Are you okay?" one of them asked.

Ellie suddenly realized how she must look, makeup smeared, sitting on the bathroom floor in a dress that definitely wasn't designed for that. Taking a shaky breath, she tried to force a reassuring smile.

"Yes, thank you." Ellie climbed awkwardly to her feet, flattening her hands against the wall when her legs shook, threatening to send her back to the floor. "I just got some bad news. A family issue."

"Oh, I'm sorry." Both women looked at her sympathetically. Now that she was on her feet, they must've decided she wasn't in need of their assistance, because they headed for the stalls. Ellie took tentative steps to one of the sinks. Her face looked pale, her skin undershot with green, and her hazel eyes were huge. She did a cursory job fixing her makeup, took several deep breaths that weren't any less shaky than the first one, and left the restroom.

Dylan was waiting where she'd left him. Although it felt like the phone call had taken hours, it had probably only been ten minutes, tops, since her cell had vibrated. She wove her way through the crowd until she was next to him and plucked her sweater off of her stool.

"Dylan," she said, leaning close to his ear so he could hear. He wrapped an arm around her waist, and she couldn't stop herself from flinching. Even shielded by the barrier of her dress, her skin felt oversensitive, as if every nerve were exposed. Ellie resisted the urge to shove away his arm, reminding herself that he was her boss's friend. Later, when her father was safe, she could gently give him the brush-off. "I'm sorry, but I have to go. Family emergency."

"Oh, that's too bad." He knocked back the rest of his drink and stood. "I'll drive you home."

She cringed inwardly. Over the past hour, she'd watched him drink two and a half martinis, and he'd just finished off the third. "Thank you, but I'll catch the L. There's a stop right by my apartment building."

"Sure?" When she nodded, Dylan sat down again. "Okay. It's been fun. I'll call you, and we can do this again sometime." When he leaned in as if to kiss her, Ellie twisted free of his arm. Boss's friend or no, he wasn't getting a kiss. Diplomacy had its limits.

"See you." After giving him a wave and a forced smile a few feet out of groping reach, she hurried toward the exit. Before she'd even left the club, Ellie had forgotten about Dylan. Her mind was filled instead with worry for another man.

The chilly air smacked her in the face as she stepped outside, and she hurried to pull on her long sweater.

The fine, soft knit didn't offer much protection from the cold Lake Michigan wind, but it was slightly better than just the thin material of her dress. Turning right, she skirted the line of people waiting to enter the club. It was still early for a Saturday night, not even eleven, and Chicago's downtown was thick with both pedestrian and vehicle traffic.

Instead of heading toward the nearest train station, Ellie decided to walk home. It was less than a mile northwest to her condo building, and she needed to move, or her anxiety would boil over. Her shoes weren't the most uncomfortable ones she owned, although they were close. She'd been walking in heels for a decade, though, so she'd had years of training in ignoring discomfort.

Ellie realized she was picking at her cuticles and quickly yanked her hands apart. She thought she'd rid herself of that nervous habit, but it apparently took only one phone call from her dad to reduce her to the anxious teenager she'd once been.

Walking wasn't enough. She needed to do something productive, or she was going to run down the street, screaming. Digging her phone out of her purse, she stared at the time on the screen for several seconds before pulling up her contacts and tapping her mom's number.

As she held the cell phone to her ear, she realized her hand was creeping up toward her mouth. Ellie dropped it to her side and made a disgusted sound. The only thing worse than picking at her cuticles was chewing on her hangnails.

"El?" Her mother's voice sounded worried. "What's wrong?"

"Hi, Mom. Sorry I'm calling so late. Did I wake you?"

"It's not quite nine here." Her mom had moved to California a few years before. "I'm not *that* old yet."

Normally, Ellie would have laughed at that, but the tight ball of nerves in her stomach wouldn't allow it. Instead, she stayed silent.

"Did the date with Chelsea's friend not go well?" her mom asked, the sharp edge of worry in her voice fading to general concern.

"No. I mean, it wasn't great, but that's not why I called." Taking a deep breath, she blurted, "Dad's in trouble."

Silence greeted her announcement. As she waited for her mom to speak, Ellie counted her footsteps, heels clicking on the pavement. *One. Two. Three. Four. Five...*

"Honey." There it was—*the tone.* Ellie had forgotten about the way her mom's words came out slow and heavy, thick with a mixture of fatigue and condescension, whenever she talked about her ex-husband. "You can't let him pull you into his drama."

"It's not drama, Mom." Her hand hovered by her mouth again, and she impatiently yanked it away. "He's sick, and he's scared, and I need to go get him."

"He'll just drag you down with him." The *tone* had sharpened with added irritation. "I know you love him, sweetie, but you can't fix him. You can't make him take his meds, and without them, he's not safe to be around."

"He's never hurt me." She closed her eyes for a second, ashamed at the sullen cast to her voice. Why did interacting with her parents reduce her to a thirteen-year-old? "I just want to bring him to a safe place. He's trying to get to Grandpa's cabin."

"Scott's cabin?" Her mom sounded startled. "In Colorado?"

"Yes. The one he took me to when I was ten." When Ellie heard the inhale on the other end of the call, she grimaced. It had been a mistake to bring that up. After their extraction from the cabin, her mother hadn't let Ellie out of her sight for days, and any mention of Baxter had turned Ellie's mom blotchy red with rage.

"What is he doing? That place isn't even accessible by car until June at the earliest. He'll have to hike—no—" Her mom interrupted herself. "I can't do this. *You* can't do this. El, you need to separate yourself from him."

"I can't just leave him," Ellie said softly, stopping at the entrance of her building. Tilting back her head, she stared, unseeing, at the layers of metal balconies above her.

"Yes." Her mother had her stern, you-will-listen-to-me voice going. "You can. You have to. Think of all the times we tried to help him and just got sucked into his mixed-up mess. For your own sanity, you need to stay clear of him."

The balconies grew blurry, and she scrubbed away tears with the hand not holding the phone. "But I haven't. I haven't tried to help him *ever*. He'd visit for an hour, looking so lost and desperate, and I'd be polite to him. When he'd leave, I'd feel relieved. If you'd heard him on the phone… Mom, he's so scared."

"There's no real threat, El. It's in his head."

"But there is a threat!" She brushed at her cheeks, but her tears flowed faster than she could wipe them away. "You said it yourself. He'll have to hike to the cabin. There's no running water, and who knows if Dad will bring food, and he's going to hide there until he feels safe. The monsters are always with him, though, so he'll *never* feel safe."

Her mom sighed loudly. "You can't save him, El."

"Not from his brain." Her breath left her lungs on a hiccup. "But I'm going to find him, and I'm going to take him somewhere where he won't freeze to death hiding from the boogeyman."

"El…"

"I'm sorry, Mom, but I have to do this. If I don't, and something happens to him, I won't be able to live with myself."

"I lived with the man for fifteen years, El. I tried, over and over, to fix him. You're just inviting heartache."

"Better heartache than regret." Ellie took a deep, shuddering breath. "Can you give me directions to Grandpa's cabin?"

"I'm not helping you chase after him, El." The *tone* was back. "I can't stop you, but I'm not going to encourage this."

Ellie was silent as she resisted the urge to whine. "Okay," she finally said. "I'll figure it out. Bye, Mom."

"El…"

Hearing a lecture approaching, Ellie ended the call.

———

That night, she lay in bed and ran the conversation with her father through her mind, over and over. When she'd asked him where he was, he'd said "Gray Goose's house." What did that mean? Was it just nonsensical rambling, and she was being an idiot for taking it literally?

He'd also mentioned "Simpson," telling her not

to come there. That sounded more logical than *Gray Goose*. She reached for her phone and pulled up the Web browser. After entering Simpson, she hesitated, then typed in "Colorado."

When the results appeared, she saw that Simpson, Colorado, was a tiny mountain town in Field County. Her heart jumped in excitement and nervousness as she stared at the small screen. There it was, the starting point for finding her father—the place that would either be the scene of a heartwarming, father-daughter reunion...or a grim tragedy.

—∽∽∽—

"You're going to do *what*?" Chelsea stared at Ellie, her mouth open. Even with her current shocked expression, Ellie's redheaded boss was beautiful—tall, slender, and perfectly polished.

"I'm going to Colorado to find my dad." Ellie focused on keeping the box-cutter blade straight, slicing a perfectly even line across the packing tape. "Since I'm off tomorrow and Tuesday, I shouldn't have to take any vacation time."

"But..." Chelsea's mouth closed with a click of teeth. "Isn't your dad, well, crazy?" She hissed the last word in a loud whisper, even though no one else was in the store with them.

"That's why I need to get him," Ellie explained, pushing back the instinctive urge to defend her father. "He's too...vulnerable to be wandering around in the middle of nowhere. I'm going to bring him back here and hopefully talk him into staying at a mental health facility in Chicago until he's back on his meds and stabilized." Saying it out loud made Ellie realize how many "ifs" were in her plan—if she found him, if she could convince him to return with her, if he'd be willing to get treatment… It was a definite long shot, this plan of hers.

"Wow." Chelsea leaned against the jewelry display case as Ellie pulled out a stack of cashmere scarves. "That's intense. I call my dad crazy, but that's just when he wears two different-colored socks, not when he runs around in the mountains, thinking the aliens want to suck out his brain or something." Reaching over to the stack of scarves, Chelsea stroked the top one. "These are gorge."

"Yes." Although her eyes were on the newly arrived merchandise, her thoughts were still on the town of Simpson.

"Hey!" Chelsea's hand left the scarf to slap Ellie on the shoulder. "You never told me how your date with Dylan went! Spill, chicklet! How was it?"

"Uh…" *Horribly boring*. "Short. My dad called early into it, so we barely got past introductions."

"Well, short or not, he liked you."

Ellie gave Chelsea a confused look. "How do you know?"

"He texted me when you were in the bathroom or something." Chelsea pulled her cell out of her pocket and tapped at the screen. "Here." She held up the phone so Ellie could read the text.

> UR frnd is HOT. Lks like chick usd 2 B on Vamp Diaries.

Her nose wrinkled involuntarily.

"What?" Chelsea demanded, turning the phone so she could read the text. "It's sweet. He thinks you look like Nina Dobrev."

"He used text-speak. And he spelled 'Diaries' wrong—unless there's a new show about bloodsucking cows that I haven't seen yet. And I look nothing like Nina Dobrev."

"Don't be such a snob." After tucking her phone back in her pocket, Chelsea put her hands on her hips. "Dylan's awesome, has a good job *and* a great body. If I hadn't stuck him in the friend zone, like, a year ago, I'd so be all over that. And you have Nina Dobrev's hair."

"It's just…" Ellie tried to smooth out her scrunched face. "He talks about his triathlon training a *lot*."

"So? That's what he's interested in."

Chelsea's tone had sharpened, and Ellie suppressed a wince. She wasn't handling the conversation well. "I know." She tried to make her voice placating. "He seems like a great guy. I was just distracted by that call from my dad."

After a long look, Chelsea's glare softened slightly. "That was probably it. Because Dylan's amazing. If you were focused on him, you'd see that."

"Sure." Normally, Chelsea was a fun boss and room-mate, but she had definite opinions and got a little contrary if she didn't get her way. Occasionally, she required careful handling. Today, with the whole Baxter situation hanging over her head, Ellie was fumbling. A subject change was in order. "You're right about these scarves—they're beautiful. How much do you want to charge for them?"

Chelsea switched topics willingly enough, but Ellie

couldn't keep her mind from wandering to her upcoming rescue mission. She'd mapped the route from her condo to Simpson, and it was just over a thousand miles. If she drove, it would take sixteen hours—without breaks. She definitely needed breaks. As much as she hated to spend some of her savings on a plane ticket and rental car, driving all that way just seemed crazy. Besides, didn't everyone in Colorado need to drive Jeeps and Hummers to navigate the mountain roads? Her beloved, middle-aged Prius probably wouldn't cut it.

"El!" Chelsea's sharp tone cut through her tumbling thoughts. "Are you listening?"

"Of course I'm listening, and you're absolutely right, Chels," Ellie soothed with the ease of long practice, her mind still running over travel plans.

Chelsea's irritated frown smoothed into a smile. "So you think that's a good idea?"

"It's brilliant." Ellie had no idea what the other woman was proposing, and honestly, she didn't really care. Her father was lost, and Ellie was going to find him—no matter what it took.

———

Squinting against the glare of the sun reflecting off snow, Ellie fumbled for her sunglasses. In Denver, the tulips and daffodils had poked their heads out of the ground already, and the day's temperature was supposed to hit seventy degrees. Who knew the mountains still had snow?

Then again, the peaks were white, which could've been a clue. Plus, her mom had said the cabin wasn't accessible by car until June. Ellie slowed her rental car as she approached a curve at the base of the pass where a flashing sign warned of possible ice on the road. It felt as if she'd reversed time two months during the three-hour drive from Denver. Maybe she should've splurged and rented an SUV at the Denver Airport rather than the more economical compact.

She sped up again as the road straightened. Although she'd been tempted to head to Simpson as soon as her shift at the boutique had ended the evening before, Ellie had gritted her teeth and bought a plane ticket—at a price that made her wince—for a flight leaving early the following morning. After being on the road for close to three hours, she was desperate to stop. It was already past noon, though, and she had only another day and a half to find her father and return them both to Chicago. Besides, there wasn't anywhere to stop. The high plains stretched in waves of white in all directions, the barren landscape unbroken until it bumped up against the surrounding mountains. Ellie carefully kept her gaze on the road so the emptiness, the feeling that she was the only person alive in this achingly lonely place, wouldn't reduce her to a useless, terrified heap.

Steering around another looping turn, she saw signs of civilization just as her GPS announced that she'd arrived at her destination. She slowed as she started passing structures—a feed store, a gas station, a ratty-looking motel—and then she abruptly turned the rental into the parking lot of a small building. A large sign above it introduced it as The Coffee Spot.

Her body craved a shot of caffeine almost as much as it desired a restroom, and this place would most likely offer both. She parked the car between two pickup trucks. As she got out of her rental, she eyed the vehicles that bracketed her. They loomed over her, making her car look miniature.

The air was thin and cold, despite the sun. Shivering, she wrapped the open sides of her cardigan around her. The single-button style was cute, but she would have appreciated several more buttons at the moment.

She closed and locked her car, then took a step toward the shop. Without warning, her heeled ankle booties slid out from under her, flying up in the air and sending her crashing onto her butt. The blow jarred her tailbone painfully, and she took a moment to shake off the shock of the fall before taking inventory. Except for her throbbing coccyx, all her other body parts seemed to be unharmed. She shifted to her hands and knees on the slick, packed snow.

An enormous hand appeared in front of her face. Startled, she glanced up at the person connected to the offered hand, first taking in his booted feet and working her way up his legs and torso before finally landing on his bearded face. He wasn't a man; he was a mountain.

The mountain was frowning, and Ellie realized she was rudely staring at her would-be helper. "Thank you," she rushed out, grabbing his gloved hand. As her fingers curled around his, she took in how small her hand looked in comparison to his oversized mitt. It reminded her of how her car appeared next to the pickups.

He pulled, easily lifting her to a standing position, and she scrambled to get her feet underneath her. The icy footing was unforgiving, and her free arm swung wildly until she latched on to the stranger's other hand. When she finally got her balance, she still clung to him, not wanting to let go of her anchor and start flailing again.

After several seconds passed, though, it started to feel a little awkward. "Sorry," she said, reluctantly loosening her grip. "And thank you. I'd be flat on my back again if it weren't for your help."

He didn't release her now-limp hands. Ellie looked from his frowning face to her captured fingers and back again.

"Uh...I think I'm okay now. You can probably let me go."

Apparently, the mountain didn't agree. Still gripping her hands, he dropped his frowning gaze to her booties.

"I know." She grimaced, interpreting his look as silent criticism of her footwear. "These were the closest thing I had to winter boots, though."

His hands finally dropped hers, and Ellie pasted on a polite smile, ready to give the giant a final thank-you and very slowly shuffle her way to the coffee shop door. Before she could open her mouth, though, his hands latched around her waist, and he lifted her as if she were a doll.

Her thank-you turned into an indrawn shriek. "What are you...? Put me down!"

Ignoring her order, he took several sure-footed strides toward the entrance of the shop and set her on the mat in front of the door. Then, without a word, he turned and walked to one of the trucks.

Openmouthed, Ellie watched as he got into the driver's seat and drove out of the lot, not even giving her another glance. When the truck disappeared, she blinked and turned toward the door. A small group of people was crowded around the glass door and window, staring at her. Startled, Ellie took a step back, and everyone inside hurried to turn away from her.

Ellie waited another few seconds as the people inside the shop pretended like they hadn't been watching the whole time she'd been carried to the door by a mountain.

"This is a weird town," she muttered, and pulled open the door.

Chapter 2

THE BLOND BARISTA LOOKED A LITTLE FLUSHED. ELLIE wasn't sure if that was from sprinting from her spot at the window to her current position behind the counter, or if it was embarrassment at being caught watching Ellie's fall and subsequent mountain transport.

"Hi." The barista's smile was friendly and completely guilt-free. "What can I get you?"

"A large latte, please," Ellie requested. She could feel the interest of the other patrons pressing in on her, and her cheeks reddened as she imagined how silly she must have looked—first sprawled across the parking lot and then hanging from the bearded man's hands with her booties dangling a foot off the ground. "Do you have a restroom?"

The barista pointed toward the bathroom door. "Right there."

With a tight smile, Ellie hurried toward it, locking herself into the tiny room with a relieved sigh. She was glad to escape the amused and curious eyes. Once she was done, she washed her hands for a long time, until she couldn't continue to delay returning to the main part of the shop. If she hid in the restroom any longer, someone was sure to come in and check on her, and that was just asking for further humiliation.

Her latte was waiting on the counter for her when she finally emerged. Ignoring the prickle on the back of her neck, telling her that everyone in the shop had refocused their gazes on her, she stood stiffly at the counter as the barista rang her up.

"So," the blond said quietly, leaning in toward Ellie, "did George actually talk to you? Because I've never gotten more than a grunt out of him."

"George?" Ellie repeated in confusion, handing the woman a twenty.

"George Holloway," the barista said, as if that clarified anything. "The man who gave you a literal lift to the door."

"Oh." Her cheeks warmed again as she accepted her change. "No. He didn't say anything, just glared at my booties like he was mad at them."

The blond woman laughed, leaning forward so she could see over the counter. Ellie took a big step back so the barista could see the ankle boots under discussion. "I don't know how he could be mad at them," she said once she'd gotten a good look. "Those are adorable. Obviously, George is not a fashionista."

Ellie had been taking a sip of her latte when she started to laugh, and she pressed the fingers of her free hand to her mouth so she didn't spew coffee everywhere. "Obviously," she echoed once she'd safely swallowed.

"I'm Lou Sparks," the barista said. "Louise, really, but please don't call me that. I always feel like I'm in trouble when I hear my full name."

"Ellie Price. And I'm the same way about my name. It's actually Eleanor, but no one calls me that." Except for her estranged father. Her mouth turned down at the memory of his panicked call.

"Nice to meet you." Lou held out a hand, and Ellie shook it. "Sorry about watching you and George. Our entertainment is the do-it-yourself variety. Some towns have film festivals, but Simpson has gossip."

"Oh." As Ellie was still trying to figure out how to respond to that, Lou's gaze shifted over Ellie's shoulder.

"Good timing." Reaching under the counter, Lou pulled out a large envelope. "George just dropped off his report on that missing-hikers call."

"Thanks, Lou." A male hand reached to accept the envelope, and Ellie shifted to the side, out of the stranger's way, turning as she did so. The man wasn't very tall, but he had a wrestler's build and a sharply defined face. After giving a Lou a smile of thanks, his gaze moved to Ellie, and his grin widened. "And who is this?" His eyes swept over her from face to feet, lingering just a little too long on her breasts. She fought the urge to cross her arms.

"This is Ellie." Lou introduced her as if the women had been childhood friends rather than having just met. "Ellie, this is Joseph Acconcio. He heads up the Field County Search and Rescue."

"Ellie." He shook her hand and then held it, not letting go even when she tried to discreetly tug free. If anything, his grip tightened. "Where are you visiting from?"

She knew better than to ask how he knew she wasn't local. In a town that tiny, everyone had to know everyone else. Plus, a quick glance around the shop showed customers dressed for warmth rather than fashion. She saw more than one Elmer Fudd earflap hat. "Chicago."

His eyes did another quick up and down of her body

before returning to meet hers. All of her internal creep radars were blaring, and she futilely tried to extract her fingers again. "Well, enjoy your stay." He squeezed her hand and then—*finally*—released it reluctantly. "Thanks for being the go-between, Lou." Joseph held up the envelope. "Whenever I nag Holloway about turning in his incident reports, he acts like I asked for one of his kidneys."

"No problem." Lou waved off his thanks. "He never comes in here otherwise, and I like to see if I can get him to talk."

"Any success?" Joseph asked with real interest.

"Nope. Not yet, but I'm determined."

He laughed. "If anyone can do it, you can. I've heard him use actual words when he's been on a call, but just when he's had to, in order to, you know, prevent death or something."

"That's good, at least."

"Well, thanks again, Lou." He turned to Ellie and gave her a smile that made her have to resist the urge to take another backward step away from him. "Nice to meet you, Ellie."

"You too," she lied.

"We'll have to get together while you're here."

Before Ellie could politely decline, Lou snorted and said jokingly, "You're a little late to the Ellie ball-game, Joseph. George Holloway has already staked his claim on the new girl, and there's no way any woman is going to turn down Mr. Silent-but-Hot. I mean, a guy with all those muscles who never contradicts you? Who could resist?"

Although Joseph held on to his smile, it went

brittle around the edges. "I've never been afraid of a little competition."

With a final stiff wave, he left the coffee shop. Lou turned to Ellie with a grin.

"He liked you."

Ellie shrugged uncomfortably. Even if Joseph hadn't set off all her internal alarms, she still wouldn't have been interested. She didn't have time for flirtations. "I'm actually here to see my dad. His name's Baxter Price. You don't happen to know him, do you?"

Lou's eyes went huge. "Baxter Price? Your dad is Baxter Price? Oh my gosh, he's on the whiteboard!"

"What?" The other woman's urgent tone made Ellie's heart pound against her ribs. "What does that mean? What whiteboard?"

"It's—" Breaking off, Lou glanced around at the crowded shop. No one was even pretending they weren't listening anymore. "Listen, I have to work until about seven thirty tonight, but would you want to grab some dinner and talk about this? Callum—the man who puts up with me—makes a mean Crock-Pot stew."

"Um...I don't know." It seemed odd to accept a dinner invitation from a woman she'd just met, but Ellie was dying to know what had caused Lou's reaction to her father's name. "My dad mentioned heading to a cabin, and I was hoping to go there this afternoon."

"A cabin?" Lou tilted her head to the side. "Where?"

Making a face, Ellie lifted one shoulder in a half shrug. "I'm not sure. I was there when I was ten, but the directions have gotten kind of fuzzy over the years."

"Do you know who owns it?" When Ellie nodded, Lou grabbed a paper napkin and a pen. "Easy-peasy, then. Just head to the County Assessor's Office, and you can get the coordinates." Passing her the napkin after sketching what looked like a rough map on it, Lou leaned in close and lowered her voice. "Come back here when you're done. Hopefully the nosy bastards will have cleared out of this place by then so we can talk."

Lou's rough map proved to be surprisingly accurate, and the women at the assessor's office were helpful and friendly. Ellie returned to The Coffee Spot less than an hour after she'd left it.

As Lou had predicted, the place was empty except for Lou and a stern-looking man in a baseball hat sitting on one of the counter stools. When Ellie spotted him, she hesitated just inside the door. The men in Simpson seemed to come in only one size—extra-large. That, plus their apparent aversion to smiling, made them a little intimidating. Ellie was more used to the guys she knew in Chicago, who seemed smaller and gentler and much less scary than these mountain men.

"Ellie!" Lou waved her toward the counter. "Awesome. This is Callum. I hope you don't mind, but I called him and told him Baxter Price's daughter was here. He has full access to the Whiteboard of Knowledge and Wild Theories, so you can talk freely in front of him."

"Uh…" Ellie had taken a step forward, but Lou's last sentence made her stop again. "I don't know what that means."

"You get used to it." A corner of Callum's mouth tucked in like he was holding back a smile, and it softened his expression slightly.

Warily, Ellie approached the counter and slid onto a stool a few down from where Callum was sitting.

"We've been trying and trying to talk to Baxter," Lou said, wiping down the counters. "He's proved to be very elusive, though. I don't think he trusts us."

"He's…" It felt strange to be talking to two strangers about her father's issues, but it sounded like they'd had contact with him, so they were her best lead at the moment. "He doesn't trust anyone, really. He's mentally ill. I haven't ever talked to any of his doctors, since I was a teenager the last time he was on meds, but I'm pretty sure he's schizophrenic. He hears voices, thinks people are after him, and has a hard time keeping his thoughts straight. He called me two nights ago, not making much sense, talking about some guys wanting to kill him and needing to hide at my grandpa's cabin until it was safe." She paused, belatedly considering Lou's last comment. "Why did you want to see him?"

Lou stopped wiping and twisted the dishcloth into a tight spiral. "That's a long and complicated story. Do you want to hear the whole thing?"

"Does it concern my father?"

"Yes."

"Then yes."

"Okay." Blowing out a hard breath, Lou rinsed the tortured dishcloth in the sink. "In early March, a body was discovered in a nearby reservoir." Callum cleared his throat mildly, and Lou gave him a look. "Fine. *I* discovered the body. We were doing dive-team training in Mission Reservoir, and I kicked him."

Ellie blinked at her.

"By accident!" Lou huffed. "I'm not a corpse abuser or anything. But it did make me feel responsible for this poor, headless John Doe."

"Headless?" Ellie asked faintly. That sounded familiar. Her father had mentioned someone's head being chopped off.

Lou winced, apparently misreading Ellie's startled reaction as general horror. "Yes. And handless. It made identification a little tricky."

"Uh…okay." Ellie's mind still spun as she tried to process this new information, wishing she hadn't dismissed most of what her dad had told her as senseless rambling. It sounded as if at least a small part of what he'd said had been based in reality.

"Since the sheriff's department wasn't making much headway identifying this guy, I took it upon myself to do some sleuthing. Callum agreed to be my sidekick." He choked on his coffee. Ellie glanced at him in concern, but Lou ignored his coughs and sputters. "When we found out that our headless dead guy was diabetic and missing some toes, we called around to some amputee and diabetes support groups in the area. We didn't find our guy, but one of the group leaders did tell me that someone else was investigating, and that his name was Baxter."

"My dad was looking into a murder?" That was unexpected. Ellie was so used to thinking that Baxter couldn't even manage his own life that the idea of him actively involving himself in someone else's was startling. She filed the information away so she could decide later whether that was encouraging or not.

"Apparently. He'd given the victim's name to the group leader, too. It was Willard. We found out later that our guy's full name was Willard Gray."

Both Lou and Callum looked at Ellie expectantly, but she shook her head. "The name doesn't ring a bell, but I haven't had much contact with Baxter since I was ten and he…um, since I was ten."

Although she looked slightly disappointed, Lou seemed to accept that. "We found out that Willard's friend, Baxter Price, had been living at Willard's house for a few weeks as he did his own investigating into his friend's disappearance. I guess they were army buddies?"

Again, Ellie turned away their expectant looks with a shrug. "Sorry, but Dad never talked about anyone named Willard. I knew my father was in the army, but it wasn't something he ever discussed with me."

"We've tried to talk to Baxter, but he keeps dodging us." Lou looked at her with hopeful eyes. "Do you think you could get him to meet with us? We want the same thing—to figure out who killed Willard Gray. It would be really helpful to combine information."

With a doubtful frown, Ellie said, "I'm not sure how much help he'd be. On the phone the other night, he sounded really disconnected with reality. He might…" Her words trailed away as a part of their conversation rang in her head. "Wait…he said he was at Gray Goose's house. Do you think that's Willard's nickname?"

"That's likely," Callum said, startling Ellie. He'd

been so quiet, she'd focused on Lou, almost forgetting that he was there.

"Is he still there?" Her heart lifted with hope. That would be so much easier than trying to run Baxter down at an unfamiliar cabin in the middle of nowhere.

"Last I heard." Lou gave Callum a questioning look, and he nodded. "Want me to draw another map?"

"No need." Callum stood. "I'll go with you. You shouldn't go there by yourself."

"He won't hurt me," Ellie protested, although a tiny part of her was relieved not to have to deal with her mentally ill father alone.

Callum didn't answer. He just gestured toward the door. Giving in easily, Ellie slid off her stool and headed toward the exit. She turned her head just in time to see Callum tugging Lou's hand so she would lean over the counter. Meeting her halfway, he gave her a short kiss that was hot enough to make the back of Ellie's neck prickle. She turned away abruptly, not wanting to be caught gawking. As she stared unseeing at one of the empty tables, she thought back to her failed date two nights earlier, with the bland and boring Dylan. That abbreviated kiss between Callum and Lou was in a whole other universe than that date.

Leaning around her, Callum pushed open the door so Ellie could walk through first.

"Bye," Lou called, and Ellie turned to give her a wave and a smile. "Tell me every single thing you discover, so I can add it to the whiteboard. I'll just be here, bored, while you two have an adventure, but that's okay. One of us has to work and bring home the bacon."

"Sparks," Callum said, his voice growly but holding an undertone of amusement.

Lou grinned at him. "Bye, sweet pea."

He gave her a stern look that softened into a smile before leaving the coffee shop.

"What's the deal with the whiteboard?" Ellie asked almost absently, distracted by the effort of walking without falling on her hind end again. To her relief, Callum seemed to notice her difficulty and took her arm. Her worry about landing on her sore tailbone overpowered any nervousness from being so close to a large, stern, and intimidating stranger.

"Lou set up a murder board when this whole thing started," he said, catching her as her feet slipped out from under her. He easily supported her weight as she scrambled to regain her footing.

"A murder board? Like on a cop show?" She bit back a curse as her legs threatened to do the splits before Callum pulled her upright again.

"Yep." When they got to the passenger side of a pickup, he opened the door and pretty much lifted her into the seat.

She opened her mouth to respond, but he closed the door before she could say anything. As soon as he climbed into the driver's seat, she asked, "And Baxter is on there?"

"Yep."

"He mentioned someone being killed." Guilt tugged at her belly. "I just thought it was one of his delusions."

"Understandable," Callum said, turning onto the main road. "You didn't know about Gray."

"Yeah. I'm just so quick to dismiss everything he

says, though." She swallowed, trying to ease the tightness in her throat.

"I don't know." Callum made another turn and slowed as he bumped over a pothole. "You came here."

"Not because I believed him. Just because I didn't want him wandering around the wilderness in his confused state."

"Doesn't matter." Shrugging, Callum maneuvered around a hole in the asphalt that was more of a crater than a pothole. "You showed up. That's the important part."

It still didn't feel right, but Ellie let it drop. They rode in silence for the rest of the ten-minute drive, until they entered a development marked with a large, engraved boulder, welcoming them to Esko Hills.

"I wasn't expecting anything quite so fancy," Ellie said, eyeing the large, elaborate houses.

"Wait," Callum grunted. Although Ellie looked at him curiously, he didn't say anything more.

Sure enough, once they crossed a gravel road at the edge of the development, a rutted driveway led to a sagging, dilapidated cabin crouched in a circle of pine trees.

"He's staying here?" Ellie asked doubtfully. The place looked like it had been abandoned for years. Callum turned the truck so it faced away from the house and then parked.

Peering at the cabin, she swallowed down bile as her stomach churned. She tried to remind herself that the ominous-looking shack held only her sweet, confused father, but that didn't loosen the clamp that was tightening around her insides. Ellie realized she was nibbling on a hangnail and yanked her hand away from her mouth. Giving herself a mental scolding not to be a chicken, she shoved her door open, almost hitting Callum in the face. He'd apparently circled the truck while she'd been cowering in her seat.

"Sorry," she said, and he waved off her apology. She appreciated having his help to get out of the truck, especially when she sank up to her shins in snow. He took her arm again as they made their way toward the sloping porch. Ice crystals found their way into the tops of her booties, making her shiver.

When they reached the door, Callum pounded his fist against it in an aggressive knock before Ellie could stop him. She gave him an exasperated look, and he raised his eyebrows.

"What?" he asked.

Shaking her head, she turned back to the closed door. "Dad?" she called, hoping the military-like knock hadn't scared him out the back door. "It's me, Ellie. Are you in there?"

There was no answer. Pressing her ear against the closed door, she didn't hear anything. Then the door swung open, and she almost fell. Callum grabbed her arm before she toppled into the cabin.

"Thanks," she said, taking a step inside.

"Wait." Tugging her back onto the porch, he moved in front of her. "Stay here."

After he stepped through the doorway, she leaned forward so she could see inside. The interior wasn't any more impressive than the exterior—just a one-room cabin with a basic kitchen along one wall and a couch along the other. A cot-like bed covered with an army blanket stood in the back corner, next to an ancient dresser. A wood stove sat in the middle of the room.

"He's not here."

"Things can never be easy, can they?" she asked, mostly to herself, although Callum gave her a half smile.

"Never."

As Ellie took another step into the cabin, Callum started pulling open the dresser drawers. Moving to the kitchen area, she opened the single cupboard. "Empty."

"These, too." Callum closed the drawers and turned to scan the cabin. "I think he's gone."

She'd pretty much figured that out as soon as she'd seen the empty structure, so she was braced for his words. "He's headed to Grandpa's cabin, then."

"You know where that is?"

Ellie patted her purse. "I just got the coordinates from the assessor's office."

"Lou has her laptop at the shop. We'll map it for you." Callum moved toward the door, but Ellie stopped him with a hand on his arm.

"Thank you." She hadn't expected to find so much help in a town of strangers.

He gave her a brisk nod. "Come on. Let's find that cabin."

A blond deputy sheriff was talking with Lou when Ellie and Callum entered the coffee shop. Even though the cop looked friendly and relaxed, Ellie felt her stomach jump with automatic nerves when she noticed his uniform.

"Ellie!" Lou called across the otherwise empty shop. "Chris saw your dad yesterday morning!"

Her eyes widening, Ellie hurried over to the counter. "You saw him? Where?"

Lifting his hands in a calming gesture, the cop gave her a smile, although his gaze stayed watchful. "I'm Deputy Chris Jennings. You're Baxter Price's daughter?"

"Yes. I'm Ellie—Eleanor—Price. Is he okay?"

"Your dad looked fine, although I wasn't able to talk to him," he said. "I was in the middle of a traffic stop on Burnt Canyon Road by the Blue Hook trailhead. When I saw Baxter, I called to him, but he ran into the trees. By the time I'd returned the driver's ID and headed after him, your dad was out of sight."

Ellie was equal parts relieved that her dad had been seen alive just a day earlier and worried. "He looked okay, though?"

"Yeah." Chris gave her another reassuring smile. "A little spooked, but that was my fault. I wasn't expecting to see him, so I acted too authoritatively. I know he has trust issues, especially with law-enforcement types." He gestured toward his badge. "He was carrying a good-sized pack. Where's he headed, do you know?"

Ellie opened her mouth but then paused and closed it again. If she told the deputy where her father was going, would the entire sheriff's department descend on the cabin, driving Baxter into another episode? As her silence lengthened, Chris's eyebrows twisted into a quizzical expression. Before she could decide what—if anything—to say, she was saved by his radio.

As the dispatcher rattled off information about a traffic accident, Chris handed a card to Ellie and hurried toward the door. "Call me if you see him," he said, making the request sound like a friendly, yet firm, order.

"We need to talk to your dad as soon as possible. His safety depends on it."

Ellie was glad the deputy left before waiting for her to answer, since she couldn't agree to make that call. If she found Baxter, she wouldn't be giving a cop her dad's location, no matter how cute and charming the deputy seemed. "Well?" Lou demanded, breaking into Ellie's thoughts. "Did you find anything at the cabin?"

A dart of remembered disappointment pricked Ellie. "No."

"Pull out your laptop, Sparks," Callum ordered. When Lou gave him a warning look, his voice softened. "Please."

"Fine," Lou agreed, retrieving her laptop from under the desk, "but not because you demanded it, Mr. Bossy-Pants. I'm only doing this to help Ellie—and because I'm dying of curiosity."

As she opened her laptop and turned it so the screen faced Callum, he smiled at Lou. It changed his entire expression from severe austerity to warm humor, and Ellie had a moment of longing—not for Callum, but to have someone look at her with such focus and devotion.

"Thank you," he said, his dry tone not matching the softness in his eyes.

His smile didn't last long. Soon, Callum was frowning at the computer screen. "That forest service road isn't maintained."

The map displayed on the laptop made Ellie feel stupid. She could read a normal map, with roads and mile markers and pins at her destination, but this was a confusing mess of shading and dotted lines. "What does that mean?"

"It's not plowed," Lou offered helpfully. "Which means you're not going to be able to access it in a vehicle."

"The closest you'll get is the end of County Road 88." Callum pointed at a spot on the map and then trailed his finger along one of the dotted lines until he reached the spot where the cabin supposedly was. "Then you'll need to go on foot to the cabin."

"That doesn't look too far." Ellie examined the few inches he'd just indicated. "Where did the deputy say he saw my dad go into the forest?"

"Burnt Canyon Road." His finger moved to a solid line that looked very close to the county road she would need to take. Her breath caught as hope surged through her. Her dad had to be headed for the cabin. Even though she'd been pretty certain before, it was good to get confirmation that this wouldn't be a wild-goose chase. If she hurried, he wouldn't be too far ahead.

"How long do you think the hiking part will take?"

"A couple of days." Callum frowned and eyed Ellie's booties with the same expression George had worn in the parking lot. "Maybe three."

"Three *days*?" She'd expected hours. Blowing out a sigh, she eyed the map, which suddenly seemed to be mocking her. "I guess I'll have to call my boss and ask for some time off."

"You're not still thinking about going, are you?" Lou asked, her face serious for once. "That might be a tiny bit insane." Although Callum didn't actually say it out loud, his expression made it obvious that he thought Ellie hiking to the cabin was a lot more than a "tiny bit" insane.

"I have to go," she said, trying to hide the way her stomach rolled in protest at the idea. Hiking through the snow for *days*? How was she going to find the cabin when she couldn't even read the stupid map? "My dad's out there. I don't have a choice."

His scowl deepening, Callum said, "You can't go by yourself. You do that, and we might as well call up search and rescue now, because they'll be pulling your body out of the snow for sure."

Lou grinned. "I know one search and rescue member who wouldn't mind pulling you out of the snow." Her grin faded, and a horrified expression took its place. "Not when you're dead, though. That just went to a really weird place."

Despite feeling overwhelmed and discouraged, Ellie gave a snort of laughter. "George?"

"Actually, I was just joking about Joseph, but George isn't a bad idea. In fact, he'd be ideal." Lou looked over at Callum. "You know him better. What do you think?"

His face thoughtful, Callum considered it and finally gave a slow nod. "Holloway's the best search and rescue's got. He knows these mountains backward and forward. I seriously doubt he'd be willing to play tour guide, though."

"I can pay him," Ellie blurted. It felt like she kept getting closer to finding Baxter and then having him snatched away from her. It would be worth the loss of her savings to know her father was somewhere safe. "And I'll get better boots."

With a sympathetic smile, Lou suggested, "Even if you're just staying in Simpson while George does his mountain-man thing, you'll need more practical boots. The Screaming Moose should be able to set you up with those, and warmer clothes, too."

"That won't work—for George to go alone, I mean."

Ellie was swamped with a feeling of hopelessness, and she had to fight back the urge to burst into tears. "He's suspicious of *everyone*. If I'm not there, he'll just hide from George—or worse." Memories of being barricaded inside that cabin flooded her mind.

Her frustration intensified when Lou and Callum exchanged a look. "George doesn't say a word to *us*," Lou explained gently. "And he knows us. There's no way he'll even talk to you about this, much less agree to go on an outdoor adventure with you."

"What about another search and rescue member?" Ellie pushed, trying to keep her voice steady. "Surely there's someone else who'd be willing to guide me."

Callum said, "They might be willing, but the mountains are a dangerous place—especially this time of year. Blizzards, wild animals, avalanches, rock slides... not to mention the human dangers. George is the only one I'd trust to get you to the cabin safely."

It was a measure of Ellie's desperation that she ignored the internal creep alarm that had sounded earlier and blurted, "How about Joseph? Isn't he the head of search and rescue? Couldn't he be my guide?"

"No," Callum said flatly, the line of his mouth even grimmer than usual.

Lou's eyebrows shot up in surprise as she looked at him. "Why not? Have you heard some juicy story about Joseph that you neglected to share with me, your gossip-loving other half?"

"Nothing specific." Despite his words, his hard expression didn't soften. "A few rumors. Enough to make me think there might be some truth underlying the gossip. Acconcio is not an option."

"Then it has to be George," Ellie said, a little relieved that the Joseph-as-guide option was off the table.

"He'll never agree." Although she looked sympathetic, Lou nodded at Callum's blunt pronouncement.

Ellie pulled her shoulders back and drew her spine straight. As well-meaning and nice as they were, Callum and Lou didn't know her. They didn't realize what she was capable of doing, the lengths she was willing to go to in order to keep her father safe. "I have to at least ask him. Do you have George's phone number?"

"No phone," Callum said.

Ellie stared at him, glanced at an equally stunned-looking Lou, and then repeated, "No...phone?"

"How does he live without a phone?" Lou breathed.

"Um...so how can I get ahold of him?" Ellie asked. "Do you know where he lives?"

Lifting his cap, Callum rubbed his short-cropped hair and then readjusted his hat. "Probably not a good idea to walk up to his place uninvited. Word has it that he has a pretty impressive gun collection." When Ellie just looked at him beseechingly, he huffed out a breath. "SAR has training tonight at seven at Station One. He should be there."

Lou pulled out her cell phone. "I'm not missing this. Jules owes me one, so I'll make her close for me tonight. We'll pick you up at five thirty, so we can go to Levi's for dinner first. Are you staying at the Black Bear Inn?"

"Um...maybe?" She wondered if that was the slightly scary-looking motel she'd passed on the way into town. "Is that the only option?"

"It's pretty much that or your car." Lou grimaced apologetically as she tapped her screen and then raised her phone to her ear.

"The Black Bear Inn it is, then."

—⁓—

As Ellie sat in her car in the parking lot of The Coffee Spot, she decided to call Chelsea and get that unpleasant task out of the way. She would probably not be happy with Ellie asking for a week of vacation time, especially at the last minute.

Chelsea answered with her usual disregard for conventional manners. "OMG, El, Dylan will not shut up about your luscious self, you temptress, you."

It took Ellie a moment to remember Dylan. Their interrupted date seemed such a long time ago. "Uh, that's nice. Anyway, Chels, I need to ask a favor."

"Did you want to borrow my adorable black mini for the next time you go out with Dylan?"

"No."

"How about my supercute red Valentino pumps, with the bows?"

"No."

"Then what about—"

"The favor isn't clothes related," Ellie interrupted before Chelsea went through the entire contents of her extensive closet. "I need some time off. It's going to take longer than I thought to get my dad."

There was a slightly ominous pause. "How long are we talking?"

Ellie winced. "I can't drive to the cabin, because the road doesn't get plowed, so I'll need to hike."

"Hike? Plow?" Chelsea's voice squeaked on the last word. "There's still snow there? Where are you, Alaska?"

"Alaska's probably warmer than it is here. The guy who looked at the map said it would probably take three days."

"Three days?" Chelsea repeated. "So you won't get back until Friday?"

Clearing her throat, Ellie said, "Um, it's three days one way."

Silence fell on the other end of the call. "A week, then?"

Chelsea sounded calmer than Ellie had expected, and she was cautiously relieved. At least there hadn't been any screaming yet. "Yes."

"El, this is sounding pretty dangerous. I mean, hiking for *days*? You should just call the police or the Mounties or whoever carries guns up there in the middle of nowhere. Let them go get your dad and bring him to you."

The memory of the last time they were at the cabin flashed through her mind again. Even though Chelsea couldn't see her, Ellie shook her head hard enough that strands of her dark hair whipped across her cheeks. "That would be bad. He doesn't trust anyone in law enforcement. He doesn't trust anyone, period. Well, except for me." She hoped. "I'll have a guide." She hoped. "I'll be fine." She really, really hoped.

After yet another long pause, Chelsea gave a heavy sigh. "Fine. Go. Leave me here with only Willow and Rylee to help. You *know* Ry doesn't fold anything with sleeves right."

Ignoring Chelsea's long-suffering tone, Ellie grinned. "Thanks, Chels. After this, I promise to never ask for time off again. Well, at least for a few months."

Chelsea snorted. "Well, just don't fall off a cliff or anything. You can't be all bruised and concussed for your next date with Dylan."

After promising to do her very best not to fall off any cliffs, Ellie managed to end the call. Blowing out a relieved breath, she started the rental. It seemed silly to drive, since the Screaming Moose was only a few blocks away from the coffee shop, but the slick lot and her still-throbbing tailbone had Ellie backing out of her parking space.

As she stepped through the door of the Screaming Moose, Ellie instantly relaxed. Although it was more touristy than high fashion, the shop made Ellie nostalgic for when they'd first opened Chelsea's boutique. It even smelled the same, like new clothes with the slightest whiff of perfumed customers. The Screaming Moose, with its mishmash of merchandise crammed into every corner, desperately needed a makeover, but Ellie immediately loved the little shop. The space was designed to resemble the interior of a mountain cabin, and the light wood was both warm and airy. The place, Ellie decided, rotating in a slow circle, had truckloads of potential.

"Hi." The greeting made her jump and turn toward the checkout counter that was tucked in the corner. The woman behind it was in her forties, with black hair pulled back into a twist. "Need some help?"

"Hello." Ellie smiled as the woman pulled off her bejeweled reading glasses and let them dangle on a chain around her neck. "Apparently, I'm ill prepared for walking across the parking lots in this town." She lifted one bootied foot.

"At least you accept responsibility for your choice

of footwear." Although her voice was tart, the woman looked amused as she stood and circled to the front of the counter. "Most visitors wearing heels just threaten to sue."

"Actually," Ellie admitted, "I'll need more than just warm boots. I'm going on a three-day hike, and I didn't even bring a coat." A little embarrassed, she gave her long sweater a tug.

The woman's perfectly arched eyebrows headed toward her hairline, but then she smiled. "My dear, this is going to be fun."

Chapter 3

IT WAS OLD AND ODD, AND THE LOCKS WERE THE manual kind with the room number on the key, but the motel room appeared to be blessedly clean. Ellie breathed a sigh of relief as she tugged her suitcase through the doorway. In her other hand, she clutched an enormous bag with an openmouthed, distressed-looking moose printed on it. Ellie had worn her new, deliciously warm boots out of the store, and walking was much easier without her booties.

The bed looked dangerously inviting after the last two abbreviated nights' sleep, but a glance at her watch told her she needed to hurry. Lou and Callum would be there to pick her up in ten minutes, and she wanted to change into some of her new clothes to prevent George from thinking she was a useless city girl. She frowned as she pulled off her boots, worried about how he'd already probably dismissed her as hopeless, but there was no harm in trying to improve his *second* impression.

After wiggling out of her skinny jeans, sweater, and blouse, she pulled out her new wicking long underwear. George wasn't going to see her underlayers, but having them on made her feel more authentic. Thick, warm socks were next. She put on her fleece pants and top after that, loving the soft, fuzzy fabric. Next, she topped it off with a waterproof jacket and pants.

When she walked to the bathroom to look in the

mirror, the top layer made a *shush*ing sound as it moved. Once she saw her reflection, she made a face. The layers were more bulky than fashionable, and her lack of heels made her look awfully short. Usually, her choice of shoes added four inches or so to her diminutive stature.

She caught a glimpse of her unhappy expression in the mirror and immediately gave herself a mental lecture. This was all to help her dad. Looking good should be so far down on her list of priorities that she shouldn't even be glancing in the mirror. Firming her mouth into a straight line, she turned away, although she couldn't resist tugging her jacket down to smooth the bulging fabric so it didn't give the illusion of a belly lump.

As she left the bathroom, she heard a sound at the door. Ellie took a step toward it, thinking it was Lou and Callum, but then she paused. The person at the door wasn't knocking. Instead, there was the metallic click of the lock releasing.

Her breath caught as she froze, starting at the door until it started to swing inward. The movement jarred her from her paralysis, and she looked around frantically. The motel phone was on the nightstand on the far side of the bed. Her racing brain tried to remember where she'd left her cell phone.

In my purse! Ellie turned toward the table by the entrance where she'd dropped all of her bags—including her cell-phone-holding purse—but then hesitated, not wanting to run closer to the slowly opening door.

Before she could decide whether to dash for her phone or to run back into the bathroom and lock herself inside, the intruder stepped through the doorway.

"Joseph?" Surprised, she paused, thrown off by his smile as he closed the door behind him.

"Hey, Ellie." He held up a motel key. "Hope you don't mind that I let myself in. Marian, the owner here, is a big fan since I rescued her grandson after he wandered away on a Boy Scout outing."

Ellie's gaze darted back and forth between Joseph's grinning face and the key. "She gave you a key to my room?"

"Sure." He leaned casually against the door, blocking her only escape route. "Oh, don't worry. I'm search and rescue—the head of it, actually. You can trust me."

If her stomach hadn't still been churning with fear, Ellie would've laughed at the ridiculousness of hearing this from the man who'd just entered her motel room without permission. "You need to leave."

"C'mon, Ellie. I just want to get to know you. Ten minutes with me, and you'll forget all about Holloway." His expression soured when he mentioned George's name. "Trust me, you want to stay far away from that weirdo. What do women see in him, anyway?"

Her eyes followed the movement as he tucked the key to her room into his coat pocket. "This isn't the way to convince me you're a great guy. Please leave now."

He slowly pushed away from the door, straightening to his full height. "No need to be scared. You're safe with me. I mean, I save people almost every day." His eyes dropped down her body again, and all her inner alarms blared. Whatever game he was playing with George Holloway, somehow she had inadvertently become the prize—and Joseph didn't strike her as a man who liked to lose. She had to get out of here. *Now*.

The exit was blocked, and her cell was right next to Joseph. The landline was on the other side of the room. There was only one option left. Spinning around, she dashed for the bathroom.

"Hey!" Joseph shouted.

She skidded once she hit the slick linoleum. Twisting, she grabbed for the door. Her sweaty fingers slipped across the wood as she slammed it closed. Relief poured through her as she fumbled for the lock. The door was thin, but hopefully it would keep Joseph out until Lou and Callum arrived. The knob was smooth, and Ellie glanced down, her newly raised hope deflating. There was no lock.

Turning, she pressed her back against the door, bracing her legs in front of her. Although she fought to hold it closed, it was no use. Her socked feet slid, refusing to find purchase, and the door opened a few feet, shoving her straining body along with it.

Wedging his compact form between the jamb and the door, Joseph grinned, and Ellie flinched. Despite her urban upbringing, she knew a predator's smile when she saw one.

"That's okay," he said. "I like playing games, too."

"I'm not playing," she panted, breathless with exertion and fear. "I want you to leave!"

Ignoring her protest, he pushed against the door again, managing to widen the opening so he could get all the way into the tiny room. Her heart pounding, Ellie backed up until she bumped into the far wall.

As Joseph stepped closer, she stared at him, trying

to hide her terror. Why hadn't she taken that self-defense class with Chelsea? Ellie had been afraid of looking clueless and weak in front of everyone, but that would've been a thousand times better than being clueless and weak in front of an advancing Joseph.

"You're so pretty." He reached toward her, ignoring her flinch, and caught a strand of dark hair between his fingers. "You're too good for Holloway."

Her breathing was fast and shallow, and her mouth so dry she wasn't sure if she could speak. She had to try, though. She couldn't just stand here like a helpless bird caught in someone's hand.

"Lou's coming here," she forced out. Her voice was almost inaudible, so she took a breath and tried again. "Lou's coming with Callum."

The words acted like a slap, making him jerk his head back and release his grip on her hair.

"They'll be here any minute now." His reaction gave her a tiny bit of confidence, and her voice got louder. "I can't imagine how much it would suck to get on Callum's bad side. It would probably be really painful, don't you think?"

His usual smug grin was gone, replaced by something a lot colder. Ellie hardly had time to be terrified before Joseph smoothed his expression and took a couple of steps back. "Why didn't you tell me you had plans?" he asked. "We can finish this another time."

"We're not finishing this." He'd already left the bathroom before she was done talking.

Ellie stayed pressed against the wall for several shaky breaths before she peeked into the room to make sure he was, indeed, gone. After quickly repacking her things, she jammed her feet in her boots, grabbed her suitcase, purse, and Screaming Moose bags, and rushed to the door.

She paused, scared that Joseph might be right outside, waiting for her. Opening the door just far enough to see that the immediate area was Joseph-free, Ellie slipped outside and hurried to the office. Her suitcase wheels caught on the ruts in the hard-packed snow, forcing her to pick it up and carry it.

No one was at the front desk when she entered. She reached to tap the ring-for-service bell and then hesitated, eyeing the keys hanging on the wall. If the owner had given Joseph her room key once, what would stop her from doing it again if Ellie changed rooms? There was no other motel in Simpson, though, so she was stuck here. Pulling back her hand, she gave a nervous glance around before darting behind the desk and snatching the key with a "3" printed on it.

Her heart thundering in her ears, she grabbed her bags again and headed for the door. She had to force herself not to run. Ellie had never stolen anything in her life. Although she reminded herself that she'd paid for a room, just a *different* room, nerves still made her hands slippery.

She'd barely locked herself into her new room when a knock on the door made her jump. Pressing a hand to her chest, she reached for her phone. Tapping 9-1-1 but not the Send button, she tiptoed toward the door and peered through the peephole.

When she saw Lou standing there, relief made her knees weak, and she canceled the call before hurrying to open the door. Lou did a double take.

"Whoa. You're much shorter than I initially thought. I'm not taller than a lot of people, but you actually make me feel vertically superior."

Although Ellie was still shaky, Lou's easy, joking manner calmed her, allowing her to answer almost lightly. "Heels. Well, a lack thereof. How'd you know what room I was in?" She worried that her key grab hadn't been so stealthy after all.

"We were headed toward where your rental car was parked, but then Eagle-Eye Callum saw you go into this one." Lou eyed her appraisingly, stepping into the motel room so the door could close behind her. "This is much better. You don't look like you're going to slip, fall into a snowbank, and freeze to death now."

The conversation was so normal and practical that it made what had happened with Joseph seem almost unreal. She opened her mouth to blurt out the whole terrifying story, but she changed her mind. At the coffee shop, it had seemed like Lou and Joseph were friends. Lou barely knew her. What if Lou didn't believe her? Would she go back on her promise to take her to talk to George? Panic flashed through her. George was her only option now for finding her dad. She couldn't risk it.

Lou was looking at her quizzically, so Ellie forced a smile. "Good. I was going for that exact look."

"Do you have a hat?"

"Oh!" At the reminder, Ellie hurried to the Screaming Moose bag. "I do. Several, in fact, of varying degrees of warmth." She pulled out a cute beanie, along with a pair of gloves. Tugging on the hat, she turned back to Lou. "What do you think?"

"Perfect." Lou grinned. "Although you might want to lose the price tag."

"Oops." She hurried to her suitcase. As she crouched next to it, digging for her toiletry bag—which held her nail clippers—there was another knock on the door, making Ellie freeze again. Lou looked through the peephole before swinging open the door.

"Did you miss me already?" she asked.

"What's the holdup?" Callum sounded grumpy. Relieved that it wasn't Joseph, Ellie turned back to her search.

"We just need to do some tag removal, and then we'll be ready to go." Lou didn't sound fazed by her boyfriend's tone. "We have plenty of time."

He responded with a wordless grumble. Ellie raised her head, blowing aside the tag that dangled in front of her eyes to see him striding toward her, knife in hand. With a squeak of alarm, she shifted away. For the second time that day, she lost her balance and tipped onto her backside. Her tailbone throbbed in protest.

Ignoring her uncoordinated retreat, Callum reached for her head, snagging the tag and slicing it off her hat with a quick jerk of his knife. Her realization of what he'd intended was quickly followed by a hot rush of embarrassment at her overreaction. He was just so very large and grim looking, and she wasn't used to the type of men who carried weapons on a daily basis. Plus, she was still on edge from her encounter with Joseph.

"Any more?" he asked, still brandishing the knife, and Ellie silently held out her left hand, where a white square dangled at her wrist. Once he sliced it off her glove, he offered his free hand to help her off the floor.

"I think that's it," she said, brushing off her seat in a nervous gesture. Barbara, the woman at the Screaming Moose, had removed most of the tags for her. Just to make sure, she did a slow-motion twirl before giving Lou a questioning look.

"If you're tagged anywhere else, it's hidden." Lou pulled open the door. "Ready?"

Ellie started to follow, but stopped and belatedly turned to Callum. "Thank you."

He acknowledged her thanks with a brisk nod as he put away his knife and ushered both women toward the door.

"I'm sorry if I made us late," Ellie apologized, a little confused by the rush. She grabbed her new room key from the table by the door as he herded her by it.

Lou snorted a laugh. "We're not late. Cal just likes to stick to a schedule." Her voice lowered to a stage whisper. "He's a little anal."

Callum's directing hand swung toward Lou's butt, connecting with a smack that made her yelp and jump out of range. She sent a glare his way, but her laugh bubbled out, ruining her show of disapproval.

They headed for Callum's pickup, and Lou climbed into the backseat, despite Ellie's protestations.

"You're already doing so much," Ellie said, reluctantly sitting in the front passenger seat when Lou didn't budge. "You don't even know me, and you're still going out of your way to help."

Leaning between the front seats, Lou gave Ellie's shoulder a light bump with her fist. "We're not doing that much. Besides, until you arrived, our investigation into Willard's death had pretty much reached a standstill. The whiteboard hadn't seen any action for a while. Helping you fits right into what we were doing anyway."

"But mapping the cabin and taking off work so you can help me arrange a guide..." Ellie shook her head. "That's going above and beyond. So, thank you. I really appreciate it."

"Don't count your guide until he's hatched out of his grumpy, monosyllabic egg," Lou warned.

After struggling with that for several seconds, Ellie finally asked, "What?"

Callum gave an amused cough. "She means that it's likely George won't agree to be your guide."

"But he's a search and rescue volunteer, right? Doesn't that mean he likes to help people?" Even as she said the words, Joseph's image popped into her head, and she shuddered.

"Yes, but I heard it was like pulling teeth to get him on the team." Lou was leaning so far forward between the seats that she was level with Callum and Ellie.

Giving her an irritated glance, Callum snapped, "Sparks, sit back and put on your seat belt."

His sharp tone would've made Ellie scramble to do his bidding, but Lou just rolled her eyes. "We're a block away from Levi's. Just don't crash the truck, and I'll be fine. Actually, please don't crash the truck, since it's currently our only mode of transport."

"You don't have a car?" Ellie asked. In the city, with the public transportation, being vehicle-less was doable. In the mountains, though, it would be almost impossible not to have a car.

"I did. It was a lovely truck, but it burned."

That was unexpected. Callum was parking the pickup as Ellie replied, "Burned? In an accident?"

"No. It was definitely on purpose."

"What happened?" Mountain living was apparently more treacherous than Ellie had imagined.

Lou made a face. "Ugh. Stupid Clay happened. Homicidal, arsonistic stalker."

"I don't think arsonistic is a word." Callum's voice came from Ellie's open door, and she jumped. Caught up in Lou's abbreviated tale, she hadn't notice him circling to her side of the truck.

"It should be," Lou said as Ellie hurried to climb out of the pickup. Callum caught her arm to steady her as she landed on the ground, but her new boots were a huge improvement on her high-heeled booties. She didn't even slip at all that time. Ellie stepped aside so Callum could help Lou out of the truck.

"Homicidal?" Ellie picked out what she felt was the most critical part of Lou's explanation. "Do you think he was the one who killed Mr. Gray?"

"Nope. Clay just tried to kill Callum and me. The timeline wasn't right for him to kill Willard."

As they walked toward an unassuming building that the critical part of Ellie would have called a shack, she stared at Lou with wide eyes. "He tried to kill you both? Is he in jail now?"

"Dead." Lou's face was grim until Callum curled an arm around her, giving her a squeeze before releasing her to reach for the door to Levi's.

"Oh." Not sure how to respond to that—should she say she was sorry? Or perhaps offer congratulations?— Ellie let it drop. "Things are very…uh, *interesting* here."

"Not usually," Lou said as she ducked under Callum's arm. "Just in the past couple of months. Otherwise, the big news around town is who is dating whom. This murder stuff is new."

"Oh." Her voice was faint as she followed Lou into the restaurant. What was she getting herself into?

"Ellie!" Joseph slid out of a booth and intercepted them. Ellie flinched and slipped behind Callum so she could use him as a shield. The eight or so people remaining at Joseph's table looked over curiously. "Hey, Callum. Good to see you again. Lou, glad you brought your hot friend."

"Hi, Joseph," Lou greeted, waving to the people he'd abandoned at his booth. "George isn't here with you guys, is he?"

He snorted. "Holloway? The day he comes to a social event is the day we'll all be ice skating in hell. The only reason he shows up for training is because it's required."

"Oh. That's okay. We'll just meet up with him at Station One. Thanks." Lou took a step toward an empty table, but Joseph shifted to block her way.

"Why do you need to talk to Holloway?" he asked.

"None of your business, you nosy Nellie." Lou shouldered past him. "I'm not fueling the gossip train tonight."

"Come on, Lou!" Joseph called after her, smiling but with an edge to his words. "Don't leave me in suspense!"

Ellie slipped past him while he was occupied with teasing Lou, hoping to sneak by unnoticed, but he caught her wrist, pulling her to a halt. Ellie's stomach twisted with nerves. Callum stopped, too, his eyes watchful.

"Want to sit with us?" Joseph asked, tipping his head

to indicate the booth he'd just left. "We can be a wild bunch, but I promise you'll be entertained."

"Thank you, but no." She tried to keep her smile polite but dismissive while attempting to tug her hand free.

His grip wasn't painful, but it was unyielding. "How long will you be in town? I have training tonight, but I'd love to take you out another time."

"Sorry." She pulled harder against his hold, and her smile was turning into more of a grimace. Usually she was smoother about deflecting unwanted male attention, but Joseph frankly terrified her. "I'm leaving tomorrow." She wasn't sure what he'd thought was going to happen when he'd let himself into her motel room, or when he'd followed her into the bathroom, or when he'd grabbed her like he somehow had the right. Whether or not he intended anything darker by his aggressive display, he was *dangerous*. Even if he never moved beyond being creepy and pushy, she planned to stay well away from him.

"Tonight after training, then?"

"Acconcio." Callum's voice was quiet, but it caught both Joseph and Ellie's attention. "Enough."

After a long moment—during which Ellie was afraid Callum's order had backfired and Joseph would cling to her more firmly in a macho hissy fit—the fingers around her wrist tightened slightly and then finally released. With a silent sigh of relief, Ellie hurried to join Lou where she was standing next to a table. As Ellie passed him, Callum fell in behind her.

"What was that?" Lou asked when they reached her. "I couldn't hear over the babble of the masses." She waved an arm to indicate the crowded, noisy restaurant.

Callum pulled out Lou's chair and then sat next to her. Across the table, Ellie sat facing them with her back to the rest of the restaurant.

"Acconcio," Callum answered when Ellie hesitated. "He's never understood the word no."

"Oh." Making a sympathetic face at Ellie, Lou said, "I've heard he thinks he's all that and a bag of chips with the ladies. He's never been pushy with me, though—probably since he knows Callum would bring the pain if he tried. Or else he doesn't think I'm hot."

"I don't see how he couldn't," Ellie said, needing to turn the conversation away from Joseph so her frantic heartbeat could slow. "Find you hot, I mean. In a purely esthetic way, of course. I'm not hitting on you or anything, so I hope my saying that didn't just make things awkward."

Lou was laughing by the time Ellie had finished her babbling monologue. "Thank you."

Even Callum was smiling, but he sobered quickly as he met Ellie's eyes. "You have to be direct with guys like that. Don't worry about hurting their feelings."

"I know." She flushed and dropped her gaze to the table, fiddling with the wire rack holding the salt and pepper shakers. "I just hate confrontation. I'm kind of a wimp."

Reaching across the table, Lou caught one of Ellie's fidgeting hands and squeezed. "I used to be the wimpiest wimp that ever wimped, and even I managed to change. Just practice being firm. It'll get easier."

"Thanks." Ellie squeezed back and then withdrew her hand, desperately wanting to switch topics. Since her father was constantly on her mind, she went with that. "I know you said you didn't have much luck talking with Baxter, but did you see him at all?"

"Nope." Lou took the abrupt subject change in stride. "I tried going to Willard's house, but your dad would never answer the door. I'm pretty sure he was there, too, since I could hear him moving around inside. Either he was home, or there's some jumbo-sized pack rats in there."

"Probably both," Callum interjected.

"He's definitely not there now." Ellie thought about the empty cabin, and she realized her fingertip was heading toward her mouth. Tucking it back into her lap, she locked her other hand around it to keep it still. "Do you think he'll even make it to the cabin?"

"Don't start thinking about possible bad scenarios," Lou told her firmly. "You'll drive yourself crazy. You have a plan—go to the cabin and see if Baxter's there. If he's not, then you can figure out the next step. No sense in worrying about it yet."

Although Ellie knew Lou was right, keeping her ricocheting thoughts in line was easier said than done.

"Sorry!" A heavy-set woman arrived at their table and began handing over menus and water glasses. "It's crazy tonight. Not that it's not crazy most nights, but the DuBois family was here earlier, so that put me behind."

Lou winced. "Man, those kids are hellions. Did they decorate the walls with the pulled pork again?"

"Hellions is a nice way to put it," the server growled in a dark voice. "And I wish redecorating was all they'd done." Her tone lightened until it was almost cheerful. "I'll be back in a minute to take your order."

"But…" Lou trailed off when the woman headed toward another table. "Shoot. Now I'm dying to know what the DuBois kids did."

"I think you'll survive the suspense," Callum said dryly.

"I know." Her tone was mournful. "But I'm just so *curious* now."

He laughed softly, reaching over to take her hand. They exchanged a look so tender that Ellie, feeling like a voyeur, had to look away.

When Lou cleared her throat, Ellie knew it was safe to focus on the couple across from her again. "So, what do you do in Chicago?" Lou asked.

"I work at a clothing boutique." Her mom had made the occasional pointed comment about her daughter being a twenty-seven-year-old college graduate still working in retail, but Ellie didn't care. Despite Chelsea's quirks and the occasional ornery customer, she enjoyed her job. She didn't make much money, but Grandpa Scott had left her an inheritance, allowing her to buy her condo, with enough left over for a decent nest egg. The rescue-Baxter project might eat a considerable chunk of that egg, though. "It reminds me a little of the Screaming Moose, although with less flannel."

Lou grinned. "Isn't Barbara great? The word around town is that she was a financial planner in New York, but then she had a nervous breakdown, moved here, and bought the Moose. Mind you, the Simpson gossip chain is kind of like a game of telephone, so the accuracy of this information is highly suspect. Anyway, the store had been a cheesy tourist place, selling T-shirts and polished rocks, things like that. She turned it into a…well, slightly less cheesy tourist place."

With a laugh, Ellie relaxed a little. "How do you like working at The Coffee Spot?"

"It's good, most of the time. Much better than lawyering."

"You used to be a lawyer?" Ellie's eyebrows shot up in surprise.

"Yes." Her shamed tone made it sound like she was confessing a crime. "Kind of. I went through all the school and even passed the bar, but I bailed before I accepted a position at a firm. I finally grew a pair and escaped from under my parents' thumbs by running out here and becoming a barista."

After considering that for a few seconds, Ellie said, "That was brave."

"The first brave thing I've done."

"Not the last, though," Callum added, drawing a sweet smile from Lou.

Watching them, Ellie desperately wished she were brave.

<hr />

Even though her stomach was churning with nerves at the thought of her upcoming conversation—or one-sided conversation, most likely—with George Holloway, Ellie found her first visit to a fire station to be interesting. Lou gave her a quick tour after Callum was pulled aside by the fire chief. Close up, the trucks were huge. There also seemed to be an inordinate number of very attractive men. After her experience with Joseph earlier, though, she kept her greetings brief and her smile impersonal when Lou introduced her to some of them.

"There he is!" Lou announced in a loud whisper, drawing the attention of several firemen standing close by.

"Who?" one of them asked, grinning.

"No one for you to be concerned about, Soup." Grabbing Ellie's hand, Lou hurried toward the other side of the training room.

"Lou!" the fireman whined, laughter in his voice. "Don't be an information tease!"

"Just a fair warning, Ellie," Lou muttered quietly, "these guys are the worst gossips in Simpson, so don't say anything in front of them that you don't want everyone and their dog to know."

"Got it. Thanks." Although she smiled, it slipped away quickly when she spotted the bearded giant who held the ability to crush her newfound hope into itty-bitty pieces. Nerves dug sharp claws into her stomach lining. This was it.

"George!" Lou greeted when they were still several feet away from him. Instead of answering, he just silently watched their approach.

Ellie swallowed, grateful that Lou was there to force her feet to move. If she'd been alone, Ellie would probably have been too chicken to even get near the intimidating man, much less speak to him. She used her free hand to tug down her jacket, hoping that it wasn't gathering in an unflattering lump at her midsection.

"Hi, George." Lou stopped right in front of him, and Ellie had to catch herself before momentum made her crash into the other woman. "This is Ellie Price. Her dad is missing, most likely heading to her grandpa's cabin on the west side of Blue Hook National Forest, and she was hoping to hire you as a wilderness guide to take her to the cabin. Ellie, this is George Holloway, who knows this area like I know the inside of The Coffee Spot." When

Lou jerked on her hand, Ellie stumbled forward another step and blushed. Why was she so uncoordinated around this man? She'd always been prone to turning red at the drop of a hat, but being around George Holloway left her especially flushed and flustered. "I'll leave you two to discuss business terms." With that, Lou walked away.

Biting her lip to keep herself from calling after Lou and begging her to stay and be a buffer, Ellie met George's gaze. "Um…hi." There was no reaction from the big man, and her heart rate ratcheted up another notch. Her hands were sweating, and she resisted the urge to rub her palms against her thighs. The waterproof material of her pants wouldn't have absorbed the sweat, anyway. "Uh, like Lou said, I need to get to this cabin." She fumbled in her purse, grateful for the chance to focus on something besides the silent man in front of her. It was almost disappointing when her fingers closed on a folded piece of paper. "Callum printed this map of the cabin's location." To her embarrassment, her fingers were shaking as she extended the paper toward him. For a horrible second, she didn't think he was going to accept it, but he finally reached out and took the map.

Ellie didn't say anything else until his eyes left the map and met hers again. "Callum thought we'd be hiking for about three days to get from the farthest point on the plowed road to the cabin. We won't be staying there, since we'll just grab my dad and go"—as long as Baxter was there and unhurt and cooperative, but she didn't let herself worry about that right then—"so it'll be about six days. I can pay you five hundred dollars a day."

After another long silence, George refolded the map carefully. Holding it out to her, he shook his head.

"Six hundred, then." When he gave another head shake, she started to sweat. "Eight hundred?" She held her breath. If she went much higher, she wouldn't have anything left for unexpected expenses, like food or a flight home.

He extended the hand holding the map another inch closer to her.

To her horror, her eyes began to burn with threatening tears. "He's not well." Now the quiver in her hands had migrated to her voice, as well. "My dad. He has delusions and hallucinations. When he called me, he said he thinks someone's after him, so he's running to the cabin to hide from them. I'm afraid..." Her voice cracked, and she swallowed. "I'm afraid for him. Not that I think someone's really trying to kill him, but he's out there on his own, seeing things that aren't there. I need to find him and get him somewhere safe."

Reaching down, he lifted her hand and gently placed the refolded map on her palm. Her fingers automatically closed around the paper as he started to turn away from her.

"Please." Despite her best efforts, tears escaped, tracking down either side of her face and thickening her words. "I can't make it to the cabin without a guide. I don't even know how to read this map." Shame burned in her chest, but her desperation was stronger than her pride. "I need your help. Please."

"You should've told me you needed a wilderness guide to find your dad." Joseph's voice made her jump and wipe hastily at her cheeks before turning. It was one thing to bare her soul to the silent George, but she couldn't stand to be that vulnerable in front of Joseph.

"I work for an outfitter during hunting season, so I do this professionally. Here, let me see."

When he reached for the map, she automatically jerked it out of his reach. "No... I... That's okay." The thought of being at Joseph's mercy in the middle of the wilderness made panic rise in her throat. "I'll figure out something."

"It's already figured out." This time, Joseph leaned over her shoulder to grab the map. "I'm taking you. I'll even offer you my *friends* and family rate. We'll track down Baxter and bring him back, safe and sound."

"No." *How does he know Dad's name? Has he been researching me?* Her fingers tightened as she twisted, holding the paper out of his reach. She was reluctant to let Joseph even see the map. A mental image of him aggressively hitting on her the whole way to the cabin, of sharing a tent with him and his roving hands, flashed through her mind. The thought was horrifying.

He caught her arm, tugging her toward him as his other hand extended toward the map. Before he could grab it, George locked his enormous mitt around Joseph's bicep and hauled him back several feet. Joseph let out a yelp, releasing her as he stumbled to catch his balance.

"What the hell, Holloway!"

George didn't respond except to place his bulk between Ellie and the other man. Relieved to have a buffer—especially such a *big* buffer—blocking the incredibly persistent Joseph, Ellie peeked around his arm. Joseph looked furious, his eyes narrow and his lips tight. The two men stared at each other for a long, tense moment while Ellie held her breath. Finally, Joseph gave a forced laugh, holding up his hands in a gesture of surrender.

"Didn't know you'd already volunteered for the job," he said, sending a fake smile in Ellie's direction. She resisted the urge to duck all the way behind George. "Since when have you started babysitting tourists?"

George didn't say a word, but something in his expression made Joseph back away from them. When he was several feet away, he dropped his hands and turned to leave the training room.

"Um..." When the big man didn't look at her or respond, she cleared her throat. "Mr. Holloway, does this mean you're going to be guiding me?"

He finally rotated until he faced her, but it was a long time before George answered. Although his beard hid the lower half of his face, his eyebrows were mashed together. Ellie wasn't sure if he was annoyed, bewildered, worried, or some completely different emotion. All she did know was that his brown eyes were very striking, and she couldn't look away from them.

It could've been a few seconds or several minutes that they stood in silence while Ellie barely breathed. Finally, *finally*, his chin dipped ever so slightly. When his short nod finally sunk into her jubilant brain, she hopped forward and hugged him around the middle. He felt as large and as hard as a tree trunk. Once she realized what she was doing, she jumped back just as quickly.

"Sorry! I'm just really glad you'll be guiding me. So, thank you. Thank you very much. When did you want to leave? I haven't bought anything yet, except for clothes." She waved a hand at her current layered outfit. "Nothing like a tent or anything, since I wasn't sure what I'd need or what you already had or…um. I'm babbling. I'm sorry. I'm just really relieved."

His shoulders dropped in a silent sigh. Reaching in his pocket, he pulled out a pen and plucked the map from her nerveless fingers. Turning over the map so it was blank-side up and using the wall as a writing surface, George scribbled a couple of lines and then handed the paper to her. As soon as she accepted it, he turned and stomped out of the training room.

"Ho-ly cow!" Lou was suddenly standing next to her. "I want every single detail of that conversation, because I couldn't hear a thing over those loud idiots." She swung an arm to indicate a cluster of men standing on the other side of the training room. "Not a single one of those useless buggers could read lips, either, so I'm dying to know—did he actually say yes?"

Still stunned, Ellie turned toward the other woman and stared at her until the final question penetrated. Only then did she start to smile. "Yes."

With a squeal of delight, Lou threw her arms around Ellie. Grinning, Ellie squeezed her just as hard. The two women bounced in a circle, still hugging. When they finally stopped, everyone in the room was staring at them.

Too happy to be embarrassed, Ellie just ignored their audience.

"When are you leaving?" Lou asked, reminding Ellie of the scribbled note on the back of the map. She flipped it over and read the scrawled words.

31490 Cty Rd 43. 6 a.m.

"Tomorrow morning." Meeting Lou's gaze, Ellie grinned and held up the paper so the other woman could read it. "I'm going to find my dad, Lou."

"Yes." Lou grabbed her in another hug, crumpling the map between them. "You are."

※

Anderson King glanced at his brother. After only two hours, Wilson was snoring, his head cocked back against the passenger seat. With a shake of his head, Anderson refocused on the motel room door. A familiar mix of exasperation and protectiveness flowed through him. It was the same feeling he'd always had for his brother, ever since his dad had shoved a scrawny, red-faced, bulgy-eyed infant into Anderson's arms with the admonition to "shut the little fucker up."

When they'd been kids, Wilson never had been any good at sitting still. He'd always been the one to make a sudden movement or a sound when they'd been hunting. It'd been Wilson who used to spook their prey, sending that fish or rabbit or pretty neighbor girl bolting for safety.

Stillness was easy for Anderson. In the service, he'd learned to turn into a statue for hours, become part of the landscape—a harmless boulder, an innocent shadow—until the target stepped into his crosshairs. He didn't need to doze like Wilson, didn't need to fidget or squirm.

So now, while his brother slept, Anderson would wait, motionless. Once she left the motel room, he'd follow. He'd be patient, and she'd lead him right to his latest prey.

Chapter 4

ALTHOUGH CLEAN, THE MOTEL BED WASN'T VERY comfortable. That plus nerves kept Ellie awake for most of the night. Between thoughts about the upcoming hike and worry that someone would pound on the door, demanding she leave her pilfered room, sleep was impossible. Despite her best efforts at keeping her hands away from her mouth during the endless dark hours she spent tossing and turning, the skin around her fingernails was raw, and her left index finger had actually bled.

In the artificial light of the motel bathroom, she wrapped her gnawed finger in a rough, generic-brand tissue. It wasn't quite five a.m., but she was already dressed and ready to go. Her bleeding hangnail had convinced her to leave early. Sitting around her dark motel room was just shredding her nerves along with her fingers.

She packed up her rental car and left the second room key on the motel room table. The front desk was manned by a tiny, gray-haired woman, who accepted the returned key with a sleepy smile. Ellie's own smile was tight as she wondered if this was the owner who had given Joseph access to her room. As she walked back out into the almost-empty parking lot, she shivered. The wind chased eddies of powdery snow across the icy surface. Besides her car, the only other vehicle was an older van parked in the shadows on the far side of the lot. Ellie walked a little faster.

Once she was in the driver's seat, she entered the address George had given her into her navigation system. Below George's scribbles, Lou had sketched another rough map, just in case her car's GPS failed. The darkness made Ellie worried about missing turns, even with the GPS's prompting, so she drove slowly. The highway was mostly empty, although she saw headlights in her rearview mirror a few times, so she wasn't the *only* one awake—it only felt that way. Despite her concerns about getting lost, the sign for the county road was clear, and reflectors bracketed both sides of the road, making the turn easy to find.

As the GPS counted down the feet remaining to the address, Ellie's hand crept toward her mouth. She caught it before her teeth could do any more damage, and she gripped the wheel tightly with both hands. When she saw an unmarked driveway on her left just as the GPS announced that she'd arrived at her destination, she swallowed hard and turned.

The driveway was longer than her headlights' reach, eventually disappearing into a cluster of pine trees. It wasn't too badly rutted, which was a relief in her low-clearance vehicle, but it was narrow, twisting and turning as she entered the trees. The coating of packed snow made her worry about her car's traction, and she slowed to a crawl. By the time a cabin came into view, she felt as if she'd been driving down the lane forever.

The house looked fairly small, although not as small as Willard Gray's former place. There was a good-sized outbuilding next to the cabin, and the large overhead doors suggested that it might contain a vehicle or two. The roof of the garage held an array of solar panels, and a wind turbine whirred on a tall pole next to the building. Ellie realized that she hadn't seen any electric poles or lines since she'd turned off the highway. She wasn't surprised George lived off-grid. It fit what she knew about him so far. The driveway widened as she approached the house, and she was able to park on the edge of the clearing so she wasn't blocking either of the garage doors.

Ellie glanced at the clock. Despite her inchworm-like speed, she was still almost a half hour early. Her fingers tightened around the steering wheel again, and she peeled off her clinging hands. Taking a deep breath, she pushed open her door and got out of the car.

As she approached the covered front porch, a light flickered on next to the door. It startled her at first, but when George didn't poke out his head, she assumed it was motion-activated. Feeling guilty for her early arrival, she walked up the porch steps, her boots thumping against the wooden risers.

By the time she reached the top, the front door opened. Interior lights silhouetted George's large form, and she hesitated for a second before taking the last few steps to meet him. Silent as usual, he stepped back, and she took that as an invitation to enter his house.

"Hi." The word sounded loud in the predawn silence. "Sorry I'm so early. It was hard to sleep, so I figured I'd give myself plenty of time in case I managed to get lost. Your place was easy to find, though, so…here I am. Early."

He shrugged off her apology as she stripped off her coat, hat, and boots. Once she was down to a more reasonable number of layers, he led the way into a good-sized kitchen. The smell of bacon made her mouth water, and her stomach grumbled as if she hadn't packed it full of barbecue the previous evening. A round table with four chairs held a plate full of food and a coffee mug.

"Oh, I'm sorry!" she apologized again. "I didn't mean to interrupt your breakfast. Go ahead and finish." Flustered, Ellie wondered if she should offer to wait out in her car.

Instead of taking his place at the table, however, he moved to the stove. She watched as he got a plate from the cupboard and loaded it with scrambled eggs, bacon, and hash browns. He laid it on the table and then returned to pour coffee into a blue mug. When he held it out to her, she accepted the coffee with a smile of thanks. Ellie normally liked her coffee milky and sweet, but she didn't want to be demanding. He was already feeding and caffeinating her. Until they were on their way to her grandpa's cabin, Ellie didn't want to risk changing George's mind about being her guide. She'd do everything she could to avoid giving him the impression that she was high-maintenance.

He put a fork by her place and pulled out the chair in front of it. When he looked at her, she slid into the seat. "Thank you."

He grunted as he took his own chair, and she looked up from her plate in surprise. That was the first vocalization he'd made in her presence. Maybe there was hope for actual conversation by the time the trip was done? She ducked her head, staring at her eggs to hide a smile.

They ate in silence. Ellie was surprised by how good the food was—the eggs fluffy and the bacon a perfect level of crispiness. Even the hash browns, which usually she didn't like very much, were tasty. The coffee, though...she took a sip and hid her wince. It was probably strong enough to put hair on her chest.

The scrape of George's chair against the floor startled her, and she almost spilled her coffee as she set the cup back on the table. He moved to the fridge and pulled out an old-fashioned-looking glass milk bottle, which he set on the table next to her elbow. She must not have hid her reaction to the coffee well enough.

"Thank you." She poured some milk into the black-as-pitch beverage, and then added some more. "The food is really good." Ellie stopped herself before thanking him again. She'd repeated it so many times in the past fifteen minutes that she was afraid she was sounding like a talking doll that could say only one thing when her string was pulled.

As usual, he shrugged off her thanks before finishing his food. Ellie eyed what was left on her own plate. George had given her a lumberjack's portion, plus nerves had tightened her stomach. When she put her fork down and sat back in her chair, he looked between her face and her unfinished food with a frown.

"It was great, but I'm really full." As she sipped her milky yet still-strong coffee, he slid the plate from her place to his and proceeded to finish off the breakfast she'd left. As she watched him eat from what had been her breakfast, a blush warmed her cheeks. She wasn't sure why, but the act of sharing food seemed almost intimate, like something an old married couple would do. Shaking off her silly thoughts, she focused on the upcoming trip.

"I couldn't get cash yesterday, since my bank doesn't have a branch here." She watched him, holding her breath, hoping he didn't immediately cancel the trip and kick her out of his house. "I can write you a check, though, if you…um, take checks."

His head shake could have meant anything from "the deal is off" to "I'll guide you for free." Ellie decided to go with one of the more optimistic translations.

"Should I just pay you after we get back, then?"

His shrug was combined with just enough of a nod for her to blow out a sigh of relief.

"Do you have winter camping gear?" she asked, and, between bites, he jerked his chin toward two professional-looking backpacks. One was huge, while the second—the one she assumed was hers—was much smaller. "Oh, good. Should I bring my suitcase in here and transfer my things?"

At his nod, she hurried toward the door.

"Wait."

The sound of an unfamiliar male voice made her stop as if she'd hit a wall. The growly rasp of that one word rippled up her spine, heating her blood and giving her goose bumps. Shocked that he'd spoken, and by her reaction to his deep, rough voice, she turned to see George had left the table and was grabbing something off the counter. He held out a flashlight.

"Oh, right. Thank you." As soon as the words left her mouth, she imagined the doll with the string on her back again. Flushing, she reached to take the light and hurried back out to her car.

Once she'd dodged through the front door, pulling it closed behind her, her shoulders relaxed. Ellie laughed at herself. How was being outside in the dark, surrounded by a predator-filled forest, less nerve-racking than being inside a warm, cozy cabin with George? He, at least, was not going to eat her.

At that thought, a hot blush warmed her cheeks, and she hurried to her car, trying to rein in her unruly imagination.

Her suitcase was small, since she'd thought she'd be in Simpson only for a night or two, so she'd crammed all of her new clothes back into the Screaming Moose bag. She grabbed the bag, her suitcase, and her purse, and then hauled the entire load into George's house. When she returned to the kitchen, he was washing dishes at the sink, but he quickly dried his hands and came over to relieve her of her burden.

"Thank you." She grimaced at his back when the words slipped out unbidden, then shrugged. There were worse things she could be repeating over and over. Ellie realized that George wasn't just piling her things next to the backpack. Instead, he'd unzipped her suitcase and was digging through it. He'd already created what she assumed was a reject pile, and her clothes were quickly finding their way into it.

Scurrying over to him, she opened her mouth to object at the intrusion of privacy and then snapped it shut. Ellie reminded herself of her vow to be as low-maintenance as possible. It was hard, though, and she couldn't hold back a whimper of embarrassed protest as her favorite push-up bra was tossed aside.

His earlier frown at her still-full plate was nothing compared to his current scowl at her now-empty suitcase.

"Most of my new clothes are in here," she told him, nudging the Screaming Moose bag with her toe. "I'm wearing the rest of them." She'd put on the same layers as she'd worn the previous evening.

Still crouching, he turned to Ellie and abruptly tugged up the waist of her fleece top, revealing the first of two underlayers. Shocked at the unexpected manhandling, she stood frozen as he lifted her second top as well, to expose her base long-underwear top below it. With what sounded like a satisfied grunt, George repeated the process on her lower half. Recovering from her startled paralysis, she stepped back, tugging the waistband of her fleece pants out of his grip.

As she stared at him with wide eyes, he turned away from her and started sorting through the contents of the Screaming Moose bag.

"You know," she started tentatively. *Low-maintenance!* her brain was screaming. *Be low-maintenance!* It was one thing not to be demanding, though, and a whole other thing to allow him to paw her, even if that pawing was well intentioned. "If you'd just *asked* what I was wearing, I would've been happy to tell you."

George did not respond to that, not even with a silent shrug. She sighed and squatted down next to him. Picking up a pair of wool socks that had landed in what she was pretty sure was the "take hiking" pile, she rolled them together and tucked them into the main section of the smaller pack.

When she picked up another pair of long-underwear bottoms, she saw George was watching her. "I read somewhere that rolling clothes instead of folding them is a more efficient way to pack." Ellie wasn't sure if that was why he was eyeing her, but she had to guess if he wasn't going to tell her. "Plus, it keeps them from wrinkling." She pulled a face. "Not that wrinkles will really be an issue on this trip."

Her explanation must have satisfied his curiosity, since he turned back to sorting her new clothes. Almost all of them ended up in the "keep" pile, and she exhaled in silent relief. He wouldn't have been happy if she hadn't had any appropriate clothes for the hike. They could've returned to the Screaming Moose, but that would've eaten up precious time. Still, the image of George accompanying her on a shopping trip almost made her smile.

Once she'd rolled and stashed all of the George-approved clothes in her pack, she tossed the contents of the reject pile back into her suitcase. While George was focused on finishing the dishwashing, she quickly tucked a couple of her bras into the pack, along with the contents of her purse. There were necessities, and then there were *necessities*, no matter what George thought.

After zipping the now-stuffed pack, she hurried to join him at the sink, snagging a folded dish towel off the counter. She took the newly rinsed plate from his hand and dried it, ignoring his raised eyebrows. After eyeing her for a few seconds, he shrugged and continued washing, handing the items to her to dry.

The sun wasn't up yet, but it was thinking about it, and gray light was creeping through the kitchen window. There was a coziness to their shared chore, and Ellie found herself smiling as she dried the mug in her hands. The first hint of peacefulness she'd felt in days wrapped around her, warming her to her core.

It was over too quickly, and the dishes were done. After George filled water bottles, some with boiling water and some with just lukewarm, Ellie screwed on the lids and tucked them into foam covers. As George attached the bottles to the packs so they hung upside down, Ellie watched curiously. She wanted to ask why he put them on with the tops down, but she figured she'd just get a grunt in response. Plus, she decided she'd better save her questions for really important things, since George was definitely not one to waste words.

He hauled both packs to the door, and they donned their hats, boots, coats, and gloves before heading outside.

"I can take mine," Ellie offered, reaching for the smaller pack, but George ignored her, carrying both easily. She closed the door behind them, hearing the wooden latch inside fall into place. The sound of the door locking made her suddenly anxious, and she turned toward his retreating back. "I didn't ask if you had your keys. Did I just lock you out?"

Without slowing, George walked through the side door of the outbuilding. Unsure of whether or not to follow, Ellie took a couple of steps after him and then hesitated. The overhead door rattled as he raised it, exposing the front of the silver pickup truck parked inside. After lifting the packs into the back of the truck, he got into the cab and started the engine.

Ellie waited, feeling useless. She wished that he would tell her what to do. Even barked orders would have been preferable to vague grunts and shrugs. Giving herself a mental slap, she cut off the surge of self-pity. Once she reminded herself that she could be stuck with bulldozer Joseph's come-ons for a week, she felt a little better about her quiet guide. As welcome as conversation would have been at the moment, there were worse things than silence.

George pulled the truck out of the garage and parked.

Climbing out of the cab, he headed back to the porch. Without moving, she watched him walk past her, figuring he'd forgotten something. He stopped at the base of the steps and turned to look at her, making a come-along gesture. She joined him on the porch just as he lifted the carved wooden "Welcome" sign.

Underneath was a cord that lay flat against the door, both ends disappearing into holes drilled through the thick wood. Slipping his fingers under the cord, George pulled, and Ellie heard the clunk of the latch disengaging.

"Cool," she breathed, a smile starting. "Guess I didn't lock you out after all."

Releasing the cord, he let the latch fall back into place, securing the door. When he replaced the welcome sign, the cord was completely hidden.

"I should've known something was up when I saw a welcome sign on your door," she said. Her eyes widened as a gloved hand flew up to cover her mouth. "Oh, that was rude. I'm sorry. I didn't mean it the way it sounded." She actually *had* meant it the way it sounded, but she just hadn't intended to say it out loud.

George didn't appear to be upset by her comment, though. In fact, he looked closer to smiling than she'd ever seen him get. His amusement slipped away quickly, however, and his usual austere expression fell into place. He motioned at the truck, and she hurried toward it. Before she reached it, she glanced at her car and hesitated.

"Is it okay to leave it here?" When he shrugged affirmatively, she looked back at the rental. "Should I lock it?"

Instead of answering, he held out an upturned hand.

"Keys?" she guessed, digging them out of her coat pocket and laying them on his palm. He headed for her car while she watched him curiously, not sure why he wanted to be the one to lock the car doors. Instead of securing the vehicle, though, he climbed into the driver's seat and started the engine.

As he drove the car into the shed where the truck had been, she thought how odd he looked—he was so big, and the car was so small. After turning off the engine, George unfolded himself from the driver's seat, and Ellie had to hold back a giggle.

"We could take my car to the trailhead," she couldn't resist suggesting, and then swallowed another laugh as his scrunched brows told her exactly what he thought about that idea.

She climbed into the passenger side of the pickup while he lowered the overhead door. His truck was older, but it was well-maintained. It reminded her of her grandpa's pickup, with the cloth bench seat and manual windows. She suddenly felt five years old again, and all her uncertainties and insecurities rushed through her. What was she doing? Why did she think she was capable of hiking for days through the wilderness in search of her father? In an effort to distract herself from her fit of nerves, Ellie leaned forward and wrote her name in the thin layer of dust on the dash.

As soon as George swung into the cab, she scrubbed the dashboard with her fist, erasing the letters and leaving just a smudged rectangle in their place. He didn't comment—of course—but just looked at the spot, glanced at her face, and then shook his head.

The truck rolled forward, and Ellie's stomach

clenched around the breakfast she'd just eaten. Their journey had begun.

Although the forty-five-minute drive was quiet, it wasn't awkward like Ellie had feared it would be. She was beginning to get used to George's silence, and it was easy to get lost in her own thoughts as the pink light of dawn outlined the mountain peaks around them.

The truck began to slow, catching her attention. "Are we close to the road's end?"

Shaking his head, George pointed. Two small, deer-like animals bounded across the road in front of them and ran through the adjoining field. Leaning forward, Ellie watched until they disappeared from sight.

"What were they? Deer?"

"Pronghorn."

Once again, his voice startled her. It was so deep, as befitted a man of his size, and rough-sounding, like his infrequent speech had caused his voice box to rust.

"Pronghorn?" she repeated.

"Antelope."

"They're so little. I always thought antelope would be bigger—when I thought about antelope, at least, which honestly wasn't very often. It was more than I thought about pronghorn, though, since I'd never heard that term before." Craning her neck as she tried to catch a final glimpse of the animals, she knocked the side of her head against the window. "Ow." Glancing over at George as she rubbed her temple, she caught the upward curl of his mouth. "Hey! No laughing at my pain."

The tiny grin disappeared as if it hadn't existed as he

let the truck roll forward again. Ellie had seen it, though, and her insides warmed with the knowledge that she'd gotten George Holloway to smile. She decided to make it a personal quest to get him to do it again.

Chapter 5

TEN MINUTES LATER, THEY SAW THE "NO ROAD Maintenance Beyond This Point" sign. George turned into a small gravel lot and parked. He immediately opened his door and got out of the truck, but Ellie took a few seconds to breathe as panic threatened to shut down her lungs. This was it. Once she started walking along that logging trail, civilization would no longer be just a short drive away. Letting out a final shuddering exhale, she opened her door and jumped out of the cab.

While she'd been attempting to stave off hyper-ventilation, George had pulled their packs out of the back of the truck. He held the smaller one, and she turned her back toward it so she could loop her arms into the straps. When George rotated her to face him and adjusted the fit, she felt strangely self-conscious and warm with each brush and tug of his large, capable hands. Since he looked at her frequently to check her reactions to the adjustments, she couldn't even avoid his gaze to reduce the awkwardness. Once he appeared to be satisfied with how the backpack rested on her, he buckled the strap across the top of her chest and the one around her waist.

Giving a final, satisfied nod, he took her hand and guided it to where one of the upside-down water bottles was within easy reach. For some stupid reason that she didn't think about too closely, Ellie blushed at the contact of his gloved hand against hers. Ducking her head, she pulled the bottle free and took a drink.

Instead of reaching for the larger backpack, George headed to the passenger side of the truck. Curious, Ellie shifted to the side so she could watch what he was doing. The backpack moved with her, a part of her, yet not. It was an odd sensation, like she'd grown a camel's hump. Although she'd felt the full weight of the pack when the straps had first pressed into her shoulders, it seemed much lighter now after the adjustments George had made.

Her attention returned from her backpack to her guide, who was fiddling with a pair of electronic doo-hickeys that looked like a cross between a handheld video game and a really big stopwatch.

"What's that?"

He held it out so she could see "Avalanche Beacon" printed on the front. He pushed the button that said "Receive," and an arrow above a ".3 M" pointed toward the second beacon.

The idea that someone might need to locate her—or her body—using this thing was rather off-putting, but she didn't say anything as her guide pushed a button marked "Send." After fiddling with the beacons for a minute longer, he tucked one into the chest pocket of her new red coat and zipped it securely. Once again, color rose in her cheeks, and she had to hold back a self-deprecating eye roll. Something about this man's size and silent presence had turned her into a flustered, blushing ninny.

To distract herself from her reaction to George, Ellie adjusted her jacket, patting the spot where the beacon sat. It didn't even create a bulge. One of the things she loved about her new coat was the plethora of pockets. Wearing it, she didn't need a purse, unless she just wanted to accessorize.

Looking at George again, she blinked. He was in the process of removing a honking huge gun from the glove compartment. Ellie must have made a noise, because he looked at her as he slid the pistol into a holster at his hip. On the other side of his belt, he tucked two ammo magazines into their own nylon case. When he dropped his hands, his coat fell to cover the holstered gun, but Ellie noticed a vent on the side seam of his jacket. She assumed it was there to allow access to his weapon, rather than being just a stylistic detail.

"Is that...um, going to be necessary?" A collage of possible scenarios requiring a firearm flashed through her mind, from mountain men crazy with cabin fever to rabid wildlife to a zombie attack...or worse—a crazed-mountain-man zombie attack. His slight nod was tempered by a half shrug, which she translated as "possible to likely." That response did nothing to settle her newly fired nerves. She looked around with a small shiver. The looming evergreen and leaf-stripped aspen trees suddenly took on added menace. She'd known about the obvious dangers—cold and hunger and getting lost—but now a new host of fears crowded into her mind.

George hoisted his oversized pack with the ease of frequent use. He fastened all the buckles in a quarter of the time it had taken to get Ellie situated. After locking the truck, he strode toward the logging trail, and she hurried to catch up with him.

She'd wondered why they weren't using the

snowshoes strapped to the backs of their packs, but the snow had a hard crust that held her weight. It was slick, and Ellie was once again grateful for the good traction her new boots supplied. Once she decided to trust that her soles would grip the surface, walking became easier, and she quit trying to do the half-shuffle, half-skate motion that wasn't getting her anywhere.

Just in that short time Ellie had taken to find her bearings, George had pulled ahead by fifteen feet.

"Don't be a burden," she muttered under her breath as she hurried to catch up with her guide. It was easier said than done, though, since she already felt winded. In Chicago, she was faithful about going to the gym four times a week, but the altitude was almost ten-thousand feet higher than what she was used to. Straightening her spine, she tried to even out her breathing and lengthen her stride.

As she rushed after George, Ellie attempted to ignore the eerie silence of their surroundings. All she could hear was her puffing breaths, and it was too easy to imagine hungry eyes watching her struggle. She had to appear to be the most catchable of prey. Her pace quickened.

It was no use, though. George's effortless gait widened the gap between them with every step. As the road tipped upward onto an incline, Ellie knew she had to say something.

"George," she panted, but he was too far ahead of her to hear. "George!" There was a slight wheeze to her shout, but it did the trick. He stopped and turned around to look at her. "Sorry…but you're…going…to have… to slow down."

By the time she'd finished her breathless sentence, she'd almost reached him. It was a lot easier to catch up with him when he was standing still. His slight nod was the only indication that he'd heard her. Turning around, he set off on the trail again. The incline leveled, and Ellie found it easier to stay right behind him. His pace seemed to have slowed, and he frequently looked back to check on her. The three-day hike suddenly felt less impossible than it had just a few minutes earlier.

The trail surface varied from a stone-hard snowdrift to bare rocks to a few inches of fluffy powder. As they were walking on a section of icy crust, Ellie's foot broke the surface, and she was suddenly one knee deep in snow.

As she pulled her leg out of the drift, her boot caught on the top crust of ice and started to slide off her foot. Bending, she caught the top of her escaping boot and jammed her heel down. Once it was in place again, she stayed leaning forward, using the opportunity to pant for oxygen.

Two enormous boots appeared in her view. Forcing herself to straighten, she tried to give the appearance of breathing normally and not sucking air like a winded racehorse. George was watching her and, no surprise, frowning.

"Okay." Her ruse was completely destroyed when she talked, since she couldn't get out more than one word at a time. "Ready…now. Let's…go."

Instead of turning and leading the way once again, he reached toward the side of his pack. By feel, he unzipped an outside pocket and pulled out a small bag. When he held it out to her, she saw that it contained trail mix.

"No, thanks." She was able to say two words without a gasp in the middle. Ellie considered that an improvement.

He didn't withdraw his hand.

Shaking her head, she added, "Still full from… breakfast."

Now he was frowning again, and he was still holding out the trail mix.

"Fine," she sighed, accepting the nuts and raisins. Jamming a few into her mouth, she chewed, wishing that it was at least the kind of mix that had chocolate in it.

"Drink, too." George gestured toward one of her water bottles.

As she obediently washed down her mouthful of trail mix, Ellie wondered if she'd ever get used to that so-infrequent bass rumble. After three more small handfuls of food, she returned the bag to George. He must have considered her intake to be sufficient, since he accepted the trail mix and promptly finished it. She watched, awed by the amount of food he was able to consume, but then figured it wasn't that surprising—his huge, muscled frame must require a lot of fuel.

After a few more swallows, she restowed her water bottle. George lifted his brows in question, and she gave a firm nod. Whether it was the food, water, or just standing still and breathing, Ellie felt… She wouldn't say energized, but at least she was slightly more prepared to keep walking.

They continued like that for a while, walking for much too long a time and then stopping for much too short a time. By the fourth break, Ellie was flushed and damp with perspiration. Barbara had promised her long underwear would wick away any moisture, but either it was failing, or she was sweating more than it could wick.

George's brow was creased with an unhappy wrinkle.

"What?" Ellie asked after she swallowed her mouthful of granola bar. "I'm eating *and* drinking"—she held up her water bottle—"so why are you cranky?"

As usual, his response was word-free. Pulling off a glove, he reached toward her. His hand slid under the bottom hem of her jacket, and his fingers dove beneath all of her layers before she could react. At the touch of his calloused skin on her bare stomach, she jumped and took a belated step back, pulling away from him. Even when the contact was broken, she could still feel the heat where his fingers had touched.

"What was…?" She stared at him. "What?"

"You're sweating."

"So?"

"You'll get cold. Take off a layer." Once again, he reached for her, as if he was going to start stripping off her clothes, and she reversed another step.

"Okay, but you could've just asked me." Still flustered, Ellie started unbuckling the straps holding on her pack. "I'm not a horse. If you want to know if I'm sweating, just say, 'Are you sweating?' and I'll answer honestly. You don't have to feel me up to find out."

Her backpack was reluctant to leave her shoulders, so she squatted until the bottom of the pack rested on a rock behind her and then attempted to wiggle loose. This time, when George approached, she let him grab the pack and slide it free.

As she took off her jacket, she debated what to remove and decided on her outer long underwear layer—just the top. Hot or not, she wasn't about to start stripping off anything from the waist down. Her zip-up fleece top came off next, and she put it on top of her coat so it didn't get snow on it. Grimacing at the dampness of the fabric, she pulled the silky second layer over her head, dislodging her hat on the way.

She bent to pick up her fleece, shivering a little in her single, slightly clammy top, and caught a glimpse of George's face as she straightened. His eyes were wide and fixed on her chest. Following his gaze, she saw that the form-fitting long underwear presented a clear view of the lines of her bra and, even better, her cold-stiffened nipples.

With a mortified intake of air, Ellie clutched her fleece to her chest. Her movement broke George's daze, and he blinked, then quickly turned so his back was to her. She scowled. Why couldn't he have done that a minute earlier?

She fumbled to stuff her arms into the sleeves and then zip it up all the way to her chin. Although the fleece wasn't in any way revealing, she didn't feel totally covered until she had the jacket on and zipped. It was only after putting on her hat and gloves that she cleared her throat.

George turned slightly, so he wasn't quite facing her but could probably see her in his peripheral vision. Her cheeks still warm, she rolled the discarded top and tucked it into an empty pocket on her pack, not wanting it to get any of her other clothes damp. Once she'd zipped the section closed, she eyed the pack. She'd be able to get it onto her back, but it would be a lot easier with help.

"Uh…George?" When he turned to face her completely, she tilted her head toward the pack sitting on the rock. "Could you...?" He moved to lift the pack, and Ellie turned her back to him, sliding her arms through the straps. His hands shifted to her biceps, and he turned her to face him so he could fasten the buckles around her chest and waist. Even though George's touch was brief and impersonal, Ellie could feel her cheeks heating again.

It was a relief when he turned and started walking, giving her some space to figure out why this silent mountain of a man flustered her so much.

Ellie peered at the position of the sun, squinting even behind her sunglasses. Although she was no ancient navigator, it sure looked like lunchtime to her. "George?"

He turned his head, not quite looking at her. Since the whole not-really-naked-but-it-felt-like-she-was incident, he hadn't made eye contact.

"What time is it?"

"Noon."

Wow, she was good. Maybe she'd missed her calling. Instead of working at a boutique, she could be letting sailors know the time. She'd have to time travel back a ways, though, since they had clocks on ships now. Ellie blinked, a little disconcerted by the trajectory of her thoughts. The high altitude must have made her punchy. "Can we stop for lunch soon?"

"Not stopping for long."

"Oh." Her legs gave a wail of complaint. So did her lungs.

"No sense in sitting a long time and getting cold."

But the sitting part sounded so *nice*. She reminded

herself to be low-maintenance. They were only a half-day's hike—a *slow* half-day's hike—away from his truck. It definitely wasn't too late for George to turn this car around if she was irritating. "Okay."

Her tone must've been mournful, since he actually looked at her and stopped. He pulled out more trail mix from what appeared to be an unending supply. Balancing her pack, she carefully sat on a chair-sized rock and immediately regretted it. There were very inconveniently located lumps that dug into her posterior. Wincing, she shifted to the other side of the rock, which was just as uncomfortable. With a sigh, she gave up and just chewed on her trail mix.

As she finished off the water remaining in the bottle, a twinge in her bladder reminded her of another biological need. She'd been dreading it, but Ellie knew that peeing outdoors—in the *cold* outdoors—was something she was just going to have to do. There was no sense in whining about it, even just in her head.

George took the empty bottle from her hand and switched it out for a full one he took from a more inconvenient spot on her pack.

"Thank you." She tried to stand, but the weight of the pack pulled her backward, and the rock behind her prevented her from taking a step back to catch her balance. As she started to topple, George caught her upper arms and pulled her upright, holding her there until she was steady. She looked at him, and their gazes caught for a long second. This time, she was the chicken who dropped her eyes first. "Thank you." With a silent sigh, she realized she'd turned back into the one-phrase-Franny doll.

He released her arms, and she waved toward a couple

of scrubby pine trees ten feet away from them. "I'm, um, just going to go to the ladies' room."

As she walked toward the dubious privacy of the trees, Ellie could feel him watching her, and she hoped he looked away before she actually got down to business. She'd never had issues with a shy bladder before, but these were new and trying circumstances.

When she reached the far side of the trees, she purposefully didn't look back at George to see if she was truly hidden. If he was watching, she didn't want to know, or she'd never be able to go. On the other hand, being out of his sight and away from his protection brought its own set of worries about hungry predators. Giving the surrounding area a hunted look, she told herself firmly to quit being a paranoid city girl. Skimming down all four bottom layers, she shivered when the cold air met her bare skin.

Belatedly, she realized she should have taken off her pack before attempting to pee. Using a nearby trunk to balance, she lowered herself carefully. It was trickier than she'd expected, and she promised herself that she'd never take a toilet seat for granted again.

By the time she was finished, her teeth were chattering, and the tops of her thighs were beginning to go numb. A movement to her left made her whip her head in that direction as she abruptly stood, almost losing her balance again. Before she even identified what had drawn her attention, she'd dragged all of her bottom layers up to her waist.

A rabbit moved cautiously out of the shelter of a tree, and Ellie's muscles relaxed. It was all white except for the black tips of its ears.

"Hey, bunny," she said very quietly, standing still so as not to scare it. "Aren't you cute?"

"Snowshoe hare."

At the deep rumble of George's voice, both she and the rabbit jumped. The hare bolted for cover, disappearing into a group of pines. Ellie, on the other hand, turned to give George a *look*.

He just raised his eyebrows back at her.

"Can't I have a little privacy?"

His eyes dropped to her fully clothed body and then returned to her face.

"You didn't know I was done," she huffed, and then remembered her pledge to not be difficult. Residual adrenaline from being startled twice—once by the rabbit and the second time by George—had made her snappy.

"You took too long."

"Sorry." She must've been behind the pines for quite a while. "We can go now."

He turned and headed back to the trail, Ellie following.

Ellie focused on George's broad back, trying to think about anything except her current misery. The top crust of snow had gradually gotten softer, the snow more powdery, and her boots sank several inches with each step. This forced her to raise her knees higher, and her quadriceps soon started complaining.

It was worth dealing with minor discomfort, she told herself grimly, since each step was bringing her closer to her father. She hoped. Instantly, she cut off that train of thought. Baxter had to be heading to her grandpa's cabin. He was just taking a less-traveled route, while they were following the logging road, which is why she hadn't spotted his trail. If her dad wasn't, and this whole miserable trek was for nothing, then she might just sink down into the snow and throw a tantrum. George would probably be annoyed by that.

Suddenly, it occurred to her that Baxter was making his own trip to the cabin. Alone. With no George to guide him. Fear quickened her breathing even more than the thin air already had. Consciously trying to slow and deepen her inhales and exhales, she reminded herself that he was an experienced camper and hiker. Before that catastrophic visit to the cabin when she was ten, he'd taken her on lots of wilderness adventures. He'd be fine. The memory of how confused and chaotic he'd seemed during their last phone call tried to surface, but she pushed it into a dark closet in her brain and slammed the door. *He'll be fine*, she repeated over and over, the words matching the rhythm of each miserable step. *He'll be fine*.

Ellie almost crashed into George before she realized that he'd stopped.

"Break time?" At his nod, she pulled off a glove and held out her hand for the inevitable trail mix. As much as she'd been eating, though, she still felt hungry. She figured that walking through the snow must burn a zillion calories an hour. It felt that way, at least.

As she chewed, he removed his pack. Ellie was a little bit jealous of how easily he handled the weight when she found getting in and out of her own backpack such a struggle. After detaching the snowshoes from his pack, he moved behind her to get that pair, as well. He crouched by her feet like a shoe salesman, and she fit her boot into the bindings. While she was on one foot, she teetered and caught his shoulder to regain her balance. Once she was steady, she realized George had gone still under her touch. She withdrew her hand, oddly reluctant to end the contact, and his hands started moving again. He ratcheted the straps until they fit snugly around her boot and then repeated the process on the other snowshoe.

When he moved away to put on his own snowshoes, she lifted one foot at a time, testing the weight of them. They were surprisingly light, and she was excited to try walking. Almost anything would be better than slogging through the shin-deep powder like they'd been doing for the past hour.

Once George ate a few giant handfuls of trail mix and shouldered his pack, they returned to hiking. Ellie quickly got the hang of the snowshoes, and the novelty of them made the next hour or so go by quickly. Yet as the late-afternoon sun dipped low and the shadows lengthened, her feeling of being watched deepened. Although she tried to tell her paranoid mind that it was only cute bunnies or happy squirrels or curious raccoons eyeing her from behind the trees, fear still soured her stomach.

Despite the snowshoes, her fatigue turned the walk into drudgery. Everything ached—her muscles, the blisters on her heels, her cold fingers. When George stopped again, she wanted to cheer, but she couldn't muster the energy.

A fallen tree sprawled across the small clearing, and Ellie made her way over to it, excited about the prospect of sitting. Before she made it, George stopped her with a hand on her arm.

"We're camping here."

"Oh." She wasn't sure why she was so surprised by this. In her misery, she'd just assumed that they would hike on and on, never stopping. "Good."

He unbuckled the straps around her front and helped her ease the pack off, then crouched to loosen the bindings on her snowshoes. Rolling her shoulders as she stepped out of them, she realized how sore she'd gotten from carrying the weight all day. After removing his own snowshoes and pack, he extracted a small shovel from it. Moving to the other side of the downed tree, where a semicircle of pines created a partially sheltered spot, he started digging.

"Can I help?" When he didn't pause in his work, she frowned. "Please? I'm getting cold just standing here." As if those were the magic words, his head came up, and he eyed her closely.

"There's another shovel in your pack," he finally said before returning to his shoveling.

As she pulled it out, she saw several other items she didn't recognize and made a mental note to ask George what they were. By the time she made it back to him with the shovel, he'd already dug out over a foot of snow in a rectangle that was about five feet by eight feet.

"What can I do?" she asked, eyeing the tidy corners. It looked so perfect that she didn't want to start digging and mess up the symmetry.

Using his shovel, he sketched out a smaller square in front of his rectangle. "Dig down another couple of feet. It'll make it easier to get in and out."

Impressed by the longest series of consecutive words she'd ever heard him utter, Ellie started digging. She soon warmed up again as she cut through the hard-packed snow. Apparently, the soft stuff was just on the trail to make walking difficult. By the time she'd finished her square, George had lowered his rectangle another foot.

He eyed her work and grunted, "Good." Ellie couldn't help but beam at the praise as she stretched her cramped fingers.

They laid a tarp over the bottom of the dug-out rectangle, and then George showed her how to fill the fabric tent anchors with snow. As she did that, he assembled the tent with impressive quickness. While he secured it, she pulled the sleeping bags out of their compression sacks.

"Pads," George grunted. When she just looked at him blankly, he jerked his head toward the packs. Ellie discovered he'd brought two pads each—one foam and one self-inflating.

"Whoa!" she said as she hauled the pads through the entrance of the tent. "I figured we'd be on the ground. This is four-star camping."

He crawled in after her with an odd expression on his face, as if he was trying to figure out if she was teasing. "The ground's what makes you cold, not the air. We need insulation."

"Plus, it'll be cushy." She unrolled them, and George showed her how the self-inflating pads worked. The foam pads went on the floor of the tent with the air-filled ones on top, followed by their sleeping bags.

Ellie looked at the oddly shaped bedrolls. "These look like cocoons."

"Mummy bags."

Tilting her head, she said, "I can see why they were named that."

When he climbed out of the tent, Ellie followed. "What's next?"

"Dinner."

He hitched his pack over one shoulder and walked away from their campsite. After staring for a second, wondering where he was going, she hoisted her own pack onto her back and hurried after him. Her feet broke through the snow, making her appreciate the snowshoes. Although her pack was lighter now, it pressed down on the sore spots it had created during the day of hiking.

As she followed George, she hoped that he hadn't meant they were going hunting for their dinner. An image of the cute bunny she'd seen earlier flashed in her mind, and she swallowed. Maybe she could convince him to stick with trail mix.

He finally stopped, placing his pack on the ground. By the time she'd reached him, he'd pulled out several items, including a small camp stove.

"What's for dinner?" she asked warily. When he handed her two foil pouches, she relaxed. "Beef stroganoff and chicken teriyaki. In a bag. This should be interesting."

His grunt actually sounded amused as he held out a small pan. "Snow."

Resisting the urge to salute, she traded him the pouches for the pan and went looking for a clean patch of snow. In the fading light, it all looked pretty good, so she filled the pan and returned to where George had fired up the cook stove. He took the pan and poured some water from one of his bottles over the snow before setting it on the burner.

"Why add water?"

"Keeps it from scorching. Watch it."

Apparently, "please" was not part of George's vernacular. She couldn't get too bothered by the lack of politeness, though, since he hadn't even been talking to her just that morning. She kept an eye on the pot while also watching George, who'd pulled a long length of thin rope from his pack. After filling a bag with snow, he tied it to the end of the rope and tossed it over a branch fifteen feet up in one of the pine trees. The snow-filled bag flew over the branch and headed toward the ground, bringing the line with it.

The water started boiling, and she hurried to pull it off the stove. "That was fast."

"High altitude." At her confused look, he clarified, "Water boils at a lower temperature up here."

"Really? Huh."

Instead of responding, he just handed her a small, soft-sided cooler and a coffee filter. When she looked at the items and then back at George, he gestured toward the food pouches.

"Right." The water would be to reconstitute the food, and she guessed that the coffee filter was to catch any dirt, tree bits, or dead bugs that might have been hanging out in the snow they'd melted. She read the directions on the back of the beef stroganoff. It looked pretty easy—add water and let it sit for nine minutes. "What time is it?"

Pulling back his coat cuff, he moved a step closer and held his watch so she could see it. He'd do anything to avoid actually speaking, she figured.

"Can you let me know when nine minutes has

passed?" At his nod, Ellie tore open the first package. Pouring hot water through the filter into the pouches was a little tricky, but her gloves were thick enough to protect her from the small amount she spilled on herself. After sealing up the first pouch, she repeated the process with the second, and then zipped them both into the insulated cooler. "There. Dinner's made." The satisfaction in her voice made her grin. There was something about camping that turned the simplest tasks into great feats of accomplishment. It was like she was a pioneer—or it would be, if they'd had Gore-Tex and Under Armor and artificial food preservatives in the 1800s.

While she'd been occupied with "cooking," George had put another pot of watered snow on the stove, and he was back to his tree-swing construction, or whatever he was doing with the rope. When the line dangled between two trees, the center loose enough to sag just five feet from the ground, he joined her by the stove.

After collecting the empty water bottles, he put a scoop of powdered energy drink in each one before filling them with the boiling water poured through the filter. Ellie closed the energy powder container as she read the label.

"Cherry flavor?"

"Freezes at a lower temperature than plain water," George explained, closing the top of the last refilled bottle.

"You know what freezes at a really low temperature?" When he raised a brow, she grinned. "Vodka. Plus, that would make us feel warm—well, until we froze to death in a drunken haze—and it would make my blisters stop hurting."

He'd been starting to smile until she mentioned the

blisters. His suddenly serious gaze went to her boots before shooting back to her face.

"It's fine." She was a little embarrassed to be whining about such a small discomfort. "I was just making a joke."

"No blisters?"

"Well, yes, blisters, but they're not a big deal."

According to his scowl, they were most certainly a big deal. "We'll take care of them tonight."

Knowing it was pointless to argue, Ellie tried not to think of how much his last comment sounded like a threat. "What time is it?"

After checking his watch, he pointed toward the cooler—or warmer, she supposed it should be called. He pulled a couple of sporks from his pack and handed her one. With a smile, she accepted it.

When he gave her a questioning look, she just shrugged. "Sporks are fun."

George shook his head and unzipped the cooler, holding the opening toward her so she got the first pick of the meals. If her assumptions about reconstituted food in a pouch were correct, neither would be a winning choice. She grabbed the chicken randomly, figuring that at least the meal would be warm. After eating trail mix all day, a change would be nice.

She gave it a stir with her spork and then took a bite. It wasn't nice. It wasn't nice at all. Since she didn't want to chew it anymore—because then she'd have to keep tasting it—Ellie swallowed it like a mouthful of medicine. It was still lumpy enough to hurt her throat going down. Staring down at the still-full pouch of food, her shoulders drooped. There was a lot in there.

Glancing up, she saw George was watching her. "Just fair warning. You're going to be stuck with a lot of this." She gave the pouch a jiggle.

He didn't look too concerned as he shoved another sporkful of beef stroganoff into his mouth. With a sigh, she dug into her own dinner.

Chapter 6

ELLIE ENDED UP MANAGING TO DOWN ALMOST HALF of her so-called chicken teriyaki before she gave up and handed the remaining food to George. He finished it quickly, and then tucked the empty pouches into a plastic bag and sealed it shut. He put that into a stuff sack, along with all the trail mix and other food he'd pulled from his pack. Once he emptied his pack of everything edible, he stripped hers of any food, as well.

He closed the stuff sack and attached it to the drooping center of the line stretched between the two trees. After he pulled the end attached to the second tree, tautening the rope and drawing the stuff sack full of food a good fifteen feet off the ground, she finally couldn't stand not knowing any longer.

"What are you doing?"

"Bears."

His one-word answer made her suck in a quick breath and look around, frantically peering through the gathering darkness. "Bears? Here?"

Pausing in the middle of securing the line, keeping the food dangling high above them, George looked at her. "Not many out yet, but no reason to take any chances."

"Yes, I think that's smart. I approve of not taking chances with bears." She couldn't stop swiveling her head side to side, though, and the growing shadows were sparking the scaredy-cat side of her imagination.

"So, should we head back to the tent now?" Not that she thought the soft-sided shelter would offer any protection from a bear's claws and teeth if it really wanted to eat them.

George did not look appropriately worried about the possibility of becoming a bear's midnight snack. In fact, although it was hard to tell under his beard, she was pretty sure he was amused by the squeaky pitch to her voice. He definitely didn't rush through packing up the stove. After giving the sporks a rudimentary cleaning with a handful of snow and then rinsing them with the remains of their quickly cooling water in the pan, he stowed them in his pack.

Quickly sliding her arms into her own backpack, she waited impatiently as he did a final check of the area. Before he put his own pack over his shoulder, he pulled out a flashlight. Once he turned on the light, Ellie realized how dark it was getting, and her desire to hide in the semi-safety of their tent doubled. At least then they wouldn't be standing by the yummy-smelling bag of food.

"Is that why we ate over here? To keep all the smells away from the tent?" she asked as George finally, *finally*, started walking back toward their main campsite.

He dipped his head. "No food in the tent." His sideways glance was almost accusatory, as if he thought she was smuggling a candy bar in her coat pocket or something. Overcome with a sudden burst of bear-induced paranoia, she quickly checked her pockets for possible forgotten tidbits. To her relief, the only things she found were the avalanche beacon and the folded map that Callum had printed out the day before.

"I'm clean," she said, earning another look from George, this one amused.

Ellie shivered. With the sunlight gone, the temperature was quickly dropping, and a cold breeze had picked up. The area outside the yellow beam of the flashlight seemed deeply dark and endless, filled with unfriendly things with fangs and claws. She stepped a little closer to George. He was just so reassuringly large. If an angry bear did happen to attack, George would have a pretty good chance of winning that fight.

When the tent reflected the light, she let out a silent exhale of relief. "Should we bring the packs inside?" she asked, looking back at him as she scurried toward the entrance. Thanks to the flashlight he carried, all she could see was a blinding circle of light. Her hand whipped up to shield her eyes.

"In the vestibule."

Ellie held in a snort. "Vestibule" was a pretty fancy word for the tiny porch area draping the entrance of the tent. With white spots still plastered across her vision, she fumbled for the zipper. Before she could climb through the opening, George tugged at her pack, and she shrugged out of the shoulder straps. After setting her pack aside, he caught her again, this time by the arm, before she could dive into the tent.

"Don't you need to"—he jerked his head to the area outside the tent—"first?"

After a second of staring at him blankly, she realized what he was asking and made a face. "Yes. Good idea." She reversed out of the vestibule and stood, accepting the flashlight and a few thin squares of camping toilet paper that George offered. The flashlight's beam seemed so puny compared to the yawning darkness that surrounded them. "Um...did you need to go, too?"

"After you're done."

There was no way to tactfully ask a near stranger if he would pee in the woods with her because she was scared of bears and whatever else lurked out there, so she just vowed to stay close to the tent. Privacy became a nonissue when carnivorous—or at least omnivorous— wild animals were about.

She ducked through the trees sheltering their tent, just twenty feet or so from the entrance. It was both easier that time, since she didn't have her pack, and more miserable, thanks to her worries and the dark and the biting wind. She'd always imagined that being in the wilderness would feel peaceful and solitary, but she just couldn't shake the feeling that she was being *watched*. Telling herself that she was being an idiot, Ellie focused on finishing what she needed to do so she could escape the phantom gaze and return to the safety of the tent and George.

Ellie hurried back, almost crashing into George halfway to the tent entrance. She wondered if he'd been watching out for her. Knowing that he'd been so close while she'd answered the call of nature was both reassuring and slightly creepy. When she tried to hand off the flashlight to him, he held up his own. She was secretly relieved not to have to spend any time in the complete darkness.

Crawling into the tent alone was eerie, the bouncing light of her flashlight creating odd shadows on the fabric walls, and she felt like she held her breath until George joined her. The sleeping bag on the left looked slightly smaller, so she scooted over to that side, attempting to keep her boots off the bed. It was difficult, though, since there wasn't much tent floor showing around the edges of the pads.

Her hand rose to her mouth, but her glove kept her teeth off her fingers. While setting up the tent earlier, she hadn't noticed how *close* the sleeping bags were to each other. Even though they'd both be wrapped with multiple layers of fabric, it would be a little disconcerting to sleep that close to a man she'd just met the day before.

The stranger in question cleared his throat, and she looked up to see him holding out two stuff sacks, one empty and one full. Although she accepted them, she gave him a questioning look.

He pointed at the full sack. "Water bottles." And then at the empty one. "Boots."

"Okay." That was strange. It wasn't like there were any snakes around in the cold weather to crawl into her boots or anything. With a shrug, she removed her gloves and unlaced her boots. When she pulled them off, her socks tried to follow, pulling loose from her blisters, and she yanked them back into place, hissing at the sting.

George made a wordless, unhappy sound as he looked at her socked feet. In the oddly shadowed illumination of the flashlight, the dried blood next to her baby toes looked black against the tan socks. From the throb at the backs of her heels, there'd be more blood there if she turned her feet to see. Instead, she focused on tucking her boots into the sack.

Once that was done, she looked at George, but he was

still scowling at her feet. When she put the stuff sack in the corner, however, he finally pulled his attention away. "In your sleeping bag."

"Really?" Once she thought about it, though, it made sense. It would be much better to stick her feet into warm boots in the morning instead of frozen ones. The thought of having to get up in eight or so hours and repeat the day of hiking was overwhelming, and she shut down that train of thought before she started whimpering. She slid the stuff sack into the bottom of her sleeping bag. "Should I put all my clothes in there with me?"

Shaking his head, he began to remove his own boots. "Just the water bottles and your gloves. Keep on your socks, long underwear, and hat."

She tucked her gloves next to the stuff sack holding her boots and added the one full of water bottles. "I thought I read somewhere that it was warmer to be naked in a down sleeping bag."

Even in the light of two flashlights, she had no idea how to interpret the look he directed at her for just a second before refocusing on his boots. He cleared his throat. "Myth."

"Oh." That was good. It was going to be uncomfortable enough sleeping right next to George without being naked. Besides, the idea of stripping to the buff in the cold air was not appealing. He put his boots in a stuff sack and then crawled to the entrance, unzipping the door so he could get something out of the packs. He reversed, zipping them in again, handing her a pair of her socks. He also had a white plastic box in his hand, which he placed next to him on his sleeping bag. Her hand went to her coat zipper, but George reached out and covered her hand with his, stilling it. She looked at him in surprise.

"Feet."

Making a face, she scooted back and pulled one foot onto her other thigh. Once again, George's hand stopped her. This time, he closed his fingers around her foot and gently tugged, turning her until she sat perpendicular to him with her feet on his lap.

He opened the white box, and Ellie leaned closer to see the contents. It looked like a first-aid kit. Taking out a few wrapped packets that she guessed were alcohol wipes, George tucked them into his waistband, momentarily revealing an inch of his hard stomach in the process. Ellie realized he was warming the wipes for her, and she felt a rush of appreciation for his thoughtfulness.

He removed her socks, and the air instantly chilled her bare skin. Her toes curled in protest.

"I'll be quick," he promised, and he was. Quick and brutal. After cleaning the blistered areas with the alcohol wipes, leaving her breathless from the burn, he dabbed on antibiotic ointment and covered all four spots with Band-Aids. He took the socks he'd just retrieved from her and slid them over her doctored feet.

"Thank you," she said as he folded her feet into his huge hands, enveloping them completely in luscious warmth. For a minute, neither of them moved. Ellie had never felt so cared for, so protected. At the same time, his gentle hold made her stomach dip and swoop with nervous excitement. It seemed as if every nerve ending in her body was based in her feet, and George's touch was setting all of them on fire. Her breath audibly caught, and self-consciousness slid over Ellie at the

sound. When she shifted uncomfortably, George immediately moved her feet back onto her sleeping bag, rotating her body in the process. This time, when she went
to remove her coat, he didn't stop her. As she tucked
it by the head of her sleeping mats, the rustle of paper
reminded her of the map.

Pulling it from her jacket pocket, she unfolded it and
held it toward George. "Could you show me where we
are on here?"

"Get in your sleeping bag and finish undressing." He
peeled off his coat and the layer beneath. "And then I will."

That was easier said than done. It took a lot of wiggling and some grunting before she was down to her
single long-underwear layer, socks, and her stocking
hat. "Okay."

He frowned. "Arms in."

When she obeyed, he zipped her sleeping bag all the
way to the top and then tugged the hood up over her
head. Once he tightened the drawstring, only her eyes,
nose, and mouth were exposed. She'd expected it to be
claustrophobia-inducing, but it felt cozy instead. Thanks
to the body heat produced by her undressing calisthen-
ics, the bag was already starting to warm.

"Don't breathe into the bag," he warned. "It'll hold
in the moisture and get cold."

"Okay." The idea of tucking her face into the sleeping bag wasn't appealing anyway. That *would* make
her claustrophobic.

"I have a bandana we can put over your nose and
mouth if your face is cold." He was watching her
closely, as if she were going to start defiantly breathing
inside her bag as soon as his back was turned.

"I'm fine. Map?" She wiggled onto her side so she could get a better view.

With a final stern glower, he picked up the map and directed the beam of a flashlight on it. After studying it for a minute, he tilted the paper and the light so she could see.

"We parked here." He pointed to a spot very close to where Callum had marked. "Followed this road." The tip of his finger traced one of the dotted lines. "Now we're here." He stopped at a point heartbreakingly close to where they'd started walking.

"The cabin is that *X*." Since her arms were bundled into her sleeping bag, she couldn't point, so she just tilted her head toward the map. "Which way do you think Dad's going? The deputy saw him at the Burnt Canyon Road trailhead."

The pause after his small shrug lasted a long time. Ellie opened her mouth to speak, figuring George was done, when he spoke, moving his fingertip along an area on the map that didn't follow any of the lines. "This way, maybe."

She resisted the urge to pull her arm out of her sleeping bag so she could trace her father's route on the map. Instead, she asked, "How long do you think it'll take us to get there?"

George studied the map for a moment before answering. "Two and a half days, if we push it."

That was longer than she'd expected and would total more days than she'd told Chelsea. She sighed. It wasn't like she could call Chels and let her know, either, since she didn't even have to turn on her phone to know that there was absolutely no cell coverage. Trying to shift her thoughts away from Chelsea's annoyance—since there was nothing Ellie could do about that anyway—she asked, "Will we just keep following the same road?" The dotted line appeared to travel in a semi-straight line before it passed close to the cabin's X.

"No." His finger left the road and made a loop, creating a half circle before ending up at the cabin.

She frowned. Although the map symbols confused her, the route he'd just indicated didn't make any sense. "Why that way? It seems a lot longer."

He tapped the map at a point between their current location and the cabin. "Avalanche area."

Her lungs compressed. After she'd tucked away the beacon in her coat pocket, she'd forgotten about that particular danger. "Avalanche? We could get buried in an avalanche?"

"Possibly. Not as likely if we go this way." He pointed at the roundabout route.

"Not as likely? That means there's still a chance?"

He offered another one of his affirmative shrugs, not looking all that concerned about the thought of being buried under tons of snow. With a sigh, she closed her eyes.

"If Dad's not at the cabin, I'm going to kill him. Or I will if I'm not buried under a hundred feet of snow or eaten by a bear first."

Something tickled her cheek, and she opened her eyes to see George's hand moving away from her face. She gave him a slightly startled look.

"Hair," he explained, brushing his fingers against his thumb as if flicking away a stray strand.

"Oh." She felt warmth and awkwardness cover her

like a heavy blanket as she looked at him, stretched out next to her, so close she could easily touch him if her arms hadn't been bound to her sides. Closing her eyes again, she pretended he was a little farther away from her to reduce the temptation to close that tiny space separating them. "Good night."

There was no response except for the rustling of fabric. She assumed that he was removing his outer layers, and her imagination supplied a full-color movie of what he probably looked like while stripping. She squeezed her eyes more tightly closed and tried to think about other things—anything except a half-naked George lying right next to her. Eventually, the sounds stopped, replaced by the clicking burr of his sleeping-bag zipper. The red glow behind her eyelids faded to black as he turned off the flashlights.

When it was quiet, drowsiness quickly overcame her. Her last thought before she slept was not of bears or avalanches or even her father. It was that tiny glimpse of George's bare stomach as he sweetly warmed her alcohol wipes.

She was flushed but smiling as she fell asleep.

Anderson could hear them breathing. Silly sheep, fast asleep.

As he circled the tent, close enough to stroke his hand across the outer surface, he thought of how easy it would be. George Holloway, the smug, self-righteous bastard, the great search and rescue tracker, wouldn't even see it coming. Anderson could take them both out before Holloway could even unzip his sleeping bag. Better yet, he'd do Baxter Price's daughter and make Holloway watch.

Anderson paused next to the tent entrance, sorely tempted. They'd followed the two all day, and the high-and-mighty Holloway hadn't had a clue. He'd been so focused on the hot piece of city tail that he wouldn't have even seen a mountain lion if it had jumped on him and started chewing on his head. Everyone thought Holloway was so great, but he didn't know shit.

His fingers twitched, wanting to reach for that tent flap. It wasn't time yet, though. The two had to serve their purpose, and then Anderson could have his fun.

"Anderson?" The wind quieted for a moment, allowing Wilson's distant whisper to echo through the night. Holloway's sleeping breaths stopped, alert stillness taking their place, and Anderson backed away soundlessly. Exasperation drew his brows together. Once again, his brother had ruined a perfectly good hunt.

Anderson slipped away as silently as he'd arrived, covering his tracks as he went. The obliging wind would erase the last hints of his presence.

It was okay. Anderson knew how to be patient. He'd get another chance at both Holloway and his city girl — maybe not tonight, but soon.

Her sleep was restless. The restriction of the mummy bag and the cold on her face kept nudging her into partial wakefulness. The sounds from outside the tent were both too quiet and too loud, giving her strange, half-alert dreams. At some point in the early morning hours, she wiggled over like an inchworm and curled against George's massive form. Tucking her face into the warm nook created by his shoulder and neck, she sighed with relief. With that last part of her finally warm, she fell asleep again and stayed unconscious until pinkish, early morning light filled the tent.

Her nighttime, half-asleep self hadn't felt self-conscious when she'd cuddled up to George. She'd just wanted to find a heat source. Her morning self, however, jolted awake at the realization that she'd taken over a slice of his sleeping pads and was plastered against him, their sleeping bags mashed together. Most embarrassing of all, though, was that her face was buried under his chin, her breath warming the skin of his neck.

By his stillness, she guessed he was already awake. Her plan to roll quietly away from her current position was therefore foiled. Instead, she inched far enough away so she could see his face.

"Good morning."

She wasn't surprised when he didn't answer. Although he'd started speaking more, he still didn't bother with the nonessentials: pleases, thank-yous, hellos, good-byes, good nights, and good mornings. Studying his face, Ellie couldn't tell whether he was annoyed or indifferent.

"Sorry about getting so close." She inched back again and slipped into the space between their sleeping pads. "My face was cold."

His slight nod told her nothing. Since her bladder was becoming quite insistent, she decided to ignore her embarrassment and focus on getting through another day of hiking. She squirmed until her elbows were bent and her hands beneath her chin, so she could tug at the drawstring on her hood.

Before she managed to loosen it, George reached over and opened it. He then opened her zipper a small amount. "Get dressed in there."

"Okay." She slid one arm out of the sleeping bag to snatch her fleece layers and pull them in with her. Just that single contact with the outside air made her wince and wish she could stay in her cozy sleeping bag all day. Maybe George could pull her on a sled?

The mental image made her smile, which, in turn, made her realize how gummy and gross her teeth felt. "You wouldn't happen to have packed a toothbrush, would you?"

Under his beard, the corner of his mouth quirked up.

"Is that a yes? Honestly?" Her voice lit with relief. "Oh, thank goodness. I thought I'd have fuzzy teeth for the next week."

Dressing in the sleeping bag was worse than undressing, and finally, annoyed and starting to sweat, she unzipped the bag and climbed out of it. When George gave her a reproving look, she just shrugged and pulled on her fleece pants over her long underwear.

She finished adding her layers as quickly as possible. Morning felt even colder than the night before, although it sounded like the wind had died. She remembered hearing it howling off and on during her frequent bouts of wakefulness. Digging out her gloves and the two stuff sacks, she hurried to pull out her boots. The cold was already seeping through the tarp and the tent floor into her socked feet, and she gratefully shoved her feet into the wonderfully warm boots.

Even when she was fully dressed, including gloves, she still felt chilled. The first thing she was going to do when she got home, she decided, was take a long, hot bath. The thought of it made her feel even colder, and she shivered.

George had been dressing right along with her, although he was much more efficient, especially when it came to putting things on in the confines of his sleeping bag. Not only was he dressed, but he'd rolled his sleeping bag and was working it into the compression sack.

"Leave that," Ellie said, unzipping the entrance. "Right after I…uh, visit a tree, I'll get everything packed in here while you cook breakfast." She hesitated. "It's not going to be reconstituted eggs and bacon, is it?"

That got an actual smile. "Oatmeal."

"Good." She sighed with relief. One gross meal in a pouch a day was plenty.

―――――

It was easier, Ellie found, to get the sleeping bag *out* of the compression sack than it was to get it back *in*. Growling, she fought the slick fabric.

"I'm cooking breakfast tomorrow morning," she muttered. "George can pack."

By the time she'd wrestled her sleeping bag into submission and rolled the mats, she knew George was probably waiting breakfast on her. Their tracks from the night before had filled in with blown snow, leaving just the faintest of trails for her to follow.

As she approached George, he held out a spork. His eyebrow was lifted quizzically, and she sighed as she accepted the utensil.

"Sorry." Since he held the pan of oatmeal between them, she assumed they weren't getting separate bowls, so she just dug in. "That sleeping bag took forever to get into the tiny sack. It's a tricky devil."

He snorted. Whether it was in agreement or in amusement at her incompetence, she wasn't sure. They ate in silence for a while, taking turns reaching into the pot for a sporkful. The oatmeal wasn't bad. She would've preferred it with milk, but he'd sweetened it with something and added pecans, so it was pretty tasty. It was a definite improvement over the previous meal.

As usual, she withdrew her spork before it was half-way gone, and George finished the oatmeal. Afterward, he cleaned the pan and sporks with melted snow, scrubbing at them with his fingers. He dried the few dishes with a small towel before stowing everything in their packs.

Eyeing the place where the food had hung overnight, she asked, "Any sign of bears?"

Although he kept his gaze on the cookstove he was packing, Ellie could tell he was trying not to smile as he shook his head. With a huff, she hoisted her pack onto her back and headed back to the tent.

While he amused himself by thinking about her fear of mauling and dismemberment, she'd get some more packing done.

Chapter 7

ONLY AN HOUR INTO THE DAY'S HIKING, ELLIE already felt wretched. Despite the Band-Aids and extra-tight lacing, her boots rubbed against the blisters. By the way they were already throbbing, she knew her feet would be raw by evening.

That morning, George had told her to store her avalanche beacon under her outermost layer, which had put her in a quandary. Her fleece didn't have pockets that zipped, and her long underwear had no pockets at all. After some dithering, she'd stored it in her bra, wincing as she'd tucked the cold device against her skin. It was the most secure place under her coat, but it definitely wasn't the most comfortable.

She wished she hadn't asked about their route the previous night. When George turned off the logging road, she followed reluctantly. It made it worse to know that they were taking such an indirect route, although she was aware that it was better than to risk walking through an area with a high likelihood of avalanches.

Her muscles were painfully stiff and sore from all of the unaccustomed exercise the day before. Even with George walking slowly, she was still falling behind. Every few minutes, she'd have to run a couple of strides to catch up with him. If she couldn't push her body to move faster, the weeklong trip was going to turn into double that.

"You are stronger than you think," she mumbled under her breath, ignoring the way her body shrieked its opposition. "This doesn't hurt. This feels wonderful. I'm out in the beauty of nature. My feet are as light as air. What blisters?" She tried to think of more positive affirmations—not that they were really helping. In fact, the words used up some of her precious oxygen, and she didn't have any to spare. "Pain is just weakness leaving the body." Ellie wasn't sure where she'd heard the last one, but she was pretty sure it hadn't been in her yoga class.

Focused on trying to convince herself how not miserable she was, she didn't notice George had stopped until she got a face full of the front of his coat. Taking a step back, she looked up to meet his gaze. If she had to take a guess, she would say his expression was a combination of bafflement and amusement.

"What?" she asked.

Shaking his head, he turned and started walking again. Now that they'd stopped, her legs refused to move again.

"George?" she called after him. He tipped his chin toward his shoulder, indicating that he was listening. "I'm sorry, but could we take a break? My legs aren't being very cooperative."

He turned and returned to where she was standing, his hand immediately going to the trail mix pocket as he eyed her water bottle meaningfully. Although she wasn't thirsty, she pulled it out and took a drink, trying not to make a face at the energy powder's bitter tang that the cherry flavor did a poor job of masking.

Her expression must have given her away, because he grabbed another bottle off his pack and exchanged it with hers. When she took a drink, the taste—or lack of taste—of plain water made her smile.

"Thank you."

With a nod of acknowledgment, George held out the bag of trail mix. "What color is your urine?"

Blinking, she tried to process the question. After the past hour of silence, he finally spoke to ask her about her pee? "Uh, what?"

"Your urine." He enunciated clearly, as if it were her hearing that was the problem, and not the question. "What color is it?"

"Um...I didn't look at it." Because she was a *normal* person.

He frowned. "Check next time."

"Why?" she asked warily. Although quiet, he hadn't seemed like a freak, but she really didn't know the guy.

"It should be light or clear. If it's dark, you're dehydrated."

"Oh." Her shoulders lowered in relief. He wasn't a freak then—at least, not about pee. "Okay." At the reminder, she took another long drink of water. When he extended the trail mix again, she tugged off a glove and took a handful.

"Are you sweating?"

Pausing a second, she took stock, but the fabric against her skin didn't feel damp as it had the day before. "Not that I can tell." A thought occurred to her, and she grinned at him. "You asked this time instead of feeling me up!"

Above his beard, his cheeks grew ruddier, and Ellie felt bad about embarrassing him. She concentrated on the food in her hand.

Finishing her handful of trail mix, she pulled on her glove and took a final drink of water. Securing the bottle in its upside down position on her pack, she bit off a resigned sigh and tried to force some enthusiasm into her voice. "Ready?"

After eyeing her closely, he started walking. Ellie forced her concrete legs to follow. To distract herself, she looked around at the scenery. Even though they'd left the main forest service road, they were on a trail of some kind, judging by the clear sweep of snow in front of them. It was narrower than the road, though, with only about three feet of space between the bordering trees. She tried to imagine it in a couple of months, when the snow would be gone and everything—not just the pine trees—would be green. It was hard to see beyond the all-encompassing white.

Ellie tried to take a step, but something was holding down her foot. When she glanced at her boots, she saw that one snowshoe had landed on the edge of the other one, pinning it. She'd barely made the realization when another struck her—she was falling.

A grunt escaped when she landed, her hip and her hand hitting the ground next to the path first. Immediately, she started to slide down the incline, her body bumping off rocks as if she were a pinball. Ellie scrambled to grab something, anything that would keep her from tumbling farther down the slope. Her hand closed around a leafless bush, but its shallow roots released their grip on the soil, sending her slipping another few feet until a large boulder halted her downward slide.

Biting back a groan, she lay still for a moment, taking inventory of her body parts. Despite an overall ache, everything seemed to be functioning, so she carefully rolled onto her side. The worst part was the embarrassment. After all, she'd tripped over her own feet. George loomed over her, adding to the humiliation.

"I'm fine," she said before he could ask. "For looking so fluffy and soft, though, snow is really freaking hard." Shoving up into a sitting position, she untangled her snowshoes, giving the culprits an accusing stare.

"Wait." His eyebrows knotted in concern, George went down onto one knee next to her and ran his hands over her, starting at her head and working down her arms and legs. Her attempt to make another I-am-not-a-horse objection came out as a croak, so she went silent as he finished his inspection. When he didn't find any broken bones or gushing wounds, he stood.

Ellie started to climb to her feet, afraid that her attempt to stand in snowshoes wasn't going to be a pretty sight, when George leaned down. Catching her under the arms, he gently hoisted her to her feet, stealing her breath for the second time in as many minutes. She made a startled sound and clutched at his forearms for balance. Once she'd gotten her bearings, she hurriedly released her grip, although a large part of her wanted to continue to hold on to him.

"Sorry...I mean, thank you." Ellie wasn't sure why she was so flustered or why her skin felt so warm. "That was efficient. Quicker than me trying to stand up on my own, I mean." Why was she babbling? For whatever reason, her mouth did not want to stay shut. "So, thank you. Um, again. Ready to go?"

Instead of releasing her, he gave her an assessing look, his eyes dropping to her snowshoes and back to her face as if checking once again for any broken or missing body parts. Ellie blushed, and her heart beat faster, even though she doubted that he'd be able to make out even a suggestion of her shape under her multiple bulky layers of clothes. When he apparently didn't see anything out of place, he removed his hands slowly, almost reluctantly, and turned to lead the way back up the slope to the trail.

With some personal space reestablished, Ellie was able to breathe again—well, as much as she *could* breathe in the thin air. She fell in behind George, alternating between watching her feet so she didn't trip herself a second time and stealing quick glances at his back. Since he kept looking over his shoulder to check on her, he caught her eyeballing him a few times. When that happened, she couldn't stop herself from ducking her head to focus on her snowshoes.

She couldn't figure out why she was behaving like a preteen girl with a crush for the first time in her life—including when she'd *actually* been a preteen girl. It was probably a good thing George was so quiet, so he couldn't comment on how silly she was acting. Tilting her head, she eyed his back as she thought. Maybe it was because he was her lifeline in an unfamiliar, dangerous situation. Or perhaps his well-honed survival skills struck a chord with her inner cavewoman. At that moment, he turned to check on her again, and she looked away, pretending to study an evergreen tree squatting next to the trail. As soon as she saw in her peripheral vision that he'd faced forward, she resumed her study of his ridiculously broad back.

Her growing crush on George wasn't *that* surprising,

really. He was a good-looking guy. The few glimpses she'd had of his body had been positive…very, very positive. Sure, he was quiet, but he was also strong and smart and very patient. It was like he was a different species from Dylan and the last few guys she'd dated. She tried to picture George in skinny jeans and had to smother a giggle. Despite her efforts, he must have heard, since he glanced back at her. Her gaze dropped to her snowshoes.

Her musings about what made George so attractive kept her going until her stomach pinged with hunger.

"George?"

He immediately stopped and turned, making her wonder if he was still jumpy because of her fall.

"Snack break?" she asked with a smile, and he reached for a pocket on his pack.

When she looked around, she made a face. There were no rocks, downed logs, or other sure-to-be-uncomfortable seats available, so she resigned herself to standing. She noticed that the trees around them were bare and blackened. Even the evergreens were stripped of their needles.

"What happened?" she asked, gesturing at the skel-etal remains of the forest. "Was there a forest fire?"

His grunt was affirmative. George presented her with jerky this time, so that was different.

"Wow." The burned areas stretched farther than she could see. "It must have been huge. Was it lightning that started it, or a campfire or something?"

"Arson."

Her gaze snapped back to his face. "Arson? Really?"

"Yes. Eat."

After taking a bite, she chewed thoughtfully. "Is this beef?"

"Venison."

"Oh." She chewed some more…and then even more. After only one bite, her jaw was already getting sore. Feeling a little dumb, she asked, "That's deer, right?"

After giving her a cautious look, he lifted his chin slightly in the barest of nods.

Unable to interpret his expression, she asked, "What?"

"Didn't want to upset you."

Her eyebrows squished together in a puzzled frown. "Why would it upset me? Oh, because it's deer? Bambi and all?" She eyed the dried meat in her hand, but then shrugged. "As long as I don't have to look into its big, innocent eyes and pull the trigger, I'm okay with eating it. Same with cows or chickens." Frowning, she looked up at George. "Does that make me a hypocrite?"

He seemed to consider this seriously before he answered. "No. I think it makes you typical of most people nowadays."

"That doesn't seem much better." Tired of chewing, she handed the remainder of her jerky to George and reached for her water bottle. Although it was heavy enough to be half-full, nothing came out when she tipped it back. Puzzled, she peered into the wide mouth.

"It's frozen." George handed her one of his bottles. When she took a drink, the not-quite-right cherry flavor hit her tongue. Grimacing, she swallowed. "Sorry," he said.

"Not your fault," she said, forcing down another drink. "It's just the laws of nature, I guess. I'll live. It is colder now, then? I thought it was, but then I figured I was just being a whiner."

He frowned at the sky. Gray clouds had covered the brilliant blue from earlier that morning.

"Think it's going to snow?" She shivered at the thought as she recapped the water bottle. When she tried to hand it back to him, George refused to take it, removing the frozen bottle off her pack instead.

"Yes."

It took her a minute to realize he was answering her question. "Like, a few snowflakes, or the storm of the century?"

He shrugged, but his expression was concerned.

Feeling bad about slowing their pace, Ellie stowed her water bottle where the frozen one had been and moved quickly toward a stand of trees. "I'll be right back, and then we can go. I'll be faster from now on, I promise."

"You're doing fine."

She made a face over her shoulder at him. "No, I've been limping along like a three-legged camel. I'll do better." Without waiting for a response, she hurried behind one of the thicker trees.

"Check the color of your urine," he called after her, and she wrinkled her nose.

"Again with the pee-color thing?" she muttered, although too softly for him to hear. Once she was done and had all her bottom layers pulled to her waist, she did look and was dismayed to see it wasn't clear or even pale yellow. George was definitely going to increase his nagging about drinking nasty cherry-flavored water. Even though he didn't say much, his chiding looks were worth a thousand words.

With a sigh, she turned…and then stopped abruptly. A moose stood a short distance from her.

Ellie could hardly believe what she was seeing. It was the most enormous animal she'd ever seen outside of a zoo. It towered over her, at least a couple of feet taller than her at the shoulder. It wasn't just tall—it was bulky, with a broad body and a wide, heavy head topped with small but thick antlers. Her muscles froze as her thoughts galloped in the most unhelpful way. It shouldn't have been scary. After all, it was just a moose, not anything with claws or fangs.

And yet… Maybe it was the animal's huge size or its proximity, but the moose *was* scary. Very, very scary.

"George." The word came out in a wheezy rasp that probably didn't carry five feet. The moose didn't look happy. The hair rose between its shoulders like a pissed-off cat, and it pinned its ears against its skull. She didn't know moose-speak, but that couldn't be good. She took a step back, and it jerked up its head, making it look even taller and more threatening.

What were you supposed to do when facing a charging moose? Run? Climb a tree? Play dead? She had no idea, and that helplessness was as terrifying as the wild animal itself. "George!" That time, her voice rose in a yelp, which probably didn't make the moose any happier.

A hand closed over her upper arm, and she almost jumped out of her skin. George moved in front of her, creating a barrier between her and the moose, and she swallowed a relieved sob. He stepped back, nudging her so she had no choice but to retreat with him.

As the moose watched, hackles still raised and ears

pinned, they slowly moved away one step at a time. Once they were parallel with a larger tree, George shifted sideways, moving Ellie with him.

When the tree was between them and the moose, he turned and quietly said, "Run."

Chapter 8

PIVOTING AROUND, SHE ALMOST TRIPPED ON HER snowshoes again, but George grabbed her pack and steadied her so she didn't fall. There was a sound behind her, and she looked over her shoulder in a horror-film-cliché move she knew she'd beat herself up over later.

The moose was charging after them. Ellie yelped and faced forward, her feet moving faster than she thought they could go. Tree branches whipped across her face, but she couldn't feel the sting, couldn't feel anything except sheer terror that she and George were going to be trampled.

She ran until the air felt like a rusty blade sawing in and out of her lungs, until bile rose up in the back of her throat, and she knew that, if she didn't stop, she'd die anyway, charging moose or no. Slowing in a few faltering steps, she stopped and immediately bent over, her hands on her thighs right above her knees, and sucked in air. Oxygen was the most critical thing at the moment. Not even her safety had priority.

When she managed to straighten, she reluctantly turned, half expecting to be face-to-face with the moose. Instead, only George stood there. There was no sign of the charging animal. She looked around frantically, her panic making her illogically worried that the moose might leap out from behind a tree.

George laid his hands on her heaving shoulders. "Its

charge was just a bluff. It ran at us for about ten feet and then stopped."

"It's…gone?" she gasped, her breathing still uneven.

When he nodded, Ellie burst into tears. She felt silly for crying over a *moose* but was unable to stop her sobs. Now George looked like *he* was about to panic, so she buried her face against his chest, not wanting him to see her meltdown. The outer layer of his coat was rough against her cheek, but he felt reassuringly solid underneath it. With their packs, the embrace was awkward, made even more so by George's obvious discomfort. He patted her lightly on the upper arms, but then seemed to settle. One hand wrapped around her head, holding her face against him, while the other rested on her hip.

Her arms were tucked between them, and she realized, as her sobs turned to sniffles and hiccupping gasps, that she was squeezing two handfuls of his coat. Once the worst of the hysterics were over, she also realized how cold her wet face was.

"Sorry," she muttered, releasing her grip on his coat. "I'm being stupid. It was just so *big*, and I had no idea what I was supposed to do."

"It's not stupid to be scared of a moose. I'd rather encounter a bear than a moose."

"Really?" She peered suspiciously at him, trying to see if he was pandering to her wimpiness or if he really meant it. He looked sincere, although it was hard to tell with George.

"Yeah. Bears are predictable. They don't want to be around us any more than we want to be around them. I get that. Nothing wrong with needing a little personal space. If you ever do run into a black bear, just back away slowly the way you came. Don't run, and don't climb a tree. They can outrun and outclimb you. You can talk to it in a calm voice, too. Let it know you're a person."

George's deep-voiced monologue was soothing, easing the last of her tears. Now that she'd calmed, she puzzled at his uncharacteristic outpouring of words. He *hated* talking; why had he turned into an infomercial now? The idea that he'd done that for her, to comfort her, made her heart squeeze with gratitude.

Despite her warm and fuzzy feelings for George, though, the thought of bears still made her nervous. "What if we run into a grizzly?"

"You won't. No grizzlies around here."

That was reassuring. She took a step back, and his hands dropped away from her. She swiped at her face with her fingers, but the nylon outer shell of her gloves didn't provide much absorption. When something soft rubbed over her cheeks, she looked up in surprise. George had pulled off his stocking hat and was using it as a handkerchief.

"I'm good." She took another step back so she was out of reach. "Sorry. Don't get your hat all wet just because I'm being a baby."

He actually rolled his eyes at that and followed her, getting another swipe in before she ducked.

"Really." She sniffed and forced a smile. "I'm fine now. Put on your hat and let's go." Glancing around, she realized that everywhere they'd been looked pretty much the same to her. She hoped nothing happened to George, or she'd be wandering the mountain until the snow melted—or she was eaten by a moose. "Did we at least run in the direction we're headed?"

As he pulled on his hat, he raised a shoulder in a gesture that Ellie interpreted as "kind of, but not really."

She sighed. "Well, lead on. You know where we are, though, right?" Her voice was still nasally from residual tears. When he gave her a look, she raised her hands in a gesture of innocence. "Sorry! Didn't mean to question your mountaineering skills. Just checking."

As they started walking, George in the lead, Ellie couldn't help but look around for more potentially hungry wildlife that might jump out at them. When a rustling noise came from a tree above them, she gave a little shriek and jumped sideways, tangling her snowshoes and falling into a heap.

While George helped her back to her feet—which basically involved him lifting her off the ground—he looked like he was fighting a smile.

"What is it?" Ellie peered at the spot on the tree where the noise had originated.

"A squirrel." He coughed into the back of his glove.

She narrowed her eyes at him. "Did you just laugh?"

He shook his head, looking suspiciously serious.

"Liar." She brushed off snow that still clung to her hip. "If it had been a bear, you'd have been thanking me for the warning."

This time, his laugh boomed out before he bit off the sound.

Unable to hold her irritation, she grinned back at him. "Just turn around and keep walking, buster," she said.

Before he did, he brushed at her pants, his hand moving over her hip and across her thigh.

"Did I miss some snow?" She twisted to look, trying to keep her pack from overbalancing her. George shot her a glance so full of joyful wickedness that she froze for a few seconds before swatting at him. "Quit copping a feel and get back to leading."

He dodged out of reach and started walking. As she followed him, Ellie found she was wearing an enormous grin.

The smile didn't last long. When the wind picked up, it carried hard granules of snow along with it, whipping them against Ellie's face like a sandblaster.

"Ow, ow, ow," she chanted under her breath, twisting her head to protect her face from the icy pellets. George stopped and turned her around so he could get something from her pack. Not really caring what he was digging out of there, Ellie was just happy to have her back to the stinging wind.

He pulled a fleece ring of fabric over her head, tucking it into her coat collar so it encircled her neck. Making a happy sound, she buried her chin into the fuzzy fabric and pulled it all the way over her nose. Her breath reflected off the fleece and spread over her cheeks, warming them.

Next, George fitted ski goggles over her eyes, adjusting the wide elastic band over her hat. With all her skin covered, she hardly felt the impact of the wind, and her shoulders lowered with relief.

"Want me to get yours?" she asked, raising her voice to be heard over the howling wind.

He shook his head and slipped off his own pack, pulling a face mask and goggles from one of the many zippered sections. When they set off again, it felt much easier, even when her breath fogged the bottom of the goggles. Although it was still early afternoon, the clouds made it feel like twilight, especially when the snow started to fall.

It took Ellie a while to realize that there were fresh snowflakes joining the existing ones the wind was whipping around her. Soon, though, her visibility was reduced so much that she could hardly see George's back five feet in front of her. A swirl of wind-driven snow hid him completely for a few seconds, and her heart thudded in panic. Hurrying forward, she grabbed a handful of his coat.

He turned his head to look at her.

"I couldn't see you," she yelled over the wind.

"We need to make camp."

"Okay," she agreed, relieved. They walked another twenty minutes, though, before finding a place sheltered enough to satisfy George. By that point, Ellie was pretty sure she would've been happy just curling up in the snow. Since her face was protected from the wind, she'd been able to concentrate on just how cold her feet were. They felt like numb blocks of ice hanging off her legs, and just sheer will and the promise of resting soon allowed her to keep moving them.

They finally stopped at a spot where a boulder and a few scrubby pines made a partial windbreak. They shed their packs and snowshoes, tucking them against the boulder. When George pulled out the shovel and started to dig, Ellie wanted to cry. Instead, she retrieved the other shovel and joined him. She decided that she'd already exceeded her quota of tears for the day.

They worked fast, not digging as deeply or as precisely as they had the previous day. The wind blew fresh snow into the spot almost as quickly as they could remove it. Finally, George grabbed the tarp, and they stretched it across the shallow indentation they'd managed.

While he worked to set up the tent, she filled the snow anchors, although she eyed them in concern. The wind was blowing so hard, she hoped they'd be enough to keep the tent secured. George gave a shout, and she moved to help him erect the tent.

He must have had the same doubts about the anchors, since he dug holes in the snow and buried them, stomping the snow down on top of them. Once Ellie saw what he was doing, she started digging holes for the other anchors, and they finished quickly.

The snow was thickening, making it hard for Ellie to see even a few feet in front of her. When they pulled the packs into the vestibule of the tent, they had to first knock off the snow that had piled on them. The shelter of the tent was welcome, but Ellie knew it was only a temporary break.

"Do we need to go hang up the food?" Her words shook along with her quivering jaw. Even with all her layers of clothing, the wind cut through to her skin.

"No. We'll take our chances."

"Good." Ellie pulled off her fogged goggles, catching her hat as it came off with it. After shaking off the snow, she shoved the hat back on her head. "If I walked five feet away from the tent, I don't think I could find my way back. It's like those stories of the olden days, when ranchers would tie a rope from the house to the barn during a blizzard, so they didn't get lost and freeze to death."

"Get in your sleeping bag."

Although a "please" would have been nice, the thought of being warm was even nicer, so she started unlacing her boots. Her blisters didn't hurt so much when her boots came off that time, mainly because she couldn't feel her feet. Her right sock pulled free with her boot, exposing her waxy, white skin.

George made an unhappy sound and caught her by the ankles, rotating her like he'd done the night before. This time, though, he pulled her left sock off and then tucked both of her feet under his coat and top layers, so they were directly against his bare stomach.

They both hissed at the contact. The heat of George's skin burned against Ellie's, and she tried to withdraw her feet, but he held her firmly in place.

"Too hot," she whimpered, although she didn't fight his hold after that first attempt.

"I know," he said. His hands wrapped around the tops of her feet—not rubbing, but just holding—while his stomach pressed against the soles, surrounding her feet with painful fire. The burn eased to a pins-and-needles tingling, and she wiggled her toes against his belly to ease the sting.

"That must be like holding a block of ice to your stomach," she said.

He gave an affirmative grunt, but he didn't move her feet away from his skin. "Why didn't you tell me your feet were cold?"

With a shrug, she said, "All of me was pretty cold by the end. I didn't want to whine."

"I need to know." He gave her a stern look. "The blisters, the cold feet, dehydration. These are serious things out here."

"Sorry." Ducking her head, she studied a seam on her glove. "I might be a little bit dehydrated, too."

Keeping her feet against his belly, he rose to his knees and shuffled toward the entrance. His movement tipped Ellie onto her back and turned her ninety degrees, making her giggle.

"I feel like an upended turtle."

He looked down at her and smiled, his eyes as warm as melted chocolate, before reaching into the vestibule to dig through his pack. His body was twisted oddly so he wouldn't dislodge her feet. He handed her a water bottle, a dry hat, and then a couple of stuff sacks. Tossing the same things onto his own side of the tent, along with the first-aid kit, he closed the entrance and returned to his spot across from her.

Ellie pushed back to a sitting position. Sensation had returned to her frozen feet, and the pain had faded to a radiating heat. She could feel the ridges of his ab muscles under her soles, and she had to resist the urge to explore more of his torso with her toes. Ducking her head to hide her flush, she gave herself a stern lecture on not being a perv.

"Drink."

She opened the water bottle and took a drink. This time, when she winced, it was because of the temperature and not the nasty taste.

"Cold?" George guessed. It was, but she took another drink anyway. "I'll make tea. We won't make hot food tonight, though."

"Bears?"

Nodding, he plucked her socks from where they'd dropped and tucked them next to her feet. The chilly knit quickly warmed. Pulling a few alcohol wipes out of the first-aid kit, he slipped them against his belly, as well. "Doubt they'll be out in this, but no reason to ask for trouble."

"I don't mind. I'd take trail mix over that nasty food in a pouch any day."

He just smiled at that, something that seemed to be happening more and more. She wondered if she'd caused his increased happiness and was unable to hold back a grin of her own at the thought. It was strange how connected she felt to this large, taciturn man whom she'd only known for a few days. Ellie wondered if it was just because she was depending on him to stay warm and fed and safe. Even as the thought crossed her mind, she dismissed it, knowing that she would've felt the same way about George if they'd met in the safety of a Chicago smoothie shop.

"Ready?"

Before she could ask him what she should be ready for, he uncovered her feet. The cold air wrapped around them, making her shiver. Instead of the sickly white from earlier, they were now a bright pink. He pulled off the bloodied Band-Aids and examined the blistered spots and her toes carefully.

"Am I frostbitten?" she asked, leaning closer so she could see.

"No." George still turned a glower on her. "Tell me next time your feet get cold." He gave them a little shake for emphasis.

"I will." She sat back, leaning on her hands, as he pulled out an alcohol wipe and tore open the package. "I just don't want to be whiny."

"Tell me once. If you tell me over and over again, then you're whiny."

She laughed and then sucked in a breath as he cleaned her blisters with the alcohol wipe. He was just as quick—and just as merciless—as the previous night. When he pulled on her socks, warm from his body, he was frowning.

"The blisters are worse." Instead of returning her feet to her, he kept them in his lap, rubbing them absently. It felt wonderful, so she didn't complain.

"Sorry?" She held in a groan of delight when he massaged the arch of her foot.

"Not your fault."

"There isn't much to do about it, though, is there?"

"You have any thin socks?"

"Mmm…" The foot rub was stealing all her attention, and she had to force herself to focus on his question. "Think so. I'll have to check my pack."

"Wear those under the wool ones."

"Mm-kay." Seriously, his hands were magical. When he returned her feet to her, she swallowed a disappointed sigh. Without his warm touch, they quickly grew cold, and she started stripping down to her long underwear. After her struggle undressing the night before, she decided to just do it fast and then hop into her sleeping bag.

It wasn't until she was zipping herself in that she caught sight of the look on George's face and realized she'd just given him a strip show. It was a show that ended with her in her long underwear, but still. Her face reddened as she concentrated on her sleeping-bag zipper. She pulled it most of the way up, but left the hood down and drew the top around her shoulders. When she fished the avalanche transceiver out of her bra, she heard George suck in a breath.

He stayed frozen for another long moment before he shook himself and headed for the packs.

It felt almost decadent to huddle in her sleeping bag as George made them tea and fed them trail mix, a granola bar, and venison jerky. He also stowed her water bottles and boots in their stuff sacks and handed them to her to tuck into the bottom of her sleeping bag. There was indeed a pair of thinner socks in her pack, which joined her gloves inside her bedroll, as well.

Only after all their gear was stowed, and she was fed and sipping tea, did George crawl into his own sleeping bag.

"Do you have a pack of cards?" she asked, pretending not to watch as he stripped off his outer layers. He shook his head. "Monopoly? Checkers?" Both received another head shake and the beginnings of a smile. "I'd suggest charades, but that would involve leaving the sleeping bag, and that's not going to happen."

He zipped himself into his own bag, and she stifled a sigh. The show was over.

"We could play 'Never Have I Ever...'"

His quizzical eyebrows made it clear he didn't know what that was.

"That's okay. It's a drinking game, and I don't think it'd be the same with tea." Shooting him a teasing smile over the top of her cup, she added, "Since you refused to bring vodka, we'll have to wait for the Saint Bernard with the flask around his neck to arrive." Taking a sip of her hot drink, she thought for a moment. "I know! Thumb wars!"

His eyebrows were knitted in confusion again.

"I'll show you." She pushed herself into a seated position, taking care not to spill any of her tea as she shifted the mug to her left hand. Even without being spiked with something alcoholic, the warmth felt really good going down. She reached out her right hand, fingers curled loosely and thumb pointing to the tent ceiling.

Instead of meeting her hand with his, George just looked at her face, then at her hand, and back at her face again.

Ellie rolled her eyes. It was like trying to play games with an alien. "Hold your hand like this."

After a long hesitation, he held out his arm, mimicking her hand position. She curled her fingers into his, marveling at how small hers looked next to his mammoth hand. She shivered at the contact , but not because her arm was out of the warmth of her sleeping bag. The way he was watching her, with his eyes narrowed and focused, made her blush and drop her eyes to their locked hands.

"Okay." Her voice was a little higher than normal, and she hoped he didn't notice. "The goal is to hold the other person's thumb down for four seconds. No using your other hand to help." Not that he was going to need any help to obliterate her in a thumb war. She eyed their hands again. This was going to be a David and Goliath kind of battle. "We start out by saying one, two, three, four"—she moved her thumb from side to side with each word—"I declare a thumb war!"

Her thumb pounced, latching around his and pressing it down as she counted to four. He allowed it, still watching her with an unreadable expression.

She frowned at him. "Okay, no pacifists allowed. You need to go after my thumb, or at least do some evasive maneuvers. Got it?" Ellie waited until he eventually nodded. "Let's go again."

After chanting the preliminary words, she pinned his thumb again.

"George." Her hands would've been on her hips if that had been possible while wrapped in a mummy bag with one hand trapped in the grip of a quiet lumberjack and the other one clutching a cup of tea. "You need to put some effort into it."

This time, she eyed him militantly as she counted off the numbers. When she stretched her thumb toward his, he moved it to the side.

"Yes! Now we're playing!"

Although he dodged, he still let her win too easily.

"Try to hold my thumb down this time," she said as they launched another war. Hers darted forward, but he mashed his giant thumb on top of hers and flattened it.

"One…"

Laughing, Ellie tried to free her thumb, to no avail.

"Two…"

Holding out her mug so it didn't slosh tea over her lap, she twisted her arm from the shoulder, trying to escape his hold.

"Three…"

If her left hand was free, she could've cheated and used it to pry up George's thumb, rules be damned. Ellie wasn't about to sacrifice her tea, though, so she impulsively went for one of the other avenues open to her.

Without thinking, she leaned forward and kissed him on the mouth.

Chapter 9

HER GIGGLES STOPPED AS SOON AS THEIR LIPS TOUCHED. What had started as a teasing move instantly turned serious. They both froze in place, thumbs still overlapped, mouths barely pressed together. Despite the light contact, her lips tingled and burned, as if he'd brought them back from the edge of frostbite. Heat rushed through her, making her flush and swallow the urge to press her mouth harder against his. It felt like forever before Ellie, eyes wide, managed to sit back, breaking the contact. George stared at her.

"Uh...sorry." She wasn't really sorry, though. As brief and light as it was, it had been nice. Really nice. Want-to-repeat-it-very-soon nice. "I was trying to cheat."

He continued to stare until she dropped her gaze to study their still-locked thumbs.

"Four."

The low-spoken word brought up her head, and it was her turn to watch him. His thumb stroked hers a single time before he released her hand. It felt instantly cold, and she withdrew it, wrapping it around her rapidly cooling mug.

Taking a sip just for something to do besides stew in the awkwardness she'd created, Ellie made a face. Lukewarm tea wasn't very tasty. Knowing that she needed the liquid, however, she knocked the rest back, finishing it in three swallows. Lowering the empty mug, she saw that George was still eyeing her, and she racked her mind for ways to keep them occupied. Unfortunately, her brain was not cooperating. It just wanted to kiss George again.

Blushing as if he could read her thoughts, she carefully set her mug between the sleeping pads and the side of the tent. With her hands empty, she had to concentrate on not reaching for George. Her eyes darted around, looking anywhere except for where she really wanted to look. Her gaze fell on her coat, and an idea popped into her head.

"Can you show me where we are on the map again?" She risked a glance at him in time to catch his nod. Moving like a caterpillar, she wiggled her way to the top of her sleeping mats and dug the folded paper out of her pocket. Inching her way back to the center of the pads, she unfolded the map and placed it between them.

He examined it and then pointed. "We camped around there last night." His finger moved a disappointingly short distance. "Now we're about here."

Shifting so she had a better view, Ellie made a face. "Sorry I was so slow today. How long do you think it'll take to get to the cabin?"

The wind picked that second to howl, the gust shoving at the tent as if intent on blowing them off the mountain. Ellie leaned closer to George.

"Depends," he said after the wind died down enough that she could hear him. "This storm might last a couple of days."

Huddling deeper in her sleeping bag, she asked, "Do you think he's out in this?"

"Baxter? Could be. When did he leave?"

"The deputy, Chris, saw him Sunday morning at the Blue Hook trailhead."

"Your dad experienced?"

"With hiking and camping, you mean? Yes. He took me with him a few times when I was little, before... I'm just worried because he seemed so confused and scared the last time we talked on the phone."

"He's most likely already there." His finger brushed the spot on the map where the cabin was located. "If not, he'll have supplies."

"That's true." Giving in to the need for contact, even if it was with two sleeping bags between them, Ellie leaned against George's side. She ignored it when he went rigid, and soon she felt some of the tension leave him. "Thanks for agreeing to be my guide. If Joseph had been the one to bring me out here, I'd probably be running out into the storm just to get away from his wandering hands."

The stiffness returned to George's body at the mention of Joseph.

"Do you not like him?" she asked, tilting her head to look at him. His face was canted away from her, though, so she couldn't see his expression. "Is that why you decided to take me?"

There was a long pause before he spoke. "He's good at what he does. You would've been safe...in that way." He put an odd emphasis on the last three words.

"So, he wouldn't have led me into an avalanche, but I might have woken up in the night with him trying to squeeze into my sleeping bag?" Her voice was teasing, her discomfort with Joseph diluted by distance and George's reassuring presence. When he turned his head to meet her eyes, though, his expression was completely serious.

"The other search and rescue people, they talk."

Unlike you, she wanted to say, but she kept her mouth shut instead. George was sharing more than he ever had before in her presence, and she didn't want to make him shut down again by cracking jokes.

"I didn't want him to take you."

There was an entire story in his two sentences, and Ellie's stomach churned a little at the thought of being trapped in the tiny tent in a snowstorm with Joseph rather than George. She wanted to think it would never have been an option, but then she remembered her desperation at the fire station two nights before.

Leaning her head against his shoulder, she said, "I'm glad it was you."

They sat in silence for a few minutes, listening to the wind shrieking outside the tent, until Ellie sighed and sat up straight.

When George looked at her in question, she admitted, "I need to pee, but I really don't want to go outside."

He reached over to grab her coat. She let the sleeping bag fall to her waist, and he held her jacket for her so she could slide her arms into the sleeves. Taking a bracing breath, she shoved the sleeping bag off her legs and yanked on her windproof pants, skipping the fleece middle layer.

As she fished the stuff sack containing her boots out of the bottom of the mummy bag, she noticed that George was pulling on his own outer layers.

"You don't have to come," she protested, pulling on her boots and wincing as they instantly pressed on her blistered spots. Dipping her head to hide her grimace, she pulled on her bootlaces.

He frowned and covered her hands with his. "Not so tight. No wonder your feet were cold." Pushing her hands aside, he loosened the laces and then tied them before repeating the process on her other boot.

"I thought they wouldn't rub as much if they were tight."

Shaking his head, he tugged on his own boots. "Not worth it. It takes away the cushion of insulating air, plus it cuts off your circulation."

"Besides, they gave me blisters anyway," she said wryly, unzipping the door. "And, seriously, I'll be okay by myself. You don't have to supervise." She dug a couple squares of camping toilet paper and a flashlight out of her pack.

"I won't watch you," he huffed, and she turned to give him an appalled look.

"I didn't think you would—at least not until you said that." His cheeks had flushed above his beard, and Ellie had to bite back a smile. "I just meant that there's no reason for both of us to get cold."

He grunted, his face still red. "I have to go, too. Move. You're letting in the cold air."

Losing the battle against her grin, she faced forward to hide it. "Yes, sir."

Once she crawled out of the vestibule, the wind smacked the smile right off her face.

"Don't go far!" George bellowed over the wail of the wind.

It was cold, windy, and she just wanted to get back into her sleeping bag, so Ellie didn't take the time to point out the ridiculousness of his warning. She barely stepped to the side of the tent before yanking down her pants. Biting back a shriek as the cold wind slapped her bare parts, she hurried as fast as she could. Her pants were scarcely back in place before she dove for the tent entrance. George followed her in just seconds later.

"Do you have any wet wipes?" she asked through chattering teeth. "I'm filthy." That morning, she'd brushed her teeth and washed her hands and face with some melted snow, but it would be nice to clean up more than once a day. She added "washing her hands" to the list of things she'd never take for granted again once she returned to civilization.

He pulled out an alcohol wipe from the first-aid kit and offered it to her, but Ellie shook her head.

"Better to keep those in case of emergencies." Her boot rubbed against her heel as she removed it, making her wince. "Or blisters."

With a nod, he returned it to the kit and started stripping off his coat.

Once they were tucked back into their sleeping bags, Ellie turned onto her side facing George and propped herself up on an elbow. "How about truth or dare?"

His eyes widened with a look of sheer terror.

"That's a no, huh?" When his look of panic didn't change, she waved her hand, dismissing the idea. "It would've been hard to think of dares we could complete without leaving our sleeping bags, anyway. Okay, what about tic-tac-toe?"

George couldn't sleep. He couldn't stop looking at her, and sleeping required closing his eyes. Therefore, sleep was not an option. He didn't mind. Once she'd collected her father and returned to the city, he'd have plenty of dull, empty nights he could fill with sleep.

After several rounds of tic-tac-toe and hangman, she'd fallen asleep while the flashlights were still on. Despite the nagging voice in his head telling him that he was wasting batteries, he left them on so he could see her. His conscience lectured him, said that he was as bad as Acconcio, leering at her as she slept.

A dark strand of hair had escaped her hood and lay against her cheek. His hand twitched, needing to brush it away from her face, but he didn't touch her. That would be crossing the line, a line he already straddled by watching her without her knowing.

She was just so pretty. When he'd first seen her sprawled in the coffee shop parking lot, with her perfectly smooth and glossy sheet of hair and impractical city clothes, he'd assumed she'd be snobbish. Then she'd met his gaze, her eyes warm and round, shining with bits of green and gold and brown, and he'd changed his mind. She wasn't a snob, but a china doll, beautiful but fragile. When he'd picked her up and carried her to the door, her lips had rounded so they'd matched the shape of her eyes, making her look even more doll-like.

He hadn't wanted to lead her into the wilderness. Something that delicate shouldn't be exposed to cold and danger and exertion. When Acconcio had pushed himself against her, though, grabbing her with that look on his face, the one that reminded George of a well-fed house cat playing with a mouse, he couldn't let it happen. He couldn't let the coyote lead the bunny into the wild.

The fragile doll had surprised him, though. Although slow and unfamiliar with things that were second nature to George, she'd listened and helped and kept on walking, no matter what.

It worried him how much he liked taking care of her, feeding her and doctoring her feet and making her tea. It gave him ideas he shouldn't be considering, like keeping her. The thought of having someone else living in his house for the first time since his father died was as seductive as the feel of her breath against his neck when she'd rolled into him the night before.

And she'd kissed him.

His breath left his lungs in a harsh exhale as he focused on her lips, the lips that had touched his, leaving him frozen while every part of him burned. As much as he reminded himself that it had been a joke, a tease, a way to win the silly game she'd insisted they play, he still couldn't shrink it down to the right size in his own mind. It was huge and important, and he'd always remember those few earth-shaking seconds.

How could he forget his first kiss?

Chapter 10

"ANDERSON?"

"What?"

"How much longer are we going to be stuck out here?" Huddled in his thin sleeping bag with only his pale face showing, Wilson looked miserably cold.

"Depends." The word was almost drowned out by the wind shaking the walls of their cheap three-season tent. When his source had told him that Baxter Price's daughter was in town, looking for her dad, Anderson hadn't thought it'd lead to winter camping, especially when he got a look at the glossy and citified Miss Price. By the time he'd figured out Holloway was taking her into Blue Hook, there hadn't been time to buy supplies. They were stuck with what they could steal out of Holloway's neighbor's storage shed. Anderson didn't have a sleeping bag. Instead, he was making do with a couple of blankets. It was fine. He'd been cold before, and he'd be cold again. Wilson, though, didn't do well with cold. He'd get bronchitis again if he had to spend many more nights outside.

"On what?"

"On how long it takes for them to lead us to Price."

Wilson turned onto his side, his bony knees pushing into the fabric, pulling it tight. "Then, once we kill him, we can go home?"

"Once we kill him, we can go home."

Wilson's sigh shuddered through chattering teeth. "Wish they'd hurry up."

Studying a loose thread on the tent's ceiling seam, Anderson thought about that. Rich satisfaction spread through him at the thought of giving Holloway a glimpse of what Anderson King was capable of. "Maybe we can give them some incentive."

Chapter 11

THE LIGHT WAS STRANGE WHEN ELLIE WOKE, DIM and eerie. Her face was once again tucked between George's shoulder and chin, and she flushed but didn't move. The desire for heat won over embarrassment, and George was wonderfully warm. His chest moved with slow, even breaths, but she knew he was awake.

"Is it morning?" she mumbled, burrowing more tightly against him before she realized what she was doing.

His chin bumped lightly against her head when he nodded—at least, she assumed he was nodding. It was hard to tell with her face mashed into his neck. With a great effort, she rolled onto her back. Yawning, she worked her sleeping-bag zipper down a little bit so she could move her arms more easily.

The silence suddenly caught her attention. "The wind stopped."

Now she could actually see George nod. He'd freed his arms from the mummy bag and had pushed himself to a seated position.

"Did it stop snowing?"

"Think so. Need to look outside."

That reminded her that he couldn't have gone outside before, because she'd been *lying* on him. Ellie blushed and busied herself with adding her second sock layer and gathering her clothes while keeping the sleeping bag wrapped around her.

"Tea?" His question brought her attention back to George.

"Sure." Taking a deep breath, she let the sleeping bag drop and scrambled into her fleece layer, followed by her coat. "Give me a minute to dress my bottom half, and I'll get snow for water while I'm outside." Her flush returned. "From a *different* spot than where I...um."

His teeth flashed in the grayish light as he grinned. It stunned Ellie for a second, so rare and unexpected. Blinking, she returned to yanking on her pants. Shoving her feet into her boots, she loosened the laces before tying them. George gave a grunt of approval.

When she glanced over at him, she saw he'd almost finished dressing already. The man was *fast*.

Once she crawled out of the tent, early morning sunlight made her squint. Standing, she saw the reason for the weird light—a thick layer of snow covered everything, including the tent. Carefully stepping over the guy wires, she swept an arm over the rounded top, knocking off the snow. George joined her.

Looking around, Ellie smiled. "It wasn't fun to walk through last night, but it sure is pretty this morning." Fresh snow was piled on every tree branch and rock, so white it had a bluish tint. "It looks like a Christmas card." Just as she said the words, a deer stepped between a pair of trees across the clearing from them. Its enormous ears swiveled toward them before it bounded through the snow to the safety of another stand of pines.

"*Release the deer*," Ellie murmured under her breath, and then laughed at George's raised eyebrow. "Movie reference. Never mind. Were that deer's ears really huge, or was it just me?"

"Mule deer."

"Oh. I see where that name came from." Her bladder started sending her the message to quit lingering over the scenery and get down to business. "I'll just head over there." She waved at the boulder next to their tent.

Her feet sank into the snow until her boots disappeared completely. She was tempted to go back for her snowshoes, but she was already halfway to her destination, so she kept going.

When she slogged through the snow on her return trip, she pondered something. "George," she called, and he looked up from where he was scooping snow into the pot. "Why was the moose so scary when the mule deer was just cute? What's the difference?"

"About eight hundred pounds and an extra fifty feet of space between it and us." He returned to his snow gathering.

She thought about that for a moment. "Makes sense."

Just in the short time they'd been out of the tent, the temperature felt as if it had warmed. Ellie scooped up a double handful of snow and was delighted that she could actually pack it into a ball. Normally, the snow was either frozen like a brick of ice or dry and powdery. This was snow she could play with.

Grinning, she launched the snowball at George, catching him on the shoulder. His befuddled expression made her giggle so hard that she almost fell. When she saw him put the pan down and start heading her way, she gave a laughing shriek and tried to run in the other direction. The deep snow made her feel like she was running in slow motion, and she was laughing so hard that it made her even less coordinated. A glance over her shoulder showed George was quickly gaining on her, his longer legs easily catching up with her much shorter ones. It was strange to think that, if he'd chased her just a few days ago, she would've run out of true fear. Now, though, after he'd warmed her feet with huge, gentle hands and sacrificed his stocking hat to mop up her tears, she couldn't even remember what she'd found so intimidating about George.

She made a sharp turn to the side, hoping that, if not faster, she was at least more maneuverable than him. On her third stride, she hit a deeper drift and floundered in snow up to her thighs, erasing the last of her lead. She didn't mind when he closed the gap between them, though—being caught by George was not a bad thing.

Grabbing her around the waist, he tossed her over his shoulder with an ease that made her breathless for several reasons she didn't want to ponder. Instead, she concentrated on clinging to the back of his coat as he spun her around.

"Okay!" Her stomach hurt from laughing so hard, which wasn't helped by her current position. "Okay! Sorry! Uncle! I'm going to puke!" The last one was the winner. As soon as it left her mouth, she was turned right side up, and her feet sank into the snow again. She panted for air, breathless from laughter. "Sorry, but I couldn't resist. The snow is just so…throwable."

Although George shook his head at her, his eyes were glinting with playful humor. "Save that energy for walking."

"But it's not nearly as much fun."

His stern look melted into a grin. Reaching toward her, he brushed the back of his fingers against her cheek.

Almost immediately, his smile fell away, and he jerked his hand back. He appeared almost stricken. "Sorry."

"Please." She rolled her eyes, trying to keep it light despite the way her cheek still burned in the best way where he'd touched it. "That was nothing. I basically flattened you in your sleep so I could use you as a face warmer. Twice."

To her relief, the tense lines of his face softened again. "I don't mind."

When she realized she was gazing at him like a soppy idiot, she dragged her eyes away from his. Clearing her throat, she asked, "So, oatmeal for breakfast?"

After a pause, he confirmed, "Oatmeal."

They moved quickly after that, working together to prepare breakfast and break camp with an efficiency that made Ellie feel like they'd been hiking together for weeks rather than days. As she hoisted her pack onto her shoulders, she paused in the middle of buckling the strap across her chest.

George looked over at her with an inquiring expression.

"I thought I heard voices." Turning her head, she strained her ears. "There wouldn't be any other hikers around here, would there?"

"Could be." She could tell he was listening, as well.

After several moments of listening to the drip of melting snow and a trilling birdsong, she returned to fastening her pack straps. "Guess I imagined it. Unless bears have developed a human call to lure us to them." George snorted, and she grinned, loving that she'd almost made him laugh.

They set off on the trail, and Ellie moved quickly, determined to cover more ground than she had over the past two days. Her soreness had eased, although the blisters still hurt. George adjusted his pace to hers, keeping a few feet ahead of her, and she wondered how quickly he'd move if she weren't along. That thought was depressing, so she banished it and focused on walking.

The trail narrowed and grew steeper. On their right, a wall of rock towered over them. Snow gathered in the nooks and crannies, but the sun was quickly melting it, and water streaked the rock face.

Despite Ellie's determination, she groaned with relief when George called for the first break.

"It'll level out soon," he promised as he offered her the trail mix.

With that to look forward to, she kept the break short. True to his word, the trail flattened and widened five minutes later. The snow cover was shallow, so they stopped again to remove their snowshoes and attach them to their packs.

After they resumed walking, the scenery changed again, and they passed through a sparsely wooded area. The sun filtered through the evergreen needles, giving the space a greenish glow. New, blindingly white snow covered everything in a blanket that sparkled when it caught the light. Small animal prints were the only patterns marring the pristine snow, and Ellie hated to ruin the perfection with her boots. The trees and snow muffled all sound, and she found that she was holding her breath at the beauty of it.

Her noisy exhale made George turn his head to look at her. His smile froze as his eyes fixed on something over her shoulder. Puzzled, she started to turn, but an arm looping around her neck stopped her midmotion.

Something pressed against her temple, and she could feel the metal, hard and cold, even through her hat.

"You move, and she's dead," a male voice rasped in her ear.

George's hands—one of which had darted to the vent at the side of his coat—raised to shoulder level, palms out, in a gesture of surrender. His gaze was fixed on where the gun met her temple, and his expression was so cold and hard that he didn't even look like himself.

Like a punch to the belly, the reality of the situation hit her, and she stiffened in the stranger's hold. In all her years living in Chicago, she'd never been mugged. The idea that it could happen to her in the middle of nowhere, in this beautiful, serene place, seemed ludicrous. There was no denying the clamp of the ropy forearm against her throat, however, or the gun barrel boring a hole in her temple.

"Don't you try anything, either, pretty girl." His voice changed when he talked to her. It slid over her, syrupy and sickening, making her shudder. "We're just going to lighten your load a little, and then we'll be on our way. If you don't make a fuss, then no one gets hurt. It's easy, see?"

Her brain locked on the "we," and her knees went soft at the thought that there was more than just one attacker. Her chin was forced up by the forearm across her throat, but her backpack required him to stand to her left, rather than directly behind her, so she could almost see him. The gun took up most of her field of vision, its looming, black shape enormous. The man was just a fuzzy form behind the gun, but she could tell he was tall. She could smell him, too, a mix of body odor, woodsmoke, and a strange, sharp chemical she didn't recognize.

"Wilson!" The stranger's barked order made her jump and swallow a shriek. "Get their packs. His first."

A man stepped into her line of sight, surprisingly close, making her jerk back. The barrel of the gun pressed harder against her temple, and pain radiated across the side of her face. The guy walking toward George was average in size and pasty pale, with streaks of red across his cheekbones from the cold. He was wearing camouflage pants and jacket, although both looked too thin to provide much warmth.

All Ellie could think was that she'd seen Wilson's face. She could describe him to the police, pick him out of a lineup. George was getting a good look at the other man. Why didn't the men wear masks? The only reason her frantic brain could come up with was that they planned to kill both her and George. Biting back a groan of terror, she struggled against the man holding her captive, but he all too easily subdued her by tightening his arm across her throat. Her need for air overwhelmed everything, and she stilled in his hold. With a cold chuckle, he loosened his grip just enough for her to breathe again.

After quickly undoing the waist and chest straps of the backpack, Wilson moved behind George and yanked the pack off his back. As the straps slid down his rigid arms, George kept his gaze on Ellie. She'd never seen anyone look so coldly pissed, and she wondered how the men didn't cower in the face of George's fury. If she'd been the object of his deadly anger, she would've immediately dropped the gun and run.

She stared back at George, trying to find reassurance and to reassure in turn, but the gun at her temple kept reminding her that they were both probably going to die. A whimper rose, but it couldn't make it past the forearm crushing her throat.

After hoisting George's pack onto his own shoulders and securing the straps, Wilson moved toward Ellie. Her heart thumped against her ribs until all she could hear was its rapid pounding. Their eyes met, his pale blue and bloodshot. She tried to silently plead with him, but Wilson dropped his gaze quickly, and he started to fumble with the strap across her chest.

When she cringed away from his hands, the arm around her neck tightened again, making bright spots flicker across her vision before the stranger behind her eased the pressure. Her throat hurt as she gasped for air, and she was so focused on sucking in oxygen that she didn't even feel the strap around her waist fall free.

Wilson moved behind her, and she felt her backpack straps sliding down her arms. Without him in the way, she had a clear view of George. His fists were by his sides but extended slightly outward, as if he were an Old West gunslinger right before the draw. His gaze was fixed on her as if he were attempting to silently shove words into her head, and she stared back at him, desperately trying to read his mind.

He wanted her to do something, but her thoughts were on fast-forward, refusing to fall into their usual logical order. Everything in her was screaming for her to run, but the gun and the stranger's hold made that impossible. Terror boiled to the surface, and she barely managed to push it down enough to focus on George again.

His eyes flickered to the ground and then back to her

face. He repeated the action, gaze down and then up again. Ellie could guess what he was trying to tell her, but it was just that—a guess. She swallowed hard, her throat pressing into the man's forearm. What if she misinterpreted him and did the wrong thing? She could be the one who got them both killed. Her vision darkened again, this time from flat-out panic.

"It's stuck," Wilson complained, tugging at the pack. "Let go for a second, Anderson."

"I can't," the man holding her growled back.

"Well, I can't get it off unless you do." Wilson gave the pack a rough yank that jerked her arm back painfully, but Anderson's body blocked the strap on her left shoulder, keeping the pack bound to her body.

With a huff, Anderson shifted his weight, putting a bare inch of room between his chest and her, while keeping the gun to her temple. His forearm shifted to an awkward angle, so it no longer pressed flat against her throat. Without allowing herself to hesitate or even think about what she was about to do, Ellie went limp.

Her neck wrenched painfully when her chin hit his arm. The barrel of the gun scraped along her hairline and across her scalp, but then she was on the ground. All sounds were suddenly muffled and strange, and there were faint, distorted shouts and then a popping noise.

Since she wasn't sure if her legs would support her, even while crawling, she rolled. Disorientated, she went in the wrong direction. Instead of moving toward safety, her body crashed into a pair of legs. Something heavy fell on her, landing painfully on her left shoulder. She cried out, but even that sound was muted, as if she were wearing earplugs.

Ellie lifted her head and found herself face-to-face with a man she didn't recognize. Blood streamed from a gash running through one eyebrow, and his eyes were dazed. It clicked in her brain that it was Anderson who'd fallen on her, and he must've hit his head as he landed. She stared at the man who'd been terrorizing her, shocked by how *normal*-looking he was. When she'd been trapped in front of him, his arm across her throat and his gun at her head, she'd pictured him as a monster. Not this.

Her random, scattered thoughts were interrupted abruptly when she remembered his gun.

Whipping her head to the side, she spotted the black pistol. It was still in his hand, but his fingers were lax, barely gripping it. Ellie lunged for it, grabbing the butt of the gun and twisting it away from him, even as comprehension returned to his eyes.

She scrambled to the side, half scooting and half crawling, trying to shift the gun so she was holding it in a more useable position. It was unexpectedly heavy, and her whole arm shook as she pointed the pistol at Anderson, so she wrapped her other hand around the grip, steadying it.

Anderson rose in a crouch, swaying as he swiped blood out of his eye. His gaze was predatory, and he shifted forward, as if preparing to pounce.

Ellie pulled the trigger.

Chapter 12

JUDGING BY THE LACK OF BLOOD SPURTING FROM A new hole on Anderson's body, she'd missed, but he still jerked away. His compromised balance sent him sprawling on his back, but he regained his feet quickly. Out of the corner of her eye, Ellie saw motion, and she shifted the gun to point it at the new threat.

Wilson skidded to a halt, his hands open and palms toward her. They were both in her field of vision, so she shifted her gaze back and forth, ready to point the gun at whoever twitched first.

"Calm down." Anderson's voice startled her, and she squeezed the trigger again, making both men duck. Weighed down by George's stolen pack, Wilson staggered, falling to his knees, but Anderson remained upright. One side of his mouth curled into a condescending smile, but his eyes were narrowed, calculating, as they slid from the gun to Ellie's face. "You're going to hurt yourself with that thing. Why don't you give it to me and—"

His weight shifted a tiny bit forward as he spoke, and Ellie fired. A chunk of the aspen tree right next to Anderson exploded, sending splinters of bark flying. He leaped to the side, barely keeping his feet.

"You bitch!" he snapped, his fake smile gone. "I'm going to fuck you up so bad, all while Holloway watches."

Although a tiny, adrenaline-crazed part of Ellie

wanted to retort, she pressed her shaking lips together silently and raised the gun higher.

"How many bullets do you have left, little girl? Bet you don't even know." The creepy, partial smile was back, looking so out of place in the tense standoff that it made her shake harder. "Enough to chase us off, do you think? Even if you manage that, we won't go far, so you'd better take Holloway and run fast like bunnies." His smile widened. "Not that it'll do you any good. I'll find you wherever you try to hide."

"Go." She forced the word through her aching throat. Instead of backing away, Anderson made a quick hand signal, and Wilson lurched forward. As she turned the gun toward the approaching man, her tense hand squeezed off another unintentional round. Instead of grazing a tree, it took a chunk out of Wilson's arm. He yelped, drawing Anderson King's full attention.

Anderson was definitely not smiling when he turned back to her that time. "Hurt my brother again, bitch, and I'm going to carve his name on your face."

Unable to hold Anderson's menacing gaze, she focused mostly on Wilson, only shooting wary glances at the other man. "Leave," she demanded. "Leave, and I won't shoot him."

The tense silence stretched for an unbearably long time. Ellie's gaze jumped from one man to the other as she tried to keep the increasingly heavy gun steady.

"Fine." Anderson's voice made her jump, and she narrowly avoided pulling the trigger yet again. His earlier words about not knowing the number of bullets gnawed at her stomach. "We're going, city bitch, but you're not free of us. You'll never be free of us until you're dead."

Anderson started backing toward the trees, his narrowed gaze locked on Ellie. Scrambling onto his feet, Wilson followed, also keeping his eyes on Ellie the whole time.

The tree coverage was thin enough to see where the two men turned and ran, lifting their knees high to clear the six inches of snow. Ellie watched, breathing in funny little gasps, her entire body shaking, until she couldn't see them anymore. Only then did she turn to look at George.

Even while everything had been happening, she'd known in the back of her mind that something was wrong. The only reason George wouldn't have come to her rescue would have been because he couldn't. Lowering the gun, she kept it by her side as she turned in a half circle.

He was sprawled on the snow, not moving. A noise escaped her throat, something that sounded more animalistic than human, and she ran to him, dropping to her knees beside him. Blood painted a vivid red halo in the snow around his head, and his eyes were closed.

When she reached for him, she realized she still held the gun in her right hand, and she jerked it back. She examined the gun, looking for what might be a safety, but she had no idea what the few buttons and levers that weren't the trigger did. Hoping it wouldn't decide to fire on its own, she gingerly placed it in her coat pocket.

Once her hands were free, she jerked off her glove and placed her fingers against George's neck, searching for a pulse. His skin was warm, making her want to cry with relief, but she didn't do that until she felt a steady throb of life under her fingers. Then she sagged over him, harsh sobs tearing at her throat.

Biting her lip hard enough to get herself back under control, she focused on finding George's injury. When she peeled back his black stocking cap, she saw a dark red furrow along the right side of his head. The hat gaped over the injury, and blood slicked the dark brown hair surrounding the wound.

"Okay," she muttered, staring between the bloody streak on his skull and his unresponsive face. "Okay, okay." Ellie forced her brain to work out the problem logically. First, she needed to stop the bleeding. Vague memories of a first-aid unit in her high school health class told her that. She swept the area with a panicked glance, as if an urgent care center was hiding behind a tree. It wasn't, but the next best thing was—her pack still lay where it had fallen during the scuffle.

She hurried to grab it, unzipping the main section as she ran back to George's unconscious body. It was awkward to carry it in front of her, and she tripped a few strides before she reached him. Her fall was broken as she landed on the pack. Instead of standing, she just crawled the rest of the way over to him, dragging the pack along with her.

As she dug inside the center compartment, she tried to remember which pack George had put the first-aid kit in that morning. When her hand closed over the smooth plastic case, she almost started to cry again. Biting her lip, wincing at the sting of her teeth, she fought off the urge to blubber like a baby and opened the case with shaking hands.

Before she started, she arranged her supplies so she wouldn't waste what she needed to wrap the wound. There were ten gauze pads but only two antiseptic wipes left, thanks to using the rest on her blisters, so Ellie grabbed one of her water bottles and one of the gauze pads. She figured she'd use water to clean the wound, and then finish with the antiseptic wipe, and hope that it would be enough to kill any germs.

She uncapped the water bottle and leaned to pour it over the gouge, but stopped and took a quick drink, making a face when she tasted fake cherry flavor. Switching to another bottle, which proved to be plain water, she poured a steady trickle over the injury.

Once some of the blood had been washed clear, the furrow didn't look very deep. Ellie bent to take a closer look, wondering if a bullet had scored his scalp. Recapping the now-empty water bottle, she slid a hand behind his head and lifted it. Using her other hand, she scooped the melting red snow away, trying not to think of how much blood had flowed out of him. Before putting his head back down, she laid a folded triangular bandage under him so his head wouldn't be directly on the snow.

George groaned deep in his chest when she cleaned the injury with an alcohol wipe. The sound made her examine his face hopefully, looking for signs that he was regaining consciousness. His eyes stayed stubbornly closed, so she shoved away her worry and disappointment and finished cleaning the wound.

One of the four-by-four gauze squares covered the entire gouge, so she added a second on top of that one and then wrapped a bandage—the kind that felt rubbery and stuck to itself—around his head several times like a headband to hold the gauze in place.

Digging in the pack once more, she pulled out one of her extra hats. It was quite girly, lavender with light green flowers, but it would keep his head warm. Ellie carefully eased it on, grateful that the fabric was extra-stretchy and encompassed his larger skull just fine, even with the additional bulk of the bandaging.

Sitting back on her heels, she did a scan of his body, belatedly checking for any other bullet holes. His tan jacket and army-green BDUs wouldn't hide blood like his dark stocking hat had, so she resisted the urge to strip him bare to look for injuries.

Her hands shook as she used snow to clean the blood from them, scrubbing the icy crystals against her skin until her fingers were as pale as the snow she was using. She repacked the depleted first-aid kit and tucked the ruined hat and bandage wrappers into one of the freezer bags they used for garbage. Then she returned everything to the pack and zipped it.

As she finished, she started to get antsy, shooting quick glances at George's unresponsive face and then scanning the area around them. What if the two men had already returned and were watching her right now? Anderson's words about chasing them rang in her ears, and she yanked her gloves onto shaking hands so she couldn't chew on her hangnails.

They needed to run, to get as far from their attackers as possible, but George wasn't moving. Her hand hovered over the pocket holding the gun. It scared her, but not as much as the two men who could return at any second. Reluctantly, she slid her hand into the pocket and closed her fingers around the grip.

"El." Her name was more of a groan, but it made her heart leap as she released the gun and leaned closer to George.

"Hey, are you awake?" Her voice shook, which made her frown. She'd been steady—well, not too shaky—while she'd played nurse, and she wasn't about to fall apart once George woke. She had an intense need to impress him with her calmness under fire, and that was not going to happen if she threw herself into his arms and bawled her eyes out...once again.

He grunted affirmatively. His eyes were just slits, as if the sun's glare was painful, but they were open. Ellie's muscles went rubbery with relief. In George-speak, a single grunt was the equivalent of an entire coherent sentence from someone else. When he started to push up to a sitting position, she grabbed his arm to help.

Once he was upright, his hand went to his head.

"I think a bullet grazed you." Her words were a little too fast and much too high-pitched. Taking a deep breath, she concentrated on speaking more slowly. "It's not deep, but you were unconscious for"—she realized that she had no idea how much time had passed—"a while. Long enough for me to clean it up a little and bandage it."

His fingers probed at the injury through the hat. It must have hurt, because the muscles in his face tensed.

"Quit poking it and it might feel better," she scolded, and then wanted to laugh when he sent her a black look. Like her tears, Ellie held in her mirth, worried that she wouldn't be able to stop once she'd started.

As if everything had returned to him in a rush, George abruptly stood, pushing her behind him as he scanned the area.

"They're gone," she said to the back of his coat.

Her voice quavered only a little. "But they might come back, so we probably want to get out of here, if you're up for it."

He glanced at her over his shoulder. "What happened?" His voice sounded extra rusty.

"Can we walk and talk?" Holding back a shiver, she peered through the trees. "I'd rather not be here anymore."

He nodded, winced, and then reached for the lone remaining pack.

Moving to block him, Ellie protested, "I've got it. You're concussed."

With a shake of his head, he nudged her to the side and shouldered the pack.

"Stubborn," she grumbled under her breath.

One corner of his mouth lifted in response.

<hr />

Despite her promise to tell him what had happened, it was hours before she had the breath to speak. Even with a head injury, George moved quickly. They stayed parallel to the path, but didn't walk directly on it. Even city girl Ellie knew that was so the men couldn't follow their boot prints in the snow.

Instead, they walked between the trees where the lighter layer of snow had already melted. When the trees thinned, George found a rocky surface that was mostly clear of snow, and they followed that for a while. Ellie tried to turn it into a game, stepping only where she wouldn't leave a print. It worked for a while, but then the adrenaline started to leave her system.

Exhaustion pulled at her, and she couldn't seem to stop shivering, despite the warm sun. It became harder and harder to keep walking, until she gave up and stopped in her tracks.

"George?"

He turned instantly and returned to where she was standing on shaky legs.

"Can we take a break?"

Nodding, he reached automatically for the side pocket where he'd kept snacks in his pack. The design of the other backpack was different, so his fingers searched unsuccessfully for a zipper before realization dawned. Unbuckling the straps, he took off the pack.

Ellie looked around for a rock or log to use as a chair, but nothing presented itself. She knew she needed to sit down before her body forced the issue by collapsing, so she plopped down on the ground. George frowned at her.

"I'm fine. Just tired. Carry on with what you were doing." She waved at the pack, surprised by how heavy her arm felt. Letting it drop back to her side, Ellie resisted the urge to lie down and sleep. If she did that, George would not believe she was okay. Instead, she watched him as he inventoried the contents of the pack. She wasn't sure if his frown meant he wasn't happy with their remaining supplies or just that he had a killer headache. Maybe it was both.

"What do we have left?" she finally asked, needing to talk before she nodded off.

"Two sleeping mats, one mummy bag, four pouch meals but no pot to heat water and no camp stove, a flashlight, four bottles of water…" He shook the one she'd used to clean his head wound. "Make that three bottles of water, avalanche probe, shovel, waterproof matches, two bags of trail mix, the first-aid kit, your extra clothes, ski goggles, your toothbrush...uh, makeup?" He shot her a puzzled look, and she eyed the toes of her boots. She'd forgotten how she'd emptied the contents of her purse into the pack before they'd left. It seemed so long ago now. "Your wallet, some... um, other things"—by the way he blushed, Ellie guessed he'd discovered the tampons, also from her purse—"and a cell phone, but no reception."

"Better than nothing, I guess." She tried not to think about the loss of the tent. "At least they didn't take this pack, too."

"How did you get them to leave?" George watched her as he closed up the pack by feel.

"Oh!" That reminded her. Ellie gingerly pulled the gun out of her pocket, keeping it pointed away from both of them. "I wasn't sure how to put on the safety. Could you do it? And maybe take it?"

He accepted the gun and immediately dropped the magazine. Opening the slide, he turned the pistol and dumped a bullet into his palm. "It's a Glock. No external safety." He inserted the loose bullet into the top of the magazine.

"Oh." Watching as he stowed the empty gun and magazine in a pocket in his coat, she was a little jealous with the ease he'd shown handling the firearm. "I've never held a gun until today."

His shock was obvious. "I'll take you to Rory's. She has a gun shop with a range."

A sour taste climbed to the back of Ellie's throat, and she swallowed. The movement reminded her of her bruised throat. "Who's Rory?" The jealous note in her voice was obvious, and she flushed. She'd known George for three days, much too short of a time for her to be getting possessive.

He looked at her warily. "I told you. She has a gun shop with a range." Each word was enunciated, as if he thought she might be slow.

Rolling her eyes, Ellie tried to shake off the foreign feeling of jealousy. Not only did she have no claim on George, but there weren't even any other females within pheromone range. Absently, she pulled off her glove and rested her hand against her bruised throat.

George strode over and crouched next to her, gently pulling her hand away. His ferociously controlled expression returned. He'd pulled off his gloves earlier to sort through the pack, so his fingers were bare when he brushed them against her neck. She shivered, but for a completely different reason that time.

"I'm okay," she said quietly. "It's just bruised. You're the one who's hurt."

At the mention of his injury, he shook his head as if to brush off her concern.

"I was so scared." Her fingers touched the silly purple hat where it covered his bullet wound. "You were lying there, not moving. I thought you were…" She couldn't say it.

"What happened?"

"I…" She tried to put the blurred sequence of events in order in her head. "We were walking, and then the first guy, Anderson, he grabbed me."

George's face was grim. "I should have known they were tracking us. I'm sorry."

Shaking her head, she dismissed his apology. "It's

not your fault. Who would've thought that two homicidal losers would mug us for our camping gear in the middle of nowhere? You were probably on the lookout for *real* threats, like moose and rabid squirrels."

He didn't even smile at her joke. Despite her reassurances, Ellie knew he blamed himself. "Don't know what the King brothers are doing out here."

"King brothers?" she repeated. "You know them?"

With a grimace, he said, "Meth dealers from Simpson."

"Why follow us all the way out to the middle of nowhere just to take our stuff?" Ellie wondered. "Couldn't they have just robbed an outdoor-gear store?"

George frowned, his eyebrows knotted. "Not sure. Did they say anything?"

"About what they're doing out here? I don't think so, although I don't know if I'm remembering everything right. When Anderson had me in a headlock, I was concentrating on you, on the way you kept looking down. I thought you wanted me to drop to the ground." She raised her eyebrows in question, and he nodded. "When Anderson moved away a little so they could take off my pack, I went limp, and he dropped me."

George gave her a look of approval, and she tried not to bask in it. Falling down should not be a point of pride, even if it was intentionally done.

"Things got weird, and I wasn't hearing right. I heard a popping sound. Was that the gun?" His nod surprised her. "It didn't sound like a shot."

"That's normal in combat."

It was strange to think of that encounter as "combat." Shaking off the stray thought, she continued. "Was that when he shot you?"

"Must've been." He looked unhappy. "You went down, I reached for my gun, and then everything went black."

Ellie shuddered as she thought about what would've happened if Anderson's aim had been a little more accurate. Since she couldn't continue on that train of thought without losing it, she forced herself to shut down that particular what-if scenario. "I tried to roll away from them, but I went the wrong way, so I tripped Anderson. He fell on me." Her shoulder gave a twinge, as if reminded of the impact. When she rolled it with a tiny wince, George's eyes immediately shot to the area.

"You're hurt?"

"Not really." To confirm that, she shrugged it and lowered it. Like her throat, there'd probably be a flashy bruise, but nothing had been seriously damaged. "Just remembering the moment."

Something unreadable flashed over his face, and he sat next to her, close enough that her unbruised shoulder bumped his arm. That contact, even through multiple layers of fabric, steadied Ellie and made it easier for her to continue.

"He must've hit his head on something—a rock, probably—when he fell, because he had a big gash through his eyebrow that was bleeding everywhere. It stunned him, and I grabbed his gun out of his hand."

George stiffened against her.

Wanting just to be done with telling the story so she could go back to deliberately not thinking about what happened, she ignored his reaction and rushed out the next words. "The other guy, Wilson, came running toward us, so I pointed the gun at him, too. I shot a few times, but I didn't hit them. Well, I might have winged Wilson's arm, but that was it." In a burst of honesty, she admitted, "Except for once. I didn't mean to pull the trigger. I just jumped, and it happened. So they backed away and then ran. I should've made them give us your backpack. Sorry. I wasn't thinking clearly. Then I saw you"—Ellie had to swallow hard before she could continue—"cleaned your head, and, after I was done, you woke." She kept the last part as brief as possible, since she wasn't ready to talk about how still he lay, bleeding into the snow, without bursting into tears.

He put his arm around her, his hand settling on her sore shoulder. Although she had to stifle a flinch, the comforting weight of his arm across her back was worth the ache. Leaning close, he put his mouth next to her ear.

"Good job, El."

Despite the entire crazy day, his simple praise made her smile. It dropped at his next words.

"This isn't a good place to camp. Can you keep going?"

Her body screamed "No!" but she nodded anyway. The farther they could get from the two men, the better. His arm slid away, and she stifled a regretful sigh. As pathetic as it was, she could've sat in the snow with George's arm around her for hours. He stood and offered a hand. She grabbed it and pulled herself to her feet, biting back a pained groan. In just the short time they'd been stopped, all her muscles had stiffened, locking into a sitting position.

George was watching her face closely, so she forced a smile and asked, "Ready?"

After a long moment, during which he studied her, he finally turned and started walking. The first few steps were the worst, but her body soon grew numb, and Ellie fell into auto mode, her feet moving without the assistance of her brain. The narrow, uphill path was full of switchback turns, and she frequently tripped on rocks protruding from the thin layer of snow. The afternoon light grew watery and then tinted with red as the sun approached the mountain peaks.

Just as Ellie started thinking tearfully that they were going to have to walk through the night, George stopped. She locked her knees to prevent herself from crumpling to the ground right where she stood. Looking around, she saw they were on a rocky apron that stretched in a half circle in front of a sheer rock wall towering above them.

As he moved toward the wall, George disappeared. Ellie blinked, sure she was hallucinating or losing time or something.

"George?" she asked, too freaked and exhausted to be embarrassed by the shrill note of panic in her voice.

His head popped out of the wall at about waist height, and she almost screamed. Then she realized that the evening shadows had hidden the entrance to a shallow cave. Forcing her legs to move just a few more steps, she reached the entrance and looked inside.

"Nice," she breathed. It was perfect—just deep enough to be sheltered from the weather, but not so deep that a bear could be hiding in the depths. George smiled at her as if she'd complimented him on a thoughtful gift. At the moment, the cave really was the most wonderful thing he could have given her.

When George shucked the backpack, she moved to grab the sleeping pads, but he frowned at her.

"Sit," he ordered, pushing a water bottle and one of the bags of trail mix into her hands. "Drink."

She did, gratefully. Although she was too tired to feel hunger, she forced down a couple of handfuls of nuts and dried fruit before taking a drink. Frowning, she studied the bottle.

"Should we conserve?"

Shaking his head, he inflated the top sleeping pad. "Plenty of snow. We'll just bring them into the sleeping bag with us."

She'd started taking another drink at his first head shake, and she choked when he said "us." Coughing, she looked up to see him watching her with a concerned frown. "I'm fine. Just went down the wrong pipe." Inwardly, she scolded herself for overreacting. Of course they were going to share the only sleeping bag. It was a matter of survival, not of lust. She took another sip, trying not to notice that he was still watching her with his eyebrows knotted together.

Despite her mental lecture, when he laid the mummy bag on top of the stacked sleeping mats, she eyed it like it was a large, flat, very venomous snake. It wasn't as big as his had been, but it was still good-sized, intended to fit a large man. She'd probably be able to squeeze in there with him, but it would be a tight fit. They would be pressed against each other, wearing just their long underwear…

Her body flushed from her feet to her hairline, and she gulped down another drink of water, hoping it would cool her. It didn't work. The sideways glances that George kept throwing her way as he set up their cave didn't help, either.

"You okay?" she finally asked, not able to handle one more unreadable look.

Instead of answering, he fiddled with something in the pack. Uncomfortable silence sat like a physical thing between them. Ellie sighed, resigned to not getting an answer, when he finally spoke. "It's... Are you...?" She watched his profile as he pressed his lips together in a grim line. "I don't know another way to..." Making a frustrated sound, he grabbed the flashlight and stomped out of the cave—as much as he could stomp bent almost in half so he didn't hit his head on the low ceiling.

Blinking, Ellie watched him leave. After he circled an outcrop, he disappeared from view, and her stomach instantly cramped with fear. She stayed for as long as she could manage, but her anxiety rose higher and higher until she was swamped in it. Sealing the water bottle, she set it aside and, ignoring her protesting body, followed him.

It was almost dark, and the gray light that remained created unnerving shadows. She stopped at the edge of the flat apron, not wanting to wander around in the near darkness and fall off a cliff. It seemed like a dumb way to die, especially after escaping getting shot just hours before.

Her ears were filled with the sound of rushing blood, and she started breathing fast—too fast. "George?"

Her call was faint, but it was enough, because he was instantly in front of her. His lips were moving, but it was hard to hear him over her heartbeat. Then her face was pressed against the front of his coat, and breathing got easier.

After a few minutes, she was recovered enough to feel embarrassed, so she took a step back, putting a few inches between them. "Sorry."

"What's wrong?" His fingers lightly touched her cheek and then were gone.

Ellie tried to figure out how to explain the panic she'd felt at being left alone, but she couldn't think of a way to say it without sounding like a childish idiot. Instead, she just shook her head. "I'm okay now. Just tired, I think."

He studied her, holding the flashlight low so it illuminated her face without shining directly into her eyes. It made him look like a campfire boogeyman, and she had to smile. As if that was the reassurance he'd needed, he stepped away. Not wanting to be far from the light—or George—Ellie followed him to a scattered pile of broken branches that he must have dropped when she'd started hyperventilating. He bent to pick them up, and she helped.

"Are we going to have a fire?" She liked the idea. It would be warm, but also cozy, making their overnight seem more like a voluntary vacation than a rescue mission derailed by supply-stealing muggers.

"Tomorrow morning." He piled the wood on the opposite side of the cave as their bed, and she added her few pieces to the stack. "Don't want anyone to see it tonight."

"Okay." She tried to hide her disappointment, but George's sharp look told her she hadn't succeeded. She sent him a smile. "It's okay, really. I was just getting nostalgic about camping trips with my dad when I was little."

He seemed to accept that, pulling out stuff sacks for their boots and water bottles.

Ellie frowned. "You haven't eaten yet *or* had anything to drink." When he brushed her off with a shake of his head, she moved over to the pack and pulled out the trail mix and one of the water bottles. Just like he'd done to her, she shoved both at him. "Eat. Drink. Don't make me check your pee color, buddy."

His teeth flashed as he grinned, and he accepted the food and water.

"Is that going to be enough for you?" she asked, eyeing his big form. Even crouched as he was, he seemed to fill the cave with his bulk. That much mass required a lot of fuel—she'd seen this firsthand. "We could try to make one of those meals with cold water." The thought made her gag inwardly. They were nasty enough hot.

"It's enough," he said between mouthfuls of trail mix. "We'll be at the cabin tomorrow, and I can do some hunting if there aren't any supplies there."

"Tomorrow?" she blinked, pulling the map from her pocket and crouching next to George so they could both see. She picked up the flashlight and directed it on the paper. "Did we make that much progress today?" It was hard to believe they'd traveled even half the distance as the day before.

"Here," he pointed. "But we'll go this way." His finger traced a line directly from their current camping spot to the cabin.

Ellie sucked in a breath. "But won't that take us right through the avalanche danger area?"

"Need to get you out of here fast. We're low on food." He looked grim. "Don't want to use the gun to hunt this close to…"

The corners of her mouth drew down as she realized what he was saying. The sound of a gunshot would carry, attracting attention from anyone who might be trying to track them.

"I could set snares for game," he continued, "but that doesn't work when we have to keep moving."

Although he didn't say it, Ellie knew he had the same need as she did to put as much distance between them and the two men who could be on their tail. A flash of guilt squeezed her lungs when she thought of how much she'd slowed them down, even today, when she'd known that danger was very likely following them.

George interrupted her mental guilt party. "We'll be cautious. If there are avalanche warning signs, I'll do some tests. I'll keep you safe."

"I know." Catching the hand pointing to the map, she gave it a squeeze, vowing to do her best to keep him safe, as well.

Chapter 13

ONCE THE NIGHTLY CHORES WERE DONE, THINGS GOT awkward again. As she stripped off her coat, Ellie caught George giving her yet another sideways glance. She turned to face him.

"We're just doing what we need to do." She figured that her earlier reaction to their revised sleeping arrangements was the reason behind his fidgety behavior. "It's basic survival. Don't worry about it."

The cold was creeping into her socked feet, so she left it at that, even though George didn't look reassured. Stripping off her fleece, she gasped when cold air hit her skin. Her long underwear was soaked with sweat, whether from the traumatic events or from a fast hike in relatively warm weather, she didn't know.

Diving for the sleeping bag, she wiggled into it. Since George hadn't taken off anything except his boots, she gave him a beguiling smile. "Could you please grab my extra set of long underwear from the pack?"

He dug through the pack, but his growing frown did not bode well for her change of clothes. Sure enough, there was an extra pair of bottoms, but her extra top was wadded into a frozen ball. As she remembered pulling it off on the first day, Ellie made a face.

"Should I leave on this top, do you think?" she asked as she accepted the long underwear pants he held out to her. She really didn't want to. It had already turned clammy and felt gross against her skin.

"No." Quickly shucking his coat and middle layers, George peeled off his top innermost layer and offered it to her.

Her mouth dropped open at the sight of his bare chest, strong and broad and furred with dark hair. When he started to smile, she realized that she was staring and brought her teeth together with a click. Shaking her head, she didn't reach for the shirt. "I can't take your clothes."

Despite her words, he dropped it right next to her and proceeded to strip off everything except his final bottom layer, his socks, and his—well, her—stocking hat. When he paused, she held up the corner of the sleeping bag.

"Get in here before you freeze, crazy man!"

Instead, he didn't move, except for a nod at his abandoned shirt.

"Fine!" she huffed, trying to peel off the damp top with the sleeping bag wrapped around her. As she struggled, a visible shiver ran through George's body, and she sat up abruptly.

Pulling the shirt over her head, she grabbed his top and yanked it on as quickly as possible. It had cooled after he'd removed it, but it was dry and smelled like him, so it was a huge improvement over her shirt. Ellie shoved the abandoned, clammy top down by her legs, trying to flatten it as much as possible so it would dry in the night.

"Now climb in before you turn into a lumberjacksicle." Ellie tried to feign casual indifference, as if she flashed her bra and invited attractive man-mountains into her sleeping bag on a regular basis. Her quick change only accounted for a small part of her rapid heartbeat, though. George's hungry stare was responsible for the rest.

After another pause and shiver, he climbed in next to her. Turning to face away from her so he could zip up the bag most of the way, his massive body pressed her against the folded side of the bedroll. Her anxiety disappeared when his icy skin shocked the nervousness right out of her.

"You're freezing!" she yelped, surprised that he'd gotten so cold in just that short time he'd knelt shirtless.

She rubbed his arm, trying to bring warmth back to his skin, and he stilled for a long moment before pulling the zipper close to the top. The tight quarters increased dramatically with the bag closed, and Ellie's nose squashed against his back.

"This will be warm," she said, her voice nasally, "but not that comfortable. Can we rearrange?"

The two of them squirmed and twisted, fighting the restraints of the sleeping bag as they switched positions. When they settled, Ellie's back was to his chest, but her face was buried in the hood, making her claustrophobic.

"That doesn't work," she said, twisting her neck as far as she could so her voice wouldn't be muffled. "I'm going to turn over." As she wiggled, trying not to elbow George in the belly—or anywhere else—he shifted onto his back. She ended up half on her side and half on her belly, staring at his neck. Once she stopped craning her neck back so as not to appear too eager to snuggle into him, she'd be in pretty much the same position she'd woken in the past two mornings.

George seemed to read her mind. "This is how you like to sleep."

"Yes. I mean, this is good." Her neck was getting tired, and her throat ached, so she let it settle onto his shoulder. "Are you comfortable?"

His amused snort confused her, and she would've looked at him if her eyelids hadn't suddenly weighed fifty pounds each. Their vigorous wriggling had warmed both of them, judging by the toasty interior of the sleeping bag. When he didn't answer beyond that wordless sound, she forced herself to stay awake.

"George? Is this okay for you?" She hated the thought of him being uncomfortable all night because he didn't want to disturb her.

"Yes. Go to sleep." There was a light pressure on the top of her head, and her eyes popped open again. Had he just kissed her hat? After a few seconds, though, exhaustion began to blanket her brain again, and she tucked away the possible affectionate gesture to overanalyze later.

Her arm protested its trapped position beneath her, so she tugged it free. Since George took up most of the room in the sleeping bag, the only place to rest her hand was on top of him. After letting her arm hover over him for a few seconds, she gingerly let it settle onto his torso.

As she began to drift into sleep, her fingers moved absently, stroking the wiry hair on his chest. His hand flattened hers beneath it, stilling her.

"Sorry," she mumbled, figuring her absentminded touch was irritating him.

He expelled a huff of air. "No need to be sorry."

"'Kay. 'Night." She was so tired, it was hard to get out even those two words.

The only answer was another slight pressure on the crown of her head.

———m———

For the first time in three days—almost a week, in fact—Ellie slept hard for the entire night. She woke to silver dawn light filtering into the cave, and she allowed her eyes to open a crack. It was different than being in the tent, less isolated from nature. She almost enjoyed her cave time, although it would've been a different story if she hadn't had her two sleeping pads and a living, breathing, jumbo-sized bed warmer.

She woke as she always did with George—plastered against his side with her face tucked into his neck. This time, though, there weren't two sleeping bags between them, and her hand rested on his bare chest. Silently, she admitted to herself that she liked this better than their solitary bags, and not just because it was warmer.

Letting out a sound that was as close as George had ever come to a snore—at least during the nights she'd been sharing a tent or cave with him—he tightened the arm wrapped around her, pulling her closer to his body. She relaxed into him, not minding. When she realized his other hand was draped across his body and was cupping her thigh, though, she couldn't help but stiffen. That small movement was enough to wake him, and she felt his muscles tense slightly with awareness.

"Morning," she said to his neck, knowing that they needed to get moving but wanting another few minutes of basking in the warm safety of their shared sleeping bag.

He grunted, and Ellie chose to interpret that as "Good morning, Ellie. Isn't it a lovely day?"

Holding back a giggle at the imaginary British accent she'd assigned him in her mind, she asked, "Did you sleep okay?"

His next grunt was affirmative, although slightly tense. Even though he hadn't removed his hands, they felt stiff, as if George was ultra-aware of touching her. In turn, it made her self-conscious, and the delicious lassitude she'd been feeling began to seep away. With a sigh, she propped herself up as much as the confines of the sleeping bag would allow.

This put her face exceedingly close to his, and she realized her mistake when their eyes met. His were a soft brown, lightening almost to amber around the pupil. His dark lashes were thick and shadowed his eyes, giving him a sleepy, sexy look.

When the word "sexy" popped into her head, she jerked her gaze away. Unfortunately, her eyes then settled on his mouth, and the memory of kissing him made a shiver track down her spine for reasons that had nothing to do with the cold. George must have felt the shudder, because that lush mouth she was staring at turned down in a frown.

"Get dressed," he said, his voice extra raspy from sleep.

Nodding, she reached down to retrieve her hopefully dry undershirt. The sleeping bag did not make her contortions easy, though, and she must have bumped something sensitive on George. He made a noise she could describe only as a squawk.

"What are you doing?"

Reemerging triumphantly with the shirt clutched in her fist, she held it up in explanation. It didn't seem to settle George, though.

It was Ellie's turn to frown. "Are you okay? You're breathing really fast."

"Fine." He practically bit off the word.

"Sure? I've never seen you out of breath."

Giving a short nod, he unzipped the sleeping bag and was out before she realized his intention. He turned away to dress in his multiple bottom layers, and Ellie stared at his back for much too long before she caught herself. Giving herself a mental shake, she took advantage of his inattention to switch out her shirts.

"Here," she said, holding out his long underwear top. "Thank you for letting me wear it. Mine is dry now."

With barely a glance, he accepted the shirt and pulled it over his head. The view was suddenly not as nice. When Ellie realized the direction of her thoughts, she flushed and concentrated on pulling on her fleece top.

George was quiet as they did morning chores. Ellie found that she didn't want to be far from the silent giant. The previous day's events had left her shaken, and she knew she hadn't even started to deal with the mental consequences. Instead of dwelling on it, she focused on the day ahead and getting to her father. It made her wonder, though, what would happen once they got to the cabin.

As George started a fire with the ease of long practice, she watched him, her brain churning with possible scenarios, each one grimmer than the last. He kept darting glances at her.

"What's wrong?" he finally asked.

She lifted one shoulder in a half shrug, and then realized that she'd just imitated one of George's mannerisms. If the trip lasted much longer, she'd probably start talking in grunts and nods. A small smile touched her lips, but it quickly slid away when she considered his question.

"Nothing...just..." She shook her head firmly. "Nothing to worry about right now."

He gave her a look, the one that told her he could sit there all day if he had to, and she *was* going to tell him whatever she was holding back. It was very wordy for a look.

"Fine." It didn't take long for him to break her. "What are we going to do once we get to the cabin? Will we immediately hike back to the truck?" Although she didn't say it, she was thinking about how the route back to where they'd parked could easily cross paths with the two terrifying men who wanted to kill them. This trip was treacherous enough without adding her mentally ill father to the mix.

"We'll see what resources are at the cabin," he answered thoughtfully. "There might be a radio, so we can call the sheriff. If not, we can hike a different route that brings us to a main road." Apparently, he was employing his mind-reading trick again.

"Okay." Her shoulders relaxed a little. George had a way of calming her, of making her believe that he could accomplish anything, and do it with a minimum of fuss. It was a reassuring quality to have in a guide.

As if to prove her point, he used the aluminum blade of the shovel as a shallow, improvised pot to melt snow and heat the water to boiling over their small campfire. The good news was that they were able to fill their bottles with hot water, but the bad news was that they were able to make the remaining pouch meals. This time, Ellie had the beef stew, which was slightly better than the chicken teriyaki, but it was still fairly nasty. She forced down half of it before turning the remainder over to George to finish.

Once their water bottles and stomachs were filled, they broke camp quickly, loading everything into the solitary backpack and erasing all traces of their short habitation. As they started down the trail, Ellie looked over her shoulder at the cave, a little sad to leave it. It had been a cozy, secure shelter for the night.

"How did you know about the cave?" she asked, hurrying to catch up to George.

Glancing back at her, he shortened his long stride to match her pace. "Grew up exploring this area. I've spent the night there a few times."

"So you've lived here all your life?"

He nodded.

"Did you always live in the house you have now?"

As he gave an affirmative grunt, he took her arm to help her over a spot where the melting snow had glazed the rocks underfoot with ice. She sent him a surprised look. The Boy-Scout-type assistance was new. Although he'd checked on her a lot as they'd hiked, he'd never helped her cross a tricky part before. She added that to the head kisses in the "overanalyze later" file in her brain.

"So your parents… Did they move somewhere else?" She had a sinking feeling that they were no longer alive, but she wasn't sure how to ask that tactfully.

"Both dead."

She blinked. That was straightforward. "I'm sorry."

When he grunted his acknowledgment, she figured

the subject was closed, so she was surprised when he spoke. "My mom died when I was a baby, so I didn't know her. Dad passed fourteen years ago."

"You were still a kid, then?"

"Seventeen."

Scrambling over a pile of rocks that had worked loose from the sheer cliff above, she gave a wary glance upward, wondering if she should add "possible rock slides" to her list of worries. "Seventeen is still a kid."

"Not for me."

It was easy to picture George as a serious, quiet teenager, old beyond his years. "Did you stay by yourself, then? After your dad died, I mean."

He gave a single nod of his head. For some reason, the thought of a young George alone in that cabin in the woods made her sad.

"What did you do to make money?" Once again, she was probably being nosy and rude, but he didn't seem to mind answering her questions, and she was dying of curiosity. His upbringing was a world away from her apartment-dwelling childhood in Chicago.

"Same as what I do now. I don't buy a lot, so I don't need much money. I do some plowing in the winter, construction in the summer, and"—he sent a sly glance her way—"occasionally babysit tourists in the mountains."

For some reason, that stung. "If you've done this before, why didn't you want to take me?"

His face went serious, even a little anxious. "I was teasing. I meant just you. Sorry. I'm not good at jokes."

As her hurt feelings dissolved, she felt a little silly. "No, I'm sorry. I didn't mean to be so touchy." She hoped her overreaction wouldn't kill any future hints of humor in him. "And what are you talking about, not being good at jokes? You're funny."

Although he didn't say anything, his expression lightened. After a minute, he said, "Knock, knock."

Ellie burst out laughing, the sound bouncing off the rocky slopes and echoing back to them. "See? You're plenty funny."

———⁓———

They didn't take a break for several hours. Ellie could tell they both felt the same urgency pushing them. As they zigzagged their way up the south-facing slope, she was grateful for the scarcity of snow. With only one pair of snowshoes between the two of them, deep snow would've slowed down their pace to a snaillike slog.

When they finally paused for water and trail mix, the sun was high in the sky, and Ellie was sweating enough to shed her fleece middle layer and tie it around her waist. Just a short time after their break, George stopped again.

"What is it?"

His answer was a silent lift of his chin at something behind her. She whirled around so fast that she almost toppled over, and George put a steadying hand on her shoulder. A gorgeous view spread out in front of them, white snow dappled with patches of evergreens. It was beautiful, and Ellie forgot about the gun and the two men and even her father for a minute as she absorbed it.

"No wonder people do this kind of thing for fun," she breathed, turning to look at George. He was watching her and smiling, and she grinned back at him, covering his hand on her shoulder with her own. As their gazes met and clung, Ellie realized she'd rather look at George than even the beautiful vista in front of them. The thought flustered her, and she broke their too-intense eye contact.

The moment over too soon, they turned their backs to the amazing view and resumed their fast pace. Ellie hadn't panted for breath as much since that first day of hiking, but she pushed through the discomfort and ignored her desire to dawdle.

Once they started descending the north side of the slope, though, they were forced to slow dramatically. There was a hard crust on top of the snow, which helped keep their boots on the surface of the drifts, but it tended to send them sliding, especially when they were going downhill.

Ellie eyed a smooth section in front of them that cut between the trees like a groomed ski slope. "Can we just sit and sled down that?"

His face was tense as he shook his head. "Terrain trap."

"What?" The smooth snow looked innocent to her.

"An avalanche could follow that. It's a natural chute."

"Oh." She eyed the slope that had suddenly taken on an ominous quality.

"We'll cross here, one at a time. You go first."

Although she would've preferred to stick together, the clear section wasn't that wide, and she trusted that George knew the best way to keep them safe. She started to cross, keeping her gaze on a pine tree directly across from them. Knowing that she was crossing a possible avalanche path made it hard to keep her feet moving. With each step, she worried that it would be the one to bring all the snow on the mountain down on them.

When she neared her goal tree, she had the opposite problem—she wanted to run to safety. Ellie forced herself to take measured steps and not fling herself at the evergreen and wrap her arms around the trunk. Finally, she reached it. As a compromise between the logical and hysterical parts of her brain, she closed her hand around a sturdy branch, leaning casually against it to hide her tight grip.

George had started across the clear slope, and it was almost harder to watch him than it had been to do the walk herself. They both had their personal beacons, but, since he had the pack that held the shovel and probe, she wouldn't have any tools to rescue him. Watching him cross, she felt a fierce determination fire inside her. If she had to dig him out with her bare hands, she would do it. She'd dig up the whole mountain if she had to, but she wouldn't stop until he was free.

Crossing the last few feet that separated them, George gave her a curious glance.

"What's that look?" he asked.

"Nothing." He'd think she was an overly attached potential stalker if she told him what she'd been thinking, so she adopted a casual tone. "I can carry the pack for a while."

Despite her attempt at sounding nonchalant, he shot her a sharp look. "No."

Frustrated, she resisted stomping her foot in a childish show of temper. With her luck, it would trigger an avalanche, and she still didn't have the shovel if George was buried. "Fine."

He sent her an unexpected grin. "Thank you."

With great effort, she held her scowl, even in the face

of his rare, contagious smile. "If you were really grateful, you'd let me carry the shovel—I mean, the pack."

"No. Let's go."

Grumbling under her breath, she followed him into the trees.

Chapter 14

GEORGE DIDN'T LIKE IT. THE OBVIOUS WARNING SIGNS weren't there. He couldn't see any evidence of previous avalanches, there were no shooting cracks, and the snow didn't sound hollow under his boots. It had been more than twenty-four hours since the last snowfall, and there weren't any rolling snowballs—that he'd seen, at least.

Still, the temperature was climbing, and his gut was churning, despite the lack of warning signs. He wanted to dig a hole to check the layers of snow, but they couldn't stop for that long just based on his bad feeling. Even though he feared a possible avalanche, the two men who'd attacked them were the greater threat.

This jumpy, tense state of worry was unfamiliar. Blowing out a breath, he shook out his arms, trying to recover his usual calm wariness. It wasn't there, though, and he knew the reason why. It was the woman a couple of steps behind him, the one who was singing under her breath. Somehow, keeping her safe had become the ulti- mate priority, and any possible threat to her made him come unglued.

To distract himself, he glanced at her. "Are you singing?"

Her eyes widened, reminding him of his first look at her face and how much she'd reminded him of a china doll. "Sorry." It came out as a loud whisper. "Could that start an avalanche?"

Turning back to face the front so he didn't walk head-first into a tree, he couldn't hold back a quick grin. She was just so darn *cute*. "No. You could yodel, and it still wouldn't trigger it."

She laughed, and he felt proud that he was the cause of it. "I promise not to yodel. For so many reasons, there will be no yodeling."

That made him smile again. George didn't think he'd ever smiled as much in his life as he had over the last three days. Considering that they'd been robbed at gunpoint, during which he'd been shot, that was pretty impressive.

"I'm singing to distract myself. It's kind of like whistling in the dark. You know, to prove I'm not afraid."

He indulged himself by looking at her again. It seemed that each time he did, she was prettier. Now that he knew how she felt pressed against him, it added another dimension to how he saw her. The night before had been torture, but wonderful, too. The memory of her hand idly stroking his chest before she fell asleep flashed through his mind, and he whipped his head around before she could see the completely smitten look on his face.

When he heard her singing softly start again, he smiled. She had a nice voice—nothing fancy, but sweet and true. It helped to relax him, too. Once again, he found himself looking over his shoulder at her. The trees had thinned, and sunlight picked up the red and gold accents in her dark brown hair. Her cheeks were pink from exertion and probably a little sunburned. She smiled when she caught him looking, and his lungs suddenly felt like a bull elk was standing on his chest. No one had ever made him feel anything like she did, and he'd only known her for four days.

Then the ground shifted beneath him, and she was gone.

Chapter 15

GEORGE LUNGED TO GRAB HER, BUT IT WAS TOO LATE. In the midst of his absolute panic, his training kicked in. Resisting the urge to chase after her, to let the slide carry him toward her, he grabbed at a pine tree with both hands as he passed it. The branch in his right hand ripped free of the trunk, but the left one held, and he stopped with a shoulder-wrenching jerk.

He grabbed at the tree again with his right hand. This time, the branch he caught was sturdy. As soon as he was secure, his eyes searched for Ellie; he saw a flash of her bright red coat before she disappeared into the white mass of snow again.

"No, no, no, no, no!" When he realized he was yelling the same word over and over, he clamped his mouth shut and concentrated on watching where she'd last disappeared.

The analytical part of his brain that terror couldn't smother was telling him that it was a small slide. Ellie had been right on top of it, though, and now it was on top of her. Bile rose in the back of his throat, and he swallowed hard. His breathing was strange, fast and shallow, and he forced his lungs to slow.

He knew the snow had to settle before he could go after her. Getting himself buried along with her would just kill them both. Still, waiting was the hardest thing he'd ever done in his life.

As soon as the slide ended, he ran, pulling out his avalanche transceiver from his inner coat pocket as he did so. As he turned it to "Receive," he glanced down at it and lost his balance. George twisted into the fall, holding the beacon out of harm's way, and landed on his belly. Skidding down the slope like a penguin, he refocused on the spot where he'd last seen Ellie.

When he was almost parallel to the place he'd glimpsed that flash of red, George flipped so his feet were downhill, and used his boots to stop his slide. Snow fanned into the air in front of him as he slowed. Using his remaining momentum, he pushed to his feet, running almost before he was upright.

As he neared the point where Ellie had disappeared, he forced himself to slow slightly. He knew he needed to be methodical to find her. There was no group of rescuers to help. It was all on him, and running around in a panic was not going to help. If he didn't find her and get her out within fifteen minutes, her chances of survival would drop dramatically.

Moving downhill, he made a zigzag pattern, his eyes looking for any sign of her. He listened, as well, but heard only the faint moan of the wind. His gaze flickered to the locator beacon, frantic to see that first arrow, that first distance on the digital display.

When it beeped, his initial thought was that it was his imagination, but the arrow flashed onto the display, along with a thirty-two. Unable to help himself, he broke into a jog, following the arrow and glancing at the screen repeatedly, watching the distance between them shrink from thirty-two meters to two.

"El!" he shouted, but his heart was beating too loudly

in his ears to hear a response, if there was one. Quickly unfastening the pack, he let it fall to the ground and unzipped it with shaking hands. He pulled out the shovel first and then the probe. Moving the transceiver in a cross shape, he pinpointed the spot within a half meter.

The probe slid easily into the snow on his first try, so he moved out about ten inches and made a circle around the original spot. With each fruitless plunge of the probe, his terror fought to break free of his tight mental grip, but he fought it back. On his second concentric circle, his third attempt sunk the probe in only two feet before stopping. He'd found her. A muffled sound came from underneath the snow, and his breath escaped him in a relieved exhale that was very close to a sob.

"El! Ellie!" Dropping to his knees, he shouted at the snow, "I'm getting you out, El!" Leaving the probe in place and shoving the transceiver into his coat pocket, he moved to the downhill side and started digging. George chopped at the hard-packed snow and flung it behind him as fast as he could, but it felt like it was taking forever. The clock in his head ticked, counting down those precious fifteen minutes.

After digging down about three feet, he dug sideways toward the probe. A spot of red showed through the snow, and his heart jumped in his chest, hope spreading through him. He shoveled with renewed determination, although he was careful not to hurt her. When her back was exposed enough that he could tell which direction she was positioned, he moved to uncover her head. Once her airway was clear, then he could concentrate on freeing the rest of her.

As soon as he was close, he dug with his hands,

clawing the snow away from her head. Her arms must
have come in front of her face before she'd been buried,
creating a pocket of air in front of her mouth and nose.
When he saw her face, his muscles wanted to go limp
in relief, but he fought it. It wasn't time to collapse yet.

She tried to twist her head toward him as soon as
he uncovered it, but he held her still with a gentle,
gloved hand.

"Wait, El. Don't move until I get you clear." She
must have heard and understood because, except for
shivering, she didn't move again until he'd uncovered
the rest of her body. Grabbing two handfuls of the back
of her coat, George supported her neck as he turned her
onto her back and dragged her out of the hole.

Once she was free, she tried to push herself to a
seated position, but he urged her back.

"Let me check first." Her eyes were huge in her pale
face, but she didn't seem to have a head injury. He ran
his hand over her arms and legs, feeling through the
multiple layers of fabric for any breaks or signs of pain.
Unzipping her coat, he quickly ran his hands over her
ribs and belly, watching her expression closely as he did
so. Although he was certified as a first responder, his
medical knowledge was limited to the ABCs—airway,
breathing, and circulation. He could give CPR, apply
compression to stop bleeding, and rig up a splint. If
anything was wrong with her internally, though, he was
useless. "Anything hurt?"

"No."

Her shivering was getting worse, and he zipped her
coat to her chin. As pale as she was, he worried that
she was in shock. He rotated her body so he could prop

her feet onto the pile of snow he'd created. Grabbing the sleeping bag off the pack, he unrolled it and laid it over her.

"No, George." She stuttered a little, thanks to her chattering teeth. "It'll get wet. I'm okay. I just need to get up and move."

Although every instinct was shouting at him to keep her still and covered, he knew they weren't in a safe place. Unlike when he was on a search and rescue call, help wasn't on its way. Flight for Life wasn't going to magically appear overhead. It was up to just the two of them to get to safety, and having her lie on the snow at the base of a recent avalanche was not the way to do it.

With a reluctant nod, he moved her legs out of their elevated position and helped her sit. "Okay?"

"Yes." Despite her resolute nod, he frowned as he eyed her face. She was still shaking and too pale, her normally pink cheeks pasty. He was so involved in checking her color that her hands on his cheeks startled him. She'd lost a glove, and her bare hand was freezing against his skin. "George. I'm okay. Help me up?"

He did, albeit unhappily, wishing he could just teleport her to a hospital. Once she was standing, he wasn't able to release his grip on her arms.

"How far to the cabin?" Her voice was shaking a little less now, and he only felt an occasional vibration shudder through her.

"We can make camp at the base of that ridge." He jerked his chin toward the area he meant, not wanting to let go of her in order to point. "There's an overhang that'll make a good shelter."

"George." She looked at him steadily. Her color was

a little better. She'd lost that blue tinge under her skin. "We're going to the cabin."

"It's too far." His fingers tightened, and he had to consciously loosen them before he hurt her arms. Where had this resolute Ellie come from? She was usually good about following orders, at least as far as hiking and camping were concerned.

"How far?"

"Four hours, if we move fast." And he didn't want her moving at all right then.

"Come on, then." She tugged loose of his hold, and he forced his hands to release her. "Let's pack and go."

Ellie bent, swaying a little, and reached for the shovel, but George hurried to grab it.

"Fine," he growled. "I'll pack. You sit." He walked toward her so she was forced to back up toward the snow pile, and then he helped her ease down so she was sitting on it. Once she was in place, he hurried to finish packing, knowing he had just a short window before she would insist on helping.

In addition to the glove, she'd also lost the fleece around her waist, and her hat was full of snow, so he dug out a pair of gloves, her last extra hat, and a fuzzy top, and handed them to her. She must have been cold, because she lost no time in stripping off her coat to pull on the additional layer. George tried very hard not to look at her during the few seconds she wore only the thin underlayer. Mentally calling himself a pervert, he forced his gaze away from her and concentrated on packing.

In the short time it took to stow the probe, shovel, and sleeping bag, he had an idea. He unstrapped the snowshoes from the pack and then headed over to where Ellie was waiting. After helping her to stand again, he eased the backpack over her shoulders. Although she looked a little surprised, she let him buckle the straps around her torso to secure the pack.

Shoving his feet into the snowshoe bindings and tightening them, George turned back to Ellie, who was eyeing him curiously. Apparently, she hadn't figured out the plan yet. He moved in front of her and turned his back, crouching a little.

"Uh...what are you doing?" she asked, her voice uncertain.

"Piggyback," he said over his shoulder. "Get on."

There was a short silence. "You're not going to carry me."

"Yes." He tried to keep the impatience out of his tone, but he was pretty certain he failed. "I am. Get on."

"I'm not going to become a literal burden."

"El." Twisting around, he gave her an even look. "You're wasting time."

After another pause, she made a wordless sound of frustration, and then her body pressed against his back. With a grunt of satisfaction, George stood and hoisted her off the ground. Her legs wrapped around his waist and her arms around his shoulders. Despite her weight—which seemed fairly insignificant at the moment, even including the pack—she felt wonderful against him. Although he was pretty sure it was his imagination, since there were six layers of clothes between them, he thought he could feel the thud of her heartbeat against his own ribs.

With a final check to make sure she was ready, George started to run.

Chapter 16

PIGGYBACK RIDES HAD BEEN A LOT MORE FUN WHEN she was a kid. To be fair, though, she'd never had an hour-long piggyback ride before. Ellie shifted slightly, searching for a more comfortable position but not wanting to throw off George's balance.

George slowed to a walk. He'd been switching off between jogging and walking, running until his breath was heavy and ragged, and then slowing to rest. She tried to help as much as she could by holding on with her arms and legs, but her own body was working against her, exhaustion pulling at her until she caught her chin drifting toward George's shoulder several times.

"Let me walk," she pleaded, but he ignored her as he had the past ten times she'd asked. "Please, George. I think it would keep me warmer." The only reason she said that was for manipulation purposes. With George at her front and the afternoon sun on her back, she wasn't cold in the least. She did feel guilty, though, hating the feeling of literally not pulling her own weight.

Under her arms, his shoulders dipped in a sigh. "Just for a little while." He stopped and let her slide off his back. When her feet hit the ground, her knees threatened to buckle, and Ellie grabbed the back of his coat to keep herself upright. Throwing a worried look at her over his shoulder, he started to crouch, as if to pick her up again, but she took a step back, shaking her head.

"No, I'm okay. My legs were just asleep, that's all." To prove she was ambulatory, she started walking. The snow was looser there, without the frozen top crust, and her boots sank almost a foot with each step.

"Wait." Bending to loosen the bindings, he stepped out of the snowshoes and motioned her toward him. "Wear these."

She reluctantly agreed, mainly because she knew they were only as fast as the slowest person, which was most definitely her. If snowshoes would give her a little more speed, they would arrive at the cabin that much sooner.

George adjusted the bindings to grip her boots and then stood, rubbing at his head under his lavender cap.

"Head hurt?" she asked, reminded that a bullet had creased his scalp just a day earlier.

"No." When she looked at him skeptically, he gave her a smile. "Itches. Headache's gone, though."

"Uh-huh." Despite his innocent expression, she didn't believe him. For him to be unconscious like he had been, it had to have been a pretty serious concussion. She was no doctor, but it made sense that his head would hurt for a while after something like that. Ellie let it go, though. "Ready?"

He shook his head and reached for the buckles on the backpack.

"I can carry it," she protested, knowing it almost certainly wouldn't change his mind. Sure enough, he didn't even answer her as he removed the pack from her shoulders and swung it onto his own back.

"Tell me if you get tired," he ordered with a stern look.

She didn't mention that she was already tired—almost unbearably tired. Instead, she just followed him as he plowed through the snow. As she suspected, George without snowshoes was just as fast as she was *with* snowshoes, so they continued at a steady pace.

"Where's the cabin?" she asked, puffing slightly. They were crossing a wide, mostly treeless valley, so they were able to walk side by side. Everything looked a little dreamlike and off-kilter, as if she'd had a couple of cocktails. She hoped it was just exhaustion and not brain damage caused by the avalanche. Her head didn't hurt, at least. Every muscle in her body did, but her brain seemed to have escaped damage.

He pointed in front of them and slightly to the right. "We'll circle around the base of that slope. It's in a clearing just beyond that."

The spot he indicated looked really far away to Ellie, but she caught herself before she whined. Since he'd just *carried* her butt for over an hour, the least she could do was keep her complaining to herself. Talking helped, though. Silence just made her concentrate on how hard it was to take each step.

"Why don't you do this more?"

"What?"

She flung out a hand to indicate the surrounding scenery. The movement made the ground tilt in an odd way, so she dropped her arm to her side. "The guide thing. I bet people would pay a lot of money for you to take them camping." *Especially if he let the women sleep in his mummy bag with him.* Even though she didn't say it out loud, the thought of those hypothetical women made her innards squirm with annoyance.

George looked like he'd just tasted something gross. "Not my thing."

"Why not? You're really good at it. I mean, I'm clue-less, and you've kept me alive so far." When he turned to look at her with a worried frown, she wished she hadn't added the "so far."

"You're easy," he finally said after finishing his glowering inspection.

That made her laugh. She could tell the second he realized what he'd implied, because he actually blushed. Ellie loved that, judging by the frequency of George's blushes, she could make him just as flustered as she was around him.

"Not like that." His cheeks burned even more brightly above his beard. "Most tourists want…things. Like talking."

With a mock gasp, she rounded her eyes and stared at him. His form went blurry, her eyes not wanting to focus correctly. She didn't want to mention her vision issues and end up being carried again, so she joked instead. "Not *talking*! The horror!"

His frown didn't lighten. "It is for me. I'd rather not be a guide and just skip buying the extras. I don't really need another rifle. The money isn't worth it."

"*Another* rifle?" she repeated. "How many do you have?"

He was quiet for a while, possibly doing a mental count, and then answered, "Twelve."

That made her choke a little. When she could speak again, she said, "Yeah, that's probably enough rifles."

His grin was back.

"What about hunting groups?" The mention of guns made her remember Joseph's side job. As she waited for George to answer, she carefully placed each snowshoe-clad step. The horizon was rocking again, tilting her like a canoe on an ocean.

Although his frown wasn't as severe as when he'd been talking about demanding tourists, it was still present. "They don't listen." He shook his head and amended, "Most of them do. Usually, there's just one or two in each group."

"The know-it-alls?" she asked sympathetically. "Yeah, I imagine that could be tough, especially when they're all armed."

They walked in silence for a few minutes, and Ellie started counting her painful, rocking steps again, so she racked her brain for another conversational topic.

"Have you ever been married?" she blurted, and then wanted to suck back the words when he gave her a startled glance. "None of my business, sorry." A horrible thought occurred to her. What if he *was* married, like, currently? An image of an outdoorsy, tall woman, with a blond ponytail and the ability to gut a deer and start a fire without matches, filled her head. Jealousy sent a sharp pain through her stomach at this imaginary woman who'd probably still been tucked up in her and George's oversized bed when Ellie had been at his house.

"No."

Ripped out of her homicidal thoughts about a made-up woman, she stared at him blankly. "What?"

He focused straight ahead, but his cheeks were red again. "I haven't been married."

"Good." Slapping a gloved hand over her mouth, she sent him a sideways glance and saw he was grinning. "I mean, that's nice. Oh, fudge, I mean...never mind."

His smile grew at her mumbled babbling.

"Can I just start over again so we can forget the question and everything that followed?" By his amused expression, she knew he wouldn't be forgetting.

After another few minutes of silence, during which Ellie couldn't stop replaying her embarrassing moment in her head, George asked, "Have you?"

"Have I what?"

"Been married."

"Oh God, no." She shook her head and then stopped quickly when the motion made her dizzy. "I haven't even come close."

After he grunted an acknowledgment, he went quiet again. His grin had returned, though, and Ellie wasn't sure why. She opened her mouth to ask another question, and the ground tilted again but didn't correct itself that time. Blinking, she looked at George's concerned face. It was at a strange angle, and it took her a few moments to realize she was lying on her back in the snow.

"That was weird," she said.

After stripping off the snowshoes, he helped her to her feet, brushing the snow from her coat. His face grim, George didn't answer, but just switched the backpack to her shoulders and strapped the snowshoes onto his own feet. Turning away from her, he crouched, waiting.

Resigning herself to being a literal burden once again, she climbed onto his back.

———m———

Time went a little strange after that.

"El!"

She jerked, her arms and legs tightening around George convulsively.

"Stay awake."

She was trying, but the blackness kept falling over her, despite her best efforts. "Sorry." Even to her own ears, her voice sounded slurred. Her body bounced with George's running strides. It was hard to tell when she kept going unconscious, but she was pretty sure he was jogging more than he was walking. His breathing was jagged, and his arms shook where they supported the backs of her thighs.

"We close?" She needed to talk to keep herself awake, but each word was a huge effort.

"Yeah," he panted. "There…soon."

Her head sagged forward until it rested on George's shoulder. The motion jarred her forehead, but her neck didn't feel strong enough to support it. "I can walk."

His snort came out more like a gasp. "You…can't… walk. You…can hardly…talk."

"Look who's talking!" she said, although her garbled words kind of proved his point. Forcing her head to lift, she cracked open her eyes. The sun was mostly gone, and everything looked gray in the twilight. There was a shape, though, crouching in the snow some distance in front of them. "That it?"

"That's…it." Despite his heaving breaths, George increased his speed.

"Made it." Dropping her head back onto his shoulder, she fell back into the darkness.

Chapter 17

WHEN ELLIE WENT LIMP, GEORGE BENT FORWARD, clutched her legs, and added another burst of speed as he ran for the cabin. Air sawed in and out of his lungs, but he couldn't get enough oxygen. Cramps ripped across his diaphragm, and his legs wobbled. His body had had just about enough of the rough treatment, but panic allowed him to finish his sprint to the cabin's porch.

The edge of the first porch step caught on the snowshoe, and he crouched to rip open the bindings. Standing proved difficult, but he managed, even with the deadweight on his back. He stepped out of the snowshoes and climbed the last five steps.

The cabin door swung inward, and George took a stumbling step toward the welcoming glow of light. He froze halfway into his forward lurch when he saw the business end of a shotgun pointed directly at his head.

A renewed burst of panic flooded him at the knowledge that Ellie's head was resting right next to his, directly in the line of fire.

"It's Ellie!" George yelled, scrambling to put space between her and the gun's barrels. He teetered on the edge of the top step, barely stopping himself from falling back and landing on El. "It's your daughter. It's Ellie."

His breath rasped in and out of his lungs, his throat tight from exertion and shock. The silhouetted man in the doorway didn't say anything, but he didn't fire either, so that was a positive.

"She came to find you." He forced out the words despite the way talking ground against his throat like a power sander. "You called her, said you were going to her grandpa's cabin, so she asked me to bring her here. She was caught in an avalanche." That was almost impossible to say, but for different reasons. Hearing the words out loud made sheer terror flood back into his muscles, making his whole body shake. "I dug...I dug her out, but something's wrong. She seemed fine, was talking, but then she went down. I carried her here, but she keeps passing out. Something's wrong. She needs medical care from someone who knows more than me."

Out of words, George just stood and gasped for air. After what felt like an infinite amount of time, the man in the doorway slowly lowered his gun. George had to resist the overpowering urge to leap forward and disarm the man. This was El's dad, and he was the most likely source of help, hopefully in the form of a radio.

"I was...I was a medic in the army," Baxter said, his eyes on where Ellie's head rested on George's shoulder. "It was a long time ago, a long time ago, but I used to know a lot about fixing broken bodies."

"Then you need to fix our girl." George shoved his way past the older man into the cabin.

Chapter 18

ELLIE FROWNED WITHOUT OPENING HER EYES, trying to figure out what had woken her. She finally realized that she was too hot. After spending the past three nights fighting to stay warm, it was an alien feeling, and she reluctantly pried open her eyelids.

The unfamiliar surroundings made her eyes pop wide as she sat up abruptly, then gave a belated groan. Every muscle in her body hurt. She was in a small cabin, similar to Willard Gray's former home. Except for a tiny wooden table and two chairs, it was empty of furniture. There was a woodstove in the corner. Judging by the red glow of the stovepipe, it was responsible for her overheating.

Her bedding was familiar. She was tucked into the sleeping bag she'd been using, and the inflated pad provided cushioning from the rough-planked floor. Morning light struggled through many years' worth of dirt on the single window opposite the door, showing that she was alone in the cabin.

Before the thought could make her nervous, the door opened, and an older man entered with his arms full of firewood, followed by George with a similar load. It took her a second before she recognized the first man, which sent a flush of shame through her. What kind of person forgot what her own father looked like? "Dad?"

His head whipped around, and he dropped the

armload into a wooden box a few feet from the stove while keeping his gaze fixed on her. "Hey, baby girl." His voice was tentative. After taking two steps toward her, he faltered and stopped. "How are you feeling?"

"Okay." Shrugging, she held back a wince. Even that small movement hurt. "A little sore. What happened last night?" She shifted to her knees. Since she still had her fleece layer on over her long underwear, she was decently covered. Pausing a moment, she let her screeching muscles adjust to the new position before starting to stand.

George was next to her in a second, offering a hand, which she accepted gratefully. Even after that first day of hiking, she'd never been so sore. Neither George nor Baxter volunteered an answer to her question, which made her extra-curious.

"I just remember bits and pieces, and I might have been dreaming some of it." As she thought about those flashes of memory, she grimaced and looked at George. "Did you have to carry me here?"

He shrugged.

"Sorry." Wrinkling her nose, she said, "I don't know what was wrong with me. I felt kind of strange, but okay, and then the world went sideways."

"No, that was you." It was always a surprise when George made a joke—a good surprise.

She couldn't help but smile as she swatted his arm. "Yeah, I figured that."

"The shock," Baxter blurted, bringing her attention back to him. "That's why…at least I think… You'll be okay. I hope… I hope you'll be okay." He was eyeing her with such intensity, such…*longing* that it made her uncomfortable. Dropping her gaze, she leaned against George's arm, not sure how to handle this father-daughter reunion.

"Still want to get you checked out by a doctor." The bass rumble of George's voice vibrated through her. It was comforting, and she leaned on him a little harder.

"Is there a radio here?" She glanced around at the bare-bones cabin, doubting that there was anything except a mouse or two in the ancient structure.

"No." George sounded grim. "I'll need to hike to the road."

Narrowing her eyes at him, she used her sternest voice. "*We'll* need to hike, you mean."

He was shaking his head before she finished the sentence. Apparently, her commanding tone needed some work.

"George—"

"No."

"But—"

"No." His mouth flattened into an inflexible line.

"But I—"

"You need to stay here with your father." He gave her a meaningful look. Torn, she glanced at Baxter and back at George. He'd make better time without having to babysit her, and she really should keep an eye on her dad. Despite the logical reasons she should stay at the cabin while George went for help, she felt an ache in her chest at the thought of being away from him. It was crazy, since she'd known him such a short time, but he'd become important to her. If something happened to him—like getting shot in the head—she wanted to be there. It would be so hard to be left behind, to wonder and worry and fret until George made it back to her. She looked between the two men and knew she didn't have a choice. Her shoulders drooped.

"Fine." Lowering her voice, she let her hand brush against his. "You'll be careful?"

Tipping his head down, he gave her a sweet smile. "Yes."

"No getting shot again. Promise?"

"Promise."

"How long do you think it'll take for you to reach the road?"

Lifting one shoulder in a half shrug, he estimated, "Tomorrow morning, if I don't stop and the weather holds."

She blinked. "I really held you back, didn't I?"

Leaning so close his lips almost touched her temple, he said quietly, "You did fine."

As always, a tiny bit of praise from George made her beam. She quickly sobered, though. "When are you leaving?"

"Now." Reaching into both coat pockets, he pulled out the gun she'd taken off the robber, as well as its magazine. He held them out to her, but she took a step back, holding her hands behind her in a gesture she knew was childish but she couldn't help. Instead of pushing the issue, he walked over to the table and laid them down before focusing on Baxter. "Show her how to use it."

Despite Ellie's protesting sound, her father nodded. Grabbing a compression sack from the backpack leaning against the wall, George headed for the sleeping bag she'd recently vacated. While he shoved it into the bag, she deflated the pad, wondering if it was the last time they'd break camp—well, sort of camp—together.

They worked silently, melting snow in a pan on top

of the woodstove and then pouring the hot water through a coffee filter into the insulated bottles. Ellie thought about how nice it would be just to turn on a faucet to get clean, unfrozen water. Baxter pulled out a half dozen foil packets from his own pack and tucked them into George's. Ellie eyed them curiously as George gave him a nod of thanks.

"What are those?"

"MREs."

She wasn't any more enlightened after George's short reply, so she kept looking at him expectantly.

"Meals Ready to Eat."

"Like what we ate?" Although she tried to keep a poker face, she could feel her nose wrinkling. "Yum."

Her voice was flat, and George shot her an amused look. "Yes, but no hot water required."

"So extra-tasty, then."

"They're not too bad."

Ellie decided that he must have very forgiving taste buds. She tucked the last water bottle upside down in its holder on the outside of George's pack. "Is that it?"

After a quick inventory, he hoisted the backpack onto his shoulders. Her stomach heavy, she grabbed her coat and shoved her arms into the sleeves. When George gave her a look, she held her hands up defensively.

"I'm just going to see you out," she told him, pulling on her boots. "I won't cling to your leg or anything."

His severe expression lightened as the corner of his mouth twitched into a half smile. After exchanging nods with Baxter, he walked out the door, Ellie close behind him.

The cold air shocked her after the toasty interior

of the cabin, and she tugged her coat sleeves down until her hands disappeared. It was still very early, and the sun had just crested the mountain peaks to the east. George descended the stairs and stepped into the snowshoes. Ellie tested the rickety, waist-high railing that surrounded the porch. Finding it fairly sturdy, she leaned against it and watched as George secured the bindings.

To her surprise, he walked over to her. Even with his excessive height and the boost of a couple of feet of snow beneath him, their eyes were on the same level as they faced each other with the railing between them.

"Be safe," she said quietly.

"I will."

"Promise?"

"Promise."

They stared at each other for another long moment, and then his lips were on hers. The kiss was sweet and simple and the most incredible thing she'd ever felt. A rush of sensations—heat and longing, affection and need—roared through her, warming her from the inside out. Ellie leaned against the railing, wanting to get closer to him, needing more than the gentle contact but, at the same time, perfectly content to stay where they were forever. Too soon, he retreated, his burning gaze holding hers for several backward steps until he turned and walked into the open expanse of white. She watched him until he disappeared, her hand pressed to her tingling lips.

"Eleanor." Baxter's voice from the doorway made her jump and quickly whip her hand to her side. "Come inside. It's cold. You'll get cold, baby girl."

She sighed and moved past him into the warmth of the cabin. "Why do you call me Eleanor? You're the only one who does."

"I remember… I remember holding you." He smiled, his gaze far away. "You were brand-new, so tiny. So tiny." When he paused, she cocked her head, wondering if he was answering her question in a roundabout way or just lost in his memories. "I looked down at you, and you were…your face was so red. I said, 'Hello, Eleanor. Hello, baby girl.'" Ellie smiled back at him. "You've always…always been Eleanor, my baby girl."

After taking off her coat and boots, she sat down in one of the chairs. It creaked ominously underneath her, and she frowned, making a mental note to hold very still so she didn't end up on the floor in a pile of splintered wood. "I was named after your grandma, right?"

He nodded. Although he'd taken a couple of steps closer to the table when she'd sat, he stayed standing. His right hand rubbed his left forearm, sparking a memory. She remembered him doing that a lot when she was little. Wondering if he was nervous, she kept her voice light. "What would I have been called if I had been a boy? Baxter Junior?"

"No." Shaking his head, he kept his serious expression despite her teasing smile. "No. I wouldn't want to have given you that, to have put that on you. It's my curse, and I'll keep it. My problem, not my baby girl's. Not hers. Not, not, not."

Her smile faded as he began to pace. "Dad, it's okay." He ignored her, walking the length of the cabin while rubbing his arm with almost violent friction. "Dad. You never answered my question."

Although she thought he was too caught up in his mental world to hear her, he looked at her. "What?"

"If I'd been a boy, what would you have named me?" It was an effort, but she kept her words slow and calm. Inside, though, her heart was pounding. She'd been a kid the last time she'd spent any amount of time with her father, and she didn't know the best way to interact with him. What if something she said sent him over the edge?

For now, at least, he stopped pacing. "Micah." His voice was quiet. "Micah James."

"I like that." Resting her chin in her cupped hands, she smiled tentatively. "I wouldn't have minded being a Micah James."

Watching her warily, he eased himself toward the other chair. "You've…you've grown up pretty. No, beautiful. I meant beautiful."

"Thanks." Ducking her head a little, she smoothed her hair below the edge of her hat. Strands were coming loose from the braid she'd twisted it into the morning before. "I'm a mess right now. I'd kill for a shower."

"No shower here, but there's… I can heat water. For washing."

"That would be wonderful," she said, her words heartfelt as she started to stand. "Want me to get some snow to melt?"

Shaking his head, he headed for the door. "No…no. I'll get it. I'll take care of you, baby girl. For once, I'll…I'll take care of you."

Ellie sank back into her chair with a nod, giving him a smile that shook around the edges. He pulled on his coat and boots and grabbed the pan before heading out the door. Her smile fading, she rested her head in her folded arms, careful to avoid touching the gun and magazine sitting on the table next to her elbow.

Being with Baxter was harder than she'd thought it would be. Actually, she mentally corrected herself; that wasn't true. She just hadn't thought about anything past the point of finding him and taking him to get help. Now, though, seeing him in person, she wasn't sure how to accomplish that. When George brought back help, would her father bolt? Was her search and rescue mission just going to drive him out of the semi-safety of the cabin?

With a groan, she rolled her forehead across her arm, feeling the twinge of sore muscles in both her neck and her arm as she did so. In the interest of not driving herself crazy, she decided to just deal with the situation as it came. She didn't know Baxter well enough to form any sort of plan.

"You okay, baby girl?" he asked, making her jump and sit up straight. She hadn't heard him come back into the cabin.

"Yeah, Dad. I'm okay." Ellie resisted rubbing the back of her neck where the muscles had protested her abrupt movement.

Baxter set the snow-filled pan on top of the woodstove and dumped in some water from one of the remaining bottles. The action made her think of George.

"I'm just a little worried about George," she admitted.

Giving her a surprisingly lucid look, her dad said, "That boy knows what he's doing. He'll be fine."

"I know." In her brain she did know, but her twisting gut was another matter.

After washing as best she could with a couple of cups of water, no soap, and her father in the room, Ellie finger-combed her hair and rebraided it. It was amazing how much better she felt after such basic ablutions. Although the toothpaste had been in George's stolen pack, she'd grabbed her toothbrush while helping George get ready to leave that morning, so she cleaned her teeth with water and bristles.

"Better?" her dad asked, and she grinned at him.

"So much."

"Ready?" He gestured toward the gun she'd been trying to ignore.

She groaned, scrunching up her face.

Although his smile was gone in a flash, it was nice to see it, as quick as it was. Leaving the magazine on the table, he picked up the gun. After pulling back the slide to make sure it was unloaded, Baxter handed the gun to her, his hand shaking a little. It seemed she wasn't getting out of learning to shoot.

"Choose...choose a target, baby. Anything. Window, knot on the wall, anything."

She stared at him, her mouth open. "You want me to shoot this *inside*?"

"No, no." He gestured toward the unloaded gun. "Dry fire. Dry."

Gazing at him helplessly, she admitted, "I don't know what that means."

He took the gun from her hand, and she happily relinquished it, hoping he'd keep it for a while. "Dry," he repeated and squinted, tilting his head so his open eye was level with the top of the pistol. His index finger pulled back on the trigger until there was a solid click. To Ellie's embarrassment, the harmless sound made her jump. He didn't seem to notice as he returned the gun to her.

It was still hard to pull the trigger. It was also hard not to let the memory of the last time she'd held the gun make her shake and swallow back bile. In contrast, Baxter seemed to be relaxing as he made small adjustments to her stance and the way she held the gun. He showed her how to line up the sights, and told her to aim for center mass. When she looked at him sideways, he clarified.

"Shoulders to hips. Aim…aim high center. Gives you the biggest target, the biggest target and the best chance of hitting something…something vital."

Her brain immediately projected a picture of the blue-eyed man, blood dripping from the cut through his eyebrow, onto the wall where she was aiming. Instead of seeing the discolored spot on the wood she'd focused on before, now she aimed at his chest. Her hands shook, the sights bouncing too much to allow her to aim.

"Okay, baby girl. Okay." Her father's hands closed over hers. For once, his were steady while hers vibrated with nerves. "Enough…enough for now."

"Sorry."

He removed the gun from her hands, and her fingers sprang away from the grip like she'd been clutching the tail of a mountain lion. "No. Don't…don't be sorry, baby girl. You're okay. Never be sorry you don't want to…hurt someone."

Giving him a grateful smile, she sat in what she was

already considering to be her chair. "What should we do now?"

"Tell me…can you tell me about…you? Your life?" He didn't meet her eyes, and his hand started rubbing his arm again.

"Sure." Once she'd agreed, her mind blanked. "What did you want to know?"

"Just…anything. Everything."

"Um…okay. I work at a boutique…" Ellie told him about her job, about Chelsea—bad and good—and about her condo. She explained what she loved about Chicago and what she hated. She told him stories about high school and college, about her mom and her friends and her teachers. The only subject she didn't touch was George, because that was too new and fragile to be discussing with anyone. She talked until she was hoarse, and Baxter absorbed the information almost hungrily, as if he'd been starved for details of her life.

She slipped a few questions in, as well, getting her dad to talk about his own life. While he was telling a story about his time in the army, he mentioned his friend, Gray Goose.

"Is that Willard Gray?" she asked tentatively, not wanting to set him off but hoping to find out about the man who'd been killed. Some of Baxter's actions were fueled by mental illness, but she needed to know how much danger he was actually facing.

His face grew sad, but he didn't seem to get agitated by the question. "Gray…he and I…we were good friends. You could trust him, trust him to watch your back, you know?"

"Yes." Even though Ellie had never really thought

about the importance of back-watching before, the past four days with George had opened her eyes. In the wilderness, they'd just had each other when things went wrong—and they'd gone so, so wrong. If anyone else had been her guide, she didn't think she'd have survived. It was a sobering thought that only George had stood between her and death.

"He'd send me letters, emails...told me things. Things that weren't right. There were all those fires... When there was nothing...nothing from Gray for months, I knew he was gone. I wanted to find out for sure, needed to be sure." He rubbed his chest like it hurt. "I knew, though. My friend was dead, and I knew."

Although she tried to hold back the question, it burst from her lips despite her best efforts. "Who killed him? You said they were after you."

Shoving back his chair, he stood and started to pace.

"Sorry, Dad." Her stomach squeezed painfully when she saw that her question had agitated him. They'd been doing so well, sharing stories and learning about each other's lives, and she'd had to ruin it with her curiosity. She nibbled on her index finger until she realized what she was doing.

"No," he said. Instead of rubbing his forearm, he was clutching it tightly, as if to restrain the motion.

Ellie looked ruefully at her own hands, one holding the other in her lap in a pose uncomfortably similar to her father's. It was genetics in action, she supposed.

"No, no. Not your fault, baby girl. Never your fault."

"You don't have to talk about it." In fact, if it made him so upset, she wished he wouldn't.

Baxter acted as if he hadn't heard her. "I shouldn't...

shouldn't have called you. Sorry, baby girl. So sorry. Now you're in danger, too, and it's my fault. They'll be coming. They'll be coming soon."

Unable to stay still while her father was so agitated, Ellie stood. "Dad. It's okay. George is getting help. He'll be back tomorrow. What time is it?"

He just stared at her, his fingers flexing on his arm.

"Dad." She was using her ultra-calm voice again. "What time is it?"

When he pulled back his sleeve to check his watch, her shoulders relaxed a little. At least he wasn't so far into his own head that she didn't exist. She remembered that happening when she was young and he was still living with them. Her mother, Ellie, their lives—they'd all disappeared from Baxter's reality while he struggled with his mental ghosts.

"Two forty-eight."

"No wonder I'm hungry." Forcing a smile, she turned toward his pack. "Should we break out the M—what were they again?"

Although he didn't return the smile, some of his twitchiness settled. "MREs."

"Right. Can I get a couple out of your pack?" It seemed rude to dig around in there without asking, as if she were barging into his bedroom and going through his dresser drawers. At his nod, she retrieved a couple of the wrapped containers and made a face. "I have to warn you—you'll probably end up eating most of mine if these taste anything like the stuff George had. Especially if we're eating it cold."

As he moved toward her, his hand released his other arm, and Ellie relaxed a little more. "They're self-heating."

"Really?" She eyed the food packet with renewed interest. "Cool. How does it work?"

He smiled for the first time since she'd brought up Willard Gray. "I'll show you."

Chapter 19

BY THE TIME THEY'D EATEN, CLEANED UP, REFILLED water bottles, and talked some more—carefully skirting the topic of his murdered friend—the light had a reddish cast as the sun disappeared behind the western peaks.

"It's so early for it to be getting dark," Ellie said, peering out the window. The snow gave an eerie glow in the fading light.

Baxter didn't look up from where he was fiddling with a loose strap on his pack. "The mountains block the sun."

"That's another weird thing." Something moved in the shadow of a pine tree. Squinting through the growing gloom, she tried to see what had caught her eye. Everything was still, and she decided it had been a trick of the light, the filthy window, and her overtaxed nerves. "In Chicago, my GPS tells me which way I'm going. Anywhere else in Colorado, the mountains are always to the east or west. Here, I have no idea which direction is which, since the mountains are all around us." That was a slight exaggeration, since the sun gave her an idea. Nighttime, though, would be another story. If she had to find her way in the dark, she knew she'd just wander in circles until a bear, dizzy from watching her, ate her.

"Come here." Moving away from the window, she walked over to where he was pulling something out of his pack. "You need...you need a compass. Here. Here."

When he pressed something cool and heavy into her hand, Ellie closed her fingers around it automatically. Bringing it close to her face so she could examine it in the fading light, she saw what looked like an old-fashioned pocket watch.

"It was your grandpa's," he said, reaching over to open it.

"Wow." She turned her entire body so the needle rotated to continue pointing north. "That's so cool." Closing the compass, she ran her thumb over the smooth metal cover before holding it out to Baxter.

He refused to accept it. "You need a compass, baby girl. So you...so you can find your way, even when you're in the mountains."

Her nose and eyes burned, and she blinked rapidly. "Thank you, Dad."

Turning so he wouldn't see the couple of tears that had escaped despite her best efforts at keeping them contained, she moved over to where her coat was hanging by the door and slipped the compass into her pocket. Although she was sure he'd given her presents when she was little, she couldn't actually remember ever getting one from him. Ellie swept the wetness off her cheeks with the heels of her hands and plastered on a wobbly smile before turning.

"What do—" The rest of what she'd intended to say was lost in a shriek as Baxter grabbed her arm and hauled her into the corner.

"Down!" he hissed, and she crouched automatically, staring at him. Scooping up the handgun from the table, he slammed in the magazine and yanked back the slide in scarily efficient motions. When he held it out to her, grip first, she made no move to take it.

"Dad…" She didn't whisper because he had, but because her throat was almost too tight to produce sound. She'd lost him. The ghosts in his head had taken over, just like seventeen years ago in this same cabin.

"Baby girl, *please*!" The desperation in his voice made her wrap her fingers gingerly around the grip.

With a satisfied nod, he moved toward the table. Flipping it onto its side, he used it to barricade her into the corner. Ellie watched, the gun clutched awkwardly in her hand, mildly surprised that she wasn't crying. She didn't feel upset, though, just numb.

When he'd arranged the table to his satisfaction, he leaned over so their faces were close. "Center mass, baby girl. Remember that." Without waiting for a response, he grabbed the shotgun from where it had been propped up next to the door and flattened himself against the wall. Moving silently, he picked up a two-by-four that Ellie hadn't even noticed and placed it into the metal brackets on either side of the doorframe, barring the door.

Because she wasn't crying, because her heart wasn't pounding with fear, but was instead thumping in a quiet, steady rhythm, because her breathing wasn't rough and raspy in her ears, because of all of those things, Ellie was able to hear a soft scuff of a boot on the porch, followed by the squeak of a wooden board.

Her first thought was that George had returned, and her heart rate did pick up at that, but common sense reminded her that George wouldn't *sneak* onto the porch. He'd stomp his monster-sized boots up the steps. Her numb despair started thawing at the realization that someone was outside, and that someone didn't want them to know.

The shadow she'd seen earlier flashed through her mind, and her gaze shot to the unprotected window. The wall containing the window made up one side of her corner, so she could see only the protruding edge of the window frame from her vantage point.

"Dad!" she whispered. When his head turned toward her, she gestured toward the window, hoping he could see her in the dim, red glow of the woodstove fire. There was a window in the cast iron door, but it was sooty and small and let out only a limited amount of light.

A crash of breaking glass had her ducking behind the table, her hand squeezing convulsively around the grip of the gun.

"Open the door, old man, or I'll shoot you from here."

The voice was horribly, gut-wrenchingly familiar, and she felt the MRE she'd eaten earlier work its way back up her esophagus. Fighting down the need to vomit, she focused on breathing, on slowing her quick pants that sounded so loud to her own ears, and peeked over the top of the table. One of the windowpanes had been broken, and the man outside had shoved a pistol into the opening.

All she could see was the vague outline of the gun and the dark-gloved hand that pointed it at her dad. Her position was almost the same, minus the snow underneath her. Instead of an unconscious George lying on the ground, her father was standing frozen, his shotgun pointed uselessly toward the barred door.

A gust of wind whistled down the stovepipe, making the flames dance and illuminating the look of grim resignation on Baxter's face. Ellie knew he wasn't going to open the door. Her dad was going to let the blue-eyed man shoot him so she would remain hidden, safely barred inside the cabin.

A surge of rage burned through her, flaring like the fire in the woodstove. Anger at her dad for trying to sacrifice himself when she was just getting him back, at the man who wouldn't stop terrorizing her, at herself for cowering in a corner while her father waited for the bullet to rip apart his insides—all of it twined together and allowed her to raise the pistol with steady hands.

The fire died down again, but there was still enough light for Ellie to see Baxter shift his weight. She just knew he was about to swing the shotgun toward the man at the window, the man who could pull the trigger so much faster than Ellie's father could aim.

Turning back toward the dark shape of the pistol protruding through the broken window, Ellie held her own gun steady. The white dot on the center sight glowed in the firelight, and she lined it up with the others, just like her dad had showed her. Letting her finger slide to the trigger, she squeezed, smooth and steady.

The flash from her gun surprised her more than the boom, as did the yelp from the man at the window. There was a thump as the pistol fell from his hand onto the cabin floor. Despite her fear and ringing ears, Ellie had to smile. That was the second gun she'd taken from the asshole.

As the man yanked his hand back, Baxter swung the shotgun toward the window but didn't fire. Long gun held snugly against his shoulder, he made his careful way toward the window. Her heart tripping in double-time, Ellie watched his slow approach. Still focused on the window, he crouched and located the fallen pistol by feel. As soon as his fingers closed around the handgun, he backed toward Ellie's corner.

"Nice shooting, baby girl," he whispered, handing her the pistol before stepping over the barricade.

Accepting the gun with a now-shaking hand, Ellie grinned. Praise from her father, she realized, was almost as nice as getting it from George. "Thanks."

"Not sure if there are more than the two brothers," he started quietly.

"I don't think so."

"Or what kind of weapons they have besides that"— his head tilted toward the handgun he'd just recovered— "but they've followed me a long way. Don't think they're giving up anytime soon."

She wasn't sure if it was the combat situation or what, but Baxter sounded as coherent as she'd ever heard him.

"I took this gun from him a few days ago when they tried to steal our packs." Ellie held up the first appropriated pistol. "So they're down two, at least."

"There was just the pair of them, then?"

"Yes. The guy in the window is Anderson, and the other is Wilson."

"Anderson and Wilson King."

"George said they're drug dealers." At Baxter's grim nod, she hesitated before asking, "Why are they after you?"

He looked sad—sad and tired. "I've put you in enough danger. If he found out you knew... I can't do that to you."

"Who is *he*?" Frustration joined the anxiety eating at her stomach lining. "Dad, tell me what's going on!"

Baxter remained stubbornly silent.

Cold air was rushing through the broken window-pane, battling with the heat radiating from the wood-stove, and Ellie gave a convulsive shiver.

"I'll get our coats." When Baxter started to stand, she laid a hand on his arm.

"You cover me, and I'll go." Before her dad could protest, she swung one leg and then the other over the sideways table. Her pulse was drumming in her ears as she kept her gaze locked on the broken window, expecting Anderson or Wilson to come crashing through at any second. Ellie had already taken several steps toward where the coats hung by the door when she realized she had a gun in each hand. *How very badass of me.* With a silent, more-than-half-hysterical giggle, she pointed both guns toward the window and rushed to the coats.

Breathing in quick, shallow gulps, she continued to watch the dark hole of a window as she dropped the pistol in her left hand into her coat pocket and yanked her jacket off the hook. Hanging her and her dad's coats over her right arm, carefully keeping her gun uncovered, she bent down and grabbed her boots in her left hand.

Every second she was in view of the window seemed to stretch into hours. Without looking away from the jagged hole in the glass, she stepped into Baxter's boots and moved as quickly as she could in the oversized footwear back to their barricaded corner. Each step threatened to trip her and send her sprawling, leaving her vulnerable to the two men watching. Despite her fear, she stayed upright for the entire dash to the corner. Her father had his shotgun aimed toward the side of the window, only easing the barrel toward the ceiling when she'd reached the table wall.

Ellie wasn't finished, though. After she stepped out of the boots and dumped them, her own boots, and the coats onto the floor, she evaded Baxter's grasping hand and slipped along the other wall. This time, she took just a few steps toward the window in order to grab Baxter's pack. Those couple of steps seemed to happen in slow motion, as everything inside of her resisted getting closer to danger. When her fingers closed around the strap, her breath emptied from her lungs in a rush. Leaving Baxter to watch the window, she pivoted and lunged for the safety of the corner. When her knees bumped against the table, she hoisted the backpack before clambering over the barricade once again.

Relief made her shaky when she was safely behind the table. Her dad didn't look happy with her. The light from the woodstove was just bright enough to see the tight, flat line of his mouth.

"Sorry," she whispered. "I just wanted to get everything we might need if we're stuck in this corner all night."

He gave a stiff nod, not looking at her. They both donned their coats and boots in silence. Ellie couldn't keep her gaze from darting to the window. After reaching into his pack, Baxter held out something toward her. Accepting it, she saw it was a stocking cap and gratefully pulled it over her head. As soon as she had it on, he extended a pair of gloves. Although she took them from him, she tucked them in her coat pockets. Adrenaline was keeping her hands warm at the moment.

Dressed for the cold, they sat with their backs pressed against the wall. Only a couple of inches separated them, but it felt like a mile as Baxter sat rigidly, his gaze fixed in front of him.

"Are you mad at me?" Ellie finally whispered. It seemed like a trivial concern with two homicidal drug dealers just a thin wooden wall away, but she couldn't hold back the question.

After a long moment, her dad sighed. "You can't risk yourself like that, Eleanor. Not for me."

That was wrong on so many levels that she didn't know how to answer it. Finally, she said, "I knew you had my back."

Baxter turned his head to look at her in the flickering light. "Always, baby girl."

Reaching for his hand, she gave it a squeeze. "Same here, Dad."

Chapter 20

MINUTES PASSED WITH PAINFUL SLOWNESS. ELLIE finally quit asking her dad what time it was, since it just made it worse to know. In her mind, she set up a countdown clock, ticking off the seconds until George's arrival.

She forced herself to drink, but she shook her head when Baxter offered her food. Ellie knew she wouldn't be able to choke it down. The cabin grew colder, and her dad slipped out of their corner hiding place to feed the woodstove. Aiming her pistol at the window, she didn't think she breathed the whole time he was exposed.

Enough time had passed that she began to wonder if the men outside had left. As soon as the thought crossed her mind, there was a scratching, scrabbling sound outside the window. Her back grew rigid, and she grabbed a handful of her dad's coat. The noise wasn't loud, but it seemed to be coming from different directions. First, it was focused outside the wall by the window, and then it sounded almost like they were on the roof above them. She and Baxter sat stiffly, listening, until silence returned. The quiet was more ominous than reassuring.

Were they just waiting them out, knowing that Ellie and her father would eventually have to leave the security of the cabin? They had enough water for a couple of days, and George would be there in less than seven hours. That thought jolted her as she imagined the men ambushing George and the rescuers he'd bring with him. There was no way to get word to him.

Her stomach soured as different scenarios, each one worse than the last, ran through her mind. She was so caught up in her nightmarish thoughts that she jumped when Baxter squeezed her arm.

"Smoke."

Once he said the word, she instantly smelled it. "Are they burning us out?"

Eyeing the thin haze starting to fill the cabin, he shook his head. "It's coming from the woodstove. They've blocked the pipe."

"That explains what they were doing on the roof," she said. "My turn. Cover me." Again, she was over the barricade before her dad could stop her. At the woodstove, she grabbed the shovel off the side of the ash can and shoveled the flaming contents into the metal container. Sparks jumped as the burning wood fell into the can, a couple hitting her bare hands. Ignoring the sting, she capped the ash container and did a final check inside the stove. Satisfied that it was out, Ellie hurried back to their corner, suppressing a cough from the smoke.

"It's going to get cold now," Baxter warned, helping her over the table.

"Cold is better than asphyxiation." Taking her place against the wall again, the rough logs at her back made her worry. "Do you think they'll try to burn the cabin?"

Her dad shrugged. "Depends on what supplies they have. The wood on this place is dry, but the snow keeps the kindling underneath it wet. I'm no fire expert, but I'd think they'd need an accelerant to get things started."

Not feeling reassured, Ellie leaned back against the

wall and stared at the haze, straining her eyes to see if it was getting thicker, indicating that another fire—possibly in the walls—was burning.

"Please tell me why these guys are after you," she said after several minutes. "I'm stuck in the middle of this, too. You're not protecting me by keeping me in the dark."

"He…he sent them," Baxter said after a long pause. His take-charge attitude had faded back to his usual tentative way of speaking, and she felt bad for having caused the change. It was important that she know all the details of their situation, though. If she was about to get burned alive inside that cabin, she had a right to know why.

"He who? And why?"

Completely ignoring the first part of the question, he said, "I got too close. He thought I knew. Thought I knew, that I had proof. He's protecting him."

That made no sense. Ellie tried to think of the best way to phrase her next question to get a clear answer in return. "What did you know?"

"About Gray Goose. He didn't deserve that. Dumped like he was nothing. He was a good soldier, a good friend."

With a huge effort, she resisted gritting her teeth in frustration. Baxter was scared, and when he got scared, his communication skills got a little shaky. Ellie knew that, but it didn't make it any easier to deal with, especially in their current perilous situation. "What did you know about Willard?"

"He killed him. Gray Goose figured it out. He knew, and now he's dead. He sent… Gray wrote me letters, told me things, so now...now he's trying to make me dead, too. I don't want you to get caught in the crossfire. Not you, baby girl."

"Little late." At his flinch, a surge of guilt flowed through her. "Sorry, Dad. It's not your fault. You told me not to come here, but I found you anyway."

Her reassurances didn't seem to ease Baxter's mind, judging by his miserable expression.

"We'll get out of this." She tried to inject confidence into her whispered words. "We've already gotten two of their guns away from them, one of them is shot in the arm, and I think the other guy's hand is hurt. George will be here tomorrow with help."

Despite her assurances, he still looked distant. Suppressing another smoke-induced cough, Ellie took a drink of water to try to quiet her irritated throat. Between the bruises and the smoke, swallowing was almost impossible. Looking around the cabin, she was pretty sure the haze had dissipated a little. She supposed that was one positive about the broken window—the air circulation was good. Cold, but good.

Her mind returned to their conversation before she'd snapped at Baxter. "Who is he? The guy who killed Willard Gray?"

He opened his mouth, but before he could speak, something flew through the broken window. It looked like a comet while it was in midair, complete with a fiery tail, and it landed with a *thunk* in the middle of the plank floor.

Ellie stared at it, unable to move, unable even to blink, her brain refusing to accept that there was a bomb right in front of them.

Chapter 21

"Go! Go! Go!" BAXTER HAULED HER TO HER FEET, almost launching her into the air. He kicked the table, sliding it forward far enough that they could run between it and the wall. At the door, she reached for the board, only then realizing that she still held the pistol in her right hand.

Her dad flung the bar to the side and yanked open the door. It was her turn to grab Baxter and shove him against the wall next to the opening. There were four sharp cracks of sound, and Ellie felt her dad's chest expand in a shocked inhale as he heard the gunshots. The men outside must have been waiting for the door to open, hoping she and Baxter would come flying outside to be picked off like the proverbial fish in a barrel.

As soon as the shooting stopped, Ellie was moving through the open doorway, gun up and blasting as she ran into the night. She pulled the trigger over and over, until the pistol went quiet and she knew it was empty. Even with the deafening booms of her own shots ringing in her ears, she heard the scream. It was a terrible sound, like nothing she'd ever heard from a human throat before. She froze in her tracks, but Baxter shoved her from behind, making her stumble back into motion.

Her feet fumbled on the steps, and she almost pitched forward, barely preventing herself from falling face-first into the snow at the base of the stairs. Baxter gave her another push to the left.

"Go!" he yelled again, so she turned and ran, that awful scream still echoing in her head. The snow was deep, slowing her pace to a nightmare-worthy slog, and she fully expected to feel the impact of a bullet at any moment.

Instead, just as she reached the first line of trees, there was a bright flash that lit up the night. Ellie felt herself flying forward toward an evergreen, weightless for just a moment before she hit the prickly boughs. The branches bent under the impact, absorbing most of her forward momentum, and she landed fairly softly on her belly in the snow. As she sank face-first into the powder, the world went dark around her, and the snow swallowed her whole. The memory of the avalanche swamped her, and she was back there, torn off the mountain and dragged along with the cascading snow and rocks and branches, helpless to stop her descent. The worst had been at the end, when the snow had hardened around her in an encapsulating body cast.

She couldn't move—then or now—not even an inch. The darkness had been so complete, and the snow had blocked almost all sounds. When something had jabbed her side, she'd cried out, more surprised than hurt, and then she'd heard the muffled but beautiful sound of George calling her name.

The thought of George jerked her back to reality, and she lurched to her hands and feet. She could move. The darkness was gone, the air lit with a dull red, and so was the silence, her sobbing breaths loud to her own ears. *It's over*, she reminded her still-panicking mind. *George dug me out. It's over*. Even as she calmed slightly, she realized that, despite being free of the snowy cage, she wasn't safe.

Scrambling to her feet, she started to run again. The ground sloped up, adding to the difficulty until her jog turned into a fast walk. When the tree coverage thickened, she allowed herself to cower behind a squatty pine and peer through the branches at the house below.

Despite the darkness, it was easy to see the cabin, since the small structure was on fire. Flames climbed the walls and licked the roof, lighting up the area around the burning building.

A body was lying on the snow, either unconscious or dead. Another pair of men were standing at the edge of the circle of light. One had a gun pointed at the other guy's chest. Her lungs seized when she recognized the unarmed man as Baxter.

Once she'd torn herself free from her momentary paralysis, she ran again, down the slope this time. The only thought in her head was to help her father. She'd just promised him that she'd have his back, but she'd run the other way, instead. If he was killed, she'd never forgive herself.

As she grew closer, logic crept into her brain, reminding her that she was out of ammo for her only weapon that hadn't been blown to bits. She remembered the other handgun she'd tucked into her coat pocket, but a quick search came up empty. Disappointment surged through her as she realized it must have fallen out of her pocket, probably when the explosion had sent her flying. Slowing her pace, she stayed in the trees, circling around until she could approach the armed man from the rear.

Her foot caught on something in the snow, and she

tripped, going down to one knee. When she pulled her foot loose, the end of a stubby, rotting branch emerged from the snow. She picked it up, testing the weight. It was light enough for her to carry without too much effort, but it was heavy enough to use as a weapon. Looking up at the sky, she mouthed a "thank you" before starting her silent jog again.

The fire was loud. She'd never known that before, but it roared, allowing her to creep up on the two men without being detected by the gun-holder. Baxter saw her. She knew because she saw his eyes widen in a moment of panic before he refocused on the stranger. Now that she was closer, she recognized the one called Anderson, so Wilson must be the man lying unmoving in the snow.

The memory of the horrifying scream flashed through her mind, but she quickly shut it down. If she had been the cause of Wilson's death, there would be time later for guilt and regret and self-recrimination and whatever else she might feel. Now, she needed to concentrate on survival—hers and her father's.

Anderson was talking, but she had to get very close to hear him over the noise of the burning cabin. When she got within branch-striking range, she wound up like she would at the batting cages but then paused.

"...said that you saw us on Second Street that night."

Baxter was shaking his head, focused on Anderson's face. Ellie figured he was trying not to glance over the armed man's shoulder at her, not wanting to give away her presence. "I wasn't even in Simpson that night."

"Why would he have said you watched us make that sale if you didn't? He said you were willing to testify against us."

"Because he killed Gray." Baxter's calm, coherent persona was back. "And I knew. He wants me dead, and he's using you to do it."

Ellie saw Anderson's back stiffen in shock. "The headless dude found in the reservoir?" Part of the cabin collapsed with a crash and a renewed roar of flames, drowning out what Anderson was saying. Once the noise died down, she caught just the tail end of his sentence. "…everyone thinks he's a hero when he's actually a fucking killer."

When he shifted his weight, she was afraid he'd turn and see her, so she swung. The branch vibrated when it connected with his head, and she almost lost her grip. Instead of falling, though, he turned and squeezed the trigger at the same time.

At the roar of the gun, Ellie's knees softened, nearly sending her to the ground. The pistol was swinging in her direction, though, so she stiffened her legs and swung the branch again, this time aiming at the hand holding the gun. There was a dark streak along the heel of his hand close to his wrist, and Ellie had a moment of disappointment that it looked like she'd only managed to nick him when she'd shot him.

Anderson blocked with his left hand. The piece of wood glanced off his forearm and connected with the barrel of the gun. It went off again as it rotated toward the ground, and Anderson yelped as it was knocked from his grip.

"You broke my fingers, bitch!" he snarled.

Taking a few scrambling steps back, she raised the branch onto her shoulder like a baseball bat. "You were going to shoot my dad, *bitch*." Even though her voice shook, she was glad she'd managed any comeback at all.

His gaze flicked to where the gun had landed by his

feet and then back to her face. After a few tense seconds, he crouched to grab the pistol. Ellie had been expecting it, and she brought the branch down on the back of his head, hoping she hit a more vulnerable spot this time. Going down on one knee, he dodged a second blow and rolled out of reach.

She saw that the gun was back in his hand, and time slowed as he raised it, the light from the burning cabin bathing him in a hellish red glow that illuminated the smug smirk on his face. He thought he'd won, and, in that moment, Ellie was pretty sure he was right.

In the fraction of a second that she stared at the pistol aimed at her, Ellie felt a jolt of sadness that she'd never see George again. Anderson pulled the trigger just as the wind settled and the fire quieted. In the sudden silence, there was a hollow click.

They froze for a startled moment, both staring at the jammed gun. Swearing, Anderson smacked the bottom of the grip and then yanked back the slide to clear it.

Move! A voice in her head commanded, and Ellie pivoted to run. The snow, half-melted by the heat of the fire, was slick underfoot, and she stumbled, falling to her knees in the slush. Turning her head, she saw Anderson was aiming at her again, and she clenched her teeth against a sob as she scrambled to her feet. *How sad*, she thought, *to have been saved by a jammed gun, just to die anyway a few seconds later*.

Movement to her right made her flinch and twist to face the newest threat. Despite the earlier awful scream and seeing a body lying still in the snow, she still expected Wilson to be standing there. Instead, it was Baxter, running toward Anderson.

Her dad tackled the bigger man, driving his shoulder into Anderson's midsection. As both men hit the ground, the gun flew into the air, dropping into a slushy drift. Terror for her father dug claws into Ellie's throat as she watched Anderson roll Baxter beneath him and land several solid punches.

Tearing her attention from the unequally matched fighters, she slogged through the melting snow toward where the gun had landed. The hole it had made on its way down was obvious, and she found it quickly.

As she shook off the wet chunks of snow, she sent a mental prayer that the gun would still work, and she aimed it at the two grappling men. Anderson shook off Baxter and rolled gracefully to his feet. As Ellie's dad weakly attempted to stand, Anderson drew back his leg as if to kick Baxter in the ribs.

"Stop," she ordered, but the word was swallowed by the renewed noise from the fire. "Stop!"

The scream worked, and Anderson spun around to face her. He ran toward her, closing the distance between them before she even realized he was moving. Her finger on the trigger tightened automatically, and the gun in her hands roared. His body jerked as if he'd been hit, but he didn't stop coming.

"Bitch!" he yelled, and then he was on her, twisting the gun from her hands with humiliating ease. He drew back his arm, and she ducked as his fist swung toward her face. There was nowhere to go, however, and she cringed as she waited for the pain of the blow.

It never came.

Baxter was suddenly between them, pushing her back so his body physically blocked her from Anderson. He landed a punch to Anderson's belly that doubled him over. A second hit to Anderson's jaw sent him to his knees. Landing strike after strike, Baxter looked possessed, his expression wild and painted in firelight.

"You do not hit my baby girl." Baxter punctuated each word with another blow. "You do not hurt my Eleanor."

Anderson tried to regain his footing, but Baxter's foot connected with the other man's throat, sending him to the ground and making Anderson lose his grip on his gun yet again. Hearing Baxter's ragged breathing even over the noise of the fire, Ellie feared her dad was tiring.

Although Anderson looked dazed, he definitely wasn't done. His clenched fists were swinging with more and more accuracy, and a pained yelp from Baxter drove Ellie toward the pair. Her boot slid on a rock that had been exposed by the melting snow, and she reached down, grabbing a stone about the size of George's fist.

Running the last few steps toward the fighters, she swung the rock toward the back of Anderson's head. It connected but didn't knock him out. Ellie pulled back her arm to try another hit, but he lurched to his feet, throwing her off-balance and making her stumble back a few steps.

With a roar like a wounded bear, he swung an arm, knocking Baxter off him and sending him flying. Ellie clutched her rock, trying not to drop it as her fingers started to shake.

Anderson's gaze focused on her, his expression turning ugly and angry. "You fucking shot my baby brother. I'm going to make it hurt when I kill you, bitch."

"No." Baxter spoke clearly, although his breath was coming fast. "You won't." He stepped closer to her, brandishing the branch she'd initially used as a weapon. Anderson's gaze flicked back and forth between father and daughter before finally stopping on Ellie.

"I will kill you." Anderson sounded like he was making a vow, and she braced herself for an attack, holding the stone in her hands more tightly. Instead of advancing, though, he backed toward the trees where he was quickly swallowed by the shadows beyond the reach of the firelight.

Ellie kept a tight grip on the rock as she moved a step closer to Baxter. "You okay?"

"Fine, baby girl." His gaze didn't leave the spot where Anderson had disappeared. "I'm just fine."

Something collapsed in the burning cabin, and the flames shot higher with a roar that made Ellie jump. It was impossible to see beyond the circle of firelight, and she shivered, feeling horribly exposed. "We need to go," she said in a hushed voice that shook with cold and a waning adrenaline rush.

"Yes." Baxter moved his head jerkily as he stared in one direction and then the other. "Yes, we need to move. He'll be back, baby girl. He'll be back, and I don't think I can protect you."

"You did great, Dad," she whispered, taking a few steps away from the fire and then pausing when she realized she had no idea where to go. Without replying, Baxter moved in the other direction, and Ellie followed, grateful that she didn't need to come up with yet another survival plan. Her body and brain and courage were just about spent.

They slogged through the snow at a jog, heading away from the cabin. The ground slanted upward, and the rocky footing was slick, slowing them to a rushed walk until they reached a limestone outcropping edged with stunted bristlecone pines. When Baxter stopped, Ellie almost bumped into his back.

"Don't we need to keep moving?" Although her words weren't loud, Ellie winced at the clear note of panic in them. Her fear overcame her need to be tough, however. "Dad? Shouldn't we go?"

"Need to wait for help," he said. "Can't keep you safe, Eleanor. I can't, but George can. We need to be here when he gets back."

As much as Ellie wanted to be George's welcoming committee, she needed to run until she couldn't feel Anderson's hateful stare burning into her back. The long night stretched in front of them, and they wouldn't be there when George arrived if Anderson managed to kill them before morning. "But, Dad—"

"We'll hide." His unusually firm tone cut off her argument. "I know this place, baby girl. I know this place, and that's how I'll keep you safe."

After a long second, she sighed. "Okay." Even as she agreed, the knots of anxiety in her belly twisted tighter.

"Okay." Baxter smiled, his teeth reflecting a tiny bit of light in the darkness. "Okay. Good. This way." He started climbing the nearly vertical side of a boulder, and Ellie, biting back a very bad word, followed. It was more manageable than she'd expected, with a rough surface that provided decent hand- and footholds. Baxter looked back to check on her often, and she managed to scramble to the top of the boulder right behind him.

Panting and sweating under her coat, she resisted the urge to unzip, knowing her temporary body heat would soon dissipate.

"This way," Baxter said in a low voice as he stepped onto a narrow path, barely wider than her feet. On one side was a wall of rock. On the other, the trail dropped off abruptly, diving into the darkness. Ellie peeked over the edge and immediately jerked back, wishing she hadn't looked. She couldn't see the bottom of the drop-off.

Her breath was coming painfully fast, but she ignored it, fighting the urge to yell and stomp and throw a complete tantrum. She didn't want to step onto a skinny ledge. She didn't want to fall off the mountainside to her probable death. She didn't want to be out in the cold another night, especially without George. She didn't want to be without George at all. She didn't want Anderson to be stalking them. She didn't want Baxter to be in danger. *She* didn't want to be in danger. So many things had gone wrong and were continuing to go wrong, and Ellie was sick of it. Unfortunately, there was nothing she could do except to step onto a skinny, slick, rock trail and follow her mentally ill father into the darkness. It was her only chance to survive the night.

Her heart beat so hard that it actually made her chest ache as she inched along the slick path. Baxter moved with surprising ease, pulling so far in front of her that he became just a shadowy outline.

"Dad!" she hissed, trying to make her feet move faster without losing her balance. Her foot slipped, only a tiny slide, but it was enough for her to flatten her back against the rock forming the safe side of the trail, her fingers searching blindly for handholds.

"It's okay, Eleanor." Baxter made his way back to her. "Almost there. Almost there, baby girl. Just…just a few more steps."

Although she strained her eyes, Ellie couldn't see the "there" about which her dad was talking. Despite her doubt, she forced herself to leave the safety of her position and start her slow shuffle along the trail again.

"Here," her dad said. It had been, Ellie felt, quite a bit farther than a "few more steps." The trail widened, opening up to a flat area not unlike the one next to the cave where she and George had spent the night. Hope of another, similar space like that cave rose in her as Baxter slid through the opening between an evergreen and the rock face.

Baxter shifted to the side, and Ellie got her first glimpse of their hiding spot. She came to a dead stop. "No."

There was no shallow, open, non-claustrophobia-inducing cave. The hiding spot that Baxter had led her into was a stone hole, no more than four feet high and deep enough that the back of the space—if there was one—was hidden by blackness.

"No," she said again, her voice rising with a sharp note of hysteria.

"Shh," Baxter warned, his gaze darting around nervously. "He could... He's out there. He's hunting us, baby girl."

Anderson suddenly seemed like the better option. "I can't, Dad." Her voice broke, and she had to look away from the narrow opening between two huge rocks. "I can't."

"You can, Eleanor." As before, the more upset she got, the calmer he stayed. "I need you to be safe. You'll be safe in there. Hidden."

"What about you?"

"I'll be with you."

Her gaze was drawn to the space between the rocks, and she shuddered. "Can't we just stay out here?"

Even before she finished asking, Baxter was shaking his head. "Too exposed." His hunted gaze scanned the rock rising above them. "Too easy to take us out if we stay here. Please, baby girl?"

The thought of Anderson "taking out" Baxter stiffened her spine. "Fine." She forced out an exhale, frustrated by the way it quavered. Her gaze never leaving that terrifying dark entrance, Ellie moved closer and closer to the hole, her breath coming in quick pants. As she reached the rocks, she didn't hesitate—she couldn't or she'd lose her nerve. Dropping to her hands and knees, she crawled into the darkness.

It took every ounce of courage she possessed to keep feeling her way into the inky space. Each time she reached forward, groping for any obstacles—rocks, holes, or hungry bears—she had to force her hand to move. Her entire being wanted to flee, to get out of this hole as fast as possible and run away.

The only thing stopping her was the man entering the claustrophobic space behind her. If she told him she couldn't do it, Baxter would let her leave. Then he'd stay outside with her, sitting ducks for Anderson to pick off during the long night. Her dad was the only reason she was able to keep shuffling forward on her palms and knees.

Her gloved fingers brushed something. A scream grew in her throat, and she clenched her teeth to hold it back. *Stay calm*, she told the part of her—a very large part of her—that was barely clinging to reason. *It's not alive. It's not going to hurt you. It's just stone.*

"I think we're at the back," she said, not even caring anymore that her voice shook. She was just happy that she wasn't running screaming through the night.

"Seems about right," Baxter responded, still sounding unusually calm. "It's been a while since I found this place, but I remember it being pretty shallow."

Ellie held back a semi-hysterical laugh. It didn't feel very shallow to her. In fact, it felt like the mountain had swallowed her, and the open air was very far away. Her breathing started to get too fast, and she consciously tried to calm herself. Shifting to sit on the uneven, rocky, and so-very-cold ground, she pushed away all thoughts of being trapped in the rock or under several feet of snow. There was a quiet rustling sound next to her as her dad sat to her left. She realized that, if she looked directly at the entrance to the cave, she could see outside. The night was lit by the dull red cast from the fire, and the sight of it took the most urgent edge off her panic.

"Sorry about Grandpa's cabin."

"Not your fault, baby girl."

They fell into silence. "Who brings a bomb camping?" she finally asked. "Although I guess they weren't out here to get in touch with nature."

"Looked improvised," her dad said. "Could've had some kind of fuel on them from a camp stove or something."

"Oh! There was a stove in George's pack, the one they stole."

Baxter hummed thoughtfully. "Runs on white gas, probably. That could've done it."

Ellie was so tired, she started seeing odd shapes and halos in the darkness. Her body swayed until her shoulder rested against her dad's.

"Try to sleep, baby girl," he said. "I know it's not the most comfortable spot, but see if you can get a few minutes of shut-eye."

"What about you?" she asked, her words slurring from exhaustion. "Do you need to sleep?"

"I'll be fine."

"But what if—"

"Sleep."

The moment she rested her cheek on her dad's shoulder and closed her eyes, she slipped into a strange half sleep. Instantly, she was back to being trapped under the snow, locked in place, unable to see or hear or move. The darkness was unrelenting. She tried to fight her way back to consciousness, but her body refused to wake completely, leaving her stuck in the horrifying memory.

Although it felt like an eternity, it could've been hours or mere minutes before something startled her and she sat up with a jolt. When she realized she was still trapped in the dark, Ellie tried to bolt to her feet. Only Baxter's hold on her arm kept her from standing and bashing her head into the low rock ceiling.

"Eleanor," he soothed in a hushed voice. "Baby girl, it's okay."

"Dad?" The uncertainty in her voice made her sound like she was ten years old again. Trying to shake off the panic that wanted to cling to her, Ellie sank back to sit on the ground. Reality was returning slowly, and the close-in walls of the cave weren't helping her twitchy nerves.

"Yeah, I'm here." Once she'd sat back down, he released her arm, giving it an awkward pat first.

She missed the contact once it was broken. "What time is it? Do you know?"

"Almost sunrise."

Her entire body went loose with relief. The sun would light up their hiding spot. Even though the narrow cave would still be too close for her liking, the brightness would help. Best of all was that George would be there soon. They sat in silence for a few minutes before Ellie gathered her courage to blurt out the question she'd come all the way to a remote cabin in the Rocky Mountains to ask him..

"Dad, will you come back to Chicago with me?"

He went still next to her. "They'll lock me up...lock me up, baby girl."

"Yeah." She didn't even try to lie to him. "It'll just be for a short time, though, while they figure out your meds and a therapy plan."

Baxter's silence sounded like a definite no, and her throat felt tight.

"Please, Dad? Don't you want to know who the real bad guys are and which ones are just in your head?"

"I know." From the sound of it, he was rubbing his forearm over his coat sleeve, and Ellie dropped her head in defeat. "You think I don't know, but I know."

"I thought you wanted another chance to be a dad— to be *my* dad?" Tears burned her eyes, making her voice thick. "You can't have my back if you don't even see me."

His breath caught audibly. "Baby girl..."

"Dad. Please."

He didn't agree, but he didn't say no. They were silent for a long time, watching the opening to the cave as the light outside changed from black to charcoal.

The cold from the rock underneath her was permeating

her clothes. Ellie started to shiver, and she wrapped her arms around her middle, desperate to hold in the heat. It didn't help that every sound made her jump.

The fact that Anderson was...somewhere, possibly close and very likely angry, did nothing to settle her nervous stomach. She worried more that he'd ambush a returning George than she fretted about Anderson finding her and Baxter, although that nightmarish scenario did run through her mind, as well.

"Sun's coming up." Baxter lifted his chin toward the cave entrance. Through it, she could see a portion of a dramatic sunrise, with a red band outlining the peaks and adding a streak of color to the dark gray sky. They were the first words he'd said since their talk about him getting medical help.

"Good." Whether or not he'd go with her to Chicago, she couldn't stay mad at him. He was who he was, and she loved her dad. It would just be easier to love him if he'd stay on his medication. "That'll warm up things."

"Cold, baby girl?"

"Of course." She gave him a rueful smile, which he returned, looking relieved. It was wonderful being able to see him again in the dawn light. "It's my permanent state of being nowadays."

Cold and hungry. Her stomach had started to hurt from emptiness as well as nervousness. She would've gratefully eaten one of Baxter's nasty MREs at that point.

"Soon," she muttered. "George'll be here soon, and I'll make him take me out for pizza as soon as we get back to Simpson." She frowned. "If Simpson has a pizza place."

"Talking to yourself, baby girl? Thought I was...I

was the crazy one." One corner of her dad's mouth quirked up as he gave her a tentative sideways glance.

She smiled back. "I think I'm suffering from delusions brought on by extreme hunger."

Shifting closer to the cave entrance, Baxter peered outside. "Want me to do some hunting? I could probably dodge Anderson long enough to get us a rabbit."

"You shouldn't risk going out there." She made a face. "Also, gross. And if I still find the thought of eating bunnies disgusting, then I'm not even close to starving. I'll let you know if that idea starts getting appetizing." Another thought occurred to her, making the idea of having Thumper for breakfast even less appealing. "Plus, we can't start a fire in here, even if we did have a way of starting one."

Her dad glanced out the entrance again. "There's probably still some smoldering pieces of the cabin. We could use one...one of those."

"If we're still here tonight, then maybe." The idea that they'd have to spend another night in the dark, stifling confines of the cave made her fight down panic. She wanted to leave the claustrophobic hole and the ruins of the cabin and a possibly lurking Anderson and the memory of how she'd killed a man, and return to civilization—and pizza. But Ellie knew it wouldn't be that easy. Her memories wouldn't be burned along with the cabin. They'd stay with her for the rest of her life.

An odd noise made her raise her head. "What's that sound?"

Baxter listened intently for a moment, and then met Ellie's eyes. A huge grin spread over his face. "That's a helicopter."

After a shocked moment, she returned his smile with interest. "George."

Her dad gave a happy laugh. "George."

With relieved excitement bubbling through her, it was hard not to abandon all caution and hurl herself down the trail to the remains of the cabin. Ellie had to keep reminding herself that Anderson was still out there, and the helicopters were still just tiny dots in the sky. They weren't safe yet.

As she cautiously followed her dad out of the cave, Ellie let out a long breath. She felt like she'd held it the entire time she'd been stuck in that dark hole. It had kept them safe, but she'd hated every second.

Baxter was serious and watchful as they emerged, his gaze constantly moving. In her excitement over help arriving, she'd forgotten the treacherous journey the night before. The narrow trail was both easier and scarier in daylight—although she was more confident about where to put her feet, Ellie could see exactly how far she'd fall if she took a wrong step. Descending the nearly vertical rock face was even scarier, although it helped to have Baxter standing at the base beneath her, quietly calling where to reach for hand- and footholds.

By the time the trail widened and headed downhill toward the blackened shell of the cabin, she was sweating and dizzy from nerves. The last part of their route was the worst. As the trees gave way to an open stretch behind the cabin's remains, Ellie felt exposed and vulnerable. It was too easy to imagine Anderson watching them from one of the many concealed hiding places, waiting for his chance to take out both her and her dad.

The two helicopters were louder now, although they

were still quite a distance away. As Ellie and Baxter circled around to what had been the front of the cabin, she saw a dark shape on the ground. Ellie's worries about their safety were temporarily forgotten as what she'd done hit her like a kick to the belly. Her boots felt weighted, but she forced them to step forward, one at a time, until she stood by the side of the man she'd killed. Darkly stained snow surrounded his body, as he'd been far enough away from the cabin that the heat hadn't melted the snow.

His eyes were fixed and cloudy, staring into the distance. There were two holes in the front of his coat.

"Center mass," she murmured, and then jumped when Baxter spoke behind her.

"Good shooting, baby girl. I...I would've ran right into a storm of bullets if you hadn't pulled me to the side."

"Was it good shooting if someone's dead?"

"Yes." There was no hesitation in her dad's voice. "You get to go home, baby girl. That's definitely good."

As she looked at the person she'd destroyed, it didn't seem like a good thing. They stood there a long time, until the helicopters were almost overhead.

In the clear light of morning, she eyed the dead man's stained jacket. "Why is his blood orange?"

"It's frozen. That's the color it turns when blood freezes."

She allowed her dad to tug her away from her victim. "I think I would've been fine never knowing that blood turns orange in the cold."

Baxter's mouth grew grim, and he kept his gaze on the helicopters above them. "And I would've given a lot for you to have never known."

Chapter 22

IT WASN'T GEORGE—NOT ON EITHER OF THE TWO helicopters—but he'd sent them. Four men wearing tan sheriff's department uniforms and carrying guns piled out of the first one as soon as it touched down. Once they'd disarmed Baxter, gotten the condensed version of what had happened, and secured the scene, the Flight for Life helicopter was finally allowed to land.

Baxter and Ellie were quickly checked by the two EMTs and then bundled on board the Flight for Life helicopter. Although George had wanted to come, according to Grace—the chattier of the medics—there wasn't room with the pilot, both EMTs, Ellie, and Baxter. As it was, it was a tight squeeze.

"With that mess of a crime scene, though, there'll be more law-enforcement people coming in on sleds," Grace said.

Ellie frowned. "Sleds?" That seemed like a slow way to travel. Maybe Grace had meant dog sleds.

"Snowmobiles," she clarified, and Ellie felt silly for picturing a team of crime scene investigators on toboggans.

She and Baxter were flown to a Denver hospital. Although she had bumps, extensive bruises, and was mildly dehydrated, the doctors didn't find any reason for her to stay overnight. Baxter, however, had firmly locked himself in his own head during the helicopter ride, and he'd been placed on a psych hold.

Ellie was talking with the on-call psychiatrist about possible in-patient treatment facilities in the area for her dad when a young, freckle-faced nurse approached and hovered next to them expectantly.

"Did you need something, Phoebe?" the psychiatrist, Dr. Kruger, asked, turning to the nurse. She blushed, the pink blending her freckles together.

"Ms. Price?" she asked. "There's a very...tall gentleman looking for you."

Now Ellie was blushing, too. "Could you tell him I'll be right there?"

Wide-eyed, the nurse hurried away, and Ellie turned back to Dr. Kruger. "So, you think the place in Armstrong would probably be the best, then?"

He looked amused. "Boyfriend?"

"Um...no."

"But you want him to be your boyfriend."

"No...maybe. I've only known him for a week—less than that, even!" She was flustered. How had they gone from talking about having her father committed to discussing her unlikely relationship with her mountain-man guide?

"Sometimes it doesn't take long before you just know," the psychiatrist said. "Trust your gut."

Ellie eyed him. "Is that your professional advice?"

Chuckling, he looked like someone's sweet grandpa who'd carry around toffee in his pockets to pass out to neighbor children. "No. That's my no-charge advice. And I think the Armstrong facility would be a good fit for your father. Now go let your not-boyfriend know you're okay. We'll finish our talk later." With an avuncular pat on the shoulder, he walked away, leaving her staring after him. Weren't doctors supposed to be impatient and rushed? Dr. Kruger was more of a fairy-godfather type.

Shaking off her whimsical thoughts, she hurried toward the waiting area and her extra-tall visitor. Once she saw him, leaning against a square support pillar, Ellie stopped. In the large open spaces of the mountains, he'd seemed big, but here, in an enclosed area, he was enormous. The freckled nurse noticed Ellie and tilted her head toward George, as if Ellie could have missed the Paul Bunyan look-alike. She gave the nurse a grateful smile anyway and walked over to her former guide. He saw her approaching and pushed away from his leaning post, straightening to an even greater height.

Although she was dying to hug him, she made herself stop a few feet away and just grin like a fool…a sleep-deprived fool. "Hi."

The corners of his mouth drew upward, his own version of a goofy smile, and she lost control over her body. Rushing the couple of steps forward, she wrapped her arms around his middle. He remained rigid in her hold for a few seconds, and then unbent enough to awkwardly return the hug. His pat on her back was vigorous enough to make her grunt.

Pulling back just enough so she could look up at his face, she asked, "Are you okay?" Ellie noticed he was no longer wearing her lavender hat, and a fresh dressing covered his head wound. It looked much more professionally done than her field bandaging hack job.

He shrugged. "You?" The backs of his fingers brushed over her cheek, and she leaned into his touch.

"A few bruises, but nothing to keep me here." Her

eyebrows drew together as her smile faded. "Baxter, though…he lost it in the helicopter. They're holding him here tonight, and then he's going to a psychiatric hospital in Armstrong, forty minutes or so north of Denver."

"That's good."

"It is." With a nod, she said with more conviction, "It really is. I wish he was going to be closer to me, but the doctor didn't advise dragging him all the way to Chicago. If Dad can stay on his meds, I think that'll help him separate reality from the demons in his head." Leaning forward, she let her cheek find George's chest again. "He really was in danger. I thought the bad guys were all just a creation of his confused brain, but they'd been sent by someone, the guy who'd killed his friend, Willard Gray. I heard Anderson admit that the murderer had told Anderson and Wilson"—the second name caught in her throat as she pictured his staring eyes and frozen, orange blood—"that my dad had witnessed some kind of sale. I'm guessing it was a drug deal. Dad won't tell me who he thinks the killer is, though. I think he's trying to protect me."

George's hand cupped the back of her head, and Ellie closed her eyes. She was pretty sure that, as tired as she was, she was perfectly capable of falling asleep, standing or not. She'd managed to doze while sitting upright on a truly uncomfortable rock, after all.

"How'd you get here?" she asked, fighting sleepiness by prying open her eyelids.

"Drove your car."

That woke her, and she pulled her head back again so she could stare at him. "My rental?"

At his nod, she started laughing, trying to imagine

George's three-hour trip to Denver, folded up in the driver's seat of the tiny car. "Why?"

"Knew you'd need to return it."

The utter sweetness of him, that he'd squash himself into the compact rental for hours to save her some hassle, made her stop laughing and tear up again. Blinking hard, she asked, "Do you have a ride back?"

That time, his shrug accompanied a shake of his head.

"Want to stay with me? I was going to get a hotel room." When she heard how her offer sounded, her face flushed with heat. "I mean, I'm too tired to drive right now, but I could give you a ride back tomorrow."

After eyeing her for a few seconds, he shrugged affirmatively.

"Good. Great." Anticipation started to bubble in her stomach. "If you have time, we maybe could do the tourist thing in the morning. Since I need to get Dad settled at Armstrong, I'll be staying here a couple of days. I've never been to Denver before, so I'd love to explore the city."

Despite the flare of panic in his eyes, his grunt sounded like a yes, and she hopped in excitement. "Awesome. We're going to have so much fun."

A male voice interrupted her tour-guide planning. "Eleanor Price?"

Turning, she saw a handsome man in a sheriff's department uniform. "Yes?"

"I'm Sheriff Rob Coughlin from the Field County Sheriff's Department, and I need to talk to you about what happened at the Blue Hook cabin site."

Leaning her shoulder into George's chest, she took comfort in his heat and strength.

"Mind if we talk over here?" Although the sheriff's

voice held command, he softened it with a slight smile. "Excuse us, George."

With a glance at George, wishing she could stay leaning on him instead of talking to an intimidatingly good-looking lawman, Ellie followed Coughlin toward the empty corner of the waiting room. As she settled into a chair, she looked toward George again. He was watching them with an unhappy expression.

After the sheriff took down all of her personal information, he asked, "Why don't you tell me what happened?" Once again, it was a gently given order.

She took a deep breath, using the few moments it took to organize her thoughts. "I got a call from my dad last Saturday evening—"

"Your dad is Baxter Price, correct?" he interrupted, scribbling notes onto a small pad of paper.

"Yes. He was talking about having to hide from someone, saying that people had been sent to kill him, so he was heading to Grandpa's cabin. I thought he was just delusional and paranoid, but I was worried about him wandering around in the mountains in his compromised mental state."

The sheriff looked up from his notebook. "Delusions and paranoia. He has a history of mental illness, then?"

"Yes. Ever since I can remember. He brought me to that cabin seventeen years ago and barricaded both of us inside."

A spark of recognition lit his gaze, but she didn't know if that was from personal experience or just hearing the story from others who had been there. He didn't clarify which one it was, but instead continued his line of questioning. "Has he been diagnosed?"

"Not that I know." If she had her way, though, that was about to change. "He'll be going to the Armstrong Psychiatric Hospital tomorrow, though."

"Tomorrow?" He tapped his pen against the notebook. "I'll need to talk to him today, then, to get his statement."

Wrinkling her nose, she said regretfully, "You won't get much out of him. He's not responding to anyone right now."

"If not, I'll deal with it. Back to your statement. What happened once you received your father's call?"

It took a long time to get through her retelling of her time in the mountains. The sheriff interrupted frequently to clarify a point or ask for additional details.

"What time was it when King threw the explosive device into the cabin?" he asked.

In her exhausted state, the name confused her for a moment before she made the connection. "That's right. Dad had said his name was Anderson King."

"Yes. Anderson Heathrow King."

She blinked. "That's a mouthful. George said they're drug dealers?"

"Yes. King and his brother, Wilson Jerome King, are—or were, in Wilson's case"—Ellie flinched—"local methamphetamine dealers. I've had quite a few encounters with both of them."

"They thought Dad witnessed a drug deal."

His gaze was piercing. "What?"

"When Anderson was holding the gun on Dad, he said something about my father witnessing a sale."

The sheriff looked thoughtful. "That would explain why the King brothers were trying to kill him."

"He—Dad—said he never saw anything, though."

Coughlin's gaze softened. "Baxter probably has a

hard time remembering what he did and did not see," he said gently.

"Maybe." When she ran through the memory in her mind, though, her father had seemed so *certain* that he was being set up. "Dad kept talking about the person who killed Willard Gray sending Anderson and Wilson after him."

The sheriff leaned forward, interest bright in his eyes. "Did Baxter tell you the name of this person?"

"No. Sorry."

"Did he say anything that might help us identify a suspect in the Gray case? Anything at all? Even the smallest detail, no matter how trivial, might be important."

Sheriff Coughlin was so serious and intent, Ellie felt a surge of disappointment that she couldn't help him, especially since Willard had been her father's friend. Renewed determination to find out whom her father suspected the killer was surged through her. Once he was on his meds, Baxter would hopefully be more lucid. In the meantime, though, she had nothing of value to offer the sheriff. Holding up her hands in an I've-got-nothing gesture, she watched as disappointment dimmed his look of sharp interest.

Shifting back in his seat, the sheriff asked, "If Baxter isn't able to talk to me today, would you be willing to try talking to him?"

She shook her head. "Sorry. When he gets locked in his head like this, he doesn't communicate with anyone."

He accepted that calmly. "I'll visit him when he's been at Armstrong for a few days, then, and let him get his mind straight first. So, what time was it when Anderson King threw the explosive device into the cabin?"

They'd gone over her statement twice when a bottle of water appeared in front of her face.

"Thank you," she said gratefully, accepting the bottle from George. Uncapping it and taking a few swallows, she realized just how dry her throat had gotten during the interview. George shifted closer to her chair, sending the sheriff a look.

Coughlin raised an eyebrow and then stood. "I think that's good for today. George, you drove Ellie's car here, right?" At George's nod, he continued. "Good. After I see Baxter, I'll give you a ride back to Simpson, and I can get your statement on the way."

Disappointment rushed through Ellie. The sheriff was ruining her plan to keep George close. "But"—she frantically racked her brain for a reason why that wouldn't work—"how can you take notes and drive at the same time?"

Apparently unaware that he was being a plan wrecker, the sheriff smiled. "That's what makes digital recorders so great. Well, one of the reasons." He gestured toward a black device on his duty belt before turning to George. "I'll be right back. This probably won't take long."

Although he didn't look happy, George lowered his chin in a nod.

"Can I be there with him?" Ellie asked as the sheriff started to turn away from her. "While you talk to him?" Even though she knew Baxter wouldn't answer any of Coughlin's questions—probably wouldn't even hear them—she felt uncomfortable just leaving him alone to be interrogated.

As expected, the sheriff shook his head. "Sorry. I need to get all the witnesses' statements individually. It's too easy for someone else's version to affect your memory of what happened."

Ellie grudgingly admitted to herself that what Coughlin said made sense. "The on-call psychiatrist is Dr. Kruger."

"Thanks."

She watched the sheriff approach the admittance desk and then turned to George. "Sit," she said, patting the seat next to her. There were no armrests separating them, so it was like an institutional, uncomfortable sofa. Although he eased his large form into the spot she'd indicated, he moved stiffly. "What's wrong?"

His one-shoulder half shrug was so familiar after their time in the mountains that nonsensical tears filled her eyes. "Too many people, too…" He glared around the waiting area. "Too enclosed." When he glanced at her then, his scowl morphed into panic. "What's the matter?"

"Nothing." Swiping at the wetness under her eyes, she was annoyed that she'd let a few tears escape. "Just tired and being silly."

To her shock, he reached over and caught hold of her arm, maneuvering her into his lap. Her heart was thumping so rapidly that the beats seemed to merge into each other. Resting one hand on her waist, George cupped her head with his other and tugged until her cheek rested on his chest.

After a frozen moment, his warmth and scent and the softness of his shirt and his total…*George*-ness overwhelmed her, and she relaxed against him, closing her eyes. "Glad you're okay," she sighed.

"Me too."

That made her grin without opening her eyes. "You're glad you're okay, too?"

He squeezed her waist. "Funny."

"Sorry." A huge yawn overtook her, and she had to wait until it had passed before she could speak again. "I know I'm more punchy than clever right now."

"You're fine." He petted her hair like she was a cat. Although she wondered if she should object, it felt too nice to interrupt. Questions niggled at her brain, mainly about his hike to get help, but it didn't seem necessary to share information at that moment. Instead, she just enjoyed the thump of his slow, steady heartbeat against her cheek, the slide of his fingers over her head, and the heat that radiated from him.

It just seemed like seconds later when George's chest moved in a deep sigh that she both felt and heard. When she lifted her head and opened her eyes, she saw the sheriff was returning. She tried to scoot off George's lap, but the hand at her waist tightened, holding her in place. Ellie subsided against his chest again.

"Any luck?" she asked the sheriff once he was close to them.

Lips drawn down in disappointment, Coughlin shook his head, and Ellie successfully resisted saying, "I told you so."

"Ready, George?"

That time, George's sigh was silent. Dropping a kiss on the top of her head, he lifted her off his lap as he stood. She was impressed by how easily he moved her.

Even though she was relatively small, that was still a hundred-plus pounds he was shuffling around like she was five pounds of feathers.

With a final press of his hand on Ellie's shoulder, he accompanied the sheriff toward the exit.

"Bye." Ellie watched them go, her shoulders sagging. It had been only a few days in the mountains and a couple of kisses, but she hadn't expected it to end so abruptly or so...soon. As she watched her mountain of a man disappear through the automatic doors, her insides collapsed in on themselves. How was she supposed to return to her life in Chicago when it was over a thousand miles away from him? The thought of home now seemed flat and gray and sadly George-less.

With a huge effort, she straightened her spine. There was nothing to be done. She belonged in the city, and George belonged in the mountains. They never would've worked together.

And yet as she turned to find the fairy godfather masquerading as a psychiatrist, she couldn't silence the tiny internal voice that was wishing they could've at least *tried*.

Chapter 23

GEORGE SLAMMED THE DOOR TO HIS CABIN SO HARD that it bounced against the frame and flew open again. He stared at the gaping door, fighting the urge to rip it off its hinges. This raging temper was unusual for him, making him feel like a stranger was occupying his body. Nothing George had done lately had gone right. Ever since he'd gotten back from Denver, ever since she'd left—

He cut off that thought immediately as he shut the door. Everything was bad enough without dwelling on El.

After shedding his outerwear, he stomped into the kitchen and stared moodily at the refrigerator. It was late afternoon, and he hadn't eaten since early that morning. The missing hiker they'd been trying to find all day turned out not to be missing after all. After the man and his girlfriend had argued while hiking, he'd walked to the trailhead and called a friend to pick him up. When his girlfriend had returned to her car and saw that he wasn't there, she'd panicked, thinking he'd gotten lost—or worse. All day, while George and the other search and rescue members had trudged around the Wyatt Wilderness Area, fighting a biting wind as they'd tried to find the missing man, the guy had been holed up at his buddy's house, playing video games and ignoring the many frantic incoming phone calls and texts.

After such a long, strenuous day, George should've been starving. Lately, though, he'd not been able to dredge up interest in anything—welding, working, playing music. He'd forced himself to eat, but nothing had tasted right. It had just made him think about how he'd finish El's leftovers.

And now he was thinking about her again. With an impatient huff, he left the kitchen. The living room wasn't any better. The mantel clock ticked too loudly, emphasizing how quiet the house was. For the first time ever, George wished he had a TV so he could turn it on and drown out the lonely silence.

His house, his *life*, seemed so...empty now.

Unable to stand the quiet any longer, he pivoted around and strode back to the front entry. If he was just going to wander the house and try—and fail—not to think about her, then he might as well do something productive. George figured he could stop by his neighbor's place and see if she needed any plowing done. Although it hadn't snowed in a few days, the wind might have caused some drifts to fill her driveway.

He automatically reached for his coat and then froze, his hand hovering in midair. The last time he'd worn that particular jacket had been to take El to the cabin. When he started to shift toward another coat, he stopped, his jaw tightening. It was stupid to turn his jacket into a shrine to Ellie. He'd been with her for less than a week; why did he feel so shattered?

Grabbing the first coat, he yanked it on, resisting the urge to tuck his nose into the collar to see if her scent lingered. Sticking his hands into the roomy pockets, he rooted around in search of gloves. Instead, he felt something so soft that he knew it was out of place. Pulling it out, he felt like he'd been punched in the chest.

It was El's hat, the purple one she'd put on him after bandaging his head. He turned the silly flowered thing over in his hands, his rough fingers snagging the fine knit. There was an almost-black stain from his blood, and he stared at it as he remembered stuffing the hat in his coat pocket while the EMT examined the bullet graze on his head.

He couldn't do this anymore.

Crumpling the hat in his fist, he stomped to the door of his cabin and wrenched it open. His neighbor's driveway was going to have to wait. He had shopping to do.

"Someone's here to see you."

Chelsea's glee was evident, which piqued Ellie's curiosity. That suggestive expression meant it was a man, and that meant it was…

A burst of excitement spread warmth through her entire body. "George?"

"What?" Chelsea's excitement turned to confusion. "No. And who's George?"

As quickly as it had hit, Ellie's jubilation died. "No one. Never mind."

"Nuh-uh." The taller woman crossed her arms over her chest. "Spill."

"Now's not really the time," Ellie hissed, sending a meaningful glance at the occupied dressing room in front of them. Several different sizes of the same two dresses were draped over her arm. "Are you okay in there, Mrs. Oakly? Do you need a different size?"

"I'm fine, dear," the woman in the changing room responded, to Ellie's disappointment. She could've used a way to escape her friend's interrogation.

"Start talking," Chelsea demanded.

With a sigh, Ellie admitted, "It's really nothing. He was my guide when I was in the mountains. That's it."

"But you want it to be more." It wasn't a question.

"What I want doesn't matter." She'd come to that realization several days ago around two a.m. "He went back to Simpson, I flew back here, and I haven't heard from him since."

"Hi." The male voice made both women turn toward the source.

"Dylan." Immediately feeling bad about her flat tone, Ellie forced a smile. "Good to see you."

"You too." He looked at Chelsea and then at the closed dressing room door. "Could we maybe talk somewhere else a little more private?"

Ellie shook her head. "I'm working."

"Right." He gave his surroundings another discomforted glance. "I was hoping we could grab some drinks again, since our last date ended so quickly."

"You came here to ask me that?"

"Well, yeah." He shifted his weight. "You weren't answering your phone."

"Sorry." Her voice was flat again, but she couldn't bring herself to apologize for the lack of sincerity. "I don't think so. But thank you for offering."

He blinked, looking a little stunned. Ellie got the impression that he wasn't turned down very often. "Oh. Okay. You sure?"

Very. She couldn't bring herself to be quite that rude, though. "Yes."

His nod was short, as his expression changed from surprise to hostility. "Fine then. Bye. See you, Chelsea."

Chelsea made a sound that could have been a response to his good-bye. They waited until the outside door jangled, indicating that he'd left. Ellie didn't want to look at Chelsea, worried that her abrupt dismissal of Dylan would bring a round of recriminations. Instead, she fussed with the dresses hanging over her arm.

"Still okay, Mrs. Oakly?" She wondered what the woman was doing in there. She had to be done trying on the two dresses she'd originally brought in with her.

"Just wonderful, dear!" There was a gleeful note in the older woman's voice that made Ellie frown.

The silence stretched until Ellie was forced to meet Chelsea's gaze. "What?"

"You just turned down Dylan. In, like, two words."

And there it was. Her nose wanted to wrinkle, but she smoothed her expression. "I'm sorry, Chels, but I just don't want to go out with Dylan again. He's so…little."

"He's six feet."

"Exactly. And he's scrawny."

"He's a triathlete. He works out a bazillion times a day."

"I know." She lost the battle with her expression, and her face scrunched. "He told me in excruciating detail."

"He's not *scrawny*."

Ignoring Chelsea's incredulous screech, Ellie just shrugged. "Plus, his face is too naked. And he probably doesn't know what to do when faced by an angry moose."

"A what?" Giving her head a shake, Chelsea visibly refocused. "I can't believe you just turned him down like that. You never turn down guys directly. You just run into the bathroom and hide until they leave."

"Once. I did that *once*."

"This is about your mountain dude, isn't it?"

"Of course not." Her blush flamed, calling her a liar.

"So he's really tall."

A small, besotted smile tilted up the corners of her mouth. She couldn't seem to force it down. "So tall."

"And muscle-y."

"Yeah." It came out as more of a dreamy sigh than a word.

"And...bearded?"

Frowning at Chelsea's judgmental tone, Ellie said defensively, "It's still cold there. I think he has it to keep his face warm." The smitten tone returned to her voice. "It's a really good beard, though. Thick and such a nice color, and it's soft. I thought it'd be scratchy."

"How do you know it's soft?" Chelsea demanded, and then her eyes widened. "Did you kiss him? OMG, you kissed him! You slut!"

"Hush!" Sending a frantic glance toward the dressing room, Ellie whispered, "Just a peck. Maybe two pecks. And Mrs. Oakly doesn't need to know about it."

"Don't mind me, ladies!" Mrs. Oakly trilled from her dressing room. "Just carry on and pretend I'm not here."

Ellie rolled her eyes. That was why the woman was taking forever to try on two dresses. She was listening to the soap opera going on outside the dressing room.

"Well, that explains a lot." Chelsea clapped her hands together. "No wonder you've been as much fun as a constipated turtle lately. You're useless to me like this. You need to go find your lumberjack, hit him over the head with your club, and drag him to Chicago by his beard. I'll even give you the rest of the day off to go accomplish that."

Ellie blinked at her and then glanced at the clock. "My shift is over in five minutes."

"And I'll give you those five minutes if you go get your man and quit moping."

"I'm not moping."

"Ha!" Chelsea pointed one perfectly manicured fingernail at her. "You are so moping. You've been moping for a week, ever since you got back from your mountain adventure. I'm getting depressed just being around you and your heavy sighs. I've had to up my visits to my therapist to twice a week because of you."

Rolling her eyes, Ellie said insincerely, "Sorry."

"You should be. I'm going to take the cost of that extra weekly visit out of your paycheck." The scary thing was that Ellie wasn't sure whether or not Chelsea was joking about that. "So, what's the problem? Why don't you call him?"

"He doesn't have a phone."

Chelsea stared at her, mouth open, for almost a full minute. "I'm sorry, what? I thought you said he didn't have a phone."

"He doesn't. No cell, no landline, nothing."

"But..." Chels looked bewildered. "It's not even possible not to own a phone, is it? I mean, how does he text? Or check his emails when he's not at home? Or take selfies?"

The thought of George taking a selfie almost made her smile. "I don't know how he does it, but he manages to survive phoneless."

"Okay." Chelsea tapped her lips with her finger. "We can work around the whole crazy no-phone thing. You'll just need to go there in person."

Ellie cringed. "That seems so...desperate. I mean, I didn't even know him a week. Plus, I hired him to be my guide. It wasn't like he wanted to spend time with me. It was just a job for him."

"It's not desperate." She hurried over to a rack of dresses and started flipping through them. "It's proactively going after what you want. And if a hairy man who shops at the Big and Tall Store is what you want, then get him you shall." Pulling out a dress, she held it up for Ellie's inspection. "We'll have you looking beautiful and then drop you on his doorstep. He won't be able to resist, especially since I imagine he doesn't see many women up there in the mountains."

Shaking her head, Ellie wasn't sure where to start refuting Chelsea's entire ridiculous plan. "First of all, there are plenty of women—*beautiful* women—in Simpson. I'm friends with one of them." She and Lou had been calling and texting since her return to Chicago. "It's a plane trip and a three-hour drive just to get there. *And* I'm not going to throw myself at George and risk being rejected. If he's interested, he knows where to find me." She paused, not sure if that was true, but then she shook her head. It was better this way. She barely knew the guy. Besides, ever since she'd left the mountains, she'd been a neurotic, jumpy freak. It would be rude to dump the shaky, nightmare-ridden mess she'd become into George's lap.

"C'mon, El." Chelsea held up a blue dress to Ellie's chin and regarded it thoughtfully. "Don't you want to see this guy?"

Gently pushing the dress aside, Ellie handed Chelsea the clothes draped over her arm before hurrying behind the counter to grab her purse. "I'm not going to hunt him down," she said, not really answering the question.

"I have to run some errands. Would you mind helping Mrs. Oakly finish up?" Without giving Chelsea a chance to reply, Ellie darted out the door and almost ran to the small lot next door where her car was parked.

Climbing into her Prius, she laid her head back against the seat and sighed. It was hard enough keeping thoughts of George at bay without Chelsea interrogating her about the man.

Her phone rang, startling her. Once she dug it out of her purse, she peered at the caller ID, fully expecting Chelsea to be calling to continue their conversation—the one Ellie had run out of the shop to avoid. It was Lou, instead, and Ellie tapped the talk button in relief.

"Hi, Lou."

"Ellie!" Even for her, Lou was talking fast—and loudly. Ellie held the phone away from her ear, wincing. "How are you? I'm just calling to chat. Hey, by the way, what's the name of the store where you work? I'm thinking of…uh, getting some new clothes. Cuter, less Simpson-y clothes."

"Chelsea's?"

"That's it! I knew it was some chick's name. So, does the shop have a website?"

The conversation was just getting stranger and stranger. "Yes," Ellie said slowly, then gave her the boutique's website address. Lou needed to lay off the coffee—or the crack.

"Perfect! Thank you! And what time do you work tomorrow? Or do you work tomorrow?"

"I do." She was starting to fear for Lou's mental health. Armstrong was working out well for her dad so far. Maybe she'd recommend it to Lou. "Ten to six."

"Wonderful! Fantastic! Hey, I have to go. Talk to you later!"

The call ended as abruptly and oddly as it had begun, and Ellie held out her phone so she could stare at it again. "Weird."

At four the next morning, she officially gave up trying to sleep and made a cup of coffee. Her vision had a strange, too-bright, halo-y thing happening that she was pretty sure was related to not sleeping for a week. When she did manage to doze, the nightmares were waiting.

Her dreams didn't feature what she'd expected, though. Instead of explosions and avalanches and gunfire and charging moose, it was little details, like orange blood in the snow and a broken window. Despite their quietness, those images were no less terrifying.

The worst, though, was the overlying feeling of her nightmares, a complete and utter loneliness that made her wake up crying more than once. As she stared at her slowly filling mug, she absently rubbed the center of her chest, feeling the memory of that terrible ache.

Once her coffee had brewed, she took her mug to the cute, whimsical chair she'd found at a downtown furniture store. It had cost more than the rest of her furniture combined, but the chair had shouted at her from the window display, and she'd returned over and over until she'd given in and bought it.

Tucking her feet underneath her, she looked out the window at the city lights and tried not to think about George. As usual, she failed.

"I hate sales," Ellie muttered under her breath as she straightened a rack of clearance tops, moving a size-two blouse out of the size-twelve section. It was midafternoon and the first chance she'd had to breathe since she'd unlocked the door at ten that morning. Chelsea had run down the block to grab salads for a belated lunch. One nice thing about the rush had been that Chelsea hadn't had a second to quiz Ellie about George, and her roommate had been out late the night before, so she hadn't had time to restart her interrogation then, either.

The bell on the door rang, and Ellie's shoulders fell. The sound marked the end of her full three minutes of quiet time. Pasting on a smile, she turned toward the arriving customer.

"Welcome to Chel—oh!" Her standard greeting cut off in the middle, leaving her mouth hanging open as she stared at the bearded man standing in the boutique, looking enormous and incongruous in the girly fluff of a shop. "George?"

He nodded, as if she'd truly been confused about who stood a few feet in front of her. Actually, she'd just been checking if he was a longing-induced hallucination. After squeezing her eyes closed and opening them again, he was still there, and her shock was starting to shift to pure, unadulterated joy.

Her first couple of steps were slow, and then she launched herself at him even as he reached for her. Her cheek hit his chest with almost painful force, but she didn't mind. It was just more proof that he was real—flesh and blood and beard and flannel. Her arms wrapped around his middle, and she squeezed.

"What are you doing here?" she asked, leaning back so she could see his face. She'd missed him. Ellie hadn't realized how much she could miss someone she'd known for such a short time.

Color darkened his cheekbones before he answered. "Wanted to see you."

Ellie couldn't have stopped her huge grin from spreading across her face even if she'd wanted to. Her cheeks were already hurting from the force of it. "Good. I wanted to see you, too."

He frowned, but his eyes were happy. "Why didn't you, then?"

"Come to Simpson?" When he shrugged affirmatively, it was her turn to blush. "I figured I'd chased you enough. I thought I was probably just a client to you."

His eyebrows rose. "Didn't you get the check?"

She had. The check she'd written and sent to his home via a delivery company, since she figured he would have a post office box for mail, had been returned to her. When she'd opened the envelope, her heart pounding with excitement at receiving something from George, all she'd found was torn pieces of the check.

Her smile faded. "Yes. You could've included a note." He gave her a look.

"How was I supposed to know what it meant?" she said defensively. "I thought you felt bad about me almost getting killed a few times, and that's why you returned the money. I didn't know." She'd *hoped*, but she didn't know.

When he rolled his eyes at her, she laughed. The

typically teenage gesture looked strange on his bearded face.

"Oh!" Her brain had belatedly started working again. "That's why Lou was acting all weird on the phone yesterday. Did you ask her to find out where I worked?"

Looking pained, he shook his head. "I asked her for your phone number."

"You got a phone?" It was almost as shocking as him showing up at the shop.

With a nod, he reached into his jacket pocket and pulled out an inexpensive prepaid phone, still in its packaging. "Lou thought it'd be better if I just came here, though."

She hugged him again. "Definitely. Much better. I like that you're in touching distance." Her face grew hot again as one corner of his mouth curled in a smile. "Um…anyway. Why here? I know you have my home address, since you mailed the shredded check there."

"It's a secured building." When she stayed silent, not sure what that had to do with anything, he continued. "Didn't know when you'd be home, and I didn't want to hang out in front."

"Right," she said as realization dawned. "My neighbors would definitely have called the cops if a hot lumberjack was lurking by the door."

His smile went from a half to a whole. "Hot?"

Her earlier blush was nothing compared to the heat that suffused her skin that time. "Uh…right. So, how long can you stay?"

His gaze dropped, and he paused before answering. "A while."

"Really?" She bounced a little on her toes in

excitement. Her arms were still looped around his waist, since she hadn't let him go yet. Ellie didn't ever want to let him go. "Does that mean a few days or a few weeks? When's your flight home?"

He raised his shoulder in his typical half shrug, and she grinned, so happy to see that familiar gesture again. "No flight. I drove."

She blinked at him. "Drove? Your truck? Here?"

His one-sided smile was back, almost distracting her from her line of questioning.

"It's a fifteen-hour drive," she said. "Without any breaks."

"Made it in fourteen." The other side of his mouth followed the first.

"Wow." She wasn't sure if she was talking about his impressive speed or just her ecstatic amazement that he was actually here. "Why didn't you fly?"

His smile turned to a grimace. "Hate planes."

"Wow," she said again. "I still can't believe you drove all the way here." *To see me.*

Changing the subject, he asked, "How's Baxter?"

"Better. I video chat with him every day. The doctors are still trying to figure out the best mix of meds for him, so sometimes he seems"—she tilted her head to the side, searching for the right description—"I don't know, dull and flat. Not like his usual self."

George opened his mouth, but whatever he was going to say was interrupted by the jingle of the doorbell. He turned toward the sound, tucking her behind him in the same movement. Ellie peeked around his arm to see who'd entered the store.

"Ho-ly mountain man," Chelsea said slowly,

checking out George from his boots to the top of his head. "You are George, and you look like the guy on the paper towels. I see why El sent Dylan packing so fast."

His head swiveled around until he was glaring at Ellie.

"What? Oh, Dylan?" She waved her hand. "We'd gone on one date—a half date, really, since my dad called that night."

George's scowl lightened, but not by much.

Giving his ridiculously large biceps a reassuring pat, she said, "He's short."

"Not really," Chelsea contradicted, looking amused.

Ignoring her, Ellie continued, "And he has little chicken arms." Her arm-patting turned to petting.

Chelsea coughed, which might have been hiding a laugh. "Triathlete."

"And his face is all"—Ellie wrinkled her nose—"naked."

George had been looking less and less upset as she'd listed Dylan's imperfections, and he grinned at the last one.

"Holy moly," Chelsea breathed, no longer appearing like she was about to laugh. "I want one. I want a George. Are there more like him in the mountains? Because we can close the store, fly to Colorado, and go George shopping, only for me this time."

By the end of the monologue, Ellie had moved in front of George, creating a human wall between him and a hungry-looking Chelsea. "Down, Chels. And no. There are no George clones in the mountains. I didn't run across any, at least. Although"—she thought back to her first night in Simpson—"there does seem to be an excessive number of hot firemen.

Oh, and the sheriff's pretty fine, too. Plus, you know...handcuffs."

Chelsea made a whimpering sound.

"Tell you what," Ellie said. "If I can have the rest of today off to hang out with George, then you can come with me next time I go to Colorado."

"But it's the first day of our big sale." Chelsea looked terrified. "They'll trample me and then complain about how my guts are splattered all over the fifty-percent-off rack."

Ellie still had an ace in her pocket, though. "I know where the Simpson fire station is."

"Fine! But you're working tomorrow, *and* we're going to sexy fireman land the second we both can take a week off." Chelsea stomped toward the checkout counter. "In fact, as soon as I drag my crumpled, mangled body off the floor after the next sale rush eases, I'm going to rearrange the schedule." She grabbed the printout of the schedule and ran her fingernail across the upcoming weeks. "When is the prime time? I want to maximize my firemen exposure."

"Wednesdays at seven."

Ellie looked at George, surprised he'd volunteered the information. She wouldn't have thought he'd participate in hooking up Chelsea with a fireman. He caught her startled glance and leaned close to her ear.

"The sooner you're back in Simpson," he rumbled, making her warm and shivery at the same time, "the better."

She felt her eyes widen as she stared at him. "Okay" was all she managed to utter.

His smile was thick with smugness and male satisfaction. Ellie was too smitten to care.

Chapter 24

SHE SMILED AS HE FOLDED HIMSELF INTO THE FRONT passenger seat of her Prius. When George caught her look and lifted his eyebrows in question, she just shook her head. There was no way she was about to explain how happy she was that her car would smell like George for days after he left. Since he'd found a parking spot for his truck a few streets over from the shop that didn't have any time restrictions, she suggested he leave his vehicle parked there for the night. Finding an open spot around her condo building was brutal.

As she started the engine, she shook off her dopey grin and tried to focus on being a good hostess. "Anything special you want to do today?" When he gave a half shrug, she ran over some options in her head. There was the zoo, but George lived where elk and bears hung out in his front yard. The zoo seemed like a pale imitation of that. She liked Millennium Park, but the wind had a sharp edge to it—not as sharp as it had been in the mountains, but cold enough to discourage outdoor play. She remembered his reaction to the enclosed waiting room at the hospital, and she mentally canceled the Art Institute and several other indoor options as being too crowded, too claustrophobic, and too not-George.

It made her stomach squirm with nervousness, but she asked the question anyway. "Want to see where I live?"

At his immediate nod, she took a deep breath and backed out of her parking space.

Her nerves reappeared when she unlocked the door to her condo. She was discomforted by the realization that she really wanted George to like her place.

Although Chelsea had been her roommate for over a year, Ellie had been the one who'd picked it out and decorated it, and it felt like George was looking inside of *her* when he turned in a circle, scanning the open living and kitchen areas of her home.

While George examined her space, Ellie tried to view the place with an outsider's eye. She hadn't had a specific decorating theme in mind when she'd first moved into the condo four years ago. Instead, she'd just picked paint colors and furniture and wall art she'd liked, which created a slightly haphazard feel, especially when Chelsea had added her things to the mix.

"Well?" she asked, unable to take the silent appraisal any longer. "What do you think?"

Turning toward her, George gave a slow nod. "It fits you."

That wasn't quite the reassurance she'd been hoping to get. "Is that good?"

One corner of his mouth twitched upward. "Yes." She thought that was all she was going to get until he spoke again a few moments later. "It's happy and bright and warm. I like that color." He gestured toward the dark orange accent wall.

"Thanks." She beamed. He'd picked out one of the aspects of her decorating that she'd never regretted. "It looks really nice when the late-afternoon light hits it. It makes it feel like the sunset is actually happening in my living room."

He smiled at her, a complete, two-sided grin, and they locked gazes for a long minute. Warmth filled her chest, pressing on her lungs and making it hard to breathe, until she dropped her gaze and cleared her throat.

"Did you want to see the rest?" When he didn't answer out loud, she looked at him just in time to catch the tail end of his nod.

As she led the way to the short hallway, she wondered what had possessed her to invite George into her bedroom. It was like she was just asking for awkwardness.

"This is the guest room." She stepped through the doorway, gesturing like a game-show hostess. "Not much to see." The room was small, just large enough for the double bed, a dresser, and a nightstand. When George entered, it felt like the already-tiny space shrank even more.

The path to the door was completely blocked by his massive form. She felt a twinge of...not nervousness, exactly, but something more along the lines of uncertain excitement. When she took a quarter step toward him, he backed against the wall, opening the space between her and the doorway. Blushing for some unknown reason, she darted back into the hall.

"Chelsea's room." She waved a hand at the next closed door. Her steps slowed as she neared her own bedroom, but she forced her feet to cross the threshold and carry her into the room. A sting next to her index finger's nail made her realize that she was chewing on her hangnail again. In the past week of sleepless nights and jumpy days, her bad habit had returned with a vengeance, and the skin around her fingernails was raw and sore. She jerked down her hand and grabbed it with her left one.

While she'd been fighting with her appendages, George had entered her bedroom and was giving it the same slow appraisal that he'd given the rest of her apartment. Her flush returned, and she felt exposed.

The guest room, although pretty with its pearl-gray and blue accents, was fairly impersonal. Her bedroom was anything but. She'd used the same dark orange color on one wall, and the room glowed with reds and oranges, as if it were the smoldering coal bed of her home. It made her happy to wake up in that visual warmth. If George didn't like it or if he made a joke about her bright color scheme, it would hurt.

When she finally got the nerve to look at his face, he was smiling. "I like it."

A rush of relief flowed through her, and she sat on the edge of the bed as her knees wobbled a little. "Good."

He gave her a curious glance, and her blush matched the red accents in the room.

Unable to explain how important it was for him to share the feeling of warmth and comfort she'd tried to create, especially in her bedroom, she stole a gesture from him and shrugged. "I like that you like my home."

He took a couple of steps toward her, hovering over her until she patted the bed next to her. After a short hesitation, he sat, making the mattress sink and toppling her toward him.

"Whoa!" Ellie laughed, putting out her hand to steady herself before she ended up sprawled across George's lap. Instead of landing on the mattress, her fingers clutched his thigh. She stared at it for a shocked second, as if her hand didn't belong to her, and then tried to snatch it back. Before she could, George's fingers settled on hers and held it in place.

She stared at him, unable to even form an apology. He started leaning toward her, advancing so slowly that it took her a long time to realize he was in motion. Once she did figure it out, Ellie didn't move.

It seemed to take forever and no time at all before his mouth was a fraction of an inch away from hers. She studied his eyes, remembering the time in the tent, in the cave, clinging to him after escaping the charging moose, seeing his frantic face after he'd freed her from her body cast of hardened snow after the avalanche, his kiss at the cabin before he'd left to get help. It felt like she'd known him for such a long time, and he'd become so precious to her, so vital to her happiness.

Her hand crept up to stroke his cheek, smoothing over skin and beard until she found the line of his jaw under the dark hair. It was firm and square, and she smiled.

"I bet you're handsome, even without this." She gave a tug on his beard.

Instead of returning her smile, he raised his hand and mirrored her gesture, stroking her cheek with warm fingers. "You're the most beautiful person I've ever seen."

Then he kissed her. It started as a gentle press of his lips against hers, similar to but longer than their first two brief pecks. Then the pressure increased, and he started exploring, kissing her upper lip and then her lower, each corner of her mouth and then back to the center.

The buzzing feeling she'd gotten from his earlier

kisses was nothing compared to that, and she gasped, her
lips parting a little beneath his. He froze for a moment
and then latched his hand around the back of her neck,
pulling her more tightly into him. Ellie went willingly.

Although the kiss was already more intense than
anything she'd ever felt before, it stayed almost
chaste, just lips to lips. The excitement building in her
belly bubbled into impatience as his mouth touched
and then lightened, never deepening into a full kiss.
Finally, with a growl of frustration, she nipped his
bottom lip. George went still.

Realizing what she'd done, Ellie opened her eyes
wide. She'd felt the give of his flesh beneath her
teeth, and she knew she'd bitten hard enough for it
to have stung.

"I'm sor—" Before she could get the whole apology out, he was on her, using his weight to push her
back until her shoulder blades met the bed. His chest
pressed against hers, flattening her against the mattress in a way that felt both exciting and secure. His
kisses were the same but different, closemouthed until
he would tug at her bottom lip with his teeth in a more
gentle, teasing imitation of what she'd done.

This was the oddest—and hottest—make-out session she'd ever had. As he kissed and nipped at her
mouth, she parted her lips and touched the place where
she'd bitten him with her tongue, silently giving the
apology she'd not been able to say.

He made a sound she'd never heard from him before,
a quiet groaning gasp as his body jerked against hers. It
was arousing and heady to make him react in that way
with barely a touch. Ellie licked that spot again, and he

imitated her, his tongue joining his teeth and lips in his campaign to drive her insane with frustration and desire.

A thought fought its way through her cloudy brain, and it was startling enough that she pulled back from him, breathing hard.

"Have you done this before?" He didn't have the sloppy, unskilled manner of a beginner, but she got the impression he was blindly feeling his way through the experience. Each time she introduced something—teeth or tongue—he enthusiastically followed her lead. It felt as if he were learning as he went, picking up cues from her on what was next.

He reacted like she'd slapped him, jerking back and twisting to sit up. Ellie grabbed his shoulders and was pulled up with him. As she eyed the red burning his skin above the line of his beard, she knew he was about to bolt. The memory of the miserable past week flashed through her mind, and she quickly threw a leg over his lap, straddling him.

That startled him enough to keep him sitting for an extra few seconds. When he moved as if to pull her off him, she wrapped her legs and arms around him like a needy monkey.

"Sorry!" She talked fast, trying to get the words out before he peeled her off of him and left. Ellie had no illusions about George's strength—the only reason she was still on his lap was because he allowed it. "I didn't mean it like it's a bad thing. When you kiss me, it's like... whoa. My brain explodes, which partially explains why I just blurted that out like I did. Just ignore it. Pretend I never said anything. Everything was amazing and wonderful and perfect until I opened my stupid mouth."

Squeezing his rigid body tighter, she pressed her face into his neck. "Please don't go."

An endless silence followed. When George finally sighed, his breath ruffling her hair, and his arms went around her, Ellie fought back relieved tears.

"Sorry." Her words were still muffled by his neck. The position reminded her of sleeping in the cold, keeping her face buried in just that spot to steal his warmth.

"It's okay." He stroked her hair, the rough skin on his hands catching a few strands. "You're right."

In her panic to stop him from leaving, her original question had lost its importance. Now, curiosity kept her quiet and waiting for more information as she melted under his gentle petting.

"I've never..." He stopped and made a frustrated sound.

"Had a girlfriend?" Ellie offered, still keeping her face hidden. She knew from experience that it was sometimes easier to talk without direct eye contact. Besides, she was enjoying the stroke of his hand too much to move. It made her want to purr like a cat.

He nodded, and she felt the motion of his chin.

"Good," she said with honest satisfaction. When he went still, she sat back so he could see the sincerity in her expression. "The idea of you with someone else is..." Her nose wrinkled as she tried to come up with a word that fully expressed the scorching jealousy that streaked through her at the thought. "Bad. Just really, really bad."

The grim set to his mouth lightened but didn't fully dissipate. Ellie tried out another one of his gestures and lifted her eyebrows in a silent question. "You could tell," he said shortly, his gaze moving until he was looking over her shoulder.

Ellie knew she was going to have to be completely, baldly honest with him, no matter how hot her blush burned in embarrassment. "When you kiss me, even just the short one at the cabin, I feel…" Her cheeks were almost painfully hot already, but he'd returned his gaze to hers, so she continued. "It's amazing. I love kissing you, and I just asked what I did because you're so take charge with everything else." She lowered her voice in a bad imitation of his. "Eat this. Don't tie your boots like that. Sit there. Tell me if you're sweating. Put that on. Take that off." By the time she finished, he was almost smiling. "With this, it felt like you were letting me lead. It just felt out of character. It was good, though. Very, very, *very* good."

After studying her for a long moment, he gave a short nod. She felt confident enough that he wasn't going to leave that she loosened her grip around his neck and let her fingers play with his hair.

"How'd that happen, though?"

He cocked his head, his eyes questioning.

"Why hasn't some harpy gotten her claws into you yet?" she clarified and then grinned, lightly scratching at his scalp with her nails. "Except for this harpy, of course."

His eyes went dark and heavy-lidded as he tilted his head. "Mmm?"

"Never mind," she laughed. "I can tell I've lost you to the scalp massage. You can tell me later how you escaped the clutches of the Simpson women. I mean, even Chelsea wants to kidnap and clone you."

His mouth kicked up in a half smile as he leaned into her touch. The enjoyment on his face made her want to kiss him again, but she was worried it would become stiff and awkward with their recent conversation hanging in the air. Instead, she leaned in close and asked, "You hungry?"

His shrug was a definite yes.

Kissing the tip of his nose because she couldn't resist the urge, she slid off his lap and stood, holding out a hand. "Let's go get some food, then."

George eyed her hand for a moment before grabbing it with his own. As he levered up, extending to his full, substantial height, he pulled her so she stumbled forward, ending up pressed front to front with him.

She blinked up at his smug face before laughing and shaking her head. "Quick learner," she muttered, pushing away so she could poke him in the stomach. "I'm going to have to watch out for you."

Leaning down, he brushed a gentle kiss on her cheek. She stared at him, knowing her expression was full-on besotted, but she didn't care that she was giving away all her feelings. Still wearing his half smile, he nudged her toward the door, his big hands wrapped over her shoulders.

Automatically, her feet carried her through the doorway. She fought the urge to lean back into him. "Would you rather go out or eat here?" Even before he answered, she knew what his response would be.

"Here."

"Okay, but we'll need to order in. My fridge is pretty much bare of anything except condiments."

His thumb swept across her collarbone, and she shivered. "You haven't been eating." It was a statement rather than a question.

She shrugged a little uncomfortably. "I've grabbed food on my way to and from work, mostly. I just haven't been very hungry." It was hard to eat when her stomach hurt all the time. Since George had arrived, though, the twisting pain had eased. She sent him a teasing look over her shoulder. "I'm starving now, though. Does pizza sound good?"

His concerned frown stayed in place, despite the mention of pizza. "Have you been sleeping?"

As she had a feeling that the honest answer to that question would earn her a serious scolding, Ellie decided to pretend she hadn't heard it. "What do you like on your pizza?" As soon as she spoke, she realized that her nonanswer was as revealing as an actual response would've been. George's frown deepened. She braced herself for the upcoming lecture, but he surprised her. Wrapping his arms around her upper chest, he pulled her against him in a backward hug.

"El," he said quietly, his lips moving against her hair. "I'm sorry."

"For what?" She tried to look up at him, but he held her too tightly, so she subsided, content to lean against him.

She felt his chest move against her back before his breath warmed the top of her head as he sighed. "Pizza's fine."

At his evasion, she deflated. She'd been ready to deny any issue with eating or sleeping, and her built-up defenses had nowhere to go when he dropped the subject.

"Um...okay. What do you like on it?"

"Any kind of meat."

Why did that not surprise her? "Venison?" she teased.

"Do they have that?" He actually sounded excited about the option.

"Um…probably not." She could almost feel his disappointment. "I could ask, though."

"It's okay." George gave her a final squeeze and let go. "Rabbit is fine."

She took a step toward the counter where she'd left her purse before his comment penetrated. When she shot a suspicious glance at him, his face was completely expressionless for several moments before he grinned.

Ellie laughed, turning back toward her purse and digging out her cell phone. "How many times do I have to tell you that I'm not eating bunnies?" Making a face, she found the contact for the pizza place and tapped the number. "MREs were bad enough without adding fluffy, adorable animals with long ears to the mix."

Although he just shrugged, a smile lingered on his face, and she had to drag her eyes off of him when someone from the pizza shop answered her call. There was no way she could concentrate on ordering when she was drooling over happy-George.

"Hi," she chirped. "Do you offer venison as a topping?"

George laughed.

Chapter 25

AFTER VENISONLESS PIZZA, WHICH WAS GOOD DESPITE the lack of wild-game toppings, they decided to go to an early movie. It was actually Ellie who decided and then cajoled George into going. Staying at the apartment was tempting, but she thought they needed a little more time before diving into another make-out session. This thing—whatever they were, or could be to each other— was too new to rush. But she wasn't sure if she could keep her hands off him without the buffer of other people.

"Is there any movie you've been wanting to see?" she asked, scrolling through the possibilities on her phone while George drove the Prius. They were heading to a theater in one of the close-in suburbs, since Ellie figured that would give George a little more breathing room than the small, crowded places close to her condo. His large frame should have looked ridiculous folded up in the driver's seat, but he managed to pull it off with his usual steady confidence. Instead of wanting to snigger and make clown-car jokes when she looked at him, Ellie just felt the urge to let out a dreamy sigh.

He shook his head, so she started reading possibilities to him. When he looked blank at the movie titles, she began giving a brief synopsis of each one. She judged his reaction to each possibility by the face he made, from total disgust to mild interest.

"Oh! This one's supposed to be good. Mostly action

but with some funny parts." Since he didn't look opposed, she looked at the movie times and saw that they'd get to the theater in time for the earlier evening showing. Tucking her phone into her purse, she settled back into her seat and allowed herself to eye George again. She couldn't believe he was sitting in her car with her, and that they were about to go on a date. Just over a week earlier, she'd only wanted to survive, bring her dad home, feel warm again, and eat pizza. They'd accomplished all four.

"Want to talk to Baxter tomorrow morning?" she asked. "I was going to call him before my shift."

When he nodded, she smiled.

"It's the next exit."

After they left the interstate, Ellie gave him directions to the theater, and George parked on the far end of the large, open lot.

She gave him an amused look. "Are you keeping my car safe from door dings?"

"I like having space," he responded before getting out of the car and circling around to open her door. Surprised at the courtesy, Ellie beamed as she offered her hand to him so George could help her out of the car. Once she was standing, he closed the door and locked the car without releasing his grip.

As they started walking toward the theater entrance, she squeezed his hand and barely stopped herself before giving a little skip of happiness. Her shoes were made more for beauty than for skipping, hopping, or jumping.

They were also not made for hiking across an enormous parking lot, and she wasn't even a quarter of the

way to the front doors when her toes started to pinch.
Although she tried to hide her discomfort, not wanting
George to feel bad for making her walk so far because
of his parking-lot claustrophobia, her ankle twisted
with a bad step, making her give a small gasp.

He looked at her as she limped a couple of steps,
walking off the twinge of pain, and then he stopped.
His hold on her hand meant that she halted, as well.

Ellie looked at him curiously. "What's—?" Her
question ended in a yelp as he swung her into his arms,
bride style, and began carrying her to the entrance of
the theater. "I'm okay." Her arms wrapped around his
neck as he strode across the lot, not even out of breath
from her weight. "George. You're always having to
carry me. My ankle's fine. Really."

Traffic noise from the main road was distant enough
that the parking lot was fairly quiet—for the city, at
least. After her time in the mountains, Ellie had a new
appreciation for true silence. George tipped his head forward, as if they were in a noisy club. When his breath
brushed the delicate skin of her ear, she couldn't hold
back a shiver. She was so distracted by his lips that it
took her a few seconds to process his words.

"I don't mind," he said quietly. "I like holding you."

Her arms tightened around his neck as she shuddered
again. "Okay." Her voice was faint, and she was pretty
sure the movement of his chest was a chuckle.

When they reached the sidewalk by the entrance,
George carefully lowered her to her feet, keeping his
hands on her upper arms until she was steady. They
stared at each other, and he started to lean closer.
Mesmerized, she didn't move. Her focus narrowed until

all she could see was George, and all she could think about was feeling his lips on hers again.

"Excuse me." A shrill voice made her jump, and Ellie realized that they were blocking the middle pair of doors. There were five other sets of doors that the irritated woman and her two friends could have chosen, but Ellie just tugged George to the side, giving the woman a smile. She looked up at George, hoping they could resume where they'd been before the interruption, but the moment was gone. Rather than kissing her, George held open the door and ushered her inside.

Although she sighed in brief disappointment, Ellie's smile returned quickly as she laced her fingers with George's. It was an amazing thing to be able to touch him like that. She wondered how she'd survive once he returned to Simpson and she was alone again. Her grip tightened on his hand. She couldn't let herself think about being separated from George, about not being able to touch him or kiss him or read from his expression all the words he couldn't say out loud. Ellie had tried being without him, and she had been miserable. An occasional phone call—if he ever took his cell out of the packaging—was no substitute for having him close. She couldn't picture George being happy living in Chicago, but she selfishly wanted to keep him with her for as long as possible. Instead of dwelling on their eventual separation, she focused on enjoying the newness of each discovery—the roughness of his fingers and the surprising softness of his lips. Her face flushed at the thought of his earlier kisses, and he gave her a questioning look.

With a flustered shake of her head, she declined to comment and directed him to a ticket kiosk instead. He insisted on paying, just as he had with the pizza, and she frowned at him.

"If you waste all your money on me," she warned, "you're going to end up having to drag a bunch of whiny tourists all over the mountain just to earn enough for next winter."

The corner of his mouth slid up in a half smile. "It's not wasted."

Grinning at him, she towed him toward the snack counter. "At least let me pay you back in sugar. What's your favorite movie food?" she asked. "Mine is cinnamon candy and popcorn eaten together." The look he slanted at her was appalled. "It's good, seriously. It tastes like a popcorn ball." She frowned. "Wait. Why am I defending my *excellent* movie-food choices to the guy who thinks pouch food is good?"

He just smirked at her, making her laugh. As they waited in line, Ellie glanced around the lobby and caught sight of the woman who'd been annoyed that they'd been blocking the doors. The blond stranger was eyeing George with a touch too much hunger in her expression for Ellie's liking. Resisting the urge to snarl, Ellie took a half step toward George. Since she was already very close to him, the move brought their sides together with their clasped hands caught between them.

When he glanced at her, eyebrows raised, she just made a face, not wanting to explain her unwarranted surge of jealousy. He released her hand, and she fought the need to cling, reluctantly relaxing her grip and letting him withdraw. Instead of pulling away, though, he circled his arm behind her back, cupping her shoulder with his hand and tugging her more tightly against his side. She relaxed into him, perfectly content to wait forever for her popcorn and cinnamon candy.

This close to George, she felt his tension. His gaze was moving constantly, scanning the groups of movie patrons, his head turning sharply at every loud noise. Ellie hated his discomfort and wished she could erase it, that she could make him as comfortable in her urban life as he was in the mountains. There was nothing she could do, though, except lean a little more fully against him so he focused on her again with a smile.

Ellie stayed plastered against George's side until they reached the front of the line. Since he hadn't told her his snack preferences, she looked at him, waiting for him to order his own food once she was done.

"Water," he grunted. That was it.

"What else?" she asked. When he just shook his head at her and reached for his wallet, she ordered another half dozen types of candy.

George blinked at her.

"You can't have just water at a movie," she explained. Really, no sugary snacks? It was almost sacrilegious. "And I'm paying, remember? That's the rule. If one person pays for tickets, the other pays for the snacks. It's movie-going etiquette." She packed the candy into her purse while she pulled out her wallet. "I got a variety, so there's sure to be *something* in there" — she poked her purse — "that you like."

He didn't say anything but just inserted his body between Ellie and the counter and paid.

"Hey!" she scolded his broad back. "That's a serious breach of movie etiquette!"

George ignored her.

With a few muttered words about stubborn men who used their mountainous size to unfair advantage, Ellie dropped her billfold back in her purse and reached for the popcorn, only to be blocked again. George tucked the water bottle into the crook of his elbow and picked up the popcorn tub and beverage. Glancing down at her empty hands, Ellie smiled wryly. Apparently, George felt strongly about carrying the bulk of the load, whether they were on a snowy trail or in a city movie theater. She decided she should be glad he didn't toss her over his shoulder before picking up the popcorn. The mental image made her laugh, and George looked at her curiously.

"Nothing," she said, pulling his water bottle free from where he'd trapped it between his arm and body. "Just a random thought. Come on." She gave his elbow a tug. "If we don't hurry, we'll miss the previews, and they're my favorite part."

<center>~~~</center>

The movie was good, but watching George was better. He looked as entranced as a little kid, his eyes never leaving the screen as he ate most of the popcorn. All of the other snacks she'd ordered had disappeared so quickly that she couldn't even determine which one he'd enjoyed the most. George seemed to be an equal-opportunity eater. She wasn't sure why she was surprised, since he'd downed MREs with all appearances of enjoyment.

An on-screen explosion lit his face with yellow light, and he jerked back in his chair. Soon he was leaning forward again, completely engrossed in the movie. He blindly reached for another handful of popcorn, and Ellie adjusted the tub so his fingers would hit its mark.

When the credits rolled across the screen, he finally turned to look at her. George glanced at the empty popcorn tub, then his buttery fingers, and he grimaced, shooting her an apologetic glance. It made her laugh.

"Don't worry about it. I usually have two bites, run out of cinnamon candy, and leave the rest of the popcorn. It's very wasteful. Besides, I'm used to you finishing my food."

His mouth quirked up at the reminder, and his eyes grew warm. From his expression, Ellie could tell he'd felt the same odd intimacy that she had when they'd shared meals. The aching loneliness that had kept her up night after night began to ease, the hollow part of her filled with George's presence. Her expression must have given away her feelings, because he leaned toward her, getting closer and closer as she forgot to breathe.

"Excuse me." The same grating voice from earlier interrupted them yet again.

"Seriously?" Ellie muttered, but twisted her legs so the woman and her friends could leave the row. Ellie hadn't even realized that the woman was watching the same movie, but she definitely noticed how the blond angled her body so her breasts were right in George's face as she passed. One bedazzled fingernail traced a line down his biceps, making him flinch and yank back his arm.

"Hi," the woman greeted him throatily, her hungry gaze running down his chest.

That was not acceptable. "Hey!"

The woman stopped, still in front of George, who had leaned as far away from the encroaching cleavage as he could. She looked at Ellie, bitch-face fully activated. "You have a problem?"

"Not if you keep moving and get your boobs out of my boyfriend's face."

"Go on, Harper," one of her friends hissed. "Move! You're going to get your extensions ripped out again."

"Shut up, Tate," the blond snapped, but she did continue past Ellie, making a big show of not touching her legs. Ellie really, really wanted to trip her.

Once she and her entourage had exited the row and were making their way toward the door, Ellie turned, slightly shamefaced, back to George. "Sorry. I usually don't start girl fights in movie theaters. I never do, actually. I'm normally a calm, easygoing person. It's just that…" She wasn't sure how to say that she was frustrated after being kiss-blocked twice by the same blond harlot who'd been ogling Ellie's lumberjack.

When she glanced at George after her words trailed off, she saw he was grinning. "I protect you from mountain predators, and you protect me from"—his head tipped toward the retreating blond—"city predators."

Ellie laughed, her gaze fixed on his face, completely entranced by his happy expression. As it always did, that gorgeous, rare smile dazzled her in the best way. Cupping her jaw with his big hand, George tipped his head to hers. As their lips touched, instant warmth spread through her, and the rapidly emptying theater disappeared. It was just her and George and a gentle, dizzying kiss.

"Excuse me."

Ellie whirled around in her seat, ready to commit blondicide, but it was a different woman. This one had a carpet sweeper and was wearing a theater-employee uniform.

"You guys have to leave the theater now," she said in a bored voice. "The movie's over."

"Fine." Her jaw clenched in frustration, Ellie grabbed George's hand and headed for the exit. They needed to get to her condo so she could get kissed before she exploded. When they passed a trash bin outside the theater, George reached across her to toss in their empty snack containers.

"Thanks for cleaning up after us," she said, feeling a little calmer now that her heartbeat wasn't racing with anticipation. Ellie gave him a teasing smile. "Even at the movies, you follow the leave-no-trace camping rules."

He smiled back, although she didn't think it was at her lame joke. Tender and painfully sweet, it was aimed directly at her.

"Ready to go home?" she asked, squeezing his hand without looking away from his face.

He nodded.

—⁂—

The ride home had given her time to get nervous again, and she started chattering when they entered her condo.

"Did you like the movie?" At his nod, she almost asked if he'd been to a theater before, but she stopped, not wanting to bring up his inexperience with *anything*, even something as innocuous as movies. "Is there a theater in Simpson?"

He shook his head. "During the summer festival, they'll set up a screen outside and show family movies. That's about it."

It was a relief to pull off her torturous shoes. If they hadn't been so darn cute, she would've pitched them right into the trash. Instead, she headed for her bedroom to stow them in her closet, asking over her shoulder, "So everyone has to make do with their televisions, huh?"

George's response was quiet, and she had to strain to hear it from the other room. "Not everyone."

Since she was in her bedroom anyway, Ellie figured she should change out of her dress. It was strange undressing with George in the next room. Even though he couldn't see her unless he had X-ray vision that he hadn't mentioned, she was still blushing as she stripped.

"Do you not have a TV?" she called, trying to make her voice as casual as possible. Except for a slight wobble, she managed pretty well.

"No." He sounded closer, as if he were right outside her bedroom, and she paused in the middle of stepping into a pair of fuzzy pajama bottoms.

Swallowing hard, she forced her body to move again. "So what do you do when you're snowed in and bored out of your mind?"

"Read." There was a pause. "Fix things. Play music. Sing."

"You sing?" She yanked on a camisole and covered that with an oversized Avalanche hoodie. As she zipped it, she made a face at the hockey team name scrawled across her chest. "Avalanche" had a whole new meaning to her now. "Why didn't you join me in my musical stylings on the trail?"

She could almost hear his shrug. "Never really sang in front of anyone before."

The residue of her popcorn, candy, and pop combination didn't taste as good in her mouth as it had several hours before, so she headed for the connecting bathroom to brush her teeth. Ellie left the door open so she could keep talking to George. It was nice getting words rather than silent gestures from him, even if she was getting pretty good at interpreting his shrugs.

"Why not?" she called, continuing the conversation through a mouthful of toothpaste. The words were garbled, so she spit and tried again. "Why not?"

There was a pause. "Never been anyone around to hear."

That struck her as so sad. Since she couldn't say anything around the lump in her throat, she concentrated on rinsing her toothbrush. After crossing her bedroom and opening the door, she found George leaning against the wall right next to the doorjamb.

"I'm sorry."

Her sympathy appeared to have confused him.

"That you were alone so much." She tried to make her voice matter-of-fact to hide that she was one sad thought away from dissolving into a weepy mess. She'd never been much of a crier, but her tears had been on a hair trigger since she'd returned from the mountains. "Especially in Simpson. Here in Chicago, there's always somewhere you can go if you don't want to be alone."

He didn't meet her gaze. Apparently, he didn't want to discuss his aloneness. That was fine with Ellie. She didn't want to turn into a soggy heap of ugly crying and make him run back to his solitary but tear-free cabin as fast as his truck could take him.

"Come on." She led the way to the living room. Instead of settling in her favorite chair, as was her habit, she sat on the couch. After all, George was here. There'd be plenty of opportunities for chair sitting when she was alone again. After a pause, he sank down next to her, leaving a person-sized gap between them. She turned to face him, drawing up her knees in front of her.

The movement brought his attention to her bare feet. "Better?" he asked.

It took Ellie a second to understand his meaning. "Oh, the blisters, do you mean? They're fine." She held up her feet and wiggled her toes. "These feet are used to abuse, though. You've seen the torture devices I call shoes."

Clasping her feet in his hands, he pulled them onto his lap. Both hands focused on her left foot, and his fingers immediately found exactly the right place to apply the perfect amount of pressure. Leaning against the sofa arm, she closed her eyes and stifled a moan of pleasure. She wondered idly how he could be so good at giving a foot massage when he'd never dated. Deciding he must be a massage savant, Ellie made a mental vow to experience a back massage from him as soon as possible. The idea of it made her warm all over.

The ball of his thumb dug into her arch. This time, she couldn't hold back a pleased groan. When his hands went still, she opened one eye and glared at him.

"Why'd you stop?" There was a slight whine to her words, but she couldn't help it. She'd been wallowing in paradise before being abruptly jerked back to achy-feet reality.

"Thought I might have hurt you." His hands resumed their work, and she closed her eye again with a happy hum.

"If it hurts, I'll say, 'Ow. Stop. That hurts.' This is heaven."

He switched feet.

"How'd you learn that a good foot massage is the key to a heel-wearing woman's heart?" she asked, settling her back more comfortably against the arm of the couch.

"I overheard Cora saying something to Janelle about her husband giving them to her when she was pregnant."

Ellie opened her eyes so she could look at him. "Who are Cora and Janelle?" she asked lazily, and then moaned. "Oh, that's nice. Right there."

"They're on the team."

"Search and rescue?" When he nodded, she let her eyes drift closed again. "Next time I visit Simpson, I'll have to meet those two ladies and thank them."

He made a soft, amused sound, but the important thing was that his hands kept moving. In fact, they'd traveled around the back of her heel and over her ankle. His fingers were working at the base of her calf, which was starting to make her squirm in a whole different way.

"Seriously, though," she said, mostly to distract herself from his wandering hands and the sensations they were creating, "I'd like to meet your team members. The only one I've been around is Joseph, and he's probably not the best ambassador."

His hands slowed, making her open her eyes. George was scowling.

"Hey," she said softly, and he met her eyes. "You okay?"

"Just thinking about him taking you to the cabin instead of me," he said. His hands wrapped around both of her feet like they had at the cabin, surrounding them in glorious warmth. Even after she'd returned to her climate-controlled life in Chicago, her feet were almost always cold.

Leaning forward, she covered his hands with hers. "He didn't. You took me, and you kept me safe and my feet unfrozen."

George looked up, and their eyes met. Suddenly, he was over her, and they were kissing. Her mouth opened a little at the shock of it, and his tongue was there, exploring her with tentative touches that were more arousing than any experience she'd had before. Recovering from her surprise, Ellie wrapped her arms around his neck and held on to him.

Everywhere his mouth touched lit up, as if he were supplying electricity to her nerve endings. His teeth tugged gently on her lower lip, and she audibly sucked in a breath at the spark of pleasure. At the sound, George pulled back a few inches, checking her expression as if to see whether it had been a good gasp or a bad gasp. Burying the fingers of both hands into his hair, Ellie yanked him back down for more kissing. She felt him smile against her mouth.

They kissed for what felt like hours, sometimes serious and sometimes playing, both of them learning what the other one liked. Ellie discovered that touching a spot under his jaw gave him goose bumps, and George's kisses developed an edge of sexy bossiness as he gained confidence, making Ellie forget everything except for him. She kept expecting his hands to wander, for him to ramp up to the next level, but he seemed content to stick with kissing for now. When Ellie realized this, her how-far-will-we-go tension eased, and she just settled in to enjoy the experience. George's kisses were even better than his foot massage, which she didn't think was possible.

The bang of her door closing interrupted them, making them jerk apart. Both she and George were on their feet within half a second.

"Oops." Chelsea dumped her purse and coat on the small table by the door. "Am I interrupting?"

"Yeah." Ellie's voice was sharper than she'd intended, but her heart was still thundering. Everything scared her lately. The fact that she was multiple states away from the last known location of Anderson King didn't stop her from jumping out of her skin at every loud noise or sudden movement.

Chelsea looked unaffected by Ellie's snappy tone. "The sooner you find me a George of my own, the sooner I'll be too busy to bother the two of you. So you might want to get on that." She sauntered over to where they stood by the couch, elbowed her way between them, and plopped down on the center cushion. "Should we watch a movie?"

As she thought about murdering her smirking roommate, Ellie glanced at an impassive George. Now that Chelsea was there, things felt a little awkward.

"Actually, I'm kind of tired." Checking the clock, she was shocked to see it was after midnight. They really had been kissing for hours. "And you were driving all night, so you've been up for"—she tried and failed to do the mental math—"days! You must be exhausted."

George moved to grab his duffel bag from where he'd dropped it near the entry when they'd first arrived.

"You two are no fun at all," Chelsea said with a pout as she thumped the cushions on either side of her. Bouncing to her feet, she headed for her bedroom.

"Good thing I was just stopping by to change before going out again. Later, kids. Be safe."

After the tornado that was Chelsea disappeared, George turned toward the guest room. Although she'd already shown him where it was, Ellie still followed him the short distance. Despite her tiredness and her sudden onset of shyness, she didn't want to say good night and leave him just yet.

He dropped the duffel at the foot of the bed and looked over to where she was hovering in the doorway.

"The bathroom's through there." She pointed toward the closed door. "It's connected to my room, but I'll try to remember to knock instead of just barging in like I usually do. Thank goodness Chelsea has her own."

Instead of smiling at her joke, his stare increased in intensity, and she wondered if he was thinking about Ellie walking in while he was in the shower. That made *her* think about walking in while he was in the shower, which made her flush bright enough to spontaneously combust. What was it about George that reduced her to a stammering, blushing teenager?

"Um…okay." Ellie looked anywhere except at those hot eyes. "Good night, then. Feel free to wander around if you need anything from the…uh, kitchen or anything." Now she was thinking about him wandering into her room, and she needed to stop it.

"Good night," he said quietly. While she'd been carefully not looking at him, he'd moved close…very close. Her eyes widened as he bent and place a light kiss on her startled mouth. His lips were gone before she could kiss him back.

The backs of his fingers brushed her cheek, and she

turned her head to kiss them. The heat in his expression ratcheted up another notch, and he took her by the shoulders. To her disappointment, he turned her around. "Better go while I can still let you." His voice was low, his lips almost touching her ear. With a final squeeze of his hands, he gave her a gentle push and released her shoulders.

"Okay," she said without turning around. "Good night. Uh...I already said that. Sorry."

There was a chuckle behind her as she scampered to her door before anything else embarrassing could leave her mouth. Once in the safety of her bedroom, she closed her door and leaned against it, smiling. George was there, in her apartment, and they'd kissed...a lot.

Resisting the urge to squeal like an overexcited kid, she bit her lip and squeezed her hands together at her heart. It was too much to hold inside, though, and her feet did a mini Snoopy dance of happiness.

Chapter 26

HE WAS OVER HER, HOLDING HER DOWN, HIS FILMY
eyes staring at nothing and orange blood crusted on
his coat.

"El!"

George! That was George's voice. Wilson had gotten
to George, ambushed him in the pine trees, shot him
in the head like his brother had, but this time Wilson
had managed to move over the few inches required to
send the bullet into his brain. Now George was the one
with the milky eyes and faraway, empty gaze. Grief rose
in her chest but couldn't escape, building and building
until her misery erupted in a scream.

"El. El, wake up."

Reality returned like the snap of a rubber band, and
George's face—complete with no bullet hole or dead
eyes—came into focus. The lamp next to her bed was on,
casting a warm, golden light over his features and high-
lighting the worried creases between his brows. He was
leaning over her, his hands gripping her upper arms.

"George?" Her voice sounded rusty, and her throat hurt.

He released her slowly, as if he wasn't sure if she
was really awake yet. As soon as her arms were free,
she launched herself at him, wrapping her arms around
his neck. She pressed her face under his chin, reveling
in each sign of life—the warmth of his skin, the rise and
fall of his chest as he breathed, the strength in his arms

as he hugged her back. Ellie wasn't sure how much time passed before her terror faded and self-consciousness began to creep in.

"Sorry," she muttered, trying to put some space between them, but George seemed reluctant to loosen his grip. After a few halfhearted attempts at pulling away from him, she allowed herself to sink back against his chest. Once she relaxed, his hands started stroking her back.

"You were screaming." His voice was so deep that the words vibrated through her. It was oddly comforting to feel him talk.

"Sorry I woke you."

"I wasn't sleeping yet."

Turning her head to see the clock on the nightstand, Ellie was surprised to see it was just after one.

"Do you get nightmares a lot?" he asked, shifting so he could sit on her bed and pull her into his lap.

Despite her embarrassment at acting like a scared little kid, she couldn't bring herself to turn down the comfort he was offering. "Not really." She could almost feel the disbelieving glare he gave the top of her head. "Most of the time, I can't fall asleep, so...no bad dreams."

"That's not better," he grumbled.

The last terrifying seconds of her nightmare replayed in her head, and she shivered. "It kind of is."

"What was your dream about?"

"Wilson."

His hand stilled on her back. "Wilson King?" he asked, and she realized that she'd never told him the whole story of what had happened after George had left to get help.

"Yeah." It was a sigh more than a word. "They threw in the bomb they'd made out of the stove fuel, and we had to get out before it exploded. I came out shooting and killed Wilson."

"You saved yourself and your dad."

She knew that when she was awake. Her sleeping self didn't quite understand it, though. "His blood was orange the next morning."

"You did what needed to be done, El. I'm proud of you."

"Thanks." His praise didn't give her the usual inner glow. Instead, she just felt tired.

"Ready to go back to sleep?"

"Can you stay?" The words escaped without her permission, and a blush immediately followed. "Sorry. Forget I asked."

Instead of answering, he just pulled back the covers and maneuvered both of them until they were tucked into her bed. It was their usual cold-weather position, facing each other so she could hide her face in the crook between his jaw and collarbone. Although her apartment was heated to seventy toasty degrees, she still sighed with appreciation as she pressed her chilled body against his warm one.

"Good night again, George." Her words were slurred a little bit from exhaustion, and her lips were close enough that they brushed his skin as she spoke. Ellie felt him shiver and tuck her a little tighter against him. Her face found that perfect spot against his neck, and she relaxed for the first time in weeks. In just the short time she'd known him, George had become her safe place. With a contented sigh, she allowed herself to sleep, knowing that he'd keep the monsters at bay.

She didn't know who looked worse the next morning during their video chat—Ellie or her dad. She'd slept dreamlessly, but she'd woken late and had to rush to get ready. There'd been no time to put concealer over the dark circles under her eyes, and she'd roughly dragged her hair into a messy ponytail. Baxter's gaze was dull, and the skin on his face was loose, like putty.

"Hi, Dad." She blew him a kiss and then settled back in her chair at her kitchen table. George offered Baxter a nod of greeting from his spot beside her. "New meds?"

Her dad met her eyes slowly before nodding. Everything he did appeared to be in slow motion. "Don't like them. They make everything…wrong."

"I'll talk to your doctor, if you like," she offered. "See if she can adjust the dosage or try something else."

His shrug was slow and halfhearted, making Ellie decide to definitely talk to her dad's doctor about changing his meds. He was barely recognizable as himself.

"Is everything else okay?" she asked. "Do you need anything?"

He shook his head after a pause, his expression heartbreakingly flat. "I'm okay. You're a good girl, Eleanor."

"Thanks, Dad."

"You still have that compass I gave you?"

"Yes." She touched it where it rested low on her sternum. When she'd found it in her coat pocket a few days after her return to Chicago, she'd hung it on a chain and wore it around her neck. It was too big and plain to be a decorative piece of jewelry, but she liked to feel the solid weight of it against her chest.

"Good. Keep it close. Don't want you getting lost in the mountains."

"I will." Annoyingly, her eyes started to burn with approaching tears. She forced them back, blinking until the threat of uncontrollable bawling was reduced to manageable levels. Although he couldn't see her face from where he was standing, George must have heard something in her voice, because he squeezed her shoulder. That gesture of comfort made her eyes well up again.

"I'm not sure..." The words trailed away as Baxter stared in front of him, his focus not quite on the laptop screen. She wondered what horrific images were replaying in his brain. When he started talking again, she jumped, startled. He'd been quiet for so long, she'd thought he was done speaking. "I don't know what part of it was real and what I just imagined."

"Want me to tell you what I know is true?" Ellie offered, but he shook his head.

"I want..." His words came out so slowly that it was almost painful to listen. Ellie caught herself leaning toward the computer with her throat and jaw tight, as if she could help her dad shove the words out of his head. "I want to tell you, in case it's real."

"Sure, Dad." She wished she could reach through the screen and grab his hand, somehow help him through this fog that had him trapped. "What is it?"

"You need to know, but it might put you in danger." His head slowly turned until his cloudy gaze met hers from the screen. "If he thinks you know but you don't... that might be worse."

"Whatever it is, I want to hear it." Even if it involved dragons and flying werewolves, Ellie wanted to know.

It might make Baxter feel better to warn her about whatever danger it was, whether his brain had conjured it or if it were a true risk to her safety. The half-heard conversation between her dad and Anderson King flashed in her mind, and her heart rate picked up. Maybe he was finally going to tell her who killed Willard Gray.

"It was the fires, Eleanor."

She frowned, confused. "The explosion at the cabin?"

"No." His head wagged from side to side. "No. Not that fire. The others."

"Dad, I don't understand."

Before he could explain, he jerked his head to the side, his attention caught by something Ellie couldn't see. "You're having a busy day already, Mr. Price," an off-screen voice chirped. "There's a visitor to see you. It's Sheriff Coughlin."

Ellie slumped in her chair. Even though Rob couldn't have known he was interrupting, she wanted to kick him for his bad timing. What her dad had shared so far wasn't sounding like a real threat, but she still wanted to clarify what he was talking about—if clarification was even possible.

"Hi, Sheriff," she said, trying to keep the disappointment out of her voice. Rob leaned over next to Baxter so his face could be seen on Ellie's computer screen.

"Ellie. George."

George silently returned his nod of greeting.

"I was hoping to talk to you about what happened at the cabin," he said to Baxter, who didn't respond. He just stared into space again. The sheriff, looking puzzled, turned toward the screen, lifting his eyebrows in question.

Making a rueful face, Ellie shrugged. "His meds have him talking and moving at half speed, but you can give it a shot, if it's okay with you, Dad?" When her father didn't respond, she sighed and blew him another kiss. Baxter must have used all his words for the day on her. "I have to go now so I'm not late for work, but I'll call again tomorrow. You can tell me the rest then."

"Was he talking about that night at the cabin?" the sheriff asked.

"Not about that." She didn't want to tell anyone else what her dad had been saying. It seemed like a betrayal. If Baxter wanted to share that with the sheriff, then he could tell Rob himself. "See you tomorrow, Dad. Bye, Sheriff."

She hurried to disconnect before he could press her for more details. With a sigh, she leaned back in her seat before catching a glimpse of the clock on the microwave display.

"Shoot," she yelped, jumping out of her chair and rushing for the door. "I was hoping to clean up a little"—she gestured at the sad mess that was her hair and makeupless face—"but I'll be lucky to make it to the shop on time. I'll have to take the car instead of the L. Did you want to drive?" At his nod, she grabbed her keys out of her purse and tossed them to him. "I'll call Dr. Choudhry on the way. I didn't like seeing Dad like that."

His face grim, George nodded in agreement.

"Nice driving," Ellie said a little breathlessly. He was pulling the Prius into the parking lot with ten minutes to spare before the shop opened.

George grinned. "This car is fun. I can fit it into really small spaces."

"I noticed." Especially when he'd squeezed her car into the tiny spot between two semitrucks on the interstate. Her heart had almost stopped.

As she slipped around to the shop's side door, she saw there were a few people milling around the front, waiting for her to open.

"Want to stay for a little while?" she asked, unlocking the door and holding it so George could follow her into the shop. She quickly pressed the alarm code into the keypad next to the doorway, and the warning beep stopped with a satisfied chirp.

Although she'd expected it, her stomach went hollow when he shook his head. "You need to work."

"Okay." Aware that the few minutes she had before she had to let the waiting customers in were ticking away quickly, she grabbed his hand, turned it palm up, and dropped her apartment keys into it. "Have fun. After you pick up your truck, explore the city until all the people drive you crazy, and then go to the condo and make yourself at home. If Chelsea's still there, don't let her annoy you too much."

He smiled. "Okay." Leaning closer, he kissed her. It started light, his lips exploring hers tentatively, and then things got intense very fast. Apparently, he was a quick learner, judging by the way he took over the kiss. His hand cupped the back of her head, holding her close as his lips and tongue and teeth did magical, mind-stealing things to her. A lack of oxygen finally made her pull away so she could breathe. Ellie went in for another kiss, but he held her off, flicking his gaze toward the front of the store.

"Right," she groaned, not able to look away from his mouth. "Work."

His smile reappeared, broader this time, and he gave her a final, short kiss. He squeezed her hand and then slipped out of the side door, leaving her leaning against the wall.

"Bye," she said to the closed door. With a sigh, she pushed herself upright and headed to the front of the shop, flicking on lights as she went. Bracing herself for another busy sale day, she turned the lock on the front door.

Chapter 27

ELLIE STARED AT THE DOOR TO HER CONDO BUILDING, clutching her cell phone to her ear with numb fingers. She knew her mouth was hanging open, but she couldn't seem to activate the correct muscles she needed to close it. She'd been so excited, so happy to be done with work and about to see George again. When she finally was able to speak, all she could manage to get out was a faint, "He left?"

"Yes." The doctor's voice oozed sympathy.

"How could he leave?"

"Mr. Price was here voluntarily," Choudhry explained. "It was within his rights to leave at any time, since he isn't a danger to himself or others. I did encourage him to stay, since we were still working to find the right combination of medication and therapy."

"When did he leave?" *Why* did he leave? And how? On his current medication, Baxter hadn't seemed able to work up the motivation to leave his chair, much less the facility.

"Today around noon."

"Why didn't you call me?"

The doctor dialed up the sympathy in her tone another notch. "Your father authorized us to share the details of his care with you. You are not, however, his guardian. He is capable of making decisions on his own."

Not very good decisions, if choosing to check out of

Armstrong and wander the streets in his current zombie-like state was one. "Do you have his new contact information? Where's he planning on staying? Did he have any money when he left? His pack burned. Everything he owned was in there. How's he going to live?" Her voice was getting higher and higher, and a person passing her on the sidewalk gave her a wary look and increased his pace.

"Deep breaths," Dr. Choudhry urged. "Long breath in, hold it, and long breath out."

Until the doctor talked her through it, Ellie hadn't realized how close she was to hyperventilating. "Sorry," she said once she'd gotten her breathing under control again. "I'm just really worried about him."

"I know." The doctor's sigh was audible. "I know."

Long after the doctor ended the call, Ellie continued to stare blindly at her building, useless phone in her hand. It wasn't until the door swung open, revealing a worried-looking George, that her paralysis broke.

"What's wro—?" Before he could even finish the question, she hurled herself at him, wrapping her arms around his reassuring bulk and pressing her forehead to his chest as she burst into tears.

"He left!" She wasn't sure how coherent she was, since she was crying so hard, but she kept babbling anyway. "He checked himself out of Armstrong today. I don't know where he went, or where he's staying, or if he has any money, or if he's okay, and he was on that awful medication, and how am I supposed to keep my promise to always have his back if I don't know where he is?" She ended on a wail that should've made her cringe in embarrassment, but she was too consumed by her worry to care.

"El." Just that one word in his calm, even tone brought her semi-hysterics down to sniffles and the occasional hiccuping inhale. "How long has your dad been like this?"

It took a moment for his question to penetrate, but George waited patiently for her to answer, his big hands stroking her back. "Mentally ill, you mean?" Her words were punctuated by a hiccup. "All my life. I th-think Mom said he first started showing symptoms in his midtwenties."

"How old is he?"

"Sixty-three." Even though she wasn't sure where George was going with it, the exchange was calming her. Having him hold her, the bass rumble of his voice vibrating against her cheek, was even more soothing.

"So he's lived almost forty years with this."

"Yes." Another hiccup turned the word into two syllables.

"And he survived all that time."

Now she knew where George was headed. "Yes."

"Why do you think he won't be able to manage now?"

"Someone really is after him," she argued. "Anderson King is still out there."

"Even if he managed to get out of Blue Hook alive, how would he be able to locate Baxter? You're his daughter, and you don't know where he's headed. A small-town drug dealer running from the cops isn't going to be able to track him."

The sense of what he was saying allowed relief to flow through her in a warm rush. "You're right." Taking in a deep breath, she released it in a shuddering exhale. "Thank you."

"He'll be okay, El."

"Yeah." She was starting to believe it.

"Want to go up to your condo?"

Pulling back, she glanced at the entry of her building, blinking. The news about Baxter, and then George's embrace, had made her forget where she was. She wondered how many of her neighbors witnessed her breakdown. "Good idea."

George kept an arm around her shoulders as they started to climb the first flight of stairs. It was hard not to sink against him, to let him carry her weight. They'd passed the door to the second level when she realized something.

"We could've taken the elevator," she said, continuing to climb stairs.

His expression was close to the one he wore when he talked about hating to fly, but he only grunted.

Her small smile disappeared quickly. "Do you think he went back to Simpson?"

"Maybe."

She sighed, her breath uneven. "I don't know where else to start looking for him."

His hand squeezed her shoulder. A thought occurred to her, and she fumbled for her purse as she stopped abruptly. Digging through the contents, she pulled out the card she needed. Her fingers were shaking, making it hard to tap the right numbers, but she finally managed to send the call.

"Coughlin."

"Sheriff." Her voice still sounded quivery from exertion and emotion. "This is Ellie Price."

"Ellie. How are you?"

"Not good." The tears were back, lurking just

behind her eyes, and she squeezed the bridge of her nose tightly to stave them off. "Dad checked himself out of Armstrong."

There was a short silence. "I'm sorry to hear that."

"Thanks. Did he say anything about leaving when you talked with him this morning? Maybe mention where he planned to stay or where he was going to go?"

"No." The single word crushed the tiny hope that had blossomed. "He didn't say anything to me."

"Did he tell you why he planned to leave?"

"You misunderstood me," Coughlin gently explained. "When I said he didn't say anything, I meant that he didn't talk to me at all. He wouldn't even make eye contact."

"But why...?" Ellie let her words trail away. She could ask *why* all she wanted, but the only person who could tell her the answer was Baxter, and she didn't know where to find him. "Could you let me know if he contacts you? Or if he returns to Simpson?"

"Of course. I'll call if I hear anything."

"Thank you, Sheriff." She needed to get off the phone before she cried again.

"Call me Rob. I hope you find him soon."

"Me too."

George looked at her as she dropped the card and her phone back in her purse. She gave a tight shake of her head. With a silent sigh, he gave her a squeeze and a kiss on the head before they started climbing stairs again.

"George?" she asked in a small voice. "I know you just drove a really long time to get here, but would you mind if we went back to Simpson? I need to look for my dad."

"Okay. Tonight?"

Relief surged through her at his easy acceptance, and she gave him a sideways hug, so glad that she wasn't alone in this. "Would that be okay?" It probably made more sense to wait until the following morning to leave, but she knew she wouldn't sleep anyway.

"Yes."

Gratitude warmed her from her toes to her ears, and she gave him another squeeze. Although anxiety still churned inside her, it would've been a thousand times worse without George. His steady, strong presence made her feel like anything was possible. They'd drive to Simpson, find Baxter, and everything would be okay. George would make sure of it.

Chapter 28

AS ELLIE CLIMBED OUT OF GEORGE'S PICKUP, careful to keep hold of the door as her feet contacted the ice covering The Coffee Spot's parking lot, a rush of déjà vu hit her. It had been just weeks since she'd first arrived in Colorado, but it felt like years had passed. Instead of being a strange and foreign place, Simpson felt almost like home. The only shadows hanging over her return were her anxiety over Baxter and the creeping knowledge that Anderson King could be lurking close by, watching her, wanting revenge for what she'd done to his brother.

Once she knew her feet were stable, she glanced over at George, who was circling the front of the truck. The closer they'd gotten to the mountains, the more he'd relaxed. It made her realize how tensely he'd held himself in Chicago, how out of place he'd seemed in the urban setting. He'd done that—put aside his dislike of the city—in order to be close to her. Her smile warmed another few degrees as she watched him stride closer.

Ellie was so wrapped up in her thoughts that she didn't realize what he intended until she was several feet off the ground.

"George!" she cried, laughing and clutching his shoulders. "What are you doing?"

"Don't want you falling," he rumbled, but the corners of his mouth were twitching. Ellie was pretty sure he was just using the excuse to carry her.

"I have on my very practical boots." She tried to sound firm, although she was pretty sure she failed.

In front of the coffee shop door, he slowly lowered her until she was standing, his warm brown eyes fixed on her face the entire time.

"Thank you, sweetie," she said, unable to hold back a smile. "But you don't need to carry me everywhere."

He stroked her cheek with the backs of his fingers, his gaze heating from warm to blazing. Ellie was pretty sure he'd only heard the first part of her sentence, but she couldn't bring herself to care—not when George was staring at her like that.

"Coffee?" she finally said, her voice rough from both emotion and a lack of sleep. She'd dozed a little in the truck when she hadn't been driving, but her limited sleep had been interrupted by nightmarish images of Anderson, Wilson, and her father.

Leaning down, George pressed a kiss to her forehead before pulling open the shop door. As Ellie ducked into The Coffee Spot, a loud *bang* echoed through the small building. She froze as her brain flipped through a vivid set of flashcard images—George lying unmoving in the snow, Wilson's staring eyes, the gun jumping in her hands as she fired at Anderson.

Warmth at her back and whispered words in her ear returned her to reality with a snap. George, his forearm wrapped around her upper chest, was responsible for both the warmth and the whispers.

"You're okay, El," he was saying, tightening his arm around her to bring her more firmly against him. "I've got you. You're safe."

"Sorry." Her voice was froggy, so she cleared her

throat and tried again. "Sorry." Glancing around, she saw Lou latching the window behind the counter—the source of the loud noise, Ellie guessed. The other patrons in the shop, though, were all looking at her. "Did I do anything embarrassing?"

"No." Keeping his voice low, George continued to murmur directly into her ear. "You just…froze for a minute."

At second glance, the other customers' faces were filled with interest and friendly curiosity, rather than the horrified, prurient, train-wreck staring she'd expected. Ellie relaxed against George. "Thanks."

Kissing her temple, he retreated, drawing away from her carefully. He stayed close, apparently intending to catch her if necessary.

"Hey, Lou," she called, forcing relaxed confidence into her voice. She wasn't sure how well she succeeded. "How's it going?"

Rushing around the counter, Lou barreled across the shop to throw her arms around Ellie. "Absolutely fabulous now that you're here!" Lou squeezed her hard and then backed up so she could look at Ellie. "Do you *know* what kind of crazy rumors are circulating? You will be telling me every single detail, including how you got the love child of Grizzly Adams and Pa Ingalls to get a cell phone. Impressive, El. Very impressive."

Even without looking behind her, Ellie knew George would be blushing under his beard, so she steered Lou back to the counter. George followed, staying close but silent. "You've heard about Baxter, then?"

"No." Lou took the redirection without offense, returning to her post and reaching for a cup. "Obviously, the fire guys are getting lax with the gossip. Is something wrong with your dad? Latte?"

"Please on the latte. And I'm not sure about Dad. He checked himself out of Armstrong, and I haven't heard anything since."

"I'm sorry, El. I thought he was doing better." Lou kept talking, even as she steamed milk. "Do you think he's come back to Simpson?"

"Maybe." In her exhausted state, Ellie couldn't hold back the rush of frustration and anxiety that flooded through her. "I'm not sure. This was the only place I could think to start looking."

Sometime during the last exchange, George had moved even closer to Ellie until he was pressed against the back of her stool with his palms resting on her shoulders. She reached up to grab one of his hands.

Lou paused in the middle of putting a lid on Ellie's coffee. "At the risk of being condescending, I have to say that you two are the cutest thing ever."

With a soundless sigh and a squeeze of Ellie's shoulders, George pulled away and headed toward the bathroom.

"So, tell me how it happened?" Lou leaned closer to Ellie as she handed over the latte, her eyes lighting with gossipy glee. "When I last saw you two together, he'd barely agreed to guide you. Next thing I know, he's sitting in The Coffee Spot for *hours*, scowling at me like I killed his kitten. He didn't order coffee or anything. I kept asking what he needed, and he kept grunting at me with that angry frown. I was about to call Callum to see if he could do some man grunt translating for me when George Holloway actually spoke to me. In words."

Ellie was fascinated. "What'd he say?"

"'What's her number?' That's what he said. I just stared at him—partly because I was in shock that George Holloway actually spoke to me and partly because I had no idea what he was talking about. He glowered at me like I was an idiot until I finally asked whose number he wanted. Then he turned all sorts of red…"

With a sigh, Ellie asked, "Isn't he cute when he blushes?"

Lou snorted, quickly turning the sound into a cough. "Right. Sure. Adorable. Anyway, he mumbles, 'El.' And I repeat, '*L*'? I was trying to think of people whose names started with the letter *L* when it finally struck me—Ellie! He wants Ellie's number. And then I thought, 'Holy moly, he wants a woman's number, and that woman is Ellie! The guys at Station One are going to flip when I tell them.'"

Ellie blinked.

Without giving her a chance to respond, Lou jumped back into her story. "So I pull up your number on my phone and give it to him. He's getting up to leave when I tell him to sit his taciturn rump down, because a phone number is pretty much useless when he doesn't have a phone, and he pulls out this prepaid one that's still in its packaging. I start imagining how the conversation will go, where he calls you, and you answer, and he's silent except for breathing and a few grunts, and you think you have some creeper on the line, hang up on him, and he crushes the phone in his huge, heartbroken hand and never leaves his cabin again."

Ellie blinked again.

"I know," Lou said, as if Ellie had uttered something. "So that's when I called you and very sneakily got you to tell me where you worked and when your next shift was. I looked up the shop's website to get an address, printed out some maps and directions for the big guy, and sent him to claim his true wuv."

"True *what*?"

Lou frowned at her. "Haven't you seen *The Princess Bride*?" When Ellie looked blank, Lou shook her head. "For shame. You need to watch it." Her scowl flipped over to a grin. "With George."

"Um…okay?"

"So what does he talk about?"

Ellie shrugged. "Um…normal stuff, I guess?"

"Oh." Lou made a disappointed face. "I figured that once George started talking, it'd be about something momentous, like the secrets of the universe or something."

Ellie laughed. "Nope. Not yet, anyway."

"Huh." Lou glanced over Ellie's shoulder. "Bearded one incoming. Tell me what's going on with your dad."

Ellie's anxiety, which had been dulled by exhaustion and too many hours of driving, returned with a vengeance. By the time she'd given Lou the basic facts about Baxter's disappearance, she was fidgeting on her stool. Even George's steadying hand on her shoulder couldn't keep her still.

"Can we go check Willard's old cabin?" she asked George, who grimaced slightly.

Lou's expression echoed his. "Do you think he'd have gone back there? It's the first place everyone will look for him, so not the stealthiest move on Baxter's part."

"I know." Not able to sit any longer, Ellie slid off her stool. "I just need to do *something*. And it's possible he could've returned. Who knows how Dad's mind works?" Even as she said the words, she could hear the doubt in her own voice. Her shoulders folded forward as helplessness overwhelmed her.

George gently squeezed the back of her neck. "We'll go now."

"To Willard's cabin?" Surprised, she looked over her shoulder at him. At the affirmative dip of his chin, Ellie turned and gave him a grateful hug. After freezing for a moment, he awkwardly patted her back. "Thank you, George. I know it's a wild-goose chase, but I need to see for myself that he's not there."

"Hey," Lou protested in a mock offended tone. "He's not the only one chasing geese with you."

Without leaving George's embrace, Ellie turned her head so she could smile at the other woman. "I know. Thank you, too."

Lou's pretend scowl dropped away. "Everyone—the divers, the fire department, search and rescue—will do their best to find your dad, El. I'm going to get the firemen to spread the word to keep an eye out for any sign of Baxter. It'll be good for them to use their gossip powers productively, for once."

Ellie turned, keeping her back resting against George's chest. It made her feel stronger to have him so close. "Just tell them not to approach him. Deputy Jennings tried to talk to him, and Dad took off. Have them keep their distance and call me if they see him."

"Right—I forgot about that." Lou's forehead wrinkled in a frown. "If Baxter ran from Chris, he'll run from anyone. Chris is a sweetheart. I'll pass it on."

"Thanks, Lou." With a final, grateful smile, Ellie headed for the door.

As they drove through the Esko Hills neighborhood, George shot a frowning glance at her.

"What?" she asked. Although she was getting pretty good at interpreting George's expressions, the meaning of this one was eluding her.

"Are you…" His voice came out even deeper and scratchier than usual. He cleared his throat. "Are you staying at my house tonight?" The last five words came out in a rushed jumble, so it took Ellie a few moments to figure out what he'd said. His frown deepened.

"Oh!" she exclaimed as she finally figured out the question. "Yes. I mean, if that's okay? I could get a room at the Black Bear Inn again, if you'd rather I do that?" The tentative cast to her words made her scrunch her nose. Where was all her confidence?

"No!" It was George's turn to wince when the word came out loudly enough to make her jump. "Staying with me is…good." Red flushed his skin above his beard.

Her uncertainty faded as she laid her cheek against the seat and eyed his profile. He really was so cute when he blushed.

The sideways look he gave her as he stopped the truck was adorable, too. She smiled, making his cheekbones redden even more. George tipped his head toward the windshield. With a jolt, Ellie realized they were parked outside the cabin. Shaking herself out of her giddy haze, she reached for her door handle. Before she could fully open her door, George was there to help her out of the truck.

"Thank you," she said absently, her eyes on the cabin. Even without going inside, she knew in her gut that it was still empty. It appeared even more forlorn than it had the first time she'd visited it with Callum. "He's not there." Her voice was flat. Although she'd known it was a long shot, the empty cabin hit her hard. It was her only possible lead in her search for Baxter.

George just gave a "maybe" shrug and started toward the derelict building. He checked out the unmarred drifts of snow in front of the structure before indicating she should stand to the side of the door. With his body between hers and the entrance, he reached for the knob. The door opened easily. Ellie peeked around his large form and saw the same empty interior as before. Despite her earlier certainty, disappointment flooded through her at the confirmation.

"Stay," George rumbled before disappearing into the cabin.

"I'm not a dog," she called after him, although she didn't move from her spot. She glanced around the surrounding trees, struck by the eerie silence. They were so close to the upscale neighborhood, but Ellie suddenly felt isolated and exposed. The cabin would be the first place Anderson King would look for Baxter…or for her. She shivered, shoving her gloved hands into her coat pockets as her gaze darted from tree to tree. The evergreens provided so many possible hiding spots, and the branches moved constantly, potentially hiding anything—or anyone—lurking in the forest. Goose bumps prickled along her spine as she stared harder at an especially ominous shadow. She knew it was her imagination, but Ellie suddenly felt the burn of malicious, watching eyes.

Fingers closed around her arm, making her jump. George looked at her questioningly, but she waved off her paranoia, even as a voice in her head whispered *like father, like daughter*.

"Anything?" she asked, her voice too bright.

A short shake of his head confirmed what she'd already known—Baxter hadn't been there.

"Oh well," she sighed, trying to force a smile. "It was a long shot. What's next?"

He eyed her closely, as if judging her reaction to the news, before reaching for her hand. Startled, she stared at their linked fingers for too long and was almost yanked off her feet when George started for the truck.

Scrambling to catch up with him, she asked again, "Where to now?"

"My house," he said. "Need to start a fire so it's warm for you." George opened the passenger door of his truck, sending her another of his bashful looks that made her heart squeeze. She guessed it was because she'd be staying at his house that night, and then she was blushing, too.

As he rounded the hood of the truck, Ellie gave the cabin a final glance and huddled deeper in her seat, drawing her coat more tightly around her.

George left Esko Hills and turned onto the main road through town. When Ellie saw the Screaming Moose sign, she sat straighter. "Stop!" He braked abruptly, giving her a startled look.

"Sorry." She waved her hands as if to erase her earlier exclamation. "I saw the store, and it reminded me that I need more Simpson-friendly clothes. Mind if we shop before doing house stuff?"

His pathetic attempt to cover his pained expression made her laugh.

"Never mind. How about you drop me off here, and then you can do the fire building without me getting in the way?"

Just the thought of some retail therapy unknotted her shoulders a little. Worry about her father and Anderson King had consumed her thoughts for days, and shopping would allow her to put those worries aside for a short time.

Although he seemed hesitant to let her out of his sight, he pulled up closer to the store entrance before jogging to the passenger side of the truck to get her door.

"Thank you." When she smiled up at him, he went still, his gaze jumping from her mouth to her eyes and back. Ellie leaned closer, ready to be kissed, when a truck passed them, reminding her of their very public location. With a wry grin, she headed to the store entrance, giving George a final look and wave over her shoulder.

As soon as Ellie stepped into the warmth of the Screaming Moose, she relaxed. The store had such a welcoming feel, despite the fact that it made her fingers itch to rearrange the crowded, poorly placed racks.

"Ellie!" The owner, Barbara, greeted her with a smile as she crossed the store. "I heard you were back in town. Any luck locating your dad?"

Fighting down a surge of worry even as she marveled at the efficiency of Simpson's gossip pipeline, Ellie tried to dredge up a return smile. "Not yet."

"Sorry to hear that."

There was a slightly awkward pause before Ellie explained, "I'm probably going to be here at least another few days, so I need a few more warm layers."

"We definitely have those." Her mouth turned down

at the corners for a moment before Barbara's professional mien returned. "Did you want help finding something, or would you rather browse?"

"I'll just browse, thank you." Ellie's smile was more authentic that time. "You've already given me a crash course in layering, so it should be safe to let me out on my own."

"Just give a shout if you need anything." Gesturing toward her raised desk in the corner of the shop, Barbara gave an exaggerated sigh. "I'm paying invoices, so I'd love to be interrupted."

"I'll do my best to interrupt, then."

As Barbara retreated, Ellie started looking through the racks. Automatically, she began sorting by size and style, thinning the overcrowded display by moving out-of-season items to another, emptier rack nearby.

"Are you trying to get hired?" Barbara asked, startling Ellie. "Because I'll do it."

Ellie looked at her absentminded organization and flushed. "I'm so sorry. I didn't even realize what I was doing. I work at a boutique in Chicago, so it's second nature."

"Don't apologize." Putting down the paper in her hand, Barbara crossed the store again and examined the newly sorted display. "It looks great. I'm so busy with the paperwork part of this that I just toss everything on a rack and hope it sells." She reached over and played with the sleeve of a flannel shirt. "To be honest, I've lost a lot of my enthusiasm for this place lately. It's beautiful here, and I love Simpson, but it's always so cold. And the snow. There's so much snow. It never stops. Sometimes it snows in *June*. Then there's trying to make purchasing decisions. The tourists want one thing, and the locals want another, so I try to make everyone happy and end up with this inventory mishmash. Plus, everything here is so much *work*. Just running to the grocery store is an exercise in winter survival. Sometimes, I want to escape to Florida, get a job at a mall, and rent an apartment, you know what I mean?"

Holding a hoodie in front of her like a shield, Ellie just blinked at Barbara. She hadn't been expecting that desperate outpouring, and she wasn't sure how to respond. "Well, I haven't been here long…" Ellie started slowly, trailing off when the other woman waved a brisk hand.

"Don't mind me," Barbara said. "That's been building up for a while, and you were the unlucky one here at exactly the wrong time. Tell me, what else would you change?"

After eyeing Barbara to see if she was going to go off on another rant, Ellie tentatively suggested, "I'd probably move these racks farther apart to create a path through here." When Barbara looked interested and there was no sign of another oncoming monologue, Ellie continued with more enthusiasm. "These cashmere sweaters are beautiful, but they're buried over here where people can't see them. I'd put shelves on that wall by the door so that they'd be the first thing customers saw when they came in. Also, the window display…" Ellie paused as she tried to think of a tactful description.

"Horrid, isn't it?"

With a startled giggle, Ellie stopped trying to be tactful. "Maybe a little. And it's actually *dusty*! How long has it been since it's been changed?"

"An embarrassingly long time," Barbara said frankly. "Hang on for a second while I grab some paper and a pen. I'm going to need to take notes."

By the time George arrived, Ellie was positively bouncing as ideas flowed into her brain faster than she could articulate them.

"George!" she called when she saw him hovering just inside the door. As she hurried toward him, she said to Barbara over her shoulder, "Husband chairs! We need husband chairs!"

His eyebrows rose to the bottom of his stocking hat. Ellie beamed at him, overflowing with excitement. She might not know how to find her dad, but she knew how to fix the Screaming Moose. Although it was only a temporary break in her worry, this distraction was just what she needed. "Hi. How'd everything go at the house?"

One shoulder raised in a shrug that Ellie translated as "okay," and she resisted the urge to hug him, loving his wordless gestures because they were so very, very *George*.

"Barbara asked for suggestions to improve the store," she explained, and his mouth tipped up in a small smile.

He looked at Barbara. "Thank you."

From her shocked look, Barbara hadn't expected to hear George speak. "Oh. Um, I should be thanking Ellie. She's really good at this."

Unable to hold back her grin, Ellie turned toward the shop owner. "Thanks. This has been so much fun. Would you mind if I came back another day?"

"Not at all." Barbara looked around the store. "In fact, I'd welcome the help. We still need to tackle the window display."

At the reminder, Ellie had to hold back a hop of

excitement. "Yes! I can't wait. I'm not sure what my schedule will be like while I'm here, though." At the reminder of her father, her excitement faded. Her work at the store had kept thoughts of Baxter at bay, but now all her worries returned in a rush, deflating her like a popped balloon.

"Whenever you can make it would be fine," Barbara assured her. "I have plenty on my plate, so all of this"—she waved the notebook containing pages of scribbled ideas—"won't get done today…or in the next few days, even."

"Okay. I'll be in when I can." With a final smile and wave, she slipped out the door as George held it for her.

They walked in silence for a few steps before George spoke. "It looked better—what you did in there, I mean."

"Thanks." She beamed at him as her enthusiasm resurged, but then she immediately felt guilty. "For a while, when I was working on the shop, I forgot about my dad. Do you think that makes me a terrible person?"

"No." His response was immediate. "I think he wants you to be happy."

"Thanks, George." Overwhelmed by a surge of affection, she swiveled toward him and caught his arm. Standing on her tiptoes, she tugged until he was tipped sideways enough that she could kiss his cheek—a cheek that reddened as she released him.

They were both quiet as they walked to the truck, but it was a happy silence.

Chapter 29

IF ELLIE THOUGHT THE STARING EYES AT The Coffee Spot had been bad, they were nothing compared to the crowd at Levi's.

As soon as they entered, the packed restaurant went silent, and all heads swiveled to stare at them.

Under the scrutiny of what felt like a hundred pairs of eyes, Ellie stopped abruptly. George bumped into her back and then caught her upper arms, steading her before she could stumble forward. Everyone's gazes moved to fix on George's fingers.

"Ellie!" Joseph stood and beckoned. "Come on over."

As much as Ellie *really* didn't want to spend time with Joseph, there were no open tables, so the alternative would be to keep standing by the door, the object of everyone's stare. There were also quite a few other—hopefully less unsettling—people at the table who should be able to act as buffers between her and Joseph.

Darting a glance at George, she mouthed, "Okay?" and he nodded, so Ellie walked over to where Joseph was pulling up additional chairs to the already-crowded table. She unzipped her coat and felt George slide it off her arms. Looking over her shoulder to thank him, she saw he'd already turned away, heading toward the coat rack just inside the entrance.

"Glad to see you made it back okay," a woman with

gray-streaked brown hair and a ruddy complexion said with a friendly smile. "I'm Janelle."

"Ellie." She smiled back, shaking the woman's proffered hand. "And I'm glad, too. That we made it out okay, I mean."

Janelle laughed. "I bet."

With a mental apology to George, she settled into the chair not next to Joseph. George, once he returned from hanging up their coats, squeezed in between Ellie and Joseph without a peep of complaint, even though it was quite a feat for him to fit his oversized body into the small space remaining. Ellie tried to shift her chair closer to Janelle to give him more room.

"George!" Janelle said, reaching around Ellie to give him a welcoming slap on the shoulder. "Finally decided to join us for something other than calls and practices, huh?"

He grunted in response.

"I'm Cora." The dark-haired woman next to Janelle leaned forward, running her eyes over Ellie in that objectively assessing way that she recognized from the EMTs in the helicopter and the medical staff at the hospital. "Any aftereffects from being caught in that avalanche?"

Ellie shook her head. "I was lucky. George said it was just a small slide." She didn't mention the nightmares about those interminable minutes before George had dug her out.

"Small or not, that had to have been traumatic." Janelle made a face. "I'm claustrophobic, and just the thought of being trapped under several feet of snow…" She shuddered.

Their names were ringing a bell of familiarity, and

she finally remembered where she'd heard them before. "Cora and Janelle! You two were the ones talking about foot massages."

The two women exchanged a glance as George cleared his throat uncomfortably.

"Uh...not recently," Cora said.

Ellie blushed. "No, sorry! It was when one of you was pregnant. George had just mentioned..." She couldn't figure out how to finish her thought without revealing *way* too much personal information about both her and George. She'd just been so happy to change the subject from the avalanche that she hadn't thought ahead. "Um, we were talking about foot rubs, and he said he'd over-heard the two of you talking about them, and so when I heard your names, that's what came to mind. Sorry, that just made no sense. I'm reinstalling my brain-to-mouth filter now. So, you're both in search and rescue?"

Both of the women blinked while George made a quiet choking sound. Cora opened her mouth and then closed it again.

"I'm Reuben," the man sitting next to Joseph inter-jected, and she gave him a wave.

"Ellie."

The rest of the people at the table went around and said their names, and Ellie smiled politely, knowing it would take a while to keep the ten or so people straight. After Frank, Cora's husband, introduced himself, the table grew quiet for a few seconds.

"So," Reuben asked with a fake casualness that had everyone leaning forward as if they knew what was coming next, "you and Holloway, huh?"

Her face instantly went red-hot, and her gaze shot

to George. He was eyeing the ceiling, possibly praying for an immediate exit out of this uncomfortable conversation. "Um…yes?" Reuben's question had been open to interpretation, but she was pretty sure that she and George were a…something. So what if there were a thousand miles between their hometowns? The incredible way she felt when she looked at George, the way her heart ached with a surplus of happiness when he smiled back at her, turned that distance into a minor, surmountable problem. Whatever she had to do to keep George, she would do it.

"'Bout time." Frank sat back, a grin on his broad face. "Didn't think George would ever get any."

"Franklin!" Cora sent an elbow into his side.

"What?" He gave his wife an injured look as he rubbed the spot where she'd connected. "I'm just saying he never seems to notice the way women are around him. That hot lady hiker a couple of weeks ago did everything short of stripping off her clothes to get his attention, and Holloway never even looked at her. All the other guys were staring at her with their tongues hanging out— except for me, of course." He glanced nervously at his wife. "But George just packed up his gear and left."

Joseph smiled reminiscently. "I remember her. That chick was *stacked*."

One of the other men laughed. "Yeah, that's right. Joseph was chasing after her like a horny puppy trying to hump her leg, but she only had eyes for George."

Glancing at Joseph, Ellie saw him clench his jaw so tightly that a line of white ran along it. When he noticed her watching, he smoothed his expression and gave her a smile that didn't reach his eyes.

"It's just not healthy, spending all that time alone in that cabin of yours." Despite his wife's pointy-looking elbow, Frank apparently wasn't done talking. Personally, Ellie was glad for the distraction. "I know you have a working right hand, but that's not the same as—ow! What'd I say now, Cora?"

Everyone around the table except for Ellie and George was snickering.

"If you want to get rid of the blow-up doll you have stashed under your bed, I'll take her off your hands," Reuben offered.

Ellie glanced at George's profile. Without looking at her, he shook his head, and her shoulders relaxed in relief. If he'd really had a blow-up doll stashed in the cabin, then that would've just been…yuck. She might have been rooming at the Black Bear Inn again.

One of the other guys stared at Reuben in disgust. "Why would you want a used blow-up doll? That's just nasty."

Reuben shrugged. "That's what Windex is for."

"No, Rube. No." The man shook his head. "That is not what Windex is for."

To Ellie's relief, the food arrived for everyone except the two newcomers, distracting them from George's hypothetical sex toys. Ellie ordered ribs, then turned to George, who was still scowling at the laminated sheet in front of him. Tucking one knee underneath her so she could reach his ear, she whispered, "Why so grim? No bunny on the menu?"

A reluctant smile curved his lips as he poked her in the ribs. It was gentle enough to tickle rather than hurt, and she twisted away, giggling.

"Is Holloway *smiling*?" one of the guys asked, bringing everyone's attention away from their food and back to the pair of them. Ellie's blush, which had just started to fade, returned in a hot rush.

"Nah." Reuben shoved a forkful of barbecued pork in his mouth. "Probably just gas."

George insisted on Ellie waiting in the warmth of the restaurant while he went to get the truck that was parked several blocks away. Since she was too tired to argue, and doing things like that seemed to make George happy, Ellie agreed. Exhaustion hit her as she waited, and she leaned against the wall by the door.

"You're Ellie Price?"

The question startled her. She turned to see a small, brown-haired woman with delicate features and huge eyes. She wasn't smiling.

"Yes," Ellie said, a little intimidated by the woman's serious expression. "Have we met?"

"No. The guys from Fire"—she jerked her head toward a group of men packed into one of the booths—"talk. You're Baxter Price's daughter?"

The mention of her father flustered Ellie, and it was a second before she answered. "Yes. He's my dad. Who are you?"

"Rory Sorenson. He okay?"

Ellie wished she knew. "I hope so. He's taken off again."

"Sorry." Although Rory's tone was flat, her mouth tightened in a grimace that made her sympathy seem sincere. "He stopped by my gun shop a few weeks ago."

She could feel her eyes widen. "Gun shop?"

With a short nod, Rory said, "He seemed...upset."

"Did he say anything?" The familiar feeling of desperation, of trying to puzzle out his thought patterns in order to understand him and find him, filled her.

"No. Well, yes, but nothing—"

"Nothing that made sense?" Ellie finished for her. "Dad was pretty bad then. He was doing better at the hospital, but he checked himself out yesterday." Her gut clenched in reaction to the words. It made it worse to hear them out loud. "I don't know where to even begin looking for him."

Reaching out, Rory gave her upper arm a quick, awkward pat. "Sorry."

"Thanks."

They stood in silence until it started to get weird. Ellie was trying to think of an excuse to leave the uncomfortable stare-off when Rory asked, "You and George?"

It seemed to be the question of the evening. "Yes."

Rory looked at her for another long minute as Ellie tried to control her nervous fidgeting. Her fingers wanted to climb toward her mouth, of course, but Ellie yanked them down and held them tightly at her waist.

"Good." With a strangely meaningful nod, like they were soldiers in battle together or something, Rory turned and walked away. Ellie watched, a little bemused, as the other woman joined the booth of firemen. An almost-too-beautiful-to-be-real man wrapped an arm around her shoulders, leaning in and saying something in her ear that made her smile at him. It was startling the way happiness transformed her face before disappearing as quickly as it had come.

Realizing she was staring at the couple, she turned

and jumped. George was right behind her. Ellie resisted the urge to hug him. It had only been a couple of minutes, and they'd been separated by only a few blocks. It wasn't like he'd been lost at sea for years.

Then he smiled at her, and all her logic went out the window. Sliding her arms around his waist, she gave him a squeeze. "Got the truck?" she asked.

He grunted affirmatively as he hugged her back, the motion slightly stiff and awkward, as if he were exercising muscles that he hadn't used in a while. Her head rested against his chest, and her tired eyes drooped. She felt like she could sleep for a week. Reluctantly, she stepped back again.

"Ready to go home?" she asked.

He smiled a broad, true smile. "Yes."

Staring at him, she basked in George's warm and gentle attention. "Me too."

***

They didn't know. If they'd known he was there, they wouldn't be looking all happy and lovey-dovey. Their obvious joy burned like salt on the wound of his brother's absence. Anderson felt raw inside, as if everything had been torn out, leaving him hollow. Wilson was gone, and the bitch who'd done it was giggling and chatting with that useless dumbass. If Holloway was such a wonderful tracker, he wouldn't have let Anderson get so close.

The passenger door closed once the murdering bitch was inside. Holloway's boots crunched on the snow as he circled the hood, and Anderson was tempted—so tempted. He could do it. All he'd need to do was slide up behind Holloway without the big guy seeing him and slit his throat. Easy-peasy.

Once that dick was bleeding out, Anderson would get in the truck and drive the city bitch somewhere remote. Out here, it wasn't hard to find a place where someone could scream and scream without anyone else hearing. When he was done making her pay for Wilson's death, he'd slip the knife between her ribs. Then, the screaming would stop.

The urge was so strong, the scene so vivid in his head, that he took a silent step out of the shadows. Just a few more feet to Holloway's truck, and the so-called tracker would be dead, and Wilson's killer would be at his mercy—or his lack of mercy.

George's footsteps grew louder, closer to Anderson's watch point. Fishing his knife out of his pocket, Anderson smiled.

"George!" The sheriff stepped under the streetlight so he was illuminated as clearly as if he were an actor under a spotlight. "Heading home?"

Disappointment flooded Anderson, so thick he could taste the bitter residue. Dropping the knife back in his pocket, he shifted back into the shadows.

"Later," he mouthed silently.

Chapter 30

ALL EVENING, ELLIE HAD WANTED TO BE ALONE WITH George. Now that they were finally in his house with no one else around, she felt anxious. Standing awkwardly in the entryway, she stepped out of her boots and unzipped her coat with more focus than the actions required.

"Thanks for being so patient today," she said to break the silence. When he shrugged off her thanks as he removed his jacket, she continued. "Really. You went above and beyond. I mean, the coffee shop *and* Levi's? That's heroic."

He smiled, reaching to help her slip out of her coat. "I like being with you."

"I like being with you, too." She winced slightly. The words were so inadequate to express how she really felt. "I mean, I *more* than like you. Being in Chicago when you weren't there…" Her voice got shaky and she stopped, not wanting to cry on him yet again.

Closing the gap between their bodies until a bare inch separated them, he reached down to take both of her hands. "I hated being here without you. Before I left for Chicago, I winterized this cabin."

Ellie blinked at him. "I'm not sure what that means."

A small smile broke the seriousness of his expression. "I drained the water pipes, unplugged the fridge, cleared out anything that shouldn't freeze—basically shut down the cabin for the rest of the winter."

"Why?"

He brought her hands to his mouth and kissed them one at a time. "Because I knew I wouldn't want to leave you once I was with you again."

Despite her determination not to cry, his simple declaration made her eyes fill. "But you hate big cities and crowds and, well, most people."

"But I don't hate you." The warmth in his gaze turned that statement into something much bigger. "I got that phone, but I knew it wouldn't be enough. I want to be with you, to touch you."

"Good," she said fiercely as she forced back her silly tears. "I want to be with you, too."

The corner of his mouth hitched up into a teasing half smile. "And touching me? Do you want that?"

His up-curved lips were too tempting, so she met his eyes, sucking in a breath when she saw the heat in them. "Uh-huh."

His slight smile grew to a full-on grin. She expected his kiss, wanted it, but he surprised her by taking a step back and releasing one of her hands. After picking up her suitcase that he'd brought inside, he led her through the kitchen and into the living room. Looking around curiously, Ellie tried to figure out what was strange about the space, and she realized that the couch and chairs were arranged around a woodstove, rather than a TV. It made the room feel old-fashioned and cozy.

She had only a few moments to look at the living room before he tugged her into the bedroom. Her socks slid on the tiled floor as she scrambled to keep up with him. He set the suitcase against the wall as she looked around the room. The bed was huge, which it had to be to fit all of George in it. The metal headboard was beautiful, incorporating the abstract shape of a tree in the center. Ellie moved toward it so she could run her fingers over the edge of a branch.

"This is wonderful." Glancing over her shoulder at him, she caught the bashful duck of his head. "Did you make it?" When he nodded, Ellie looked back at the metalwork with a new appreciation. "You're talented."

Her hand moved from the frame to brush the intricate quilt that covered the bed.

"You didn't make this, too, did you?" If he said yes, she was going to feel very inferior. She couldn't even sew a button on straight.

"No. I plow Mrs. Johnson's driveway each winter, and she gave me that."

Ellie smiled at him. "That's nice of you."

He shrugged, still not looking at her. "Her husband died a few years ago. Her kids are in Denver and want her to move there, but she's lived in that house for fifty years."

Moving closer to him, she raised her hand to his forearm, but he shifted unexpectedly, and her palm landed on his stomach. She felt his muscles tense under the fabric of his shirt. "That's really nice of you, then."

"She makes me pies, too." His voice was a little hoarser than just a sentence before, and Ellie bit back a proud smile that she could create this reaction in him with just a simple touch.

She lost all track of their conversation then, as her other hand moved to join the first one. Her fingers slid up his torso and then back down to play with the edge of his shirt where it was tucked into his waistband. His chest was moving rapidly, like it had when he'd carried her for miles after digging her out of her snowy prison.

The memories of the many times he'd protected her, kept her safe, *saved* her, warmed her from the inside out. It wasn't just passion, but also affection, that pushed her to unbutton his shirt.

She'd only freed three buttons before his hands covered hers, stopping her upward progress.

"What's wrong?"

He bowed his head until his forehead rested against hers. "It's too... I feel like I'm going to explode."

"Bad explode or good explode?"

"Good. I think."

Ellie smiled. "Good is good." She took a step back, watching disappointment cloud his gaze for the moment before she unzipped and shed her hoodie, leaving her in only her thin, silky camisole. She wanted to shed that, as well, but his sharp intake of breath distracted her. George was staring, his eyes locked on her with an expression that made her feel like the most beautiful woman in the world.

As the seconds ticked past, she started to fidget. The longer he looked at her with that awed expression, the more she wanted him. When George stayed frozen, she took a step forward and kissed him. It was a simple, light kiss, but it seemed to snap something in George. He wrapped a huge hand around the back of her head, pulling her closer as he kissed her hard and thoroughly. Any hesitation was gone. After Ellie's first start of surprise, she wrapped her arms around his neck and eagerly participated.

As he hungrily explored her mouth, his free hand

dropped to her waist and slid under her top. The burn of his fingers against the bare skin of her side reminded her of that first day on the trail when he'd checked to see if she'd been sweating. The memory made her smile into the kiss. George must have felt her lips curve, since he made an inquiring sound that vibrated against her mouth.

Pulling back just far enough to speak, Ellie teased breathlessly, "I was just thinking about the first time you felt me up."

His eyebrows shot up even higher, and she laughed, the sound still raspy from desire.

"You were checking if I was sweaty." Dropping her grip around his neck, she burrowed both hands beneath his bottom hem and flattened her palms against his belly like she had a few minutes earlier, only with no fabric to block her touch this time. When color darkened his cheeks, she was pretty sure it wasn't from bashfulness. "Without using your words."

She yelped in surprise as he swept her up with an arm around her hips, lifting her off the floor as her hands pulled from under his shirt to clutch his shoulders. Carrying her to the bed, he held her easily with one arm as his other hand yanked down the covers. Although she expected to be tossed onto the mattress, George lowered her carefully, placing her on the flannel sheet with the same exquisite care he would use when handling something precious and fragile.

Once she was sitting on the bed, he stepped back and stripped off his semi-unbuttoned shirt. She watched with interest, enjoying the view as the entirety of his broad, muscled chest was revealed. When his hand went to his belt, her breath caught in anticipation.

He unbuckled it and pulled it from the belt loops, the leather making a hissing sound as it slid free. Instead of hanging it in the wardrobe, he dropped it, and the metal buckle hit the floor with a sharp sound.

Ellie knew how neatly he kept his life—his home, tent, packs, and everything else in it—so his casual clothes-tossing was out of character and extremely hot. She leaned forward as his hand found the top button of his BDUs, but then he paused. Biting her lip to hold in a disappointed groan, she just tilted her head in silent question.

"Sure?" he asked, his voice rough.

"Very sure." And she was. Ellie was more certain that she wanted George than she'd been about anything. Ever.

His chest was expanding in quick bursts as he waited another few seconds. Ellie was ready to jump off the bed and tackle him when he thumbed the button loose and lowered the zip on his pants. In a fast motion, he shoved the BDUs over his hips, bending to free his feet from the puddled fabric of his pants as well as his socks.

As he stood, wearing only his black boxer briefs, Ellie stared. Except for that short time in the cave, she'd been used to seeing George in his thermal long underwear, so his bare skin was something of a shock. A dusting of dark hair covered his limbs and chest, and she smiled.

When his eyebrows drew together, she explained, "I never knew I liked hairy guys so much." She held out a hand toward him. When he took it, she drew him toward her. His legs hit the side of the mattress and box springs, forcing him to stop, but he was close enough to touch, and that was the important thing. "I do. I really, really do."

Laying her hands flat against his chest, she felt his

heart beat against her palms. She let her fingers slide lower and leaned forward so she could rest her cheek where her hands had been. For a long moment, she listened to his heart, strong and steady, just like him. George stood still and let her feel him.

When she finally began to move her hands, his heart picked up under her cheek, making her smile. Although she wanted to continue listening to his reaction to her touch, she wanted to see him, too, so she sat back on her heels. His abs flinched under the brush of her hand. Despite his lack of clothing, he was sweating, a thin sheen of moisture that made her fingers slide easily across his skin.

While she was exploring, George watched her, his hands hovering in midair between them. When she leaned forward and kissed his chest, he finally moved, his palms settling on her shoulder blades. The delicate fabric of her camisole caught on his rough-skinned fingers as his hands stroked down her back, one on either side of her spine.

Gathering handfuls of her top, he eased it up, and she raised her arms so he could pull it off her body completely. Impatient and not wanting any barrier between them, she unhooked her bra and let it drop. His stare earlier was nothing compared to how his gaze was now fixed on her bare upper body. Self-consciousness made her flush.

Resisting the urge to cross her arms over her chest, she asked, "Is everything...um, okay? I know the, ah, the girls aren't very big..."

His eyes met hers, the intense heat in them closing her throat and stopping the flow of words. "You're perfect."

Ellie flushed with a mixture of embarrassment, lust, and pleasure, and she squirmed, unsure of how to respond. The way he was looking at her, as if she was the focus of his universe, was both heady and over-whelming. He shifted closer, and her breath caught.

"Did you want to turn off the light?" He didn't move toward the lamp. "Are you sure? Don't you need to save electricity?"

"I want to see you." The words were barely more than a growl, and she shivered again. It definitely wasn't from the cold; her body felt as if it were burning from the inside out. His hands grasped her hips as his knee depressed the mattress. Pulling her bottom half toward him as his upper body leaned forward, he eased her into a reclining position. He unfastened her pants and slid them and her underwear over her legs, slipping off her socks at the same time and tossing everything aside before he knelt between her thighs. "You're too beautiful to be in the dark."

He kissed her then, and she forgot about the light. As usual, his mouth made everything but George fade into oblivion. His hands were stroking along her ribs, the tips of his fingers barely brushing the sides of her breasts. When they finally covered them completely, she almost levitated off the bed.

Lifting his head slightly, he asked, "Okay?"

"Very." Arching into his touch, she could barely get the words out. "Yes. Please. More."

His chest vibrated with a chuckle as he kissed her again. His hands and mouth were everywhere, caressing and teasing, finding the places on her body where she was the most sensitive. Whenever she would gasp or give a low moan, he would explore the trigger spot in great detail, until she was clutching him and pleading for more.

He left her for a moment to shuck his last piece of clothing and grab a condom from the top drawer of the dresser. Raising herself onto an elbow to watch, Ellie felt the neediness that made blood roar in her ears subside slightly. He fumbled a little while donning the prophylactic, and she was reminded of his inexperience. Instead of putting her off, she loved that she'd be his first. A fierce surge of possessiveness rocked through her at the thought of George touching another woman. The intensity of the emotion scared her.

"You didn't buy those locally, did you?" she teased, needing to lighten the moment before she burst. "Does everyone in town know what we're doing?"

He returned to her before answering, straddling her hips with his knees and bending forward to nuzzle beneath her ear. Giggling, Ellie hunched a shoulder to fend off his tickling beard.

"Ordered them online."

"Good." His playful teasing had changed to small, biting kisses on her neck, turning her laughter into a needy sigh.

"Everyone in town probably still knows what we're doing," he said with his mouth against her skin, the words turning into their own caress.

"Don't care," she breathed, pulling him closer, with her arms over his shoulders and her legs hooked around his hips, loving the feel of his body shaking with laughter. His mouth found hers again as he shifted, and then he was inside her.

George groaned, the sound thick with desire, and

she clutched him tighter as he went still. Opening her eyes, she watched his face, saw his expression change from surprise to pleasure to absolute wonder, and she was glad they'd left on the light. The idea that she was the first woman to make him feel this way was amazing and overwhelming.

"Okay?" she asked, stroking her hands over the broad planes of his back. Although his expression was shouting that it was more than okay, the vulnerable part of her needed to hear the words.

"No." Her heart seized at his answer, but he wasn't finished. "Not just okay. Incredible." He kissed her, a chaste touch of his lips that contrasted with his carnal possession of her. "Perfect."

"Oh." The word was barely there, just an exhaled breath as he started to move. She clung to him as he began tentatively, like his first kisses, while watching her face closely. The wonderful friction, combined with his complete concentration on her reactions, made the pleasure quickly build inside her.

George moved faster, harder, focused on her the entire time. Pulling his head down, she kissed him, needing the connection of his mouth as everything— feelings for him, pleasure, desire—grew scarily huge within her. Her body and lips locked to George's, Ellie allowed herself to let go and flew over the edge, trusting him to keep her safe once again.

Within a few more strokes, he followed, his low groan blending with hers as his arms held her almost painfully tight. Ellie didn't mind the pressure, even as the rush of pleasure settled, and she tightened her own arms and legs, keeping him as close to her as she could.

As their breathing slowed, his grip eased. Turning onto his back, he removed the condom, dropping it into a small trash can next to the bed. Ellie followed him, not ready to be away from him yet, but he didn't seem to mind. He just tucked her close, and her face nuzzled into her usual spot against his neck. It was different this time, though, better. They were skin to skin, their muscles lax in the aftermath of pleasure. George's fingers traced patterns on her back, running up and down the length of her spine before leaving to play with her hair.

"So," Ellie finally asked, not wanting to break the peaceful silence, but needing to know, once again needing the words. "How was it?"

His laugh was just a huff of air against the crown of her head. "It was…amazing. *You*'re amazing." He pressed a kiss on her hair. "I never knew anyone could feel that good."

"Same here." That earned her another kiss. His roaming hands moved more purposefully, and she tilted her head back to look at him. George immediately claimed her lips with his. When he left her mouth to explore her throat, she tried to catch her breath enough to ask, "Again?"

Pausing, he looked at her. "Is that okay?"

Ellie gave him a cat-in-the-cream smile. "Very okay."

⌐⌐⌐

Waking with her nose buried in George's neck was wonderful yet disorienting. It was too warm, and the surface underneath her was too soft for them to be in the tent, and it took several sleepy moments before Ellie remembered the events—good and bad—of the past few days.

Her eyes popped open, and she must have stiffened, since George stirred. Making a grumbly, sleepy sound, he rolled onto his back, his arms tightening around her so that she was pulled on top of him as he went.

With a giggly yelp, she held on to him as they rolled, and then lifted her head so she could see him. His expression of heavy-lidded satisfaction was a good look for him, she decided.

"Good morning."

His wordless response was to drag her higher so he could kiss her. By the time she pulled her head back so she could breathe, she'd lost her ability to speak, so they just grinned at each other in mutual silence for a while. When George tried to tug her back for another kiss, though, a mussed hank of hair tumbled into her eyes, reminding her of something that absolutely could not wait.

"Could I use your shower?" After a fifteen-hour road trip and their energetic night, she knew she was in desperate need of some soap and water. Although George's face showed disappointment, he released her. Before she could change her mind and sink back against him, she slid off him and out of bed.

The chilly air touched her bare skin, and she grabbed for the first piece of clothing within reach—George's flannel shirt. As she buttoned the front, there was a snort from behind her. She looked over her shoulder to see George smirking at her.

"I know," she sighed, lifting her arms and doing a twirl. "It's so big that it's not a dress on me. It's a tent."

Shifting to the side of the bed, he reached out to grab one of her outstretched hands. "Looks good on you." He tugged her toward him, holding her gaze. Mesmerized by the heat in his eyes, Ellie took a step closer to him, leaning down for a kiss. Before their lips could meet, she jumped away from temptation.

"No," she said firmly. "If I kiss you, then I'm going to end up right back in bed with you."

His expression said he heartily approved of that plan. Laughing, Ellie backed toward the door. Blowing him a kiss, she turned and headed to the bathroom. Once she closed the door behind her, she leaned against it, closing her eyes and smiling as she recalled her night with George. It took a while before she shook herself out of her happy daydream and looked around the good-sized bathroom.

It smelled nice, like cedar, and the shower was huge, tiled in an intricate pattern that looked like rolling waves. She wondered if George had done the tile work, and then she remembered that he did construction during the summer. He or his dad had probably built the whole house.

George's self-sufficiency made her feel a little useless. She wondered if he'd expect her to know how to garden and can food and sew their clothes. Crossing her arms over her stomach, she hugged herself under a sudden surge of insecurity. She wondered why he hadn't dated that strong, practical, *tall* mountain woman she'd imagined him with when they'd first met, but instead had waited for Ellie. Her hand itched to travel to her mouth, so she tightened her arms around her middle.

"Stop," she hissed at her errant thoughts. If he *had* wanted that mountain woman who could deliver a baby and then cook dinner from scratch the same day, he'd had plenty of opportunities to find one. The search and rescue guys had made it clear that potential dates were throwing themselves at George on a regular basis.

Instead, though, he had picked her. Ellie. She couldn't sew or can vegetables or chop wood or even walk across an icy parking lot in most of her shoes, but he'd still picked her. She was his first and only, and she needed to remember that before the self-doubt ruined what had been a wonderful night.

She gave herself a firm nod in the mirror and then jumped a foot when there was a soft knock on the door.

"Yes?" Despite her inner pep talk, her voice still contained a quaver, and she scowled.

In wordless response, the door cracked open, and her toiletry bag slipped through the opening.

"Thank you." Once she took the bag, the door eased shut. Meeting her own eyes in the mirror again, she reminded herself that she was there, at George's house, in George's bathroom, and soon to be back in George's bed. Her jittery insecurity faded, erased by a growing warmth, and her reflection gave her an excited smile.

―――――

The shower felt wonderful. After her return from her first visit to Simpson, she'd appreciated each and every experience with indoor plumbing, but hot showers were by far the best. The only thing that kept her from luxuriating in the steamy heat for an hour was the knowledge that there was only one bathroom, and George was probably waiting for his turn.

Frowning, she smoothed a hand over her still-damp locks. She'd brought a hair dryer, but she knew George wasn't connected to any power lines, and she wasn't sure how much juice his off-grid system would supply. She'd cringed at the thought of causing a cabin-wide blackout by trying to dry her hair, so she'd just toweled it off and then combed it, leaving the dry air to do the rest. It made her feel a little vulnerable, though, to have a makeup-free face and damp hair.

She turned away from the mirror, trying to dismiss her worries. George had seen her after days of not showering—stinky, makeup free, and with braided, unwashed hair. Just being *clean* was a huge improvement to how he was used to seeing her.

After her insecure dithering in the bathroom, it was a bit of a letdown to step out of the small room and not have George waiting. By the sounds coming from the kitchen, she assumed he was cooking breakfast. Feeling oddly shy again, she darted for the bedroom.

As she dressed, she debated whether to go more for warmth or style. Since she wasn't sure where their search for Baxter would take them, she compromised by wearing cute new lingerie under a couple of practical layers. Tugging down her fleece top, she headed for the kitchen. George's figure at the stove made her pause.

He was just so *big*. Sure, he was handsome and hairy, as well—both things that she liked—but it was his size that made her feel so safe, like he could handle anything that came across his path. Silently, she crossed the kitchen in her socked feet. Once she reached him, she slid her arms around his waist and rested her cheek against his back, loving the contrast of the soft flannel covering the hard wall of muscle. He didn't jump, so he must have known she was there.

Peeking around his arm, which required leaning quite a ways to the side, her smile grew even larger. "Mmm... are you making us breakfast in a bag?"

His back shook a little when he chuckled. "No. Oatmeal."

"Good." She returned to her original position, pressing her cheek against his spine. "I love your oatmeal." In fact, she loved everything that reminded her of George. He covered one of her hands with his, ran up the length of her forearm and then back again. "What's the plan? Any ideas where to start looking for Baxter this time?" As the words left her mouth, she shivered, reminded of her dad and the man quite possibly hunting him. It had been easier when she'd been in Chicago, and Baxter had been at Armstrong, to reassure herself that Anderson King couldn't find them. Being back in Simpson made her feel like he could be around every corner.

Turning, George wrapped his arms around her. It was hard to be scared of anything when he held her like that. "Thought we'd talk to Rob first."

"The sheriff?" Her voice was muffled by his shirt, but she wasn't about to complain about how tightly he was holding her. There were much worse problems to have than being snuggle-squashed by George.

"Yeah. Then we can look for his trail, starting in the woods around Gray's old cabin."

"Sounds good."

"And you can spend more time making that store look better."

"But—" She stiffened, starting pull away from him.

Instead of arguing, George just kissed her until she melted into him. When he finally lifted his head, she blinked up at him. "Are you going to kiss me every time I start arguing with you?" she asked when she had enough oxygen to speak again.

"Yes." Although he looked smug, Ellie couldn't work up any annoyance. His smile was too beautiful to do anything but beam back at him.

Chapter 31

ROB WAS STRIDING TOWARD THEM AS THEY ENTERED the main sheriff department doors.

"Good. You saved me a trip." His voice was clipped. "George, you need to get a phone."

"He has one," Ellie said when it was clear that George wasn't going to say a word. "It's just not, well, out of the packaging yet. Unless you've opened it?" When she raised questioning eyebrows at him over her shoulder, he gave her a look. "Guess not. I have a phone. Did you want my number?" When George made an unhappy sound, she waved her hands. "Not like that. Rob knows we're together." Ellie sent the sheriff an uncertain glance. "You know we're together, right?"

Rob stared at the ceiling for several seconds, possibly praying for patience. "That's…nice, but I just need a way to reach you that doesn't involve a twenty-minute drive. Anderson King was spotted in the area."

Taking a step back, Ellie bumped into George. He put a solid arm across her upper chest and pulled her back against him. Although her heartbeat still raced, feeling George behind her helped, reminding her that she wasn't alone. "Where? Who saw him? Could they be mistaken?"

"It was one of my deputies, so I'm considering this a legitimate sighting."

Her stomach churned, and Ellie had to swallow the

bile that rose in her throat. "But why? He knows everyone's searching for him. Shouldn't he be trying to leave the country? Why is he back in Simpson? Is he still hunting my dad? Or...me?"

Rob's worried expression ramped up her fears. "I don't know what his motives are, but the fact is that he *is* here. My concern is for your safety—and Baxter's. Have you located him yet?" At Ellie's head shake, Rob frowned. "I don't want you to be alone, especially at George's place. It's too isolated."

George pulled her closer, his arm tightening until if felt like iron. She leaned more heavily against him. "George will be with me."

"If he's not, if he gets a search-and-rescue call or needs to leave for any reason, you call me. I'll send a deputy to stay with you until George gets back."

She stuffed her hands into her pockets, trying to hide how hard they were shaking. "Okay."

"What's your number?" He jotted it on a small notepad as she rattled it off. "Call if you see *anything*, understand? Even if you just have a bad feeling, call me. I'd much rather have a hundred false alarms than get there too late when it's the real thing. Got it?"

"Got it." Pulling a hand from her pocket, she curled it around George's forearm. "I promise I'll call."

"Good." With a final stern nod, he said, "Be safe."

"Thank you." Her voice quivered a little on the words as they turned to go. With a final squeeze, George reluctantly loosened his grip, dropping his arm from her shoulders and taking her hand. They stepped through the doors, and her eyes darted around the parking lot, seeing furtive movements and shapes behind every vehicle and tree.

"We should go back to Chicago," George said, his sudden words making her jump.

"No." She set her chin stubbornly. "We need to look for my dad. I'm not letting a drug-dealing killer chase me away if Dad needs me. I promised I'd be there to watch his back."

"El." Since he was still holding her hand, George pulled Ellie to a halt when he stopped abruptly. "You need to stay safe."

Meeting his gaze, Ellie felt a rush of determination. "I will. If I'm not with you, I'll ask Rob to send a deputy. I won't be stupid about this, but I'm not going to let Anderson King chase me away from my dad." *Not again.*

George cupped her face with both hands, worry digging deep creases between his eyebrows.

Wrapping her hands around his wrists, she assured him, "Nothing will happen to me. I promise."

He stared at her for a long moment before heaving a sigh and pulling her into a hard hug. She returned his embrace fiercely, knowing that she hadn't convinced him she'd be safe in Simpson. Ellie hadn't even convinced herself.

Chapter 32

AFTER THEIR VISIT TO THE SHERIFF'S OFFICE, THEY'D checked the area around Willard's cabin for signs of Baxter, but they hadn't found anything. The news about Anderson King had made Ellie jumpy, seeing shadows around every tree. Each time she'd spooked at a sound or imagined movement, George had shifted closer and closer. She could see how he was restraining his urge to snatch her up, stuff her in his truck, and drive them both back to Chicago.

Rob had called her after they'd finished at the cabin to tell her that he was scheduling a meeting for the next day. People from the fire department, search and rescue, the sheriff's department, and anyone else who wanted to volunteer would be assigned sections of the area around Simpson to search for Baxter. Everyone's kindness took her breath away, and she blinked back tears as she thanked the sheriff.

After that, the second-best highlight of the day so far was the two hours spent at the Screaming Moose. Ellie tackled the window display, immersing herself in the project to the point that she was able to push Baxter and Anderson King to the back of her mind for a short time. George stayed at the shop for most of the time, although he made a quick grocery-store visit after she gave Rob a call and, a short time later, Chris parked his squad car in front of the shop.

As she was tugging a plastic hand through a sweater sleeve, muttering bad things under her breath about Barbara's hard-to-dress, old-school mannequins, movement outside caught her eye. Joseph was walking up to Chris's car door, and Ellie groaned. Her first instinct was to hurry to the back of the shop to hide, but Joseph's gaze was already locked on her, even as he spoke with Chris through the rolled-down window. Ellie had to settle for continuing dressing the mannequin and pretending that she hadn't seen Joseph. As she fussed with the knit sleeve, she watched him out of the corner of her eye, praying he'd leave.

He patted the top of the squad car and walked around the hood.

"Go away, go away, go away," Ellie chanted quietly without moving her lips. She tensed when, instead of leaving, Joseph walked toward the store entrance, never taking his eyes off of her. "C'mon, Deputy. You're supposed to be protecting me. So protect me from Mr. Grabby-Hands." Chris didn't seem to share her reservations about Joseph, though, since he wasn't making any move to stop him.

Just as Joseph reached for the shop door, George pulled his truck up behind the squad car. Ellie gave a silent cheer as Joseph spotted George and quickly turned to walk away from the store entrance. His gaze locked on the retreating man, George got out of the truck.

After Joseph was out of sight, George stood in front of the store and studied the window for several minutes. Ellie had used bright layers that contrasted cheerily with a sparkling "snowy" backdrop. While she'd been occupied with Joseph's approach, it had started snowing for real—fat, wet flakes that stuck to George's hat and beard. When she couldn't take the suspense any longer, she called through the glass, "What do you think?"

After a final few seconds of silent perusal, he turned back to her. "Nice."

That one word from him made her glow with pride. Hurrying to the door, she held it open, giving the departing deputy a quick wave before refocusing on George. "Come in out of the snow."

George walked toward her, eyes warm, and she bounced on her toes. He was looking at her with such heat and sweetness that she could barely restrain herself from running to meet him. As he passed through the doorway, he bent his head to give her a quick, hard kiss that sent warmth running through her entire body.

"Hi, George," Barbara greeted from where she was installing shelves next to the entrance. "Are you taking off then, Ellie?"

"Yes," she said. That short kiss had made her antsy to get George alone at his cabin. "The window is almost done, but I thought I'd finish tomorrow, if that's okay with you?"

Barbara stood, stretching the kinks out of her back. "Of course. It looks amazing. Thank you so much. You're really transforming this place. I wish you'd let me pay you."

"It's fun," Ellie said, leaning against George as he wrapped his arm over her shoulders. "Just what I need to get my mind off things. I should be paying you for the therapy."

With a laugh, Barbara returned to her shelves. "See you tomorrow, then."

"Bye." Ellie grabbed her coat, and George immediately took it from her so he could hold it while she slid her arms into the sleeves. Suppressing the urge to kiss him, she had to satisfy herself with a thank-you.

His "you're welcome" grunt made her smile so hard her cheeks hurt.

The flakes thickened as they drove to the cabin, making Ellie glad they were in the four-wheel-drive pickup and not her Prius. By the time they reached his driveway, there was a heavy layer of snow blanketing everything, turning the landscape into a perfect postcard representation of winter even as the truck's tires scrabbled for purchase on the slick surface.

As George pulled the pickup into the pole barn, Ellie gave a silent sigh of relief that they'd made it home safely. She hopped out and waited outside for him to lower the overhead door, looking around at the surrounding forest. The snow muffled all sound, reminding her of the woods right before the Kings had attacked. The clouds darkened the late-afternoon sun, bringing an early twilight. Tucking her chin into the collar of her coat, she stepped closer to the side of the barn, wishing George would hurry.

When he finally came out, loaded with grocery bags, she moved to help. Of course, George being George, he refused to hand over any of the sacks.

"Get the door," he said, and she rushed toward the cabin, trying to hide her relief that they were going inside, out of sight of the watching, too-quiet forest. Flipping up the "welcome" sign, she pulled the cord to lift the latch and pushed open the door. As George brushed by her, she smiled. He gave her a questioning

look, but she could only smile bigger, unable to explain
the random rush of happiness that had just struck her
because she was with George at his house.

Closing the door behind them, she heard the solid
thunk of the latch falling into place.

———— ∿ ————

After dinner was over and the dishes were washed, Ellie
wandered into the living room. Since they'd gotten home,
the atmosphere had been heavy with expectation, just
needing a spark to burst into a full conflagration. She'd
figured the awkward part would be over after the previous night, but she still caught George sneaking peeks at
her—and she was guilty of doing the same thing. She was
enjoying the suspense, though, the excitement and anticipation. She examined a beautiful coffee table as George
leaned against the wall, watching her with hooded eyes.

"Did you make this, too?" she asked, moving closer to
examine the carved surface.

"My dad. I'm better at working with metal than wood."

The design was intricate and obviously had been
time intensive. "I guess you can create some pretty
amazing things when you don't waste all your time
watching TV." She smiled at him over her shoulder. As
her gaze returned to the table, her attention was caught
by a guitar case propped against the side of the couch.
"When you said you played music, you meant that you
really played."

When she looked at him, he was frowning in confusion. "What else would I've meant?"

Ellie laughed. "I thought you meant that you played
music, like on an iPod." Remembering that it was

George, she amended her words. "Or CDs." She paused. "Or maybe a record player? A radio?"

He ignored her progressive downgrading of his technological devices and shook his head, walking over to the guitar case. "I like playing more than listening."

As he laid the case flat on the floor and unfastened the clasps, she grinned. "Does this mean you're going to play now?"

Giving her a teasing look, he lifted the guitar from its case. "If I do, will you sing?"

"Will you?" she shot back, delighted when he nodded. She sat in the corner of the couch, pulling up her socked feet so she could sit cross-legged.

George sat in the middle of the sofa, his leg just a few inches from her knee. His head was tilted down as he tuned the guitar, giving it a melodic strum when he'd adjusted it to his satisfaction.

As he began to pick out a tune, the notes quiet but sweet, Ellie hugged herself. The music and the fire and the cozy old-fashioned room and the man next to her... everything merged together inside of her, filling her with a glowing contentment that rivaled the warmth of the flames in the woodstove.

Then he started to sing, and Ellie could only stare. His bass voice had a slight rasp, giving a rough edge to his words that just added to his appeal. She wondered why a guitar and a decent voice upped a man's hotness level exponentially. George gave her an encouraging nod, but she shrugged helplessly. The tune sounded vaguely familiar, but she didn't know the words. She didn't mind listening, though, losing herself in the music and the man singing.

"You said you'd sing," he grumbled as the final notes faded.

"I need to know the words in order to sing." She grinned at him. "Otherwise, I could hum. Or whistle."

He was thoughtful for a few moments before picking up the opening bars to "You Are My Sunshine."

"Seriously?" she asked, laughing, but she jumped right in when he started singing. It made her feel like a third-grader but, at the same time, she couldn't stop smiling. He wrapped it up with a flourish of chords, making her laugh.

Without pausing, George transitioned to the next song. Recognizing the introductory chords, she reached over and slapped his arm.

"You *do* have an iPod, you liar." It was a fun, folksy rock song that had just debuted on the charts. She had it on her own phone.

He shook his head. "Radio in the truck."

"How'd you learn how to play it?" she asked suspiciously.

His eyebrows showed confusion. "I heard it a couple times," he said, as if explaining the obvious.

Ellie blinked. "You heard it, so you know how to play it?"

"Sure."

"Whoa." As they'd been talking, he'd been improvising, changing the melody slightly and then circling around to the original introduction. "You're a guitar savant, as well as a foot-massage savant!"

Narrowing his eyes, he sent her a suspicious look without missing a note. "That doesn't sound like a compliment."

"It is. Being able to play something after just hearing it

a few times… That's incredible." She smiled at him. "I'll add it to your list of talents."

Looking a little flustered, he dropped his gaze to the guitar and started to sing. Ellie tried to join him, but she only knew the chorus and a few words in the verses, so she improvised. Gradually, when she saw how her incorrect lyrics were amusing him, she gave up trying to be accurate at all and just went for the humor.

By the end of the song, George was laughing too hard to play. It was the first time she'd ever seen him belly laugh, and the sight was entrancing. Smiling, she watched him, happiness filling her until she felt ready to burst.

"What?" George asked, carefully setting the guitar on the floor so he could wipe tears of hilarity from his eyes.

"You're just…" Stopping, she bit her lip. "Perfect."

His smile slipped away, and they stared at each other for a long minute. Before she even realized what she was doing, Ellie had lunged toward him. Despite her tiny relative size, she must have taken him by surprise, because he toppled backward as she hit. He'd been sitting twisted sideways so that he could face her, and he fell onto the cushions, his head barely missing the sofa arm.

Lying on top of him, Ellie was almost as surprised as he looked by her impulsive tackle. Feeling a little shy now that she had him trapped beneath her, she almost apologized and got off him. Instead, she gave into the temptation that his so-close mouth presented and kissed him fiercely.

It wasn't even a full second before he responded, cradling the back of her head to pull her impossibly closer.

He took over the kiss, and Ellie reflected again what a quick learner he was, before everything was lost except for the feel of his mouth on hers.

Her hands roamed as she kissed him. Frustrated by the layers, she fumbled for his shirt buttons. When her hands slid directly against the skin of his chest, he jerked in reaction, before wrapping his arms around her and rolling them right off the couch.

There was a moment of weightlessness before Ellie figured out that they were headed to the floor. He must have realized the same thing, because he reached out with one hand and pushed away from the couch. Twisting in midair, his other arm wrapped firmly around her middle, George barely managed to avoid crushing her and the guitar. Instead, he landed on his side and quickly turned to his back, so she was above him again.

"Sorry," he panted. Ellie wasn't sure if he was winded from the fall and landing or from the kiss. "Forgot where we were."

Propping herself up with a hand on either side of his broad chest, she grinned at him. "Me too." She eased her weight down until her body was plastered against his once more. "I think we're pretty stable now, though." Her experimental side-to-side rocking motion elicited a rumbling groan from George.

Apparently, he agreed with her comment, since he pulled her head down to his. This time, when he rolled them both over, it was more successful. Even though he was supporting the majority of his weight on his arms, Ellie still felt flattened in the best way.

Her top layers felt intrusive, blocking her from feeling his bare chest against hers, so she worked them toward her shoulders. Reluctantly, she broke their kiss for the few seconds it took to pull everything up and off. Her sleeves turned inside out in her struggle to peel her sweatshirt and underlayer off her arms, but she finally worked herself free from the imprisoning fabric.

Raising her head, she attempted to resume the kiss, but George wasn't focused on her mouth anymore. His gaze was fixed lower, where her bra—her pretty, stupidly expensive bra she'd just bought with George in mind—was the only thing covering her above the waist. He stared at her so long that she started to feel self-conscious.

"You've already seen everything there is to see," she teased, tilting his head so their eyes met. "Aren't you getting bored of looking at me?"

"Never." Although she was smiling, he remained serious, and the single word came out like a vow. Her breath caught as they stared at each other. She wasn't sure who moved first, but suddenly their lips met again, and everything faded away except for George.

As they kissed, her bare stomach pressed against his hair-roughened skin. Wrapping her arms around his shoulders, she fought to get closer. If she could have climbed inside him, she would have. His hands brushed lightly over her sides, making her shudder and cling even harder.

When his lips left hers, she made a protesting sound. He ignored her squirms as she tried to get his mouth to return. Instead, he laid a trail of featherlight kisses over her jaw and across her throat. She arched, giving him better access. Every so often, his tongue would touch her skin, raising goose bumps that radiated from the spot until they covered her entire body.

His mouth followed the line of her breastbone, skipped over the center of her bra, and landed on the sensitive flesh of her belly. She sucked in a breath, her stomach curving away from his touch in a reflexive flinch, but he followed, tracing a line to her belly button. When his tongue darted into the indentation, she couldn't hold back a ticklish giggle.

Turning his head, he rested his bearded cheek against her stomach. She reached down with both hands to burrow her fingers into his hair, and she felt his breath brushing her bare skin with each of his exhales. She'd been almost frantically aroused just seconds before, but there was an alluring peace to the moment, to the weight of his head lifting with her breath, to the slip of his hair through her fingers. To her surprise, Ellie realized that she was just as happy to lie there peacefully as she would've been to continue kissing him.

It was George. Whenever she was with him, no matter what they were doing, she was content.

"I love how you smell," he said. Although his words were quiet, she still jumped a little. "Even if I never saw you again after today, I'd always remember how you smelled."

Her fingers tightened in his hair. "You won't need to remember. Even after we find Baxter—*if* we find Baxter—we'll be together. We'll figure it out."

He nodded, his beard rough against her belly.

"Good." Her fingers began moving through his hair again, scratching at his scalp and making him sigh across her skin. "I've got you now. You're not escaping that easily, buster."

She could feel his face move as he smiled. The

sensation turned up the corners of her own mouth, as well.

"Good," she said again.

The floor beneath her back was beginning to distract her from the serenity of the moment. One shoulder blade was on a rug, but the other was pressing directly against the tile floor. It wasn't cold, but it was hard... very hard. With a regretful sigh, she withdrew her hands from his head so she could prop her elbows on the floor and push into a half-seated position.

"Mind if we move this to a softer surface?" she asked, and he nodded against her stomach again, making her laugh. "Yes, we can move, or yes, you mind?"

He rolled to sitting and then to his feet in a smooth movement. "We can move," he said, reaching down a hand. She accepted it, and he helped her stand with such enthusiasm that she was almost pulled off the floor.

"Thanks," she said dryly, but he just smiled. As they moved toward the bedroom door, Ellie frowned at the tile beneath her socked feet. "Why isn't your floor cold?"

"Radiant heat." At her puzzled frown, he elaborated. "Hot water runs in pipes beneath the tile."

"Oh." She crouched so she could flatten her palms against it, and he almost tripped over her, catching his balance just before they both went flying. "I like it."

With an amused snort, he bent and picked her up, tossing her over his shoulder in a fireman's carry. Except for an unladylike grunt, she was quiet as he carried her into the bedroom. George's playfulness was rare and precious, and she didn't want to do anything to discourage it. When he carefully set her back on her feet, his expression was concerned.

She grinned at him, and relief spread across his face. "I'm fine. I should be used to you hauling me around."

His gaze dipped below her neck, his expression heating again, and she was reminded of her shirtless state. He reached for her just as there was a pounding knock on the door.

Ellie jumped, her arms crossing over her chest as if whoever was at the entrance could see into George's bedroom.

"Stay," he ordered, wearing a ferocious scowl as he left the room.

Diving for her suitcase, Ellie pulled on a long-sleeve top and then a hoodie for good measure. As she zipped the front, she headed for the door. Even though she knew that Anderson King most likely would not be knocking, she still found her heart beating quickly as she crossed the kitchen. When she heard a male voice in the entry, tension left her muscles, leaving her shaky with relief. That voice was not Anderson's.

Poking her head into the entry, she saw Deputy Chris Jennings talking to an unhappy-looking George. Both men looked at her—Chris with a smile and George with a deepening frown. Ellie shrugged off George's reaction. He couldn't expect her always to obey.

"Hi, Chris," she said, stepping into the entry. George reached out and caught her hand, tugging her until she butted up against his side. "What's going on?" Now that the relief that Chris was not Anderson had faded a little, a new curl of anxiety rose inside her.

"Nothing bad," Chris soothed, apparently having heard the worry in her voice. "The guy who plows the city streets in Simpson is down with pneumonia, so

Rob sent me to stay here with you while George rode to the rescue."

George's hand tightened around hers as she looked at his face. She couldn't tell if he was just frustrated by the evening's change in plans or if he was reluctant to leave her with the deputy. She did remember that plowing was his main winter job, and she didn't want her issues to keep George from working.

Forcing a smile, she said, "You'd better get going then. The citizens of Simpson are depending on you to dig them out so they can get food and supplies and stuff."

With an amused cough, Chris said, "More likely they're wanting to get to the bar."

"So you'll be saving them from hunger or boredom," she amended. "Either way, you'll be their hero."

George didn't look impressed by that idea. Curling an arm around her, he squeezed her against his side.

"I know," she sighed, feeling the same reluctance to be separated. "But the sooner you leave, the sooner you'll be back, and the sooner we can…" With a sideways look at a grinning Chris, she trailed off. The small twitch of George's mouth told her he'd followed her unfinished thought just fine.

"I'm just going to grab…uh, something from my squad."

As soon as the door closed behind a smirking Chris, George had her pressed against the wall. He kissed her thoroughly, with a slight edge of desperation that just added to the hotness. Ellie melted against him, clutching handfuls of his shirt to keep him close. As always, she lost herself in him, forgetting everything except George and the wonderful way he made her feel. In the back of her mind, she knew she had to stop, that he had to leave, but then he'd find that sensitive spot on her neck, and she'd lose track of time again.

"Okay! So I guess I'm going to grab something *else* now."

Ellie barely heard the deputy's words or the bang of the door closing again. She was too caught up in George—the feel of his body flattening her against the wall, the way his mouth was starting to know hers, the path his huge yet gentle hands were taking along her sides. Too soon, he was pulling away.

She sighed, forcing her hands to let him go. "Drive carefully."

"I will."

Unable to resist leaning in for a final quick kiss, she said against his lips, "Those Simpsonites are lucky I'm willing to share you."

She felt his chuckle rumble through his chest and against her mouth. "See you soon," Ellie added.

It was his turn to give her a short, hard kiss. "Be careful. Stay inside."

"I will."

"Promise?"

"Promise."

Reluctantly, he released her and started pulling on his outerwear. Ellie watched, keeping her hands away from her mouth with extreme effort. Jamming his hat on his head, he bent for a final, *final* kiss and yanked open the door. Chris, standing just outside, looked startled.

"I figured I'd just wait out here until you were...uh, finished," the deputy explained, waiting until George had stomped through the doorway before stepping into the entry. "I'll stay until you get back."

George fixed him with a hard look. "Protect her."

The cheerful deputy looked suddenly serious. "I will."

After another few seconds, George gave a short nod and headed for the pole barn. Ellie moved to the doorway and watched him walk away until his form was swallowed by the swirling snow.

"So," Chris said, "do you know how to play poker?"

~~~~

Ellie slapped down her final card. "Speed!"

With a groan, Chris let the last four of his cards flop out of his hands. "This is a dumb game. Are you sure you don't want to learn to play poker?"

"You only think it's dumb because you suck so very hard at it." Gathering up the deck, Ellie started to shuffle, trying to keep her eyes off the window. It wouldn't show her anything anyway, just a dimming rectangle dusted with snow.

"I do," Chris readily agreed, leaning back in his chair and stretching. A chirp from the portable radio on his belt made Ellie jump. He pulled it free of the holder, frowning. "Low battery. Shit. I just charged it, too. This one must be going bad."

As he stood, Ellie felt a flutter of panic. "Where are you going?"

"Just out to the squad." Chris moved to the entry. "I have an extra battery stashed in the car."

Following him to the door, Ellie tried to quiet her screaming nerves. Chris would be right outside. It wasn't like he was going back to town or anything. Despite her mental reassurances, she felt very alone when the door closed behind Chris, shutting her in the empty cabin.

When she realized she was staring at the door, waiting for him to return, she moved back to the kitchen table and picked up the cards. Unenthusiastically, she started a game of solitaire, figuring that it would occupy her hands, at least.

She couldn't keep her attention on the game, however. The wind was muffled, but it made the cabin give small creaks and rattles, and Ellie twitched nervously at every sound. The storm blocked most of the early evening sunlight, darkening the kitchen and making it hard to see the cards.

Pushing to her feet, she made her way over to the light switch. As she reached to turn on the overhead light, she paused. The light would illuminate the kitchen and, with the window uncovered, leave her exposed to the gaze of anyone outside.

"It's just Chris out there, silly," she scolded herself, but her hand still dropped away from the switch. It was too easy to imagine vengeful eyes watching her. Ellie decided to wait until the deputy returned to the kitchen before she turned on any lights.

Returning to her chair, she tried to pick up her game, but she couldn't concentrate. The seconds ticked past, making her wonder what was delaying Chris. He was just going to grab a battery from his car. How long could that take?

Something caught her attention, and she raised her head, listening. She'd thought it sounded like a car engine, but the wind battered against the cabin, making it hard to hear anything. Dismissing it as her imagination—which currently seemed to be operating on overdrive—Ellie forced herself to focus on her game. In between gusts of wind, the kitchen clock ticked loudly, as if reminding her of how very long Chris had been gone.

The knock on the door startled her into giving a small shriek. Her arm jerked, scattering the cards as she jumped to her feet. A second later, she realized it was just Chris, who didn't know the welcome-sign trick.

Hurrying to the door, she opened it. "Did you lock—oh!"

It wasn't Chris.

It was Joseph.

"Hey, Ellie." He smiled, taking a step forward as if to enter the house. She moved so that her body blocked him, keeping him outside. "How's it going?"

"What are you doing here?" she asked, skipping any niceties as she peered through the snow, trying to see Chris or his squad car. Neither was in sight.

"I'm here to see Holloway." His smile was strange, too wide and forced looking. "He around?"

Ellie didn't want to share any information with Joseph, but he was George's search and rescue team leader. Plus, Chris would be back inside the house any minute—at least, she hoped he would. "He's plowing."

With a frown, Joseph shook his head. "In Simpson? He wrapped things up over an hour ago. He should've gotten home by now."

Fear instantly filled Ellie. "Are you sure?"

"I saw him on his way out of town," Joseph confirmed. "He was in his pickup, so he'd already dropped the plow truck off at the city maintenance building. There's no way I could've beat him here unless…"

"Unless what?" Her voice sounded too high.

"Well, the roads are pretty slick."

Ellie stared at him, her stomach twisting into a knot. "Do you think he had an accident? Wait. Wouldn't you have seen his truck on your way here if he had?"

With a frowning glance upward, Joseph rubbed his jaw with his gloved hand. "The snow is still coming down pretty good. Plus, there are spots where someone could go off the road and there'd be no way to see them unless you were looking."

Taking a half step forward, wanting so badly to run outside and start searching for George, Ellie made herself stop and think. "Chris is here. He can get the other deputies to start searching."

"I passed Jennings as I turned into Holloway's driveway. He left."

"What?" Chris was gone? Why had he left? Her breath was coming fast, and she made a conscious effort to slow down and think. Her phone! She needed to get her phone off the kitchen table. She didn't have Chris's direct number, since she'd lost his card sometime during the past few weeks, but she could call Rob. He'd know what was going on with Chris, and he could start the search for George. As she turned, she saw Joseph start to step through the doorway.

"Don't come in." Ellie turned back to block him, her desire to call for help vying with the equally urgent need to keep Joseph out of the house.

"Ellie," he cajoled. "I'll just wait inside with you until George is found. You shouldn't be alone right now. Unless you want to search for him? We can take my car. It'd be nice to have some time alone with you. We never really got a chance—you never gave *me* a chance." As he spoke, he tried to take a step forward, but Ellie held her ground, refusing to give even an inch. A flush of rage ran up her neck and heated her face. How dare he waste time being inappropriate and slimy when George could be hurt?

"Get out." She gave him a two-handed shove to the chest. Surprise more than force sent him stumbling back a few steps, just far enough for Ellie to swing the door closed. Ignoring his indignant yelp, she muscled through the last couple of inches until the latch fell into place.

She hurried into the kitchen. Her phone was where she'd left it, and she gave a shaky exhale of relief as she grabbed it. Her happiness was short-lived, however, when she saw the "no service" message in the top left corner of her screen.

She hesitated for a second, tugging on a hangnail with her teeth as she tried to calm her brain enough to consider her options. The first priority was getting help for George. Joseph, no matter how uncomfortable he made her, was a trusted member of the emergency services team. Even more importantly now, he had a vehicle. He could drive her to town—or at least close enough that she could get cell reception. The idea of getting into his SUV made her shudder. Everything inside of her was screaming that it was a bad idea.

Okay. Besides Joseph, what was her next option? Before she could figure it out, a raised voice from outside caught her attention. Was Chris back? Maybe even George? Hope mixed with anxiety as she rushed for the front door. After carefully checking to make sure Joseph wasn't still on the porch, she pulled it open just far enough to see outside.

Snow was still falling heavily, and the motion-activated light reflected off the flakes, making it hard to see much past the porch. She peered through the snow and then had to bite back a gasp as she spotted Anderson standing just a few feet from Joseph. Sucking in a breath, she opened her mouth to call to Joseph, to warn him that he was within reach of a killer, but something about their body language wasn't right. Ellie closed her mouth without making a sound.

"What are you doing here?" Joseph asked, sounding annoyed. "I told you we'd meet up later. You're going to ruin everything."

Anderson didn't say anything. There was a small flash and a loud *crack*, and Joseph crumpled onto the snow.

Ellie froze. She knew that sound, that flare of light. It was a gun firing. The snowy scene in front of her wavered and blurred, and she forced herself to blink several times. *Don't pass out*. Her breath tried to escape on a sob, so she clamped her lips together. *Don't lose it, and don't pass out*.

She shuffled one foot back a half step, followed by the other. Just as the door closed, she saw Anderson start toward the cabin.

A high-pitched sound was trapped in her chest, and she sucked in shallow, rapid breaths through her nose. If she opened her mouth, she would start screaming, and she wasn't sure if she'd be able to stop. The door bumped against the jamb, and the latch locked into place, the sound echoing in the silence and jolting her out of her paralysis.

Spinning around, she ran through the kitchen, bumping a chair with her hip as she passed. Her thoughts were useless, careening at breakneck speed. In the living room, she forced herself to stop running blindly. Standing in the flickering red light of the woodstove, she bit the skin next to her thumbnail hard enough to draw blood. Strangely, though, the pain allowed her to push aside her building panic and focus. She couldn't just hide in the bedroom closet, as tempting as that was. Pressing her hands against her temples, she whispered, "Think, think, think..."

What if she did hide? The cabin was solid, and the door locked. She could just wait it out until someone showed up. Who, though? George might be unconscious in a ditch somewhere, Rob was unreachable, Chris had left her, Joseph was bleeding into the snow, and no one else knew she was in danger.

The thought of George solidified her determination. She needed to get out and go somewhere with cell reception. Escaping through the front door was not an option, and there was no back door. Her darting gaze settled on one of the windows, her feet moving in that direction before she actually made the decision.

As she unlocked the window, there was a horribly familiar *thunk* from the front door. Anderson had pulled the cord and unlocked the door. Terror made her freeze for a precious second before she yanked up the window. Her fingers fumbled with the storm-window fastening, but she finally heard a click and popped it out of the frame. Ellie didn't bother trying to be careful removing the screen. She just shoved at it until the soft aluminum frame bent, and then she pulled it free.

Swinging one leg over the sill and then the other, she dropped to the ground below. Her socked feet sank into the snow, and she instantly wished she'd grabbed her boots—and coat—when she'd torn blindly out of the entry. Although the ground was lower than the floor had been, she was just able to reach the bottom of the window. Her sweaty fingers slipped as she tried to pull it closed. If she could shut it, maybe Anderson would waste time searching the house for her, giving her a precious head start.

Ellie heard the heavy *thud-thud-thud* of footsteps crossing the floor, each one getting louder as he drew near. It was too late to hide the open window. Her hands went numb with fear, falling to her sides, and she plastered her body against the rough log exterior of the cabin.

Run, dummy! some drill sergeant in her brain screamed at her. *Don't just stand here, waiting to get caught!* Her feet obeyed that voice almost before the words registered. She ran along the back of the cabin, staying close to the wall where the roof overhang had blocked most of the snow from collecting. When she reached the corner of the house, she didn't allow herself to hesitate, but plowed into the drifts, sinking knee-deep in the snow with every stride.

It slowed her to a nightmare pace, sweat beading at her hairline even as her feet went numb with cold, but she pushed grimly toward the trees. She knew she was leaving a trail that even a kindergartner could follow, but there was no other choice. With each step, she expected to feel hands grabbing for her or a bullet ripping through her, but she didn't allow herself to look back—not even a glance over her shoulder. She kept her eyes locked on the tree line that was slowly—much too slowly—getting closer.

Each ragged breath clawed at her lungs, and she

forced herself not to think of the snowshoes she'd left behind at the cabin with her boots and coat. The forest was only five floundering strides away, and then three and then, with an adrenaline-fueled lunge, she was in the trees.

The snow cover was shallower, even nonexistent at the base of some evergreens. Ellie made herself slow, rather than tearing through the woods in a mindless panic. Remembering the first time she'd run from Anderson King, she started placing her feet with care, finding bare spots and rocks where she could step in order to disguise her trail.

"Run, killer," Anderson's mocking voice called from somewhere, sounding too, too close. Her breathing was loud, and she covered her mouth and nose with her hand to muffle it. "It'll make it more fun to track you down. And once I do catch you, you'll die a lot slower than my brother did."

The darkness was deepening, with just enough light to create terror-inducing shadows behind every pine tree and clump of aspen. Branches caught her hair and scratched her face, and Ellie was glad her feet were numb, since she knew they'd be hurting unbearably otherwise. Every so often, she forced herself to stop and hold her breath, listening for sounds of pursuit. Anderson was stealthy. She knew that from when he'd snuck up on them without George noticing. That didn't stop her from pausing to check for any sounds—a branch brushing a coat sleeve or a boot crunching on snow—just in case he had a careless moment.

There was nothing.

The trees opened to a small clearing, and Ellie skirted

the edge, trying to place her feet where they wouldn't leave a print. She slid on an icy patch, grabbing at branches and barely managing to stay upright. The abrupt movement made her compass thump against her breastbone, reminding her of its presence.

Fumbling with cold fingers, she finally opened it and tilted the compass to catch the last bit of daylight. North was behind her, so she turned to her left. If she headed east, she'd eventually run into the county road. Hopefully, her phone would get reception there. If not, she'd at least have a chance at flagging down a car.

With renewed determination, she increased her pace, ignoring her frozen, increasingly clumsy feet and her painful, burning hands. The trees thinned, allowing her to jog. Panic was a constant presence at the back of her mind, pushing her faster and faster. She forced herself to stop, panting from exertion and fear, to check her compass again. After reorienting herself, she set off again, knowing she was getting closer and closer to that county road.

A crunch of underbrush made her stop abruptly, scrambling to keep her feet underneath her. She went completely still, straining her ears and mentally cursing the loud heartbeat that drowned out all other sounds. The crackle of breaking twigs came again from directly in front of her. Her frantic gaze darted from side to side as she tried to decide which way to dodge. Ellie pushed back a building hopelessness. Whatever way she went, Anderson was going to follow.

An enormous dark shape pushed past pine branches and came to an abrupt halt just twenty or so feet in front of her. A strong, musky smell hit her along with the realization that it wasn't Anderson King standing there.

It was a bear.

The sheer unfairness of it all nearly made her knees give out. She was running for her life, trying to escape a vengeful killer, and now there was a *bear*?

After the initial rush of rage and panic, George's voice echoed in her ears, as clearly as if he were there with her. *Back away slowly. Talk calmly.* She'd survived an avalanche, an exploding cabin, multiple attacks by Anderson King, and a night in a claustrophobic hole. Compared to all that, a bear should be easy.

"Hey, bear." Her voice quavered, climbing to a high note, and she swallowed and tried again as she slid her foot back. "Hello, Mr. Bear. Or Ms. Bear—and if you're a Ms. Bear, I really hope you don't have your baby bears with you, as cute as they might be, since you probably won't be in a very good mood if there are little ones around." The bear huffed, and her next backward step turned into a startled scramble. She froze, hoping the movement hadn't made her look too prey-like. That's what she felt like, though—a scared, about-to-be-eaten bunny.

"Stop that," she said to herself more than the bear as she tried to keep her backward steps slow and steady. "I'm not going to be eaten by this nice bear. I might get shot by Anderson King, but I'm not going to be eaten. George wouldn't have told me not to be worried about bears if there was a chance I'd be eaten."

The bear stood up on its hind legs.

"Oh shit." Ellie stopped breathing, stopped moving, stopped thinking. After endless seconds, the animal returned to four legs, his front paws slapping the ground.

Either the sound or the motion broke her from her paralysis. She began to ease backward again, fighting with every slow step not to turn and run. "Don't run, don't run," she chanted. "George said not to run and not to climb a tree. Don't run, don't run, don't run."

She didn't run. Instead, she backed up until the bear disappeared, its dark shape blending with the shadows. Only then did she turn and walk—quickly, but still walking—away from the bear. Her breath hitched with every exhale, but she ignored the persistent sobs and focused on getting as far away as she could without running.

Her feet felt like cement blocks attached to her ankles, making her stumble with almost every step. Now that she couldn't head east anymore—the bear was east—she didn't have another plan.

"Think," she muttered between chattering teeth. "Think. You can't help George if you freeze to death out here." Her foot caught on something, and she went down to her hands and knees. When she tossed her hair out of her eyes, she saw she'd stumbled into the same small meadow she'd passed earlier, and tears burned her eyes. After all that—her care not to leave a trail, the cold, and the bear—she hadn't gotten anywhere.

A dark shadow detached itself from the edge of the clearing. Blinking, she tried to sharpen her blurry, tear-washed vision. By the time her eyes cleared and she realized Anderson King was stalking toward her, it was too late.

Ellie scrambled to her feet, turning to run in the same motion, but he lunged forward to catch the back of her sweatshirt, stopping her forward momentum with a rough jerk. Instead of keeping his grip on her, he swung his arm and released her, making her stumble against a low-hanging aspen branch. The unyielding wood slammed into her back, but she didn't feel any pain. Too much adrenaline was coursing through her.

Ellie couldn't take her eyes off the gun Anderson was pointing at her. The weapon was less than ten feet away from her vulnerable chest, and she knew he wouldn't hesitate to pull the trigger. A rapid-fire list of escape plans ran through her head, each one more likely to get her killed than the last. It was a moot point, anyway, since the only thing she seemed capable of doing was staring at the gun and trying to breathe.

"Caught you," Anderson sneered. His hands were unnervingly steady around the pistol grip. "Murdering bitch."

"I'm sorry." No sound actually emerged from her throat on the first try. Anderson scowled at her, so she tried again, slightly more successfully. "I didn't want to kill him."

"Lying bitch." She could see his knuckles whiten as his fingers tightened, and her panting breaths came quicker. "You pointed a gun at him and shot him in the chest. Did you hear him scream? Because I did. And I'm going to make sure your screams make his seem like nothing."

"He tried to kill my dad!" Her words were coming more loudly now, but her voice had raised a few octaves in pitch. "He shot first. I had to protect my dad—protect both of us."

"Where is Baxter?"

Thrown off by the abrupt subject change, she stayed quiet.

"Bitch, I asked you a question."

"I don't know."

"Liar."

"I'm not lying!" She almost shouted the words, her nerves stretched beyond endurance. "He checked himself out and disappeared. I don't even know where to start looking. He's just…gone." Even with a gun aimed at her heart, she felt a pang at saying the words.

Several heavy seconds dragged by while King studied her as if he was trying to decide whether he believed her. "He has proof I need."

"I don't know where he is."

"Did he tell you? About who killed the floater?"

It took a while to process what King had said. "No. Do you know?"

With a harsh crack of laughter, King said, "Yeah, I do, and that's going to be my ticket out once I deal with the bitch who killed my brother."

"Who did it? And what proof does Dad have?" Talking was calming her slightly, allowing her to think more than *Oh my God, oh my God!* and she tried to keep her voice calm and quiet. Maybe she could talk him down and get King to leave peacefully. It worked on bears, why not on killers? Her cell phone was sitting uselessly in her pocket. Even if she could've reached for it without him shooting her, it wouldn't have gotten a signal.

"That's what I need to talk to Baxter about," King said with insulting slowness. It didn't seem fair that the guy holding a gun on her should get to be condescending, too.

"I don't know where he is," she repeated.

"Then you're not much use to me, are you?" The gun

rose just a fraction of an inch, but it was enough to catch and hold Ellie's full attention. "As much as I want to make you suffer, your joke of a tracker boyfriend will be here soon, and I promised my brother I'd kill the bitch who shot him."

He pulled the trigger.

Chapter 33

WHEN GEORGE FINALLY TURNED INTO HIS DRIVEWAY, he was unable to control the grin that had taken over his face. He knew he probably looked like a crazy mountain man, smiling at nothing, but he couldn't help it. It was Ellie's fault.

Memories of the previous night made his grin widen until it was creeping into manic territory. It wasn't just the sex, either, although he hadn't known pleasure like that existed. Just having her in the cabin had changed his world. Singing with her, lying with his head on her bare stomach, watching her trace the shape of a metal leaf on the headboard of his bed… She'd made it impossible for him to live alone anymore now that he'd gotten a glimpse of what a life with El would be like. When he'd gone into the bathroom after she'd left it steamy and smelling like fruity shampoo, he'd just stood there, breathing it in and desperately wanting to keep her.

He'd plowed the city streets faster than he ever had before. At the same time he'd been mocking himself for acting like a love-struck fool, his foot had been pushing harder on the accelerator.

As he rounded the curve and his house came into view, the bottom dropped out of his stomach. Flashing emergency lights lit up his yard. When he saw the ambulance, he stopped breathing. He jumped out of the truck almost before his vehicle slid to a complete stop.

"El!" he shouted even as his eyes searched the scene, trying to find her. There was something—*someone*—lying on the ground, surrounded by bright yellow police tape. His vision narrowed to the blanket-covered form as he ran toward it.

"George!" Someone grabbed his arm. George shook him off, determined to get to that body, to see if it was her. More hands grabbed and held. Balling his fist, he swung blindly, but there were too many holding him back.

"George!" Firefighter Ian Walsh grabbed both sides of his coat collar, forcing George to look at him. "It's not her. It's Joseph Acconcio. It's not your Ellie."

It took several seconds for his words to sink in. When they finally registered, he sucked in a shaking breath.

"It's not Ellie," Ian repeated.

"Where is she?" The words grated painfully against his throat.

Ian pressed his lips together, glancing to the side.

"Where is she?" George roared, trying to grab Ian, to shake the answer out of him, but the multiple hands tightened, holding him back.

"We don't know," Ian said. "It looks like she went out one of the windows and ran into the woods, but her trail ended when she got to the trees. Rob and a bunch of his guys are searching for her, but we can't send out anyone who's not armed until we know it's safe."

Safe. If Ellie had to go through a window and run into the woods, then someone was after her. Someone was *still* after her. His blood ran cold and then exploded with heat. Twisting around, he shook off the four men holding him as if they were nothing. George ran for the woods.

How had the others managed to lose her trail? To him, her sign was obvious. So was the fact that she was in socks. Ellie had been fleeing in terror in only her socks. Rage like he'd never felt began to build as he ran, following her trail. He dodged tree branches and protruding roots, each sign that she'd slid or tripped feeding his blinding anger. The only thing allowing him to keep from losing it completely was that he didn't see any sign of Anderson following her.

George had just glimpsed a clearing through the trees when he heard the gunshot.

He froze, stumbling to a halt at the sound, so foreign in this snowy fairyland of a forest.

It had only been a fraction of a second as his thoughts tumbled through his brain before his body was moving, dodging through the trees until they thinned at the edge of the meadow. His boots plunged into the drifts covering the clearing, closing the distance between him and the man holding the gun. As George got closer, he took in the scene in one horrifying second.

El was on the snowy ground, her body curled away from him. Anderson King turned his head, saw George barreling toward him, and twisted his body so he could swing the gun toward him. Before Anderson could aim, George tackled him, both men hitting the ground hard. The gun flew from Anderson's hand, flying end over end before landing and immediately sinking into a drift. A small portion of George's brain automatically noted the gun's position before he had to duck Anderson's swinging fist.

George grabbed for Anderson's arm. Even as he managed to pin one of the other man's hands against the ground, Anderson twisted his lower body and kneed George in the thigh. Ignoring the numbness that spread over his outer quad, George lifted his free hand and brought it down. Anderson jerked his head to the side, and George's fist merely grazed his cheekbone.

Using his non-pinned arm, Anderson rotated his body and sent an elbow into George's gut, forcing out all his air in a pained grunt. Barely dodging the next blow, George lost his grip on Anderson's arm and the two men rolled over and over across the snow until George's back slammed into an aspen trunk.

His head snapping back, George bit his tongue as Anderson's next punch connected solidly. "Useless," Anderson grunted as he swung again. "Pathetic piece of shit. Couldn't even save your city girl, could you, *Tracker*?" His voice was thick with sarcasm and scorn. "Got here too late to stop me from putting a bullet through her heart. What happened? Couldn't you follow her trail?" Cocking his fist, Anderson launched another swing toward George's face.

The image of El lying on the ground, so tiny and still, had burned itself into his brain. He'd barely had her, and now she was gone. Horror and grief and guilt hit him, but everything was drowned out by the blinding fury that surged through him. He'd never experienced such rage, never felt such a bone-deep urge to hurt, never wanted to kill someone until that moment.

With a fleshy smack, Anderson's punch landed in George's palm. A red haze settled over his vision as George pushed the other man's hand back. Anderson's smirk wavered and then disappeared completely as his fist was forced away from George's face and toward the

ground. Despite the way Anderson's entire body shook
with effort, he couldn't stop the inexorable retreat of his
clenched fist.

With a roar, George shoved away from the tree, rolling Anderson beneath him. His anger fed his strength,
and George pinned Anderson easily, his fists pounding
into flesh, needing desperately to hurt the fucker who'd
killed his El. George didn't even feel anymore when
the other man's fists connected. There was no pain, no
fear, no anything except for this mad rage. Even when
Anderson's strikes started losing their power, George's
fury-fueled punches didn't slow. He struck again and
again until a low moan from El made him freeze.

He stared at her motionless form, holding his breath,
praying that he hadn't imagined the sound. A hard shove
knocked him sideways, and Anderson scrambled out
from underneath him. George reached for the fugitive,
grabbing Anderson's ankle and yanking it so the fleeing
man fell face-first into the snow.

Anderson kicked at the same time Ellie released a
second tiny groan, making George's head whip around
so he could stare at her still-unmoving form. Distracted,
George didn't see the boot until it slammed into his
temple, dazing him for a moment. He shook his head,
blinking away the stars threatening to overwhelm his
vision, and saw Anderson shove to his feet and take off
toward the trees at a shambling, limping jog.

George started to charge after Anderson, but Ellie's
whimper made him turn in midlunge and rush to her,
instead, his mad rage shoved aside by hope and fear and
a bottomless joy that she was alive. As he knelt next
to her crumpled form, George felt all those battling

emotions rising to choke him, making his voice even rougher than normal as he said her name.

"El?" He supported her head as he turned her onto her back. Her eyes were open, wide and focused on him, but her breathing was too rapid and shallow. George ran his hands over her arms and jerked up her shirt and sweatshirt, searching desperately for where the bullet had entered her body. There was no hole gushing blood, though, and he moved his search lower, checking her hips and legs. The soft, light-blue fleece of her pants was unmarked, and he moved to check her chest again. There had been a gunshot, and she'd been on the ground. She had to have been hit.

"What's the status?" At Rob's shouted question, George whipped his head around to see the sheriff and Chris running through the snow toward them.

"King shot her at close range with a forty-caliber pistol," George clipped. "She's conscious but having difficulty breathing." He glared at them as he shucked his coat, wrapping it around her. "Where were you? You said you'd protect her if I wasn't there. She ran through the snow in her socks! In her fucking socks!"

"There's no radio or cell reception out here." Chris reached toward Ellie's wrist, as if to take her pulse, but George knocked the other man's hand away. "That granite bluff to the south blocks everything. I had to drive a mile just to check in with dispatch."

"What are you talking about?" Rob stared at the deputy. "The radios work just fine out here."

"But—" Chris started.

"We'll discuss this later," Rob interrupted. "Which way did King go?"

George jerked his head toward the spot where Anderson had disappeared into the trees.

"Chris, get Medical out here and send Lawrence and Macavoy to back me up." Rob took off running for the trees as Chris hurried toward the cabin.

George refocused on Ellie, trying to keep her as covered as possible while resuming his frantic search for injuries. He still hadn't found a bullet wound, but there was a dark red and purple circle in the center of her upper chest. Frowning, he touched it lightly. El jolted and gasped when his finger barely connected with the spot.

"Hurts," she panted, tears overflowing her eyes and running down her temples.

George wiped the salty wetness from her chilled skin. "God, El. I thought you were dead. You can't leave me. Don't ever leave me. I love you so much, El."

Her cold fingers brushed his cheek. "Love…you… too," she managed between quick, shallow breaths.

Even as the words burrowed into an empty place in his heart, a gleam of brass caught his eye, and George lifted Baxter's compass from where it had slid in the angle between her shoulder and neck. He carefully eased it along the chain until he could flip it over and see the dented, mangled mess that used to be the front of the compass.

Raising his eyes to meet El's panicked gaze, he held up the mutilated brass object so she could see it.

She stared at it for several seconds before giving a wheezing gasp of a laugh. "Dad…had my…back."

His laugh was just as rough as hers as he pulled down her sweatshirt and tucked his coat more tightly around her. "Yeah, El." He blinked rapidly as moisture burned his eyes. "He did."

Chapter 34

"WHOA. IT'S BROKEN?" LOU LEANED EVEN FARTHER over the counter toward Ellie to get a better view. The bells on the door jangled, announcing the arrival of a customer. Before that, they'd been the only two in the coffee shop. Ellie flushed, releasing the pulled-down collar of her shirt so the circular, multicolored bruise was hidden again.

"Sternal fracture," Ellie said, turning to see who'd just entered. It was Rory, and Ellie gave her a slightly nervous smile. The woman still intimidated her. "It hurts like a mother, but they gave me good drugs. Plus, it's better than a bullet through the heart."

"That's for sure. Hey, Rory."

Rory gave them both a somber nod and settled onto one of the stools at the counter. "Have they found Anderson yet?"

Shaking her head, Lou started to wipe down the counter. "Not that I've heard, and I have a guy on the inside. Okay, I kind of have a guy on the inside. He tells me things occasionally. Very occasionally. I do know that the manhunt is huge. Rob is pissed and taking this personally. Besides everything Anderson did to you"—she gestured toward Ellie's chest—"he's the main suspect in both Joseph's and Willard Gray's murders. And despite his...sketchy behavior, Joseph was part of search and rescue for years. He was one of ours."

KATIE RUGGLE

Ellie shook her head. "I don't think Anderson did it—not Willard's murder. At the cabin, Dad was talking about someone else being the killer, and A-Anderson"— she closed her eyes for a second, hating that she'd stuttered over his name, hating even more that he had the power to make her wake up screaming—"wasn't even sure who Gray was at first."

"You're just determined to stop me from tying up the case in a tidy little bow, aren't you?" Lou gave her a mock scowl before her expression became serious and her voice lowered. "Do you think Joseph was the killer, then? It's so strange to think that someone in search and rescue could be capable of that."

"I'm not sure." Ellie shivered. "He was a little off, but a killer? Joseph lied about seeing George head home that night, but I figured he was just being his gross and pervy self. He did talk to Anderson like they knew each other, though, right before…"

"Anderson shot him?" Lou finished with a wince.

Pushing back the nightmarish image of Joseph crumpling to the ground, Ellie gave a frustrated huff. "I'm pretty sure Dad could tell us who killed Gray, but who knows where he is."

"Still no word?" Rory asked, and Ellie shook her head. Her heart hurt every time she thought of him.

"As soon as this is better"—Ellie gestured toward her chest—"I'm going to start searching for him again. I will find my dad."

"I know you will." Spinning the tip jar in distracted circles, Lou said, "So, Baxter Price knows who killed Gray—and the murderer knows it—so the murderer tells Anderson King that Baxter witnessed a drug deal.

That way, King would take out Baxter, and the killer isn't involved."

"Smart," Rory said. When the other women stared at her, she lifted her hands defensively. "I'm not saying it was *right*. Just…smart."

Lou snorted, looking amused. Her expression quickly faded to thoughtfulness. "And your dad didn't tell you anything? No hints about who it might be? There's tons of blank space on my whiteboard that's dying to be filled."

"I thought it was Callum's whiteboard," Rory said dryly.

Lou shrugged. "It was a gift. Some women want jewelry, but I just wanted a dry-erase board and a Glock."

Rory grinned at that, the same startling, quick smile that Ellie had seen her give Ian at Levi's.

"He said a lot," Ellie belatedly answered Lou's question, "but it's so hard figuring out what's real and what's not with him."

Making a face of exaggerated frustration, Lou replaced the tip jar to its original position with a thump. "Since we're getting exactly nowhere with this conversation, let's move on." A sly grin warned Ellie exactly where they were about to move on to. "How is it staying with George? Where is your extra-large shadow, by the way?"

"He's on a SAR call. And things are…" There was no way to stop the sappy smile from creeping over her face.

"That good, huh?" Lou laughed. "I'm not surprised. He gets the same look whenever he sees you."

"Are you staying?" Rory asked abruptly. "After you're healed, I mean."

"I'd like to, and George hasn't mentioned kicking me out anytime soon." She shrugged, trying to hide how very,

very much she wanted to stay. "I talked to Chelsea—my boss and roommate back home—and she said she knew she'd lose me to George since she didn't have enough facial hair to compete with him. I think she's enjoying having the condo to herself, too. She said she'd be interested in buying it from me if I end up staying in Simpson."

"Yay! We get to keep Ellie!" Lou did a funny little dance in place, making Ellie laugh. She immediately regretted it. Usually, her chest didn't hurt when she talked, but laughing, coughing, or sneezing still sent sharp splinters of agony through her.

"Oh, ow." She breathed shallowly for a moment, allowing the pain to fade. Vaguely, she heard the bells on the door jangle again.

"You okay?" Lou asked. Both women were looking at her with concern.

"Yeah," Ellie said when the worst had passed. "Just quit being funny."

"Impossible," Lou said, deadpan, making Ellie laugh again.

"Ow."

Two muscled arms bracketed her, the hands catching the edge of the counter. He bent over her, surrounding her in a sort of George-tent, making her insides warm.

"Okay?" he said quietly, and she smiled at him reassuringly.

"Lou's just making me laugh."

"Hey!" Lou crossed her arms over her chest. "Don't give me that nasty look, Mr. Holloway. I can't help it if I'm hilarious."

He snorted before leaning close to Ellie's ear again. "Ready to go?"

"Sure." She eased off her stool as George lightly gripped her arms, trying to help her without hurting her. It would've been easier for her to do it alone, but she didn't say that. She liked his efforts to be kind and thoughtful, and she didn't want to discourage him. As she made her slow way across the shop, she called her good-byes to the other women.

"Did you find the special-needs boy who wandered away from his group?" she asked as he held the door for her. At his nod, she smiled. "He okay?"

"Yeah. Scared and cold but not hurt."

"Good."

When she stepped onto the ice-glazed parking lot, her foot slipped. It was just a small slide, but her body jerked in an effort to keep her balance. A small, pained sound escaped her before she clamped her lips together, but it was apparently enough for George. With a displeased grunt, he wrapped his hands around her waist and picked her up. She grabbed his shoulders for balance as he carried her to the passenger door of the truck and set her carefully on her feet again.

Although she tried to give him a stern frown, his concerned expression made it hard to hold it. "I am not a doll for you to always be carrying around."

He didn't look too bothered. "You look like one." His thumb brushed over her bottom lip.

"No, I don't." The touch had distracted her, and the words came out absently.

"You do." He brushed her lip again, then bent to kiss her lightly. With a happy sigh, she tried to deepen it, but he pulled away much too soon. This time, her sigh was disappointed. The additional two weeks it was going

to take her sternum to heal stretched endlessly in front
of her.

Ellie waved at the deputy leaving the parking lot.
When George had gotten the call that morning, she'd let
Rob know and asked if her temporary bodyguard could
be someone other than Chris. Although he had seemed
truly torn up about what had happened with Anderson,
Ellie couldn't get past the fact that Chris had left her
alone that day at the cabin. As much as she wanted to,
she just couldn't trust him.

George unlocked her door and helped her into the
cab. Just that movement alone hurt enough to make
black dots dance across her vision. Once the pain had
faded, Ellie reached for the radio, messing with the
knob until she found the only slightly staticky sound
of one of her favorite songs. "Wow, we can get Denver
radio here?"

"A few stations." His glance flicked from the radio
back to her. "Apparently."

"Smart-ass." She bit the inside of her cheek so she
didn't laugh and send pain radiating through her chest
again. She sang along for a few words. "I love this song.
Will you play it tonight?"

"Okay."

With a grin, she settled deeper in her seat. "It's so
awesome you can do that."

His eyes stayed focused on the road, but the corner
of his mouth lifted.

He turned onto the highway, heading toward his
house—*their* house, at least for now. She reached for
the hand that was resting on the gearshift, threading their
fingers together. "Guess what?"

Lifting his eyebrows, he gave her a quick, questioning look before refocusing on the road.

"Barbara at the Screaming Moose offered me a job as the store manager. She wants to move to Florida, where things are apparently more civilized than Simpson."

His fingers tightened around hers. "Did you..." He visibly swallowed. "Did you take it?"

"I said I'd need to talk to you." Nerves made her gaze bounce around the truck, landing on everything except George's profile. "I know we haven't talked about what the plan is after I've healed, and...too tight! Still too tight. Little looser. Okay, better." She exhaled as his grip on her hand eased slightly. When she stole a look at his face, Ellie wasn't sure how to interpret the way his jaw was working. He remained silent, so she rushed to fill the quiet. "I didn't want to just assume that you wanted me to stay. I mean, you're used to your privacy and routine, and I'm kind of messy. Like this morning, when I'd washed my underwear and had it hanging over the shower rod and forgot about it until..."

He freed his hand from hers and jerked the wheel, abruptly turning into a gravel pull-off. The truck stopped with a lurch forward that pressed her chest into the seatbelt, making her gasp.

"Ow."

"Sorry."

There was an endless moment of silence, during which George stared through the windshield.

"Stay." The word came out harsh and thick, as if he'd dragged it out of his throat by force. "I want you to stay."

"Really?" His intent look was all the answer she needed. Ellie smiled. "Okay."

"Okay?"

"Okay."

His fingers clutched the steering wheel so hard that the skin over his knuckles glowed white. With an audible exhale, he loosened his grip, and his hands turned a normal color again. "Good."

As he eased the truck back onto the highway, Ellie looked out her window and smiled.

Chapter 35

ANDERSON KING PUNCHED THE NUMBERS INTO THE burner phone. As it rang, he resisted the urge to pace. The shadows of the lawn shed hid him, but movement could catch someone's attention. It rang twice more, and King was starting to think he'd be sent to voice mail when someone finally answered.

"It's me," King said quietly.

There was a pause. "A lot of people are looking for you."

"That's why I need to get out of here."

"Why are you calling me?"

"Because"—he eyed the light seeping out around the edges of the closed blinds in the upstairs window—"to leave, I need money."

"Again, why are you calling me?"

"I found Price. We had an interesting talk."

The silence on the other end continued too long, forcing King to speak again.

"He told me some things about you."

"What do you want?"

"Just to have a chat." King grinned. The conversation was going exactly as he'd imagined. "Meet me tomorrow at that empty white house on Alpine Lane with the for-sale sign out front. Two a.m. I'll make sure the back door is open for you."

He ended the call, still smiling. With a final glance at the window, he turned and disappeared into the shadows.

———m———

The killer was late.

Anderson King prided himself on his patience, but his stomach had begun to curdle at the thought of his plan going to hell. It was one thing to leave the country with money, and a whole other thing to go on the run broke. No brother, no cash, cops on a county-wide manhunt, sleeping on the floor of a vacant house, his body bruised and aching from George Holloway's fists… How had everything gone so wrong?

Nervous energy forced him to pace the living room until Anderson realized his boots were clomping against the hardwood floor. Appalled, he stopped abruptly. A final echo of the sound reverberated through the empty space. How had he gotten so sloppy? Was he losing his stealth and nerve along with everything else?

"Anderson."

He whirled toward the voice. Anderson had been so preoccupied that he hadn't heard anyone else enter the house. The moonlight filtering through the windows wasn't very bright, but Anderson had no problem making out the handgun and its attached silencer. He reached for his own pistol holstered at the small of his back.

"Don't." The single word wasn't loud, but there was an authoritative crack to it. That and the gun pointed at him made Anderson reconsider drawing his weapon.

"About time you got here," he blustered, having a hard time looking away from the gun barrel. "I was beginning to think you didn't care if I handed all this evidence over to the state investigators."

"What evidence?"

As the other voice calmed, growing quieter and more conversational, Anderson found himself getting more and more agitated. *Relax*, he told himself. *You're holding all the cards here.* "Photographs Willard Gray took."

"Of what?"

Anderson leaned a shoulder against the fireplace mantel. "Pretty, pretty fires."

"That proves nothing."

"There are letters, too."

The silence stretched an uncomfortably long time, and Anderson forced himself not to fidget. During poker games, he'd always been good at bluffing. Now was not the time to develop a tell.

"Letters?"

And there's the tug on the baited line. Biting back a triumphant grin, Anderson confirmed, "Yep. Gray sent them to that crazy buddy of his, Baxter Price. There's all sorts of interesting information in those letters. It's funny. He may be dead, but Gray still can give his eyewitness testimony."

"Where are they?"

That was the flaw in his plan. With Baxter Price missing, there were no letters or pictures—at least not in Anderson's possession. No one had to know that, though. "In a safe place."

That disconcerting silence fell again.

"You don't have any letters." He sounded certain.

"Sure, I d—"

Time slowed for Anderson as he saw the gun flash and felt the punch of the bullet entering his chest, cutting off the lie midword. This was it, then. The gun fired once more, and he began to topple face-first toward the floor. At least he'd get to see his brother again soon.

———※———

With a sigh, Rob lowered his gun. He was tired, and it was late. The last thing he wanted to do was deal with yet another body. There wasn't any alternative, though. He'd made the mess, so he'd clean it up. That's what responsible people did.

Quietly, methodically, he got to work.

*Keep reading for an excerpt from the
final book in the Search & Rescue series*

IN SAFE HANDS

IT WAS ALMOST MAY, AND IT WAS STILL SNOWING. Daisy made a face at the fat flakes clinging to the window. It wasn't like she had to go out into the snow, but she hated that it drove everyone else *inside*. With her neighbors sheltering against the cold, her own special version of reality television had been reduced to what she could see through the windows of the few houses in her line of sight.

There was no use whining about it, though. It would have to do until spring finally came to the Rockies.

She peered through the curtain of snow at the house directly across the street from hers. It looked like most of the Storvicks were in their family room, watching a movie. Only the oldest son, Corbin, was missing. Daisy spotted him through one of the upstairs windows, talking on a cell phone while pacing his bedroom. From the way he yanked on his hair with his free hand, there was more drama happening between him and the tall, redheaded girl who visited his house on an off-again/on-again basis.

As she watched the teenager end the call by throwing

his phone against the wall, Daisy leaned closer to the window, making a mental note to tell Chris that Corbin and his girlfriend were fighting again. Last time they'd split, Corbin had spray-painted misspelled epithets on the girl's garage door. Daisy wasn't sure why his girlfriend had taken him back after that. Maybe Corbin was a good apologizer.

Since the teen had crammed in his earbuds and thrown himself on his bed, Daisy figured he'd be moping for at least a few hours. With the excitement at the Storvick house over for the night, she checked out Ian Walsh's place. To her disappointment, the new shutters had been closed, blocking her view.

The window coverings and the girlfriend had been installed around the same time. Although she was happy that Ian had found someone, those shutters had put a definite damper on any vicarious thrills. Firefighter Ian Walsh had been in the habit of walking around in nothing but boxer briefs, and Daisy missed her personal Chippendales show.

The house to the right of the Storvicks', 304 Alpine Lane, was empty and had been for almost eight months. The for-sale sign was looking a little faded, especially with the frosting of new, bright-white snow lining the top. Daisy wished someone would move in soon and give her one more channel of neighbor TV. It looked like tonight's entertainment would be a book or the internet, neither which excited her.

With a resigned sigh, she started to turn away from the window, but a movement in her peripheral vision brought Daisy's focus back to the empty house. She squinted through the falling snow. There might have been a flicker of motion by the back corner of the house, but the darkness and the veil of snow made it hard to see. As her gaze traveled over the shadowed edges of the yard, she shivered and wrapped her arms around her middle. Without any moonlight, the forest on the far side of Number 304 disappeared into absolute blackness. Anything or anyone could be lurking just past the treeline, and Daisy would never know.

Dragging her gaze away from the encompassing darkness, she forced herself to leave her window seat.

"No more horror movies for you," she muttered under her breath. Ever since her friend, Chris, had told her about the headless body found in a nearby reservoir a few months ago, Daisy had been even more on edge than usual. As she scanned her bookcase for something light and funny to read, Daisy couldn't help shooting a wary glance at the window. There were dangerous, terrifying things in the world beyond the safe walls and locked doors of her home. She knew this all too well. If she let herself dwell on those horrors, though, the nightmares would get even worse.

Picking one of her comfort reads, Daisy sat on her bed with her back toward the window. As she started on the first chapter, she was quickly lost in the book, and Daisy was almost able to shove away any worries about the unknown dangers creeping around outside her safe haven.

Almost.

Daisy recognized the knock, but she still pushed the intercom button. Messing with Chris was one of her few pleasures in life.

"May I help you?"

"Dais. Let me in." He sounded crabby. That was unusual.

"Is that how you announce yourself? Shouldn't you be shouting, 'Sheriff's Department' or something?"

"I'm not serving a warrant." Chris was *definitely* cranky. "If you don't let me in right now, you're not getting your very heavy present."

"Present?" She hit the button to unlock the exterior door. "Why didn't you say so? You know 'present' is the magic word." Tipping her head close to the wood panel, she listened for the dull thud of the outer door closing and the click of the lock reengaging. Once it was secure, she opened the four dead-bolt locks and two chains as quickly as possible. Finally yanking open the interior door, she grinned when she saw the big box Chris was carrying.

"Out of the way," he grunted, walking forward so she was forced to retreat a few steps. As soon as he was through the doorway, she closed the interior door, careful not to look at the outer one. Just the sight of that flimsy barrier between her and the outside world made her dizzy.

After refastening the locks, she turned toward her gift and its bearer. Chris had set the box on the kitchen floor and returned to the door to remove his boots. As Daisy hurried toward the mystery box, she stepped on a chunk of melting snow. With a yelp, she hopped over the remainder of what Chris had tracked in.

"I think the cows already escaped," she said, watching through the arched doorway between the kitchen and the entry as he pulled off his boots.

He blinked up at her. "What?"

"Closing the barn door? Boots? Snow on the floor?"

With a snort, he unzipped his coat. "You're a strange one, Daisy May."

"You do know that's not my middle name, right?"

"Sure." He offered her a crooked grin. His bad mood seemed to have disappeared as soon as he was inside. "*Daisy May* is just more fun to say than *Daisy Josephine*."

"If you say so." She curled her fingers under the box's cardboard flaps and looked at Chris, waiting anxiously for his okay to open it. When he waved a hand, smile tugging at his mouth, she flipped them over, revealing a sheet of bubble wrap. Pushing it aside, she spotted the flesh-colored torso and shrieked with excitement. "Grapple Man!"

Wrapping her arms around the dummy, she pulled him out of the box, scattering packing material as she did so. He was heavier than she expected, probably about fifty pounds, and Daisy grunted as she hoisted him upright. Looking at Chris, she saw he was wearing a proud grin.

"This is awesome, Chris! If I didn't have my arms full of this marvelous specimen of fake manhood, I would hug you so hard! Where'd you get him?"

"The Department upgraded, so I snagged this one for you." He leaned against the counter and crossed his arms over his chest. "He needed a new sparring partner, and I figured you could use a training buddy for times when I'm not here."

Distracted for a second by the way Chris's biceps bulged, stretching the tan fabric of his uniform shirt, it took a moment for his answer to penetrate. "He's the best present ever. Thank you, Chris." She hugged the dummy, since the man she really wanted to hug was several feet away and didn't always accept physical affection gracefully. "I shall call him...Maximillian.

Unless…" Daisy looked over the dummy's shoulder so she could see Chris. "Did you guys already name him?"

Smirking, he shook his head.

"Huh." Bending her knees, she heaved Max over her shoulder into a fireman's carry. "How could you have worked with him for *years* without naming him? It's unnatural."

"Unnatural? Naming some dummy you're about to kick in the face is what's unnatural. I'll get him, Dais." Chris reached to take Max, but Daisy spun out of reach, tottering slightly before catching her balance.

"We're good." She patted Max's behind as she headed for the training room. "I can't wait to practice my kicks on him. With the bag, I never know if I'm landing them in the right spot. Did I mention that this is the best gift *ever*?"

"I think you did a couple of times." He followed her through the doorway.

"Well, thank you again." She eyed the hook dangling from a chain next to the heavy bag. "That should be a good height for Mr. Max, don't you think?"

"Looks about right." Chris maneuvered the dummy so the ring at the back of his neck slid onto the hook. Max's feet almost touched the ground.

"Perfect." Eyeing her new piece of training equipment, Daisy excitedly bounced on her toes before turning back to Chris. "He's so great. *You're* so great. Thank you, thank you, thank you!"

She couldn't stop herself from reaching to hug him, but he dodged and grabbed her outstretched hands instead. Although she felt the usual dart of hurt, Daisy's delight in Max was too great to be squashed so easily. She squeezed his hands, instead.

"You're, uh, welcome," he said, glancing away. Ever since she'd given into a moment of impulsive stupidity and tried to kiss him a few months earlier, awkward moments had occurred between them on a regular basis. Daisy hated that.

"Are you hungry?" she asked, releasing his hands and turning toward the doorway. "I can make us some lunch."

"That's okay." He followed her out of the training room. "I'll just swing by my house and grab something quick."

Disappointment settled over her, and she fought to keep her smile. "Since you used your break to bring me my new favorite man, the least I can do is feed you. Plus, then you can fill me in on all the latest Simpson gossip."

"Gossip?" he grumbled. "I don't gossip. I'm with the Sheriff's Department, not Fire."

Daisy laughed. "If we call it 'important local news,' instead, will you tell me the latest on the hermit guy's new girlfriend?"

Although his affable smile stayed in place, a shadow darkened his expression for just a second before he reached for his coat. "Sorry, Dais. No time. Got to keep Field County safe from jaywalking tourists and vagrant bighorn sheep. I'll stop by on one of my days off so we can train."

"Sure? There are leftover crab cakes from last night. Not to toot my own crustacean-cooking horn, but they're pretty tasty."

His smile widened, but he didn't pause as he pulled on his boots. "I'll have to try them another time."

"Okay." Daisy watched as he unfastened the multiple locks. Although she wanted to push him again to stay, it would just make her seem lonely and desperate. "Thanks again for Max."

"You're welcome again." With a final crooked smile, he was gone.

And she was alone once more.

———— ᴡ ————

Sweat ran in her eyes, making them sting. Her knee connected with Max's outer thigh. If he'd been a real boy, the nerve strike would've rendered that leg useless for a while. Moving back, she practiced front and side kicks until her legs were noodle-y, and then moved to punches and palm-heel strikes.

When her wrapped hands felt too heavy to lift, she leaned against Max and gasped for breath. He swung away from her weight, so she wrapped her arms around his middle to stabilize them both. When she realized how they must look, Daisy gave a breathless laugh and forced her body to straighten.

"You really are the perfect man, Max," she said, patting his belly. "I wake you up at two in the morning, beat you to a pulp, and you're still willing to cuddle. How many men would be willing to put up with that?" A certain deputy sheriff came to mind, but she pushed the thought away before she got mopey. Looking down, she made a face as she pulled her sweat-soaked tank away from her skin. "Now I'm disgusting and need a shower. Good night, Max. Thanks for letting me assault you."

The stairs loomed in front of her, mocking her with their steepness. Daisy wished she'd left a little juice in her leg muscles for the climb. With a whimper that almost made her glad no one else was within earshot, she forced her wobbly quads to lift high enough for her feet to clear each step.

She stopped in her room to get clean pajamas. As she

passed the front window, the one she referred to as her "TV screen," she stopped and moved closer. There was a Sheriff's Department SUV parked at the curb in front of the Storvicks' house.

"Corbin, you budding little psycho," she muttered. "What did you do this time?"

Forgetting her aching legs, she scurried over to turn off the overhead light and then returned to her window seat. All the windows in the Storvicks' house were dark, and Daisy frowned. Had the deputy not gone up to the house yet? She'd been expecting shouting parents and a crying Corbin, not the current sleepy silence.

No one was in the driver's seat of the SUV, though, so the deputy had to be somewhere. Maybe Corbin hadn't done anything to his ex-girlfriend after all. She looked around the area. Despite her immediate assumption that Corbin was the reason for the deputy's visit, the squad SUV was actually parked closer to the for-sale house than the Storvicks'. Daisy thought of the movement she'd seen the other night, and she wondered if there was a homeless person living there. The deputy could be responding to a trespassing call.

Daisy drummed her fingertips on the wall next to the window, trying to remember when Chris's days off started. If he was working, then his shift started at seven a.m., so she could call him in a few hours and he wouldn't threaten to kill her. If he *wasn't* working, however, he tended to sleep late to start getting his body ready for the approaching night shift. She knew from experience that, when woken, Chris was as grumpy as a bear that had been kicked in the face.

Besides, his recent standoffishness had pushed her

off-center. Daisy wasn't sure where they stood at the moment. He'd been her friend—her only real-life, in-person friend—since she'd been sixteen. After eight years, they'd developed an easy, comfortable comradery, but she'd managed to mess that up in one impulsive second that she'd regretted ever since. It'd been movie night a few months ago, and they'd laughed in unison at some funny line. When she'd turned to look at Chris, she'd caught him staring at her with a strange, almost hungry, expression. Her amusement died, replaced by a longing so intense that she couldn't stop herself from leaning closer and closer until their lips barely touched. She could have sworn he wanted to kiss her as much as she wanted to kiss him.

But then he'd jerked back as if she'd given him a static shock. Muttering some excuse, he'd escaped from her house as quickly as possible, leaving her to wallow in regret and humiliation. Ever since that night, Chris had been acting…weird. Except for the day of her mother's murder, Daisy had never wished so hard for a do-over.

The thought of losing Chris was scary, so she shoved it out of her head and concentrated on the scene in front of her instead. An almost-full moon and a couple of streetlights illuminated the SUV and the yard immediately next to it. If she squinted, Daisy could make out the shadowed impressions of footprints in the day-old snow, leading around the far side of the house. Those must've been made by the Deputy, she decided.

Daisy tried to figure out why uneasiness was simmering in her belly. Everything was so quiet and still, with everyone sleeping—everyone except for her, at least. The squad vehicle just didn't fit with that peace. In her experience, cop cars brought action and noise and movement—or at least a visit from Chris. That must've been why the empty SUV seemed so eerie.

She shivered and blamed it on her sweaty, quickly drying tank top. Darting across the room, she grabbed the hoodie draped over her desk chair and pulled it on as fast as possible so she wouldn't miss anything that might happen outside. As she was about to rush back to the window, her cell caught her eye, and she reached for it, sliding the phone into her hoodie pocket.

Daisy curled up on the window seat again. She knew from experience that she wouldn't sleep if she tried to go back to bed after exercising, plus that odd, uneasy feeling hadn't gone away. Resting her chin on her up-drawn knee, she watched, waiting for the deputy's return.

The wind picked up, rushing past her window and making the pine tree branches scratch against the side of Daisy's house. She pulled the hoodie more tightly around her and tucked her fingers under her arms to keep them warm. Clouds crept over the moon, darkening the shadows surrounding the house.

"No," Daisy groaned. The streetlights mostly just lit the narrow circle of space around their poles, so it was much more difficult to see anything with the moonlight gone. The encroaching darkness sent her imagination into overdrive, making it too easy to picture all sorts of things hiding in the shadows. She leaned toward the glass, trying to make up for the dim lighting by getting as close as she could to the action—or lack of action.

She'd resisted getting binoculars in the past, since that always seemed like it would've pushed her neighborhood-watch activities out of "quirky" and right into "creepy." Now, she regretted having qualms. In fact, a pair of night-vision binoculars would've been even better. So what if that shoved her squarely into creeper-hood? At least she'd be able to see what was happening.

A break in the clouds revealed someone walking along the side of the empty house. Sucking in a startled breath, Daisy rose to her knees and pressed her forehead against the cold glass. She stared hard at the furtive figure.

The person's shape was wrong. It wasn't just the distortion of the shadows. Either an ogre was walking next to the empty house, or... Wishing once again for binoculars, she shifted, trying to find a better angle.

Then the wind cleared the clouds away from the moon, and she could see more clearly. The misshapen form was actually someone with a large bundle over his or her shoulder. Peering at the person, she decided from his size and the way he moved that he was definitely male.

After a half-step of hesitation, he walked into the puddle of light circling one of the streetlamps. The lights on the SUV flashed and the back hatch door lifted. Balancing the burden over his shoulder with one hand, he reached with the other to move something around, maybe making room.

"What?" Daisy muttered, confused. The man next to the Sheriff's Department vehicle wasn't wearing a uniform. He was dressed head to toe in black, rather than the tan deputy uniform. Even their Department-issued winter coats were tan. The wrapped bundle over his shoulder caught the glow of the streetlight, gleaming a familiar, semi-glossy blue. Whatever the guy was carrying was wrapped in a tarp.

Closing her fingers around her phone, she pulled it out and tapped on the video app. The scene was strange enough that she felt like she needed to record it, even if it was just so she could watch it in the morning. In the light of day, the ominous feeling would be gone, and she could laugh at the way her overactive imagination had turned something innocuous into a nebulous threat.

No matter how she shifted, raising up or dropping low, Daisy couldn't find the right angle to get a glimpse of the man in black's face. Even if she had gotten a clear view, though, she probably wouldn't have been able to identify him. She only knew Chris's coworkers through his work anecdotes. She zoomed in her phone camera, but the image just got darker and grainer, rather than clearer.

Leaning forward, the man half-dropped, half-shoved the large bundle into the back of the SUV. The rear of the vehicle sagged a little, which meant the object must be heavy. There was an unsettling familiarity in the way that the tarp-wrapped item fell, bulky and weighted, that sent a shiver across the back of her neck.

The black-clad man shoved at the bottom of the bundle. He'd managed to tuck the majority of it into the SUV when something dark fell from the bottom of the rolled tarp, tumbled over the rear bumper and fell to the ground.

Daisy sucked in a breath hard enough to scrape her throat. From her vantage point, that dropped item looked very much like a boot.

About the Author

A fan of the old adage "write what you know," Katie Ruggle lived in an off-grid, solar- and wind-powered house in the Rocky Mountains until her family lured her back to Minnesota. When she's not writing, Katie rides horses, shoots guns, cross-country skis (badly), and travels to warm places where she can scuba dive. A graduate of the police academy, Katie received her ice-rescue certification and can attest that the reservoirs in the Colorado mountains really are that cold. A fan of anything that makes her feel like a badass, she has trained in Krav Maga, boxing, and gymnastics. You can connect with Katie at katieruggle.com, www.facebook.com/katierugglebooks, or on Twitter @KatieRuggle.

Made in the USA
Columbia, SC
29 October 2021

THE HIGHER EDUCATION OF A COTTONMOUTH

by

Richard Joyce

Edited by:
Julie Frederick   UK
Stephanie J. Beavers   USA

Illustrated by:
Rachael Flora
Sarah Bellian
Richard Joyce

Middleman Publishing

ISBN: 979-8-5116-9244-9

CONTENTS

INTRODUCTION

Dear Reader,

"The Higher Education of a Cottonmouth" is the tale of Mick Lee and his grandfather John Pierce, a man both renowned and reviled for his many acts. The events take place over the course of two days, when Mick, preparing for a final confrontation with the Devil himself, writes his most important memories of his grandfather and how he came to inherit his conflict with "Ole Scratch." John Pierce was a man who could be mean as a snake, but always appeared larger than life. Even though he was an "outsider," committing rather creative heists and landing himself in prison (what he called "state college," hence the story's title), his deeds of rebellion earned him fame and the love of his grandson. Through his journal entry, Mick tells the story of how his rebellious grandfather shaped his character and made him the man he is. After Mick completes writing in his journal, he must go out and fight the devil—or so he believes. Is the devil real or is Ole Scratch nothing more than his own restless mind?

The shorter stories included in this book are intended to be just a few of the other journal entries that Mick Lee scribes about his family. They are lighthearted comedies that don't reflect the spiritual conundrum faced in the main story. Mick's stories go on to tell of his parents, and of his grandfather, and one very personal incident that occurred after he became a parent himself.

The illustrations I included in this book were done strictly against the advice of everyone I know—their position being never use multiple styles of artwork throughout a story. But, as I mention early in the first story, these tales are adventures written by the main character, about his life and the people closest to him. Also, you are told within his journal you find rough sketches and old photographs inserted randomly throughout its pages. I think of these illustrations as those sketches and photographs. I'm not sure if I was successful at establishing that. But it's my book, so I did what I wanted.

I wish to market this book to the Young Adult Religious market. I am the first to agree this is not the typical book expected for such an audience and some of the language used here may be offensive to some readers. All I can say about that is, "Get over it!" There is nothing said here that you haven't heard before, and when describing the mannerisms of certain unlikeable people, I find facing the problem the most honest approach. It takes a bit more grit but at the end of the day you tend to have less to complain about.

Maybe this book is best given to the independent, spunky kid who trips up and lands in a little hot water occasionally. The Israelite, Samson, was no stranger to conflict but found true strength in his service to our Lord. And this story, too, tells of another troubled man who stumbled and fell more than once, but still managed to find his way and persevere. These warring men serve as an example of how you can overcome any obstacle by surrendering to the Holy Spirit—confirming a troubled past can be forgiven.

I hope my writings don't prove to be terribly unpleasant to read. And with any luck you might even chuckle once or twice. One can only keep their fingers crossed. Maybe I'll do better the next go round? Thank you for taking a look.

Best wishes,

R. K. Joyce

CHAPTER ONE:
THE REVERAND

There's a fight soon to come—a long overdue fight. And Mick Lee plans to be right in the thick of it. This isn't his first go-round getting ready to kick ass. Back in the day, he'd been in a scrap or two—standing up to bullies and their kind who made sport preying on those weaker than they were. But beyond doubt, this exchange will be a full-on, knockdown, drag-out, winner-takes-all nightmare—and he knows it. And he also knows that if all hell goes wrong, this might very well be his last battle ever.

It might surprise you to know that Mick doesn't look as though he's ready to trade blows with anybody, let alone throw himself into a brawl such as this. He always appears well groomed and finely clad. Pushed-back dishwater-blond hair weaves naturally into a curl and rests loosely over the neckline of his lightly starched, French-cuffed shirt. Mick normally wears a suit, but when relaxing at home, like today, the tailored jacket comes off and he is quick to unbutton the matching

vest for comfort. By and large, he is considered to be handsome, sporting classically good-looking features with a physique to match. It's obvious he stays fit, but he lacks any real heavy muscle mass, particularly the kind of bulk you would expect to see on a serious combatant. Don't be deceived, however: Mick is tough—tough as leather when necessary. Make no mistake about that.

Mick is smart too, especially when it comes to investing. A persuasive negotiator, he is brilliantly gifted. Many have sought his peerless, down-to-earth advice. And it's that advice that has made a lot of people a lot of money—including Mick.

The secret of Mick's success rests in one simple truth— the power of the spoken word. Simply put, from an early age he came to understand when he should talk and when it was time to shut up and listen. No need to blather incessantly, to wax on using fancy talk and obscure references, when you can make a point in a clear, simple tongue: that's Mick's motto. Keep the refined repartee up your sleeve for the moment of truth. If you can predict how your mark will respond when placed in certain situations, then the right turn of phrase could deliver the final blow in your favor. He was taught that lesson in wordplay a long time ago—back when he was a kid—by someone he held in utmost reverence.

Cussing has never fit into Mick's vocabulary, but that's not to say he doesn't create a new colorful word or two when provoked. It's more likely, however, that he'll rely on the power of prayer to guide him through the more difficult situations. For him, prayer is the be-all and end-

all; it is his only recourse when times are tough, and he trusts that the boss at the other end is listening. Today, Mick is a well-respected man of the cloth, a beloved Christian minister. To many of his friends, neighbors, and business associates, he is a trusted confidante.

It's never been said that Mick's life has been without controversy. Like many a young man, he fell victim to the usual vices, turning to alcohol and, on occasion, brute force to deal with problems. The drinking started innocently enough. After all, it's not the end of the world if a kid tries to cop a taste from an abandoned beer can or sneaks a sip from a forgotten wine glass. But during his rebellious teenage years it quickly escalated beyond his control. Granted, Mick's proudly been clean and sober for the past sixteen-plus years without a slip, though the stigma from the drinking and the problems that followed haunt him to this day. The AA recovery chip he carries in his pocket serves as a constant reminder of the slippery slope he treads.

Folks readily take to Mick, and they embrace the man that he has matured to become. It's his simple origins, his honesty, and his gallant, selfless heart that win people over. Friends know that they can turn to Mick in troubled times, and he's just as likely to help strangers too. He sees his wealth as a blessing to be shared—which he does, liberally, and without judgment.

Owing to firsthand experience, Mick has come to understand that occasionally doing the wrong thing is the right thing to do; that, to ease a person's pain, you may have to feed their disease; that even a wan,

ailing drunk might truly gain from a good, stiff drink sometimes—instead of another humiliating public sermon. He bears no prejudice if a person's misery is self-inflicted as a result of bad life choices. Retribution for yesterday's ignorance isn't always just desserts—often it's just callous. A wayward man is better led by a guiding hand than by a harsh word.

These benevolent acts are exemplary of a love for all humanity at its purest. And it is this love that drives a noble man to fight tooth and nail, understanding he might not survive. Much to the reverend's dismay, his prayers for spiritual guidance of late have left him perplexed. He has received no clear answers—or, if he has, they have been clouded by an indefatigable sense of destiny that this battle is inevitable. Mick isn't precisely sure why, but he is intent on bringing this vendetta to an end. It's time.

Absorbed by the gravity of his circumstances, Mick slowly paces the hardwood floor in his home library. Lost in thought, the saucer and cup of Earl Grey he carries wobbles unsteadily. Mick usually savors his tea, steaming hot with a bit of cream and honey. But today, his incidental sips are more from habit than deliberate enjoyment. His soul searching, engrossed as he is with the plight he must face, is interrupted when at last he hears the comforting pitter-patter of rain on the library windows. He finds the sound soothing, as it helps ease his anxiety.

Grateful for the distraction, he slurps his tea purposefully, then sets the cup on the edge of his desk.

He pulls out the chair and sits, leaning forward with his elbows resting on the blotter. His journal lies closed in front of him. He lifts the front cover and idly thumbs through the book, scanning his collection of stories. Every once in a while, he pauses, holding his finger on a page where he'd attempted a rough sketch or inserted an old photograph. His mind whirls with all the anecdotes and hair-raising events contained within. He shakes his head in disbelief of the words he himself put to paper; the anecdotes that defy logic but which are, hand on heart, God's own truth.

Writing is Mick's means of escape. An old fountain pen and a blank sheet of paper are all he needs to revisit the times when life was exhilarating and responsibilities were few. These are his memoirs, his existence captured in words. He has written about his loving mother and dutiful father. Occasionally, he relates tales of notable excursions with family and friends. But most of his writing is devoted to his childhood exploits. And in these, one figure stands out more than anyone else: that of a powerful mountain of a man, a rascal, a rogue—his grandfather—whose presence made Mick feel invincible.

Midway through, Mick unveils the first of numerous blank sheets and stops flipping. As he removes the cap from his pen, he feels a pressing urge to document yet another episode of his life—to immortalize one more untold story—before it is too late. With his future hanging in the balance, Mick yearns to articulate how his rebellious grandfather shaped his character and made him the man he is and to disclose how he came to inherit this conflict. But where should he begin? How ought the story be told?

After a deep breath and modest pause of silent reflection, Mick Lee holds the pen in his left hand and titles the page as uncertainty succumbs to inspiration. Words flood his mind, the pen flowing gracefully over the paper. And he writes...

CHAPTER TWO:
HIS STORY – PART ONE

The Higher Education of a Cottonmouth

If speaking ill of the dead doesn't meet your approval, you'll soon discover you can't talk long about my grandfather John Pierce and still be recounting the truth. Virtually everyone came to know him as "the Cottonmouth," for his temperament was the human equivalent of that of a venomous viper. Unlike the Cottonmouth snake, however, whose nickname comes from its gaping cotton-white mouth, visible just before it strikes for the kill, my grandfather tended to keep his jaw clamped shut to preserve what few teeth he had left. His manner of striking was not to bite, at least literally, but to slash his unwitting opponents with his wiles— and occasionally his fists. John was my mother's father and very possibly the most grievous man who had ever walked God's good earth. But I liked him.

My grandfather was born and raised in a shotgun shack buried deep in the pines of northern Georgia, miles away from the nearest town. As years passed, civilization gradually encroached on John's place, but it took a while. By then, he was too old to give a damn about the influences of a modern society that had considerately, and conveniently, passed him by for so many years. John's backcountry upbringing suited him, with its simplicity and few demands. That's not to say his life was without strife. Even living the "simple life" requires some basic necessities, which, of course, entails the means to acquire them.

The old homestead, as it is today

It goes without saying a supplemental procurement policy was covertly devised. Some have quietly suggested that my grandfather cheated when he gambled, shot hunting dogs that couldn't keep their mouths shut while poaching, robbed graves, participated in the bushwhacking of revenuers, and swiped shirts from unguarded clotheslines when he wanted something clean to wear. Others claim Grandpa flimflammed a banker into a position of embezzlement, but none of these accusations have ever been proven, and I'll leave you to draw your own conclusions.

I will concede, however, that it's undeniable he hijacked a locomotive, kept company with convicts, loathed the entire state of Alabama, and built a rampart to defend his homestead and his sanity. John lost that fight temporarily when he became a reclusive moonshiner and turned feral from his self-imposed isolation. The thought of decent food and indecent women snapped him out of it, though. And it's true— once, during a family reunion, overcome with rage at a cousin's snide comment, John got his comeuppance, silencing him with a cooked turkey slapped over his head. He also knocked out the local reverend's teeth with a bowl of peas, was known to cuss in front of small children, and regularly invited the Devil over for a drink on Sundays. Yet, from these adversities arose a truly spectacular man.

Let me be clear: What follows is not a testimonial to the truth. Nor is it fiction, to be dismissed as nothing but yarns and tall tales. It is the composite story, to the best of my ability, that explains what made my grandfather

tick, and how he came to be so extraordinary. It is up to you to decide what is real, and what is not.

∗

Education was deemed a true luxury in Grandfather's world. Those who graduated from the eighth grade had something mighty fine to brag about. John was many things, but not a braggart, so he didn't see any need to study beyond the three R's: reading, writing, and raising hell. Why did he need school when he could get by with his wiles? Although he was a brute in stature, honest hard work didn't fit into his agenda—in fact, there wasn't an honest bone in his body. He never actually experienced the rewards of manual labor until he was sent away to the state penitentiary, the consequence of his first business venture as a self-employed train robber.

Grandpa wasn't real complicated with his train robbing. And, to tell it right, his early attempts were more comical than clever. In the beginning, he planned his brazen assault to commence around dusk, at one of several locations throughout the Appalachians and its foothills where the winding train would slow to a crawl. It was at this point that John would try jumping from a bluff onto the top of one of the train's boxcars. The next phase of his brilliant plan involved him rappelling down the side of the car with a rope (carefully tucked inside his shirt); then he'd open the door, slide in, and dump the cargo. His next objective was to hop from the train at a prearranged location, where he'd have a horse and wagon ready. From there, he would go back and retrieve whatever merchandise he could gather before dawn.

John's first crack at this scheme almost flattened him. Instead of landing on top of the train, he ricocheted off the painted logo on the near side of the boxcar and was hurled to the roadbed below, mere inches from the steel rail. In my neck of the woods, we'd call that "a swing and a miss."

His second go at it was no better. This time, taking a running start, John overshot his target and slid off the other side of the car. Even though it must have been agonizing, his landing in thick blackberry briers probably kept him from being killed—and the profanities he spewed would no doubt have made the Devil himself cover his ears.

A trio of hobos, who regularly fished at a ramshackle makeshift camp next to a stream, witnessed each failed attempt with total bemusement. On the occasions where John arrived atop the bluff, the men would discard their fishing gear and watch him with keen interest, rubbing their hands together in anticipation of the show to come. It was more entertainment than they could have asked for. When my grandfather constructed a rope swing and swooped down upon the train as it went by, a raucous round of applause erupted. In his haste to dismount the swing, he was launched back into the air, whirling chaotically in circles as soon as his foot touched the top of a moving boxcar. Like a stooge, he spun helplessly above the train while it chugged on its way. This nightly entertainment lasted little more than a week, but I'm convinced it must have been top-class.

It didn't take Grandpa long to realize that there must be an easier way to steal things from boxcars. Perhaps, he thought, rubbing his aching muscles and picking the last of the briars from his punctured skin, it would be safer to perform his illicit campaigns from the ground. So, he concocted a strategy to hide from view several miles up the line, where the late-night trains stopped for coal and water. With the aid of a confederate who probably worked for the railroad, he broke the seal on a selected boxcar and climbed aboard. He then rode the train until he got to home territory, where he pitched out the whole lot.

This rudimentary method went unbeaten weeks on end, without a hitch. However, always looking for a new challenge, John decided to steal a locomotive and everything it was coupled to. It was a dark, moonless night when he slipped into the railroad yard and commandeered an engine. But, not surprisingly, there was no place for him to take sixteen cars of rolling stock except where the tracks were leading, so they caught him pretty easily.

That's when Grandpa was imprisoned and educated by the state. As a derogatory epithet, he brusquely referred to the penitentiary as a college, because everyone there, especially the guards, seemed eager to teach him a thing or two. Despite their best efforts, respect for authority was one course John outright failed. Somebody should have warned him that it wasn't clever to be the class clown at that pernickety school.

Clearly, he lacked the finer social skills that most people take for granted. Grandpa John had a hard time understanding what was appropriately viewed as funny and what wasn't. Not long after his arrival on campus, he made himself famous and soon got inducted into a notorious chain-gang fraternity. I'm not certain why John sought the warden's attention, but I do know that when he borrowed the captain's brand-new Chevrolet and drove it downtown in the May Day parade, he got all the attention he could stand, along with a new set of irons. Grandpa said they never played nice after that.

John's antics quickly gained the esteem of the other inmates—excluding a few who got jealous of his notoriety and conspired to cause him some trouble. Once he got word of their intentions, John knew he had to address the problem directly. A master of the art of tomfoolery, he decided to leave a lasting impression by handling the situation in a manner befitting his unique sense of humor.

One afternoon, as John was spreading gravel for the county with his work crew, he realized it was becoming ever more imperative to take a badly needed water break. Policy mandated he first humbly ask Boss for permission but continue working until "the Man" gave an answer. You've probably figured out by now that Gramps never did things by the book. And, besides, he was in the mood for some fun. Eager to liven things up a bit, John took an unauthorized water break by pulling down his britches and relieving himself on the legs of those jealous, conniving troublemakers who refused to appreciate his refined sense of humor. Boss nearly choked on his stogie in disbelief. Needless to say, the act didn't win over his piss-stained opponents.

The fight that ensued would go down as one of the biggest and the best in the history of the college. John presumably was having such a good time that hardly a soul there could resist the temptation to join in. One ole boy peed on the guy next to him, and they got into a fight. Then some of the other men got baptized by the holy water and began throwing fists. Soon, everybody was prancing around holding their peckers, punching and pissing, pissing and punching. It might not have been the proudest moment in their lives, but it sure beat the hell out of spreading gravel on that dry, dusty road. Boss was aiming to shoot my grandfather in the butt with a shell of rock salt he had loaded in his scattergun, but he couldn't get a clear shot.

As luck would have it, some pencil-neck deputy driving by saw the goings-on, and in his report to the head office, the patrolman called it an "orgy riot."

Nobody snitched on how the altercation began, but the warden knew sure as hell who the culprit behind the mess was. So the next day, John was moved to another work boss as a consequence of the first one being obviously unable to control him. A sign of sure victory, according to Gramps. In exchange, his original boss was assigned two inbred Alabama brothers, Melvin and Marvin Purser, to become esteemed new members of his crew. These boys weren't infamous desperados; they were just a couple of big, dumb galoots considered among the guards as shameful, for it was downright embarrassing to be in the company of anyone that ignorant. To get stuck with them on your crew was, in principle, thought of as punishment.

Marvin Purser

The Purser brothers had been incarcerated after stealing a brooding sow from a rich widow, Alma Roulaine Cantrell. The old woman may have been without a husband, but she definitely wasn't without influence. Among her twelve children was not only the local sheriff, but also, conveniently, a district court judge.

One night, the Pursers had parked their manure wagon about a half mile down the road from her place and slipped in behind the barn. After nabbing the sow, they tied a pair of red long-handled underwear around its neck and used that as a collar to lead it away. Being thick-headed, they became confused in the dark and set out in the wrong direction; soon enough, they were lost and walking aimlessly.

The sheriff and his posse found the brothers the next morning sleeping on benches in the town square. The sow, still being held hostage, was lying on the ground between them, tied up in the red undergarment. The lawman took a turn poking the two buffoons with his billy club and ordered them to rise as slow as his wife's biscuits in the oven or he'd knocked 'em down for another try at it. Melvin looked at his brother, Marvin, and Marvin looked at the bristle-haired hog. Marvin reached over and gave her a poke in the belly, to which the fat sow replied with a squeal. "Wake up, Momma, and put your skivvies back on. We got company," Marvin uttered.

You had to admit that the pig did bear a strong resemblance to the brothers, and some of the sheriff's men joshed that perhaps it was a relation of theirs.

Not only did the Pursers look like the sow, they pretty much smelled like it too. But when a deputy made a wisecrack about how the ole girl had more than one set of tits flopping out from under her flannels, the sheriff reminded them that it was his dear widowed mother's hog, then promptly arrested the boys. He had no qualms about teasing the Pursers, but he wasn't about to sit idly by and listen to anyone badmouth his momma's pig.

* * *

It's said that the time my grandfather spent incarcerated was, by far, more unpleasant for the warden than it was for him. John was, after all, a smooth criminal, a slick schemer, and, more often than not, the warden couldn't find the hard evidence to convict my grandfather of his petty crimes. There was one instance when laxatives were covertly placed in the mess hall coffee, prompting a sudden surge of convicts returning to their cell house toilets. It only took a few flushes for the ugly realization to dawn: Someone had earlier managed to shove a bed sheet into the sewer line and obstruct the drainage pipes. What followed I will only politely describe as a fragrant deluge of overflowing toilets. And, as expected, it generated some measure of anxiety when there wasn't enough paper available to meet the demand.

That evening at laundry exchange, officials issued the inmates clean undershorts, only to notice they had been mysteriously processed with a heavy starch, which only added to the inmates' despair. The clothing better resembled wood roofing shingles than something you

could comfortably wear. In anticipation of the ensuing mutiny, John had stealthily stashed a dozen pairs of untreated underpants in his cell, spreading word that he alone held the remedy for sore bottoms—for a price, of course. With the guarantee that the undergarments would be "as soft as a lamb's ear," he advertised one pair could be had for a full pack of store-bought smokes. Needless to say, business was good.

His antics didn't always come with a price tag; sometimes it was just for the sheer hell of it. And he became all but ecstatic when others happened to join in on his charades. A spur-of-the-moment gag he played on the staff employed in the infirmary became one of his most notable calamities. He and a few other inmates had been brought to the clinic to remove some antiquated furnishings and equipment. A notoriously unpopular, crabby nurse, dressed in her usual unkempt, stained uniform, assembled the men and gave them a visual once-over. The irony of her scrutiny was not lost on the men as they stood in line in their spotless, starched stripes. Still she turned up her nose in flagrant disapproval, all the while trying—and failing—to smooth out the creases in her blouse and hide the blotches on her skirt. Incensed, she turned her interest toward the unpaid help and spitefully dispatched orders.

While receiving work instructions, for no apparent reason at all, John suddenly grabbed a ragged blanket off a stretcher and yelled, "Watch it, men!" He then dove headfirst under a lopsided gurney with the blanket flung out in front of him. With acting skills to match those of a trained performer, John pretended to grapple with some

wily, elusive critter that he had trapped underneath it. The wobbly table thumped and jittered to and fro, until he concluded this exaggerated sideshow act. He then rose from the floor, tightly gripping the shabby blanket, akin to the way you'd show a proverbial pig-in-a-poke, and announced, "It's okay, everybody. I've caught this one!" Holding the cover high over his head, Grandpa displayed his prize as if it were a well-earned trophy.

By now, he had captured everyone's rapt attention. Just as the other work-crew inmates were wondering whether John had truly gone nuts, his signature cagey grin and wink of the eye dispelled their fears. Over the years, they had all become accustomed to that expression on John's face, and it was all the confirmation they needed to know the diversion was going to be engaging. The willing pranksters eagerly awaited their chance to become his partners in crime.

The disheveled nurse in charge fretfully conjured herself into a dreadful panic. "What is it you're holdin' there?" she panted. "Oh, my lord. What you got there, mister?"

"Looks to be a baby skunk, ma'am," John answered calmly. "Probably a litter of them come in under a loose floorboard or from back behind a wall somewhere."

With that said, the hooligans quickly rallied. To keep the ruse going, one of Grandpa's cohorts alerted his pals, declaring that he, too, had spotted a skunk running along the baseboard. He scurried wildly in pursuit, grabbed a stool, and thrust it about. This heralded a

ridiculous slapstick act in which he gallantly satirized a daring young lion tamer starring in a big top circus. He bellowed with authority, commanding the unseen creature to "stay back, or face certain death."

Another con swore he saw two more coming his way, and he knocked over a stack of chairs and a tray of medical instruments to get at 'em. Slick as a whistle, the rest of the men cut loose and chased nonexistent skunks, causing total pandemonium. The nurse screamed as if a bloody murder were taking place and ran for her life, abandoning what she thought was a varmint-ridden clinic and scattering boxes across the room on her way out. The power of suggestion had her seeing skunks everywhere, and neither hell nor God's pestilence was going to slow her down. In the end, the skunk-in-the-infirmary show landed each participant ten days in the hole, but they figured the inconvenience was well worth it for the look of madness on that nurse's face.

There seemed to be no end to Grandfather's stream of hoaxes, many of which were initiated chiefly for his own selfish pleasure. The dead fish found rotting beneath the vanity cabinet in the women's lavatory at the visitors' reception center, and the gallon of hooch mailed to the governor on his birthday, accompanied by a special note of congratulations hand-signed by the warden, were only the tip of the iceberg. The cancellation of the order for the kegs of beer intended for the employee picnic, the flower bouquets sent to the secretaries working in the administration office, the unending saga of bees nesting under the warden's porch, and the official requisitions for tons of fresh farm produce to be delivered to the

penitentiary were yet more examples of my grandpa's artistry. The truth is, he was bored to death, and being blessed with a resourceful mind, he needed an outlet to express himself. Contrary to popular belief, it was nothing personal.

Still and all, John enjoyed the benefits of an early parole. When the Pursers were released from prison, the warden surreptitiously arranged to throw him on the bus, too, and declared it a holiday. By the time John had any clue as to what was taking place, he found himself marching in a procession behind Marvin and Melvin, en route to the Inmate Discharge Sally Port where collectively they were loaded for transport.

The brothers sat across from John and attempted to get better acquainted. Marvin wanted to know if John had a girl waiting or if he was returning home a lonely man. Melvin offered to swap his sack lunch in exchange for John's sincere opinion of matrimony. Grandpa was not someone who felt comfortable bonding emotionally. The bus hadn't made it past the penitentiary's gates before he was trying to force the door open, screaming for the guards to take him back. Another second spent around those two boys was far worse than the thought of incarceration with convicted thieves and killers. By John's estimation, the warden had neatly executed his supreme revenge. And what stuck deepest in his craw— John never saw it coming. For that sake alone, he would have preferred to serve the duration of his sentence than concede to the warden scoring the ultimate win.

My grandfather said that was the longest damned ride of his life. When he finally stepped off the bus, a feeling of utter relief washed over him as he observed Melvin and Marvin, their faces pushed up against the windows, teary eyed and waving bye-bye. As a condition of their release, the Pursers were returning to Alabama and were ordered never to enter the sovereign state of Georgia again. Yelling through the glass, Melvin promised John they would sneak back for a visit someday, and he'd bring their unwed sister with them.

Taking their promise as a word of warning, John returned to his old homestead, isolated in the woods, and built a stone wall complete with gun ports along the western boundary of his property. It gave Grandfather peace of mind knowing there was a fortified barrier between him and the state of Alabama, protecting him from whatever those boys might bring back his way.

For years, John lived in seclusion, privately digesting all he had experienced while he was away. To be candid, that's not all he digested. Grandpa was secretly making his own whiskey. He turned wild for a spell and almost stayed that way. But John, being a man, in time got a strong craving for decent groceries—in other words, food that wasn't something he had to shoot, trap, or grow himself. With no real culinary talents to speak of, he started thinking about the women he knew who could cook. Then, he pondered about women who couldn't cook but wore fancy dresses and smelled of beer.

At last, John ventured out in search of a suitable girl who could make suitable meals. It didn't take him long to find one. But it did take him a mite longer to reel her in for the catch. Once, back in grade school, John had teased his fated wife-to-be on the playground. In response, she deservedly gave him a shiner from a swift right cross. From then on, there was no more teasing to be had.

When it served his objective, John was gifted with a silver tongue. In the case of my grandmother, I know his pursuit was earnest. She came to appreciate this, too, and so they were betrothed and later wed at the courthouse. Soon thereafter, by grace there came a daughter, Juanita—my mother. To John, his baby girl was a living, breathing angel—a true blessing. He cherished her from the day she arrived, and Juanita adored him with all her heart. Between the two, there existed an unbreakable bond that proved strong enough to weather even the fiercest storms. And, believe me, as you'll see, that man received more than his fair share of troubles.

Unquestionably, John would have sacrificed himself for his daughter at any time if ever the need arose. But love doesn't put food on the table; nor does it buy the necessities or keep a roof on the house. Any extras, such as a new doll or a pretty dress, were just dreams in a catalog. So, to make ends meet, John kept brewing his moonshine whiskey. He sold more than he consumed, but he still consumed more than one man should.

Unlike her father, Juanita soon grew restless living in such secluded surroundings. The more she learned of the world, the more Juanita realized she had to experience the life written about in books. Eventually, my mother met my father and married him; he was a military man, and he took her to the places she had only dared to dream of.

The newlyweds were very much in love and shared countless adventures together. They were stationed throughout the United States and fortunate enough to spend a year overseas in Japan. Still, as expected, Juanita may have left her father's home, but she never left his heart. And he was in her heart, too, at all times.

Somewhere along the way Juanita gave birth to a healthy, feisty boy—me. Having been a spunky, high-spirited kid, I know I wasn't always the ideal son. Nevertheless, and without a doubt, mine was the perfect mother, and together, my parents raised me in an amazingly loving home. As it usually happens with military families, we were posted to a different location just about every other year. I had to continually make new friends and playmates, so I learned at an early age to be outgoing (a showoff) and assertive (a big showoff). Other than that, I had a rather normal childhood, but Mother was adamant that I attend Sunday school and church services, no matter where we were. Owing to my rambunctious ways, it's possible she felt that I needed to do some extra praying for forgiveness.

Although I met my mother's father several times when I was very young, our visits were so sporadic that

I scarcely recall those meetings. Our transient lifestyle made it difficult for us to visit regularly, but Mother vowed this was going to change. And she made good on her promise. Before long, it became custom for Mother and me, and Dad when he could, to visit our relatives in Georgia during the summer and on major holidays.

Whenever I was in John's presence, I was in awe of him. From where I stood, that man looked as tall as the trees. I quickly discovered Grandfather's homemade shine periodically brought out another, more volatile, side of him. At times he even became dangerous, but that seemed to only heighten the excitement I felt around him. Fights at his kitchen table were a bonus, since nobody ever did that at our house. The brawls mostly happened during card games and the like—but hardly ever during a meal. Fortunately, my grandmother's legendary cooking skills could usually quell my grandfather's rage with just a few mouthfuls. It wasn't easy to stay irritated over a trivial issue once you started eating her lip-smacking cuisine.

In all my visits to my grandparents' house, I can bring to mind only two disturbances that ever involved food. Both occurred on Thanksgiving Day, 1963. I was a mere nine years old, and on that fateful Thanksgiving, we were invited to have dinner at John's place. President Kennedy had been assassinated a week earlier. My grandfather didn't much care for presidents, but he approved of that one, and the shocking announcement of his murder angered him terribly. We all huddled around Grandpa's old-fashioned tube-type radio with its makeshift wire antenna, straining to hear the news.

Broadcast reception in the sticks was weak at best and often altogether unobtainable.

   As he fine-tuned the station knob, Grandpa put his ear to the radio but could barely hear the static crackling from its speaker thanks to the incessant moans of my cousin Hank who was bellyaching in the kitchen. Hank had grown impatient for something to eat; thus, he began making obnoxious noises mimicking the gurgling of a gigantic stomach starving to death.

Full of liquor and frustration, John stormed into the kitchen, grabbed the turkey cooling on the stovetop, and smashed the ass end of the carcass plum over the boy's head. Firmly wedged there, Hank couldn't pull it off. Now, mind you, this prize-winning bird wasn't your standard twenty-pounder; our farm-raised tom, fully dressed, tipped the scale at a whopping forty-plus pounds. I can only assume the dressing inside the turkey must have been mighty hot, too, because Hank sprung to his feet and bawled like a bull caught in a bear trap. Long, excruciating howls echoed pitifully through the bird's severed neck, alerting Scout and Sayer, the coon dogs, who assumed they were being called to go for a hunt. Hank wasn't waiting around for the gravy to be served, so he lit out.

You can imagine that being engulfed by a gigantic turkey is more than a slight hinderance. Hank didn't get very far before he missed the doorway, ran smack-dab into the wall, and collapsed to the floor. Christmas had come early for the dogs, who had him the second he hit the throw rug. Apparently the savory meat wasn't too hot for them. They each bit into a turkey leg, and in an impressive show of canine strength, they jerked that poor boy out of the kitchen and through the screen door. He lost the rug going down the porch steps, and his britches slid below his knees as he was hauled across the graveled drive. Scout and Sayer, determined the feast was theirs for keeps, dragged the overstuffed fowl past the water cistern and well beyond all four corners of the yard. When the hounds straddled a crabapple stump, the impact forced Cousin Hank's head out of the turkey's butt.

The brawl that ensued on the lawn between Hank and the dogs was priceless. Having gotten a fair taste himself of the glazed bird, Hank wasn't going to give it up without a fight. Ultimately, however, it was two hounds against one boy, and in the end Hank left with just a wing and a chunk of breast.

The second altercation started after the visiting reverend—an unwitting witness to this barbaric display—scolded Grandpa. Our distinguished guest had a particular liking for turkey and had patiently waited for that mouth-watering moment when the fowl was to be carved and served up on a platter with all the trimmings. Now, because of a temper-fit, his holiday dinner was ruined. Pointing a tattered Bible at John, the reverend informed him that his behavior was "absolutely abominable" and "utterly despicable to civil decorum." (He enjoyed showing off by using uppity words such as these.) Cradling his beloved Bible in his arms, the reverend then took his place in the chair positioned at the head of the kitchen table, where John usually sat.

John's bloodshot eyes spat fire as the sweat rolling down his neck turned to steam. From previous experience, when the veins in his temples bulged, I knew to step back—way back. This time, much to my surprise, Grandfather, with complete self-control and sincere Southern hospitality, picked up a large crockery bowl full of peas and, offering it, said, "Sir, you want some?"

Tossing his pompous nose in the air, His Holiness replied, "No, Mister Pierce, I don't believe I do."

Now, let me make something real clear. It was difficult sometimes to determine whether John was actually asking a genuine question or cynically touting an announcement avowing his intentions. Generally, John's inquiries were harmless. A sarcastic, rhetorical statement such as this one, however, usually preceded trouble—big trouble.

Without warning, Grandpa swung the hefty bowl into the reverend's face, knocking out his front teeth. Arms flailing, blood splattering, the reverend sprawled backward onto the wood floor, landing hard enough to bounce. For a second, he looked as though he was

creating snow—or, more aptly, pea—angels on the floor. John towered over the downed man and thundered, "No. I said, 'Sir, you want some!'" Yep, John was definitely speaking his mind and wasn't asking any damn questions about who might've wanted peas.

We all sat with bated breath as the reverend pulled a jackknife from the inside pocket of his frock coat and chased John through the house, slashing him several times. The dogs were in the yard eating turkey, so Grandpa was on his own. Ahead of the ruckus, Grandma had cleared a wide path, shoving furniture aside, to aid the reverend in his quest for justice. From hatch to slaughter, she had diligently labored to produce that magnificent gobbler specially for this holiday meal—only to watch in disbelief as a couple of mangy hound dogs devoured the exquisite feast and a knife-wielding man of God pursued her good-for-nothing husband.

Believe it or not, that's the day John found religion and discovered the power of spiritual testimony spoken in tongues. The reverend swore to high heaven he'd cut that son of a backwoods bum into fishing bait. John countered elegantly with a seamless medley comprising fragments of the Lord's Prayer interspersed with various recognizable phrases from "Rock of Ages" and "Jingle Bells," all the while brandishing a brass spittoon in self-defense. The reverend relented, dropping his knife. In exchange for clemency, John agreed to attend the next Sunday's worship. When all was said and done, they both got drunk on John's whiskey, babbled incoherently about the pleasures of drinking holy spirits as opposed to sinful liquor, and passed out.

That Sunday would go down in Pierce family history as the one and only occasion my grandfather ever attended a church service. And, true to form, Grandpa didn't disappoint. Debilitated from the Thanksgiving fiasco, our reverend had the senior elder assist him behind the pulpit to deliver that week's sermon, while he sat on the far right side of the chancel and recovered.

It's common practice for members of our congregation to joyously request praise if they are inspired by the message being shared, thus invoking everyone—parishioners and clergy alike—to appropriately respond in unison with an exuberant "Amen!" Hence, on this day, whenever praises were called for, the reverend's inflated split lips displayed a gaping hole where his front teeth had been, making more than one churchgoer wonder what trouble the good man had gotten himself into. In a futile attempt to shield himself from the humiliation,

he feigned a cough each time an "Amen" was required, cupping his hand over his mouth. It was a temptation too hard for Grandpa to resist. Evidently filled with the spirit, John stood up in the front row and freely requested a bunch of those "amens." Like the pure-hearted Baptist he had never been, he gyrated about the church, praising, "Amen to God. Amen to the glory of Jesus. Amen to Mother Mary, Joseph, and Moses' tired, sore feet!" I was in tears when he started blessing all of Noah's little animals two by two. So was our reverend.

Numerous people complained of my grandfather's shenanigans, but I don't think anybody walked away from the service without having laughed some. To protect the reverend's reputation, it was conveniently rumored that the obstinate donkey recently acquired for use in the church's living nativity scene had kicked him

in the chops. Naturally, everyone suspected they knew who the real jackass was.

Later that same afternoon, Grandpa's incoherent rantings drew me to the front porch. Who was the culprit this time? I wondered. Surely the reverend had learned his lesson about what happened when he provoked my grandfather's wrath. As quietly as I could manage, I opened the screen door to find Grandpa bickering with what appeared to be no one at all. I craned my neck left and right, seeing nothing but an empty space beside him, but still the rant continued. Granted, we all knew Grandpa had a few screws loose, but usually the target of his anger had a physical presence—not some invisible person. As I listened, I heard John called this apparition by name: It was none other than the Devil himself. At first I froze, stunned, but then terror seized me, and in a flash, I bolted inside the house and hid. That proved to be a wise decision. Not a minute later, an explosion of temper detonated from the front porch as John and the Devil commenced what sounded like a fistfight. From what I could gather, the points of contention were politics and the death of our president, 'cause Grandpa was cussing mad, calling Lucifer a no-good, carpet-bagging Republican. Only after it got quiet as a graveyard did I muster the courage to crawl out from under the furniture and check on him. I reckon John kicked the bastard's pointed tail that day. Grandpa didn't look any worse for wear, and it appeared Beelzebub had done took off.

Reflecting now on these episodes, I concede that the manifestations that often haunted John may have been

nothing more than the torment of his own subconscious. But at that age, as a young boy, I was positively convinced the Devil really was there—I just couldn't see him. John could, though. John would see all kinds of spooks and haints when he was drunk. Then he'd get the shakes and see even worse things when it was necessary for him to dry out. I think this one had come to visit in response to his conduct in church earlier that morning.

* * *

As kids, we cousins would dare each other to sneak up on "the man who was so mean the Devil wouldn't have him" and try to get near enough to poke his shadow with a stick. We made sure not to play this game when he was real drunk and knew it was best to wait until the evening hours when shadows were long. In spite of that, one evening, several hours before sundown, John was strolling about the yard, and I was acting cocky, strutting behind him tapping at his shadow with a small willow switch. Watching with amazement, the other kids stood on the edge of the porch, leaning over the railing, practically breathless. Soaking up the newfound attention, I neglected to watch where I was going. Suddenly, John stopped on a dime. I stumbled into him, colliding with thighs as solid as pillars of stone and an arm that felt as if it were forged from iron. The impact knocked the wind from my chest as I collapsed backward onto the dirt, staring up in terror as he stood over me with his scarred knuckles on his hips and growled, "You got a problem, boy!"

Lord, how I prayed: Please let that be a question and not another declaration. The puny Cub Scout pocketknife tucked in my boot was just a toy compared to the reverend's jackknife, but all the same I pulled it out and opened the blade. I whimpered a feeble reply. "Sir, I sure hope not." Mercifully, he spared me, at least for the time being.

Grandpa noticed before I did that my nose was bloody. He pulled a handkerchief from his bibs and tossed it at me. "Get up and stand like a man when you're in front of me," he demanded. I got up, but if my feet had been working correctly at that moment, I would have been running faster than a deer caught in the crosshairs. Still, I'm thankful I faced the hateful ogre—for this marked the start of my formal education about John.

As I wiped my nose, he bent over and asked warily, so only I could hear, "You like me, boy?" Considering the fact that I didn't want to die, I nodded my head "yes" so vigorously that cherry-red bubbles of snot blew from both nostrils. "Well, you're okay by me too," he whispered. "You've got a measure of grit in you. Probably got it from my little girl. Like mother, like son, you know."

I tried to hide my surprise at this unprecedented show of affection. Regardless of his flaws, the wicked tyrant standing there revealed himself to be a proud daddy who truly loved his daughter, and he wanted me to know it. I'm guessing loving my mother was one of the only things he ever got right in his life. Suddenly, with a burst of rage, he threatened, "But don't you tell nobody I said

so, you hear!" This time I nodded my head "yes" rapidly enough to bounce my eyeballs inside my skull and rattle my brains loose.

My grandfather straightened his posture and smiled peaceably. I kept up my guard, knowing his temper was as volatile as the weather. Everyone was watching when, hesitatingly, he offered his hand to me. "Don't worry, sir, I won't bite," I promised as I grabbed several of his huge fingers and held them. As John quietly led me around the yard, I kept my knife open in my other hand—just in case. I wasn't taking any chances, and truth be known, I had lied about the biting. One wrong move from him and I'd sink my teeth in his arm like it was a chicken drumstick.

Grandpa glanced at the children on the porch and said, "This probably makes you top dog with the other boys." A nervous chuckle escaped my lips; I had, of course, been trying to impress them. "This also puts you in good with the girls too, you reckon?" he asked. I tried to answer, but the combination of shock and pride had stunned me to silence.

It seemed as though I held Grandpa's hand for hours that evening. Cousin Hank later enlightened me it was only for ten or twenty minutes at most. But how I figured it, nobody else my size had ever touched him for that long and survived the experience, so it felt pretty darn good all the same. I never did hold Cottonmouth's hand again—not in that way. He said we were both getting too old for that sort of thing and told me not to bother him about it any further. The man wasn't fond

of elaborating, and I didn't want to push the issue. When John suggested something, it was best you listened the first time. Nevertheless, something happened that day that made me rise in my grandfather's estimation. I had proven my worth. He and I soon became inseparable during my visits. In his company, I felt a profound sense of kinship and pride, and to this day, I still marvel that he found me worthy of his attention.

* * *

The following summer welcomed a season full of long days, bare feet, sweet tea, barbeques, skinny-dipping, mischief, and quandaries. By then, I had seen my tenth birthday. I had begged to be allowed to spend that time vacationing with my grandparents, and my parents had conceded. As subtly as I could manage, I took every opportunity to be with Grandfather. Needless to say, mischief and quandaries reigned.

John's aggressive temperament was multifaceted. His demeanor brought on troubles by the score, but every so often, his personality did help to serve his needs. Not an overly handsome man by any stretch, his bold, assertive qualities nevertheless kept him from being bashful with the ladies. John appreciated the ladies just fine, and rumor has it they appreciated him pretty good too.

Now and then, when he'd had too much to drink or had an itch, he would stagger his way into a known house of ill repute. Early one morning, John invited me to accompany him to the brothel so that I could make a little extra pocket change. He mentioned there was some

light yard work that needed doing. I later learned he was just fulfilling another whiskey run, delivering a fresh supply of liquid enticement to offer to gullible patrons—for a hefty price. Grandpa apparently used me as cover in order to give the impression that all was innocent.

At first I didn't understand exactly what the place was all about, and I wasn't about to ask. All I knew is that the girls working there dressed in fancy laced undergarments, which were commonly worn as exterior apparel. They all sprayed themselves with cheap perfumes and patted their soft, beautiful faces with powders the color of alabaster. Throughout the warmer months of the year, the windows of the house were left open to provide relief from the sultry Georgia air, their fragrances wafting into the susceptible hearts of innocent—and not so innocent—men who casually passed by outside.

I was introduced to a young lady who John referred to as my Aunt Thelma, and together they sat on the porch while I mowed grass that required scarcely a trim. I couldn't hear exactly what was being said between them, but it must have been awfully funny because she giggled a lot. It wasn't long before they went into the house, leaving me to do the purported yard work. Soon thereafter, Aunt Thelma came back outside and gave me a Coca-Cola. She told me John would be awhile and that I should find a cool place in the shade if I was going to wait for him.

Even though to John many of the ladies there were more compassionate friends than hired lovers, they did request money when they knew he had it. And when he

had the product, they were keen to barter their services for that too. But most of what he sold them was a diluted adaptation of his distinctive noxious recipe. He very well knew that a strong dose of the pure distilled brew might make men behave wildly. In a house where so many vulnerable women resided, that would be sinful even by John's standards.

My dear Aunt Thelma

It's my speculation that at some point someone had told Grandmother where we were, bearing in mind she was waiting for us on the lawn when we finally got home. I guess using me as a diversion wasn't so clever after all. That simply peeved her off all the more. In my naivete, I tried coming to Grandpa's defense and told Grandmother we were just visiting dear Aunt Thelma. Grandma stared her husband straight in the eyes and scowled. "We ain't got no Aunt Thelma in the family," she snapped. John's face grimaced so tight, the backside of his pants puckered.

Hell hath no fury like a woman scorned—and Granny was no exception. Out of thin air, Grandma brandished a wide leather strap and tore into her unsuspecting husband. Stunned by the attack, John started to hightail it much too late to save himself from the brutal onslaught. Meaner than a swarm of hornets, she relentlessly whipped him about the head. Thank goodness he had the agility to bob and weave as he ran for his life or it would've been even worse. John could occasionally fend off the Devil, but he could never take Grandma in a fair fight. Not that John ever fought fair. He just didn't want Granny fighting dirty.

After a couple days, John still hadn't returned. Grandmother tried to hide her worry, but I could see it etched in her face as she ordered me to fetch him. She explicitly advised me to track him down and not just canvass around town shouting his name for all to hear. Grandma feared he would be too drunk to steer his way alone, and, come hell or high water, I was to personally cart his old bones back to her. Little did I know it was hell that would be coming.

Miss Susie

CHAPTER THREE:
MICK'S MINISTRY

Reverend Mick pushes his journal aside and tosses the fountain pen aimlessly onto the desk blotter. A dollop of ink is cast from the pen's nib, contributing another black speck to the fifty or so previously absorbed there. Lolling back in his chair, he rubs his left wrist and forefinger to relax them. Writing by hand not only frees his mind to recall years gone by, but it also brings on some respectable cramps. "I'll finish this tomorrow," he grumbles. "My story can surely wait one more day to finish—it has to. I need to do some tending before this hellish fight takes place." Looking up, he pleads, "Please—just one more day."

Unannounced, a pretty young lady in her mid-twenties—considerably younger than Mick—opens the door to the library and enters the room. Her auburn hair conjures autumn leaves, and her eyes are as green as Ireland itself. Immediately upon seeing

Mick sitting at his desk, she gasps, "Oh, I'm sorry, sir. I didn't realize you were here. I just came back from the square and wanted to do some dusting. I thought you would have already left to make your usual rounds— after all, it is a quarter past four."

"Past four—already?" he asks. "Susie, how is it I'm always losing track of the time?"

"Reverend," she says playfully, "if you weren't always two steps behind yourself, what in the world would you need me for—I mean besides the cooking, when you're here to eat it, not to mention the cleaning, the laundry, ironing, making of beds, and ensuring you are properly dressed and buttoned down for your appointments . . . and," she goes on to say, "you'd be downright perfectly miserable if I weren't around to put a great big smile on that solemn face of yours. You know I'm the most delightful part of your day." Mick chuckles. "I do love the way your face brightens when you laugh. You are a handsome man, reverend . . ." she says with a wink. Pausing to make a quick observation, she adds, ". . . and now I've made you flush. I'm sorry—it wasn't my intention to embarrass you. I was only flirting—again."

"I'm not embarrassed, dear girl. The flattery is sweet. It's just not something I am accustomed to; not lately, anyway." With a hint of vanity, Mick reflects, "I charmed a few hearts in my day." He confides, "And through His guidance I hope to have another day or two left ahead of me." At this point, Mick isn't absolutely certain what he's referring to—another chance at love or another day to live. After all, what's one without the other?

Not wanting to fixate on the plight to be, Mick hastily makes a request. "Susie, do me a huge favor and skip the library this evening. I'd rather nothing was disturbed until I'm finished here. This room will survive a day without being cleaned—don't you agree, dear?"

With a sharp nod of her head, she replies, "As you wish. But if the dust starts you sneezing, you've got nobody but yourself to blame."

"I swear on my word as a gentleman, you shall be fully absolved from the slightest criticism if I sneeze my head and tail right off."

"Okay, Sir Reverend," she says, smiling. "It's best to be on your way or your fan club will start to wonder what has delayed you." Looking out the window, she remarks, "It was raining this morning, but the clouds broke well before noon, and now it's actually quite pleasant. But we have scattered showers in the forecast for the next few days, so enjoy the beautiful weather while we have it. Tomorrow will bring much cooler temperatures. There's a notable cold front soon to knock upon our door, and you can bet another freeze will come of it."

Mick quips, "Susie, I do believe you've missed your true calling. You should have become one of those TV weather girl personalities. Thanks to your in-depth report, I believe my rubber galoshes will stay at home this evening."

Susie twists the cleaning rag in her hands and gives it a quick flick toward the backside of Mick's britches.

The rag pops as loud as the crack of a whip, getting his undivided attention. "Uh-huh . . . and one more snide remark like that, mister, and I'll show you who missed their calling to become a bare-knuckle pugilist too," she smartly responds. "Now off with you. Go do your duty. People are expecting to see you out and about."

"On my way and out the door, ma'am!" Mick says with as much enthusiasm as he can muster. Susie giggles under her breath and leaves Mick to prepare for his daily practice.

Precisely as Susie said, it is very pleasant outdoors. The rain has left everything smelling fresh. A breeze rustles the trees, loosing withered leaves that dance in the air. There are no more puddles to be found—those have long disappeared. Mick relishes the warmth of the late afternoon sun sitting above the horizon, bathing everything in gold. This is his neighborhood, and he courteously waves at everyone he sees. Mick is a prominent figure on these streets, and the locals pay him homage.

Walking toward the downtown district, Mick approaches a home he is well acquainted with. The house closed for business long ago, and now it serves as a retirement domiciliary for many of the ladies who once worked there. "Hey, mister preacher man!" comes a brusque gibe from one of the residents seated in a wicker chair on the veranda. "Don't ever walk past here without paying proper respects. I know who you are! You greet me by saying 'good day, madam.' You understand?"

"As you wish, Madame Abigail," Mick says deferentially. "You know I never stroll past this house without saying good day to you and the other ladies. Now, why do you believe today would be any different?"

"Are you back-talking, you opulent little shit? I'll wash your mouth out," the old woman threatens while pounding her fist to her lap. "I watch you prance around these parts acting all uppity. That ain't going to fly with me, boy. I remember where you come from. You're that fighting, trouble-making, snot-nosed kid that likes his drink. Don't think for a minute that I've forgotten. My mind is sharp—sharp as the day your grandpappy first brung you here."

"Yeah, and your tongue is sharper than broken glass," Mick murmurs.

"What did you say to me, boy? I say, speak up!" Madame Abigail demands, cupping her ear with her palm.

"I said 'yes ma'am,' Madame Abigail. Simply said 'yes ma'am,' nothing more," Mick answers.

"Good! See to it I never hear anything to the contrary. I expect all men who come calling to show respect for me and my girls." With a curious glance around, she asks, "Speaking of the men, where is that grandpappy of yours? That crackpot thrills me to no end," she says with a cackle.

"My grandfather passed some years back, Madame Abigail—surely you remember. I saw you at his funeral service," Mick explains.

"Don't try to pull the wool over my eyes, boy," the old woman barks. "John stopped by the other day—just to visit, he said. For the better part of an hour, he sat right there next to me telling jokes and spinning yarns. The rascal had me laughing so hard I pissed myself."

Mick suspects that at her advanced age, Madame Abigail's memory must be playing tricks on her. Of course his grandfather had sat on her porch many a time with many a lady, but that was years back. Understanding it would be rude to contradict her and also unkind, he bites his tongue and nods his head.

As if saved by the bell, the current matriarch of the house and dear friend to Mick opens the screen door, steps out onto the veranda, and joins them. She's a full fourteen years older than him, but her natural beauty and charm easily hide every one of those years. "I was wondering what all the commotion was. I might have known it was you, Reverend Lee. Only you can get Momma Abigail riled enough to spit. For a preacher, you sure have a strange effect on the ladies," she says in jest, "picking on helpless old women the way you do."

Mick takes a step forward, dropping both hands down to his sides. "Good day, Aunt Thelma," he says to her. "It's a pleasure to see you."

"It's good to see you, reverend. How's your mother— well, I hope?"

"Yes, very well," he replies. "Thank you for asking."

"You're going to call her later—yes?" she asks, already knowing his answer.

"Yes, ma'am. I plan to do that this evening."

"You're a good son to her, reverend. I'm sure she's so proud of you." Glancing downward, she sheepishly adds, "If it's appropriate, would you please tell her that I inquired? I'd consider it a personal favor if you would."

"Of course I will, ma'am—of course I will," he says.

"Thank you, sir. You've always been more than kind."

With that, she turns toward the older woman. "Okay, Momma Abigail, we need to get you inside. It's time for supper. And, as I recall, it's your turn to say grace." Aunt Thelma leans close to Madame Abigail and talks softly. "For dessert, I made your favorite—banana pudding with vanilla wafer cookies and whipped cream. So, I want you to behave yourself and say goodbye to the reverend."

"Hey, boy, you going to pray for me tonight—aren't you?" asks Madame Abigail in an uncharacteristically humble tone.

"Yes, madame, just as I do every night," Mick assures her.

"I bless you, reverend. You hear, I bless you," says Madame Abigail. "You take notice I did that."

"I bless you, too, reverend," says Aunt Thelma. "May peace be yours."

"Thank you, ladies," says Mick. "And may peace be with you." He remains standing almost at attention until the women are safely in the house. It's only after the front door closes securely that he adopts a more relaxed posture. Public exchanges commonly occur during his walks, but few are as contentious as those with Madame Abigail. He breathes deeply to reset his focus and once again sets his sights toward downtown.

On such a momentous day as this, Mick muses on why he is doing something so routine. Shouldn't he concentrate his efforts on accomplishing some grandiose

task before his final hour is thrust upon him? Was he not meant for greater things? Mick is contemplating these questions about his purpose when he reaches the shopping district. He hardly notices that day has turned to dusk until the slamming of a dumpster lid startles him back to the here and now. Peering down a dimly lit passageway, he discerns someone's silhouette—a vagrant rummaging through the garbage behind a popular restaurant, loudly cursing the scraps he is finding.

"Hey, you there!" Mick shouts. "What business do you have being so disruptive? These are civilized streets with civilized people. And that kind of language will not be tolerated here. You understand?"

"Screw off, Mac," the man responds. "Or I'll make my business with you."

"Then come out and give it your best," Mick says. "Or I'll come down there. Either way . . ."

"Ease up, mister," the man pleas. "I'm hungry. Can't you see I'm only trying to find something to eat?"

"Step out, then," demands Mick, "and let's get a better look at you."

A ragged, disconcerted man reluctantly steps forward into the light of an overhead streetlamp. "Please, mister, I want no trouble. I'll be on my way."

Fearing the authorities are about to be summoned, the drifter tries to skirt around Mick to make his leave.

Mick gently reaches for the man's shoulder and stops him. The man is shocked that someone so finely dressed would actually place a hand on a filthy bum such as himself. "What do you want, mister—I ain't nobody," the man says.

"I want to know your name, sir," Mick says.

"Name's Smith," he says but doesn't ask for a name in return.

"When was the last time you've eaten? I mean, a decent meal," Mick asks.

The man gives no reply. Mick can see he is not only embarrassed by his inquiry but also suspicious. "I'm going in for supper," Mick says, "and it's my experience eating alone is bad for the digestion. Please do me the honor of being my guest, won't you?"

With his hand still on the man's shoulder, Mick guides him to the front door. Rendered speechless, the man straggles along, not fully knowing what to think. Although the hostess raises her eyebrows at the sight of the well-dressed reverend and the straggler, she seats them at an unoccupied table off to one side in the dining area. Mick requests hot tea for two, and they each order an entrée. When the food arrives, Mick allows the man to eat without interruption. No barrage of uncomfortable questions. No proselytizing in an attempt to save him. Fortunately, the restaurant is quiet, and the customers don't pay too much notice to the unlikely pair.

After they've dined, the men relax in their chairs as they enjoy one last cup of tea. Finally, the man asks, "What's your game, mister? Don't you think it's time you play your hand? What is it you're after? Everybody always wants something, and it's my hunch you ain't no different."

"I do want something. I want to ask a favor of you," Mick says plainly. "Fulfill my one simple request, and we'll call it even."

"You talk nonsense. You know I'm a bum. I got nothing."

"Yes, you do," insists Mick. "And what I want I can't have unless you give it to me."

"Oh yeah? What might that be?" the man asks skeptically.

"I want your blessing," Mick says, looking the man directly in the eyes.

"What? You want my blessing?" the man says with a hearty laugh. "I got no such thing to give you or anyone else. Mister, people like me are found at the bottom of the barrel—and you want a blessing from me?"

"Yes, sir, Mr. Smith, that's exactly what I want from you. And I'll settle for nothing less."

Taken aback by Mick's sincerity, the man asks, "But how—why? Why me?"

"Why?" Mick replies. "Because you have seen adversity. I know what it is to be troubled and lost. And as to 'how'—simply tell me that you bless me. But you have to mean it—you have to truly mean it from your soul."

"Mister, who am I to bless you or anyone else? If you knew where my soul has been and what I done, you wouldn't ask this of me," the man confesses.

"Our lord made you for a reason," Mick says. "I passionately testify that he's not the kind of God who willingly gives up simply because you go astray. Believe in him or not, he believes in you. And when you open your heart to him, his presence is soon realized. So, invite him to work through you. Allow him to use you however he sees fit. Serve him however he calls upon you."

"I'm a ruined man, and hell is where I'm headin'! You spend another minute in my company, and you're likely to end up there right alongside me."

"If hell is the only alternative, then we're going there together because I refuse to step aside and let the Devil do his bidding. But know this—if there is any good left in you, salvation awaits at the tip of your tongue. Bless me, brother, before the Beast takes us both! Do it and be saved," Mick insists. "Speak, man!"

Upon hearing that, the man breaks down and openly weeps. It's been forever and a day since anyone has shown any regard for his well-being—his salvation. And now Mick shows it publicly without indecision. Unable to control his sobbing, he blesses Mick repeatedly—over and over. The other patrons, who have since neglected their meals, watch the scene unfold in silence. A few whisper short prayers on the man's behalf, blessing him.

"Thank you, sir," Mick says, placing his hand upon the man's shoulder once again. Letting a moment pass for the man to compose himself, Mick then reaches into his vest pocket and pulls out a business card. "I want you to take this to the person working the reception desk at the Saint Michael Hotel on Main Street. They will put you up for a couple of nights—that is, until they can place you into a room at the shelter if you want one. I have it on good authority there is a major cold wave about to hammer us, and I don't want you outside unprotected. Take a hot shower and enjoy the comforts of a bed. Tomorrow, take this same card to the Salvation Army Family Store. If you don't know where it is, ask for directions. It's not far. They'll replace your clothing with something clean and suitable. If interested, you can apply for work there. That's strictly up to you. But they are always looking for help."

Wiping tears from his cheeks, the man takes the card and reads it aloud. "So, you are that reverend fella everyone talks about. I've been in town but a few days and have already heard tell of you. Please forgive my earlier behavior. All I can say—I was desperate and half out of my mind." With that, he graciously thanks Mick and excuses himself from the table. The offer to lie in a real bed has him dizzy with the thought— maybe tomorrow can be different?

"I'm praying for you, Mr. Smith," Mick says as the man leaves.

The man stops, faces Mick, and admits, "My name is Jackson—Lonnie Jackson."

"It was my privilege to have met you, Mr. Jackson. Good night to you, sir," Mick says.

"And a very good night to you, reverend," bids Mr. Jackson. "May you fare well."

Mr. Jackson departs, and the restaurant gradually returns to normal. Customers go back to nibbling on their meals and engage in trivial chitchat; the order pick-up bell in the cook's window dings; the cash register's drawer pops open, rattling the change; a fork drops to the floor; someone laughs a little too loud. The waitress working their table delivers the bill to Mick. Without looking at it, he pulls his credit card from his wallet and hands it to her. She promptly returns with his card and a receipt requiring his signature. But instead of going about her duties, she pauses for a second or two before speaking.

"Sir, I mean, Father. May I ask you a question?" Not waiting for his reply, she inquires, "Don't you have it all backward? I mean, I've seen you bring people in here, and it always puzzles me. Aren't you supposed to bless them? What good does it do to have people like that bless you? You're a priest, aren't you?"

"No, I am not a priest," Mick corrects her. "I am an ordained minister. I know some find my style unorthodox at times, but make no mistake—ministering is what I do." He invites her to have a seat, promising that she won't get in trouble if she does because he's good friends with the owner of the restaurant. She sits on a chair across from Mick and listens intently. "You see, periodically the people I deal with either come from a questionable past or have done something they are very ashamed of—something they believe can never be forgiven. Often they are truly in fear of spending the rest of eternity burning in hell. It is my belief—indeed, my aim—to help them realize that they, too, possess the ultimate power to bless others, to help save someone else from the Devil's grasp. By exerting their ability, I am hopeful they will come to understand that they themselves can never be taken by Satan."

Mick goes on to explain, "Let me clarify what I'm saying. If you are personally given the divine qualification and the capability to bless another's soul, then how is it logically possible that you yourself are damned? If you become a chosen instrument doing God's will, you cannot be susceptible to the ills of eternal damnation. What I attempt to do is awaken people's sensibilities to the idea that they are loved by God no matter their transgressions. God may be disappointed by

our past behaviors, but he is a loyal parent, and his love for his children is unconditional."

"If the people you help are saved from hell's fire," the waitress asks, "then why do some of them shy away from your aid and continue to choose their miserable impoverished lifestyles?"

"We can do a terrible wrong and be saved. This gift is through grace and grace alone. But some will continue to bear the onus of that wrong for the rest of their lives, even though they know they've been forgiven. Their conscience will not allow them to shed it. They choose to punish themselves even when others do not."

"Well, then, maybe saving people doesn't work every time. Shouldn't a person who's been saved be incapable of self-destructive tendencies? And how can a person who's been saved be hurt by anything? How is it they are not impervious to any threat whatsoever?"

"I'll tell you how," Mick says. "A saved person can stub their own toe on the couch or bang their thumb while striking a nail. We may succumb to a disease. A mind may go insane. You can be bitten by a mad dog or maybe even be brutally murdered. As long as we are human and alive on this earth, we will always be receptive to pleasure and vulnerable to pain. If you don't believe that, look at how our lord was crucified—his divine blessing came about with insufferable agony. He was ridiculed, beaten, pierced, whipped. But even though his body was badly broken, his love for us survives to this very day. It was his death that ultimately made all this possible.

And if you accept Jesus and help others to accept him, I'm here to say there will be a place for you at the table when it's your time."

Although Mick's cup is empty, he lifts it to his mouth and tries to sip a last drop of tea from the bottom. "I'll tell you something that I just realized. If I didn't aspire to help my fellow man find his way, I would be as empty as this cup. I think it's the most important thing that I have ever done, and that's why I'm here today. I've been successful at giving business and investment advice, but that only provides a means to deliver my ministry. I almost feel as though the solitary purpose for my existence is to find people to bless me so they might have the good fortune to go on to do great deeds." Looking toward the waitress, he searches for some reaction. "I hope that doesn't sound too mysterious?"

"Well, that certainly gives me something to weigh," she says, her brow furrowed in deep thought. "At least I now understand why you do what you do. Thank you for spending the time explaining things. But I really need to go back to work. There are tables to wait, and I can't afford to get any bad tips. I have three kids to raise, and it's hard enough when the tips are good."

Wearily she returns to her assigned station, making her rounds to accommodate everyone's needs. Wise to the hardships many endure, the reverend signs his name to the receipt and, without a second thought, leaves a one-hundred-dollar gratuity.

With Aunt Thelma's reminder to call his mother ringing in his ears, Mick exits the restaurant. On his way out, several people acknowledge him with a wave or a pleasant smile and nod. He returns the gesture and sets home to where he knows Susie is sure to be waiting. As Mick crosses the street, he hears the waitress call to him from the front door of the restaurant. "I bless you, reverend! I do; I really do bless you," she says, waving the receipt in her hand.

Home again, and just as Mick presumed, Susie is quick to greet him at the door as she always does. Mick doesn't wear house slippers or smoke a pipe, but if he did, you can be confident she would have them ready.

"I notice a spot of sauce on your tie—you've had your supper?" she asks.

"Yes, I did have a delightful meal," he says. "Met another new friend. I hope to see him again. I think I can help this one—he seems to have promise."

"Then I'll expect him for lunch someday soon." Concerned that Mick forgets when he becomes preoccupied in thought, she adds, "But you do have one more duty to attend to this evening. Now, go call your mother. Don't be wasting any more of your time gabbing with me—she's waiting to hear from you. And be certain to tell her I said hello. I know she'll inquire about me, and you're to say I'm doing my best with you."

"Yes, dear—without a doubt," Mick assures her. "But just one more thing, Susie. I have a very important

appointment tomorrow night—I mustn't be late," he says with some gravity in his voice. "I'll be busy in my library throughout the day, and I would appreciate it if you reminded me when the hour is near. Later, I will post the time on my schedule so you'll know when."

"Reverend, I've never allowed you to be late for an appointment yet. I'll check your appointment board before I turn in for the night," she says. "I'll see to it you're on time." With a gentle nudge, Susie urges, "Now go make the call. And if I don't see you before bedtime, good night to you, sir. Don't be staying up all night either or you won't be worth a plug nickel tomorrow."

"Good night, Susie. If I haven't already said it a thousand times, please know I immensely appreciate everything you do." Leaning against the doorframe to the library, he observes how orderly the house is kept and the serenity that fills the halls. Mick ponders aloud, "How difficult it must be for you here. I regularly show up with unexpected guests, but everyone who enters our door is made to feel welcome. I'm in and out all hours of the day and night—I miss your fabulous meals so that I can dine with street people. On the best of days, I'm incessantly in need of more and more of your time, and on the worst of days . . . let's indeed profess you are the one who makes this house a home. Thank you—thank you from the bottom of my heart," Mick says. "I'm not sure how I was able to manage successfully before you came along. You accomplish so much in a single day— your efforts make me look good, and I am grateful. Your assistance with daily matters keeps operations flowing like a well-oiled machine. My entire day would

be a total shambles if it weren't for the attention to detail you apply."

"I wouldn't have it any other way, Mick. But you can shower me with adulation later. Now, for the last time," Susie implores, "no more dillydallying. Call your mother!"

She leaves the room, closing the door gently behind her. Before he has a chance to get mired in his own thoughts again, Mick picks up the phone, dials his mother's number, and waits for her to pick up. He has so much to tell her, and so much that will have to wait.

Mick in his library

CHAPTER THREE:
HIS STORY – PART TWO

The next morning, Mick arises with only one thing on his agenda: to try to complete the unfinished story in his journal before evening. After showering and prepping for the day, he heads straight to his library without so much as a bite of breakfast or cup of tea. He didn't sleep well, and his stomach is too unsettled for him to consider eating.

Looking out the library's windows, Mick notices a dreary overcast spitting an airy mist—a perfect setting for the trouble he's about to face. "Guess I'll be getting a little wet tonight. My rubber galoshes might not remain in the closet as long as I had hoped," he says, chuckling, making light of his predicament.

Atop his desk, Mick finds the journal lying open next to yesterday's teacup. He picks up his pen from the blotter and sees that ink has dried in its tines. He

stirs the tip in what remains of his tea and wipes the nib with a tissue. Ink flows from the reservoir, wetting the tissue and coloring his fingertips. "Thank goodness I don't have to rinse this thing out," Mick says to himself. "I was half afraid I'd find it clogged. And I would have deserved it too—not taking care to cap it."

With the pen in hand, he sits at his desk and reads aloud the last passage he'd written the day before. "'Grandma feared he would be too drunk to steer his way alone, and come hell or high water, I was to personally cart his old bones back to her. Little did I know it was hell that would be coming.'

"Oh yes, I remember. I was told to find my grandfather—I was supposed to fetch him home. But I never realized hell was an actual place and that I would observe him peddling his recipe there." A vision of that day and the events that followed slowly overtakes his thoughts. Intuitively, Mick readies his pen. "Now it's coming back to me. When Grandma set me on my way, what did I do? I went searching . . . revisiting Grandfather's regular haunts and asking around. It took some time, but I was persistent, wasn't I? Yes, it took a while." With his thoughts fully immersed in the past, Mick puts the pen to work. And once again the words flow as his hand nimbly writes a conclusion . . .

* * *

Consequent to a few inquiries, I found John selling his shine to drifters and tramps by the edge of the woods at a hobo camp under the train trestle. It soon

became evident that no amount of pleading could get him to leave with me, so I stayed to keep an eye on him. Everybody there was awfully drunk and ominous looking. The night was dark—so dark the moon was lost. A faint glow amid the smoke of a smoldering brushwood fire cast the men's faces in a jaundiced blush. Heavy black shadows swallowed the dealings of renegade vagabonds who hid in unseen recesses. The air was thick and damp, tainted with a putrid stench of mold and unwashed bodies.

Most sensible men wouldn't drink John's venomous spirits because of the bad apparitions it conjured, but these camps weren't generally populated by intellects. Here the alcohol was openly purchased and passed among them. I saw a jar of it sitting unattended, so I picked it up. It looked as clear and sweet as fresh spring water. One and all watched to see if I would taste it. John had wandered off—probably to go piss. Otherwise I knew he would have stopped me. Seizing the opportunity, I had to sample what it was everyone had a hankering for.

A generous mouthful proved more than necessary to ignite my guts and paralyze my virgin throat. It sucked the breath right out of me. I tried to draw in air, but only wretched gasps escaped. Panic paralyzed me.

I woke up crumpled on the ground, with no idea of how long I was unconscious. My head swam from the lack of oxygen, but I managed ragged breaths. From the slime saturating my hair, I could tell I had fallen on my face, but someone had at least turned me over to

stop me drowning in the mud. My vision hazed, slightly out of focus. I looked up with a start. I didn't know for certain whether I was seeing a whiskey hallucination or a hollow-eyed, flesh-and-blood creature vacant of soul. By his guise, I knew he had to be the Beast: ole Scratch Beelzebub. Dressed in a frayed black suit and string tie filthy with sweat, he hunched over me like a scavenger bird ready to take a pungent bite of death. With a cannibalistic grin that bubbled with brown tobacco spit from the upturned corners of his mouth, he exhaled a decadent sigh.

"I see you came to play, boy," I heard him rasp. "Come with me now," he sneered. "I'll be sure to take you home, child." I wasn't going anywhere with that malevolent bastard. Suddenly, he grabbed a fistful of my shirt and jerked me to my feet, pulling me close to his chest. Worse than his breath, his body reeked of burnt sulfur—of fire and brimstone. "You come along this instant, boy!" he demanded.

The other men there slowly stepped away. A few turned and ran blindly into the night. I knew instinctively I was helpless in his grip. Nonetheless I resisted and squirmed to get free. Using only the one hand, the demon lifted me off my heels. My toes stabbed at the ground in a futile attempt to keep contact. His stench was suffocating.

"Let the boy down!" a voice bellowed.

The words were John's, and he sounded insane. With a clenched fist knotting my shirt, the Fiend didn't balk. Then, a colossal figure stormed out of the darkness toward the smoldering embers of the fire and lurched through the smoke. Devil be damned—he took hold of Scratch by the wrist.

"I said now!" John's voice boomed, so cold it would give unyielding ears frostbite on a hot summer's day.

With a hellish stare, the vile monster turned his eyes toward Grandfather. The Beast raised a brow. "You alone, John?"

"Not alone today, Beelz," John replied sharply.

"Oh, yes, your grandson here. But surely you don't expect . . ." He laughed boisterously in disbelief. "You expect help from the imp?" he howled. I was set loose and pushed aside, relieved to be standing on my feet again. Grandpa released his grasp, too, but neither he nor Beelzebub gave ground.

"Are you forgetting I sometimes whip you, Scratch?" said John.

"Nobody ever gets the best of me," Beelzebub roared. "Nobody!"

"You won't admit it, old boy, but I do . . . sometimes," Grandpa reminded him. "How do you think that's possible, Beelz?"

Scratch took a moment to reflect. The truth was, I think he did recognize that John had the muscle to take him in a fight. Some days my grandfather was just too tough, and now he was standing up to him again. With a bemused expression, Beelz persisted.

"What is your righteous authority, John?" he asked, and I could hear sincere interest in his voice. "You ain't no church-goin' man. You ain't no real family man." My grandfather stood silently, his expression inscrutable. Beelz continued his attentive probe. "What's your essence, John? What do you have that's better than most?"

After a calculated pause, John smirked. He lifted his hand and held it over his shirt pocket. "It's what I got

folded up in my pocket, boy," said John. He sounded more self-assured with every word. "And in my pocket, I've got the end of you."

"In your pocket?" scoffed Beelz. "No, no, no," he countered. "Nothing's there that could be a fret to me." But his expression betrayed his suspicion. "What you got there? Some voodoo charm? Snake oil?" His stare was no longer fixed on John's eyes—the gaze now remained steadfast on John's shirt pocket clad over his heart.

"What I got here is purity, a gift so precious merely touching it would nauseate even the Lord of Sin into convulsions," Grandpa pledged. "And I'm going to kill you with it, Beelz."

I had never been aware of any such gift. John owned nothing of actual value that I knew of. I recall doubting him: Did he really have something there in his pocket, or was he bluffing again, spewing another one of his lies?

"Let's see if it's real," said Scratch, "and I'll be done with the boy. Now show it to me!"

John waved a dismissive hand in response as if swooshing a pesky fly.

Flustered by his insolence, the soulless spirit balled his hands into fists and cursed. "You have no God, and you are of depraved character. Your deceitful tongue would twist itself into knots if it ever tasted the truth. Hence I lend no credence to your idle threat!" He thrust a shaky finger at John's chest. "And I say you have nothing there."

"I'll tell you how I am going to end you," said Grandpa. "It's true I am worthless. I amount to almost nothing, and I've never denied it. But I'm not battling you with the power of my sanctity, my moral fiber, or my adherence to honor. We both know I possess none of these."

Scratch gave a sinister hiss. I watched the deviant swine rub his hands together with perverse satisfaction. Snickering, he snubbed, "Tell us something we don't know, you louse."

In a burst, John unveiled a father's pride, responding, "Damn you. I'll tell ya! You see, I've got a devout daughter. She is virtuous and gentle—everything I'm not. How I feel about her could never be expressed by its proper measure." He touched his hand to his breast again. "And here in my pocket is a silly little handkerchief—one she handcrafted special for me as a Christmas gift when she was a child."

My grandfather took a moment to compose himself, as we all watched the riveting scene unfold. "That dismal winter we had nothing, and I mean absolutely nothing. It crushed me to see my baby girl living in conditions so dire. It was all we could do just to make it from day to day." He gazed at the ground, lost in the grief of his own thoughts. "I had nothing to give her for Christmas." The recollection of it clearly devastated John. A deep sorrow showed in every crease that furrowed his face as his voice trembled with the confession. Revisiting the past had him reliving the pain.

Grandpa cocked his head toward Scratch; only now his sights were keenly set on the devil man. "Even in our despair, my daughter was the perfect angel. She realized our troubles. But she never complained—not once."

Standing tall—taller than I'd ever seen him stand before—John spoke. "So, instead of crying, what did she rise to do? That Christmas my loving baby made this handkerchief, fashioned from a threadbare cloth, for me in her Sunday school class. With crayons, she colored a likeness of me on it so that I would always know it was mine. It's the only gift I've ever gotten in my life that has brought me to my knees. And to me, it is blessed. It's the most valued thing I own. Such a humble, innocent girl— she is my strength. And this simple, tattered rag serves as my essence, representing everything that is sacred. She saved me that day." Scratch was visibly ill at ease, and Grandpa kept him on edge by refusing to yield. Boldly, he suggested, "Maybe you'd enjoy kissing it?"

Startled by the proposal, Scratch yelped. "No. I can feel it now! I can feel it from here. You leave that trash in your pocket."

John's assertion became resolute. He reached into his shirt pocket and charged straight toward Scratch in an explosive rage, shouting, "Well, maybe you'd prefer I force you to eat this trash!" This time, it was unmistakably explicit; John wasn't asking any darn fool question about what was to be eaten. His terms were a categorical declaration of things to be, and there wasn't going to be any more dispute about it. Hell, even I understood that. As did Scratch.

In a fright, Scratch retreated—stammered toward the fire and awkwardly tripped, falling dead center into the smoldering coals. I saw no indication of discomfort as he swiftly rolled backward through it. His maneuver generated a powerful swoof of hot air, kicking up a blinding eruption of embers and smoke. Flickering red and yellow sparks rose in abundance while John darted around the fire to catch him on the other side. With his fists ready for combat, Grandpa was aghast to find Beelz had vanished. The insidious phantom had doubtless slithered his way to the wooded umbra and escaped. John yelled into the thick, murky night, "You feel free to come back and finish this anytime you're game! You hear? Anytime you crave a piece of me!"

As I looked on, he positioned himself like an imposing, battle-ready warrior. My head became dizzy with it all. Was any of this actually happening? Did Grandpa truly just fight Beelzebub and win? I wondered. Was Beelz even real? Or was this incubus nothing more than the perception of my enervated state, induced by Grandfather's poisonous liquor?

Now that I was regaining my sanity, I felt sick. My unsettled nerves and the burn of the whiskey had my stomach churning. I wanted desperately to sit down, but in truth, I couldn't quit on my grandfather—not after everything he had done. So, I pulled myself together the best I knew how and silently stood next to him.

At daybreak, it was plain to see that nobody was left in the camp except John and me. The others had found their way out during the night and would probably never

return to that cursed place. I glanced up at Grandpa and asked, "Can I see it?" I didn't need to explain. He knew exactly what I was referring to.

"You mean this?" John pulled a stained handkerchief from his shirt pocket, shook open the rag, and handed it to me. I examined the fabric and found there was no adornment of any kind. Upon closer inspection, I realized it was simply just another one of his plain old hankies that he carried with him every day. Maybe even the same handkerchief he had tossed to me the day I stumbled into him out in the yard and bloodied my nose. Bewildered, I asked, "But where's the one from Mom?"

"Oh, that." Grandfather gave another one of his sly winks. "Sorry, kid, but I kinda made all that stuff up."

I gawked. I couldn't believe my ears. Was the man really so clever and brave that he had faced down ole Scratch with nothing more than his wit?

* * *

It was a long walk home that morning. Both of us were worn to a frazzle, and neither of us was looking forward to the wrath that awaited us. I had fulfilled Grandma's request, bringing back her wayward husband in one piece, but I wasn't sure he would remain so after she was finished with him. I felt good about myself, though. I considered that we had done something momentous. Illusion or not, it was a grand adventure. And to think I had witnessed the most astounding bluff ever played. Trapped into a war, by virtue of fortitude

and guile, Grandpa had proved to be as cunning as the Devil himself. The gamble of a lifetime was shrewdly won purely by his skillful spinning of a yarn, one of tragedy and triumph so moving it had Scratch running for the hills.

I didn't confess it to John right away, but I was a little disappointed he had made up the story of my mother's Christmas gift. I guess I was really hoping his tale was true—maybe not the painful parts, but at least the rest of it. After dinner that night, duly put in his place by Grandma, John retired early. I decided I'd try to talk to him about it. Despite what we had been through together, I knew I wasn't permitted to barge in on him unexpectedly and start a conversation. So, I walked quietly down the hall and saw his bedroom door was ajar. Peering in, I saw John sitting in his chair, leaning forward, his elbows on his knees. He was holding a crayon-colored piece of cloth, and was smiling from ear to ear.

I knew at once that John's story was not mere fabrication. The top drawer in his dresser bureau was resting open, and it didn't take me long to figure out that it was there that he kept my mother's handkerchief secretly tucked away. As usual, there was more to Grandpa than meets the eye. I like to think bringing it out late at night and admiring the gift in private brought him immense peace. It was too precious for him to carry around every day in his pocket, but he did carry the love of my mother every day in his heart. That one small swath of cloth contained enough love to save both our souls.

Since the Devil never truly understood what real love was, Scratch believed the power radiating from John's chest must have been the handkerchief folded in his shirt. Absent of affection, Beelz had only the capacity to comprehend material things you could touch and hold with your hands, and that had proven to be his undoing.

I marveled at how my grandfather had manipulated Scratch's imagination and used the Devil's own doubts and limitations to defeat him—a skill honed when he was incarcerated at the "state college." Using the power of suggestion, similar to how he had duped the infirmary nurse with the make-believe skunk roundup, he had Beelz nourishing his worst fears.

While in prison, often against insurmountable odds, Gramps had learned to tackle difficult situations head-on. Most troubles that came John's way were brought on by his own ill temper and admittedly sometimes by bad luck or boredom. In any case, he had fought with tenacious grit to win, be it by brain or by brawn. To him, taking on Scratch was just another day.

I wanted to leave out a part of this story, but I'm finding that difficult to do. Living in the company of John taught me that not every experience is pleasant—far from it. That's just the way of life, and this became one of those times . . .

A few days after the altercation with Scratch, a friend of John's came to the house. The man's name was Mr. Luther Payne, and truth be told, his reputation as the town drunk preceded him. His outward appearance did

nothing to help his cause, and his involuntary twitches spoke of a man well attuned to his drink.

You could describe Luther as a squalid-looking man with blemished leather skin and decaying brown teeth. If you stood too close when he spoke, his breath would blister your eyes. In the unforgiving light of day, he looked to be a century old. Slouched over a balding head was a weather-beaten fedora that looked as haggard and kicked around as he did. But he had not always held such low standing. The way I heard it told, Mr. Payne once had an adoring wife and young son. He had been a devoted husband, a tender father, and a steadfast provider. But after losing them both to the influenza, he had given up on life itself. Their passing shattered his mind and his body.

On rare occasions, a woeful tragedy or an insufferable experience can damage a person's psyche. This alteration could falsely be perceived as an evolution. But I know it's more of a regression to man's primal origins. In the case of Mr. Payne, the shock and terror of it all caused some kind of rewiring of his brain. He became a seer—a bizarre type of soothsayer who could foresee inauspicious comings and goings. A few believers interpreted his "gift" as a creditable divine guidance. Most others tried to convince themselves it was only an uncanny ability to predict ruinous circumstances. Regardless, no one denied his heightened perception, and if he came to you with a word of caution, you would be a fool to have discounted it.

This, I believe, was why people tended to avoid Luther. He gained a reputation as the bearer of bad news, which angered the very people he was trying to help. But, like it or not, Mr. Payne spoke truth, and often the solemn truth is more than most well-mannered folks can stomach. For this, he spent the rest of his life shunned, spit on, jeered, and even hated. His unusual gift was viewed as more a curse.

I find it hilarious how we smugly proclaim to be a culture of people dead set against bullying and discrimination, but when it comes to people like Mr. Payne, we customarily expect them to step aside or just disappear. I don't understand why no one ever offered to help Luther. Maybe his presence made them feel threatened. Or maybe it's common for certain people to try to elevate their own status by pretending to be better than someone else. Many a self-righteous person scoffed and poked fun at Luther unremittingly for no other purpose than to make himself feel empowered. John quipped that you'd resurrect more hypocrites in a house of worship than a house of whores. I wonder how correct he might have been about that.

Stories abounded about how Luther wandered the streets, crying out in torment for his dead family, blaspheming God at every opportunity. In an effort to ease the pain of grief rending his soul, he ingested poisons that destroyed his body in some of the worst ways imaginable. Eventually, his innards became ulcerated as a cancer spread through him. What remained of his nerves produced erratic muscle seizures that were paralyzing at times.

That particular day, however, we found Mr. Payne standing quietly in the front yard waiting to be noticed. Too ashamed to step up on the porch and knock and too timid to call out and let us know he was there, he could have been there for hours until John eventually saw him and invited Luther in to take a load off his feet. Mr. Payne refused and pleaded for John to "please" come out. Grandpa joined him, and the two men shook hands. I sought to remain unseen behind the screen door and eavesdropped. As I watched from within the house, I was roughly able to hear what they said.

"What brings you here, friend?" asked John.

"I come to warn you, John," replied Luther. "There's something you got to know." He was shaking now, and it seemed to be more than his typical tremors. Our frail oracle appeared to be seized by terror.

John was almost at a loss for words. "You came to warn me about what?" Mr. Payne was shaking so much at this point, I'm not sure he even heard Grandfather's query. To make the man feel more at ease, John again invited, "Luther, have a seat with me on the stoop, and let's talk over a cold lemonade."

By his rigid stance, I could tell there was no way Mr. Payne was setting foot on our porch. And now it seemed as if he was apprehensive about being here at all. "I come here to tell you, John. Then I'm leaving and I'll not speak of it again."

"Say your piece, Luther. Spit it out," said John plainly yet with respect.

"I was there the other night—the night you had that standoff with . . . him." I saw John's posture stiffen. "There's something you need to know—something you didn't see."

"What would that be?" John pressed, this time more insistent.

"Everybody was drinking your product," said Luther. "Hell, John, you even gave me some yourself—free of charge." He would never intentionally criticize John's act of kindness but continued, "Your drink is hard. I'm not sure what I saw or what was real. But more than one of us watched that bastard fall into the fire. And I know you rushed around to the other side to catch him." By now, he had a deranged look on his face and he could not quell the shakes. I watched as his body went into uncontrolled spasms.

"Yeah, that slippery devil rolled off into the darkness so damned fast, I couldn't catch him," John said.

"No, he didn't. He never came out of the fire!"

I gawked, eagerly anticipating Grandfather's response. He responded to this implausible news with uncharacteristic stoicism, but still I cowered on the floor.

"It's true, John," he said. "We all saw you facing him that night and cursing him. But he was behind you,

still in the fire, down in the embers, hiding beneath the smoke." Luther suddenly doubled over, grabbing at his gut. Clearly something was gravely wrong with him. Even from inside the doorway, I could hear a suppressed groan escape his mouth.

"You need a drink of shine, Luther?" Question or declaration—it didn't matter. Mr. Payne didn't acknowledge him.

"His hand . . ." Luther said, wheezing. "His hand reached out of the burning coals. He was reaching to pull you into those smoldering flames, reaching for your leg. I believe the fire gave him strength. And the flames would have burned anything you had folded in your pocket."

His voice wavering, Luther carried on. "You weren't so clever. He tricked you into coming close—nearer to the fire. But when the boy joined you and stood at your side, the Fiend ceased his ambush and slowly pulled his arm back into the ashes. Rarely is that evil one daunted, but he wasn't prepared for the two of you— together, as family."

Luther paused and took a badly needed breath that rattled with a sick, asthmatic rasp. "I'm not the only one who saw it; others say the same thing, but I can't recollect all the details. We were drinking your brew," he reminded once more. "Real or not, word of it spread quick to the rest who were there. Soon, all and sundry set heels into gear and bugged out fast. That's how it come to be that by morning, everyone was gone."

Panting like a wormy cur, Mr. Payne concluded, "He's coming back for murder, John. I see it! He abhors the very thought of you." Desperate to get the words out, he gasped through coughs, "And I know he's going to be enraged because I told you—he'll be looking to settle up with me about that too. But you're my friend, and you've always been square with me. I felt I owed you this much. You deserved to be told."

When he turned to leave, Luther's stride revealed a crippling hobble. Over a drooped shoulder, he warned, "That wicked soul wants you to think he is gone. Up from behind—that's how he will come at you. Heed my advice

and be wary." His gaze reached beyond John when he spoke those last words, seeming to bore into me, though I remained well out of sight. Scared as a mouse in a barn full of cats, I crouched even lower.

John watched hopelessly as Mr. Payne left. He had been a good friend to Grandpa. Sadly, two days later, in the rear alley of the Five and Dime, he was found lying dead in the trash. Some say they smelled a stench of burnt sulfur about him. I presume it's conceivable that filthy dead people, rotted inside and out, might emit such an odor. There was no funeral. It's reputed a hole was dug somewhere and they simply threw him in it. As it normally was with my grandfather, this became something else we never spoke of. That's how he dealt with things.

* * *

My grandfather has long since passed away, but I still feel his presence everywhere. This inadequate attempt to reveal a few short chapters of his life may not be the gospel truth, but it is the way I choose to recall it. I learned to love him despite his flaws, and I miss him dearly. Now and again I fantasize that he is nearby, swaying my judgment, guiding me through troubled waters whenever the need arises, just as he always did. His staunch support and unconventional ideology have left a profound impression upon my self-concept and how I view the plight of the impoverished. Be that as it may, I'm sure he'd climb out of his grave and get me if he knew I told on him like this. Six feet of dirt isn't deep enough to keep our John down once he gets riled. The

Cottonmouth started off mean, and the bane of white lightning kept him that way. I wonder where he is right now, heaven or hell. I can't imagine either place taking him voluntarily.

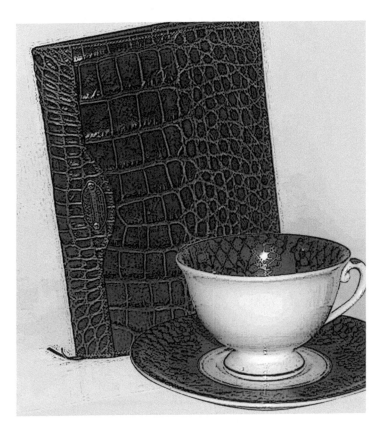

CHAPTER FIVE:
THE FIGHT

Mick Lee hears a gentle knock on the library door. The delicate rapping interrupts his concentration, jogging his memory that there's a more pressing situation yet to be attended to this evening. He looks up at the clock on the mantelpiece, sees the time, and grudgingly relents to the inevitable. The fountain pen is capped and his journal closed. "I suppose that will be all the writing for today," he whispers to himself, then calls out, "Come in, Susie. You're not interrupting. I'm not busy."

"I'm sorry to bother you, sir, but you asked me earlier to remind you of this evening's appointment . . . to be sure you weren't late," Susie says upon entering.

"Yes, that's fine, dear. I do remember," he says. "I am running a mite behind, so I guess I shouldn't delay any longer. I've absolutely got to be on my way."

Susie walks to a coatrack and retrieves Mick's suit jacket from its hook. He stands, flashes an appreciative smile, and turns his back as she helps him slip it on. Her eyes fall onto the journal lying on the desk, next to the unfinished cup of tea from the day before. The journal clearly rouses Susie's interest. "I see you've been writing again—about your grandfather?" Not waiting for his reply, she gives Mick a brisk tap on the back of his shoulder. He turns to face her, pretending to be annoyed by all the attention and huffs as she fusses over his appearance. "Stop stammering," Susie orders with a pleasant titter in her voice as she fixes his tie and buttons his vest.

"Yes," Mick stutters with a certain shyness in answer to her question. "Writing about him— and about me, too, I guess. I just wanted to scribble down a few thoughts to pass the time—nothing more to it than that."

Gently, she prods, "The truth is, you usually write when you're anxious or distraught about something. And these past few days, you've been a bit on edge. Is everything okay?"

Susie doesn't know what his twilight rendezvous has in store, and he plans to keep it that way. Whatever the outcome, this fight is his. He intentionally changes the subject and puts on his best full-face grin. Teasingly, he proclaims, "I declare, you've gotten to know me fairly well, haven't you, ma'am? When are you going to marry me, girl?"

"Hmm . . . would tomorrow be too soon? I'm available. Or maybe the next day? I need to buy a dress first—and there are those pesky invitations to be sent to all our friends and family." She willingly plays along. "Oh, a cake! Let's have a very big cake, at least four tiers. And champagne—the finest."

With a blush lighting her face, she gives the most charming giggle. "Reverend, you better behave, or I might take you seriously one day and keep you all for myself." She then chicly practices saying her name, taking his surname as her own. "Susie Lee? Mrs. Lee?" She pauses to consider. "No, those don't sound fitting—not enough syllables. Let's see—something a tad more formal, something on the lines of 'Mrs. Susie Lee, the good reverend's wife.' Yes, I think that one favors me best, don't you?"

Mick is moved by Susie's performance, as if she were actually announcing her eligibility to an appropriate suitor. Not wishing to take improper advantage of her innocence, Mick chokes on his words as he suggests, "Darling, one of these days I will preside over your wedding. You'll soon find the right young man to complement you. I promise you that." He goes on to say, "And besides, why would someone as beautiful as you want to waste her youth pandering to an older man such as me? You have your entire life ahead of you."

Has she just heard him correctly? The difference in their ages has him so insecure that he denies any potential of a relationship. Susie's posture, now erect with fists on hips, suggests to Mick that he should have

simply admired her dress after expressing his gratitude for her humor and not said anything further. Before Susie is able to protest, he again conveniently notices the clock. "Dear lord, look at the time—sorry to rush, Susie, but I have to go. And be sure to lock up when I leave. I may be gone awhile, so don't bother to wait up."

"Yes, Reverend Mick," she snips and scrunches her nose, making fun of his mother-hen attitude. Susie's willing to put this discussion on hold, but there's plenty more to be said on the subject, and soon. "You be sure to remember your Mackintosh topcoat. It stopped raining a while ago, but it's damp out. I do not want you catching your death of cold," she warns, then collects the disregarded teacup and saucer off the corner of his desk and bids him a peaceful night.

Alone again in his library, Mick chuckles lightly at the phrase "catching your death." Indeed, it is not the damp that worries him; tonight's contender is adept at delivering a lethal beating no matter the weather. With that in mind, he unlocks the center drawer to the desk and pulls it open to reveal a neatly folded, crayon-colored threadbare rag. He removes it and carefully tucks it under his jacket, inside his left breast pocket— over his heart.

Reaching into his trouser pocket, Mick then pulls out the AA sobriety chip, holding it flat in his palm, taking a second or two to regard what it represents. "I don't expect I'll be needing this trophy tonight," he says, and he gives it a casual toss. The medallion lands on top of the hard cover of his journal, bouncing several times.

The sound of it resounds in his mind—tap tap tap tap tap—as he envisions the Devil's cloven hoofs tap dancing on his manuscript.

After offering a silent prayer, he grabs a box of matches from the mantel and exits the library. On his way out of the house, the reverend picks up the thick Sunday edition newspaper off the console table in the foyer and slips it under his arm. With Susie out of sight, he opts to do without his Mackintosh, leaving

it draped over the banister by the front door where she left it for him.

Mick is serene as he walks through his neighborhood, taking a good look around at the world he has become so much a part of. The temperature has dropped considerably from the day before, and the air is crisp. Few people remain out on the streets. He feels vulnerable—as he should. Nobody's riding shotgun for him on this one. He is as alone as he's ever been. But, to his credit, Mick is prepared. And, he figures, his chances are fair.

Before long, he finds himself walking beside an old, familiar road leading to the outer reaches of town—down by the bordering tree line where the train trestle crosses. There, beneath a pool of mud, he discerns the scattered remains of a long-forsaken hobo encampment, as dark and menacing as the first day he saw it some thirty years ago. As he approaches, he shouts, "I know you are here, you bastard. I know you're here, and I've come for you!"

Standing solitary in the friendless mire, he receives no reply to his threat. "All right, then," he says. "Let's do this your way." He gathers brushwood—enough to make a fire. Even though the sticks are damp, by piling them high and using his newspaper as kindling, he eventually gets them to burn. And when the fire is sizzling, he throws on another bundle of wood for good measure. He then stands and waits—facing the darkness just as he once did with his grandfather.

It's not long before the fire is reduced to nothing more than a dim, smoldering heap. Glowing embers seethe at its center. Impatient for any type of challenge, Mick daringly casts a boisterous taunt into the pitch-black recesses. "Well, I guess it's time, ole Scratch. Let's get this party started. You ready for me, Beelz?"

He pulls an antique silver whiskey flask from his hip, unscrews the cap, holds it up high, and offers a spiteful toast. "Here's to seeing you again so that I can kick your pointed tail butt! Come out, come out, wherever you are." Mick then throws back a mouthful of Grandfather John's homemade shine.

Mick has not tasted his grandfather's poison since that fateful night decades ago—and he's escaped the influences of all alcoholic beverages for the last sixteen years. The drink instantly steals his breath, igniting his guts. No matter how nobly he resists, he can't keep his balance. Various muscles tremor while the rest of his body grows numb. A brief onslaught of vertigo brings him to his knees. Overwhelmed, Mick thinks he sees the muddy hollow slowly transforming into a ravenous pool of quicksand—craving to devour him whole—a sensation that momentarily all but unhinges his sanity.

Abaft the trestle pylons, a wicked, sinister figure lies in wait. The Beast suppresses a heinous laugh so as to not reveal his presence. He stealthily prowls closer for a better look but stays vigilant to not spoil his impending ambush. At the sight of the great reverend Mick Lee on his knees, wallowing like a pig, the concealed fiend becomes euphoric. A gob of tobacco spit spews out of Beelzebub's mouth and seeps down his bristled chin. His gangling fingers rattle as he rubs his hands together in jubilation. Although difficult to contain his exhilaration, in an inaudible voice, the Devil sneers, "I see you came to play, boy."

"I can beat this," Mick says as he struggles to regain his senses. Beset by nausea from a head reeling in every direction and a blistering stomach, he manages thoughts as best he can, pulling himself back to his feet and locking both knees to keep his body upright. Jaws clenched, he grunts, "I am stronger than this!" The liquor is impiously potent, but his determination is uncompromising. Mick knew well he would be tested

tonight, and there's no way he is going to quit this fight before it begins.

Unimpressed by Mick's resilience, Beelzebub is confident his exertion is merely a feeble act of opposition and moves even closer to waylay him from behind. The rogue knows he can quell the reverend if he acts fast—attacking now while Mick is still physically overcome by the rancid whiskey.

Cloaked in shadow, Beelz initiates his assault. He casts no more than a vague silhouette created by the dull glow of the brushwood fire. Mick stands alert as the approaching assassin creeps even nearer. Beelz slumps to his haunches and effortlessly glides across the slimy mud, similar to the way a marauding serpent navigates a shallow bog while hunting prey. Upon the confines of the sweltering coals, he crawls underneath the embers. Once there, he maneuvers straight toward his adversary. Yellow and red cinders soar high above the fire, spiraling as he tunnels through.

"Mick? Is that you over there?" A familiar female voice echoes from somewhere in the darkness. Stunned, Mick thinks the whiskey may be playing tricks with his imagination. The unexpected voice also startles Beelz, who promptly ceases all movement to avoid detection.

On impulse, Mick inquires aloud, "Susie? Is that you, dear? I'm here by the fire." She doesn't answer right away, sending Mick into a panic. "Where are you?"

Someone cautiously steps out from the darkness and wades through the mud, and he sees it is her—his dear Susie. Somehow she has found him. Over her right forearm is his silly Mac. With a trembling smile, she hands it to him and says in the sweetest voice he has ever heard, "You left this in the foyer. I was worried."

Tipsy from the drink, he takes his coat and tosses it over one shoulder. Even this slight motion upsets his footing, and he wobbles breadthways to steady himself. An electrifying surge of adrenaline races down his spine, further playing havoc with his brain. Woozy-headed and desperate for any logical explanation for her presence, he asks, "But how in the world did you find me? How is it that you are here?" He doubts what is real and tries to make sense of it all. "But how is it possible that you are . . ."

Susie puts both her hands up in front of him, and with a "stop" gesture, she calmly interrupts. "After you left this evening, I decided to finish cleaning the house and started putting things away before going to bed," she explains. "I came across your topcoat lying on the stair railing and knew you were just being your stubborn self again, intentionally leaving it. By then, you were long gone, but for some inexplicable reason, I grabbed the darned thing anyway and stood out on the porch, wondering if I could somehow find you. That's when I happened to see two men passing by. One of them asked if I was looking for the reverend, and I said that I was. He mentioned that they had seen you recently, and if I wished, they would gladly bring me to where you were. So, without another thought, I put on my jacket and joined them."

"No, Susie," Mick scolds, unable to believe how naive she has been. "How could you trust two complete strangers, and in the middle of the night? Who knows what could have happened to you!"

"Hush, Mick; I know what you mean," Susie replies. "But they weren't strangers. I'm certain I have seen them both before. I don't remember from where, exactly, but I could just sense that they were good, kind men—in the same way that you see the good in people."

"Well, where are they now?" Mick asks. "Your companions seem to have abandoned you."

"Yes, they were with me almost all the way," she says. "But when we arrived at the turnoff to the trestle, they told me they had urgent business farther down the road, but that I would find you here. After that, they were gone so suddenly I didn't even have time to thank them properly. It's almost like they disappeared. But their directions to find you were very easy to follow, so here I am." Bewildered, she affirms, "The entire incident has been . . . enchanting. And to be perfectly honest, it wouldn't take much to persuade me that this has all just been a daydream—as if I might somehow be spellbound. But when I pinch myself," she says, wincing as she does just that, "I can feel it. So this must be real."

Beelz has heard enough of this tiring chitchat. Nothing about this prattling twit puts him at risk. The butcher is going to have his way with the reverend, and no one can deny him this satisfaction. In fact, her presence makes his appetite all the more ravenous, as now his plan involves not only smiting the reverend, but also reveling

in his dear companion Susie's suffering as she watches the diabolical deed. Making his move, inch by inch Beelz slithers out from the pile of soot to pull Mick into the fire by his legs. The thought of listening to the holy man scream in horrifying agony is a temptation impossible to resist, but now he wants the bitch to hear it just as badly. "Using tooth and jaw," he muses, "I'll chew the flesh from this Good Samaritan's body and relish the tang of his seared sinews." In closure, he gloats, "She's welcome to have what is left of his cadaver once I'm done munching on his divine bones." The hand of the Devil at last touches the back of Mick's shoe. A crooked thumb firmly clamps his heel while four fungus-blighted tentacles clasp the sole. Ole Scratch is hell-bent to kill.

CHAPTER SIX:
GOING HOME

Mick detects something soft envelop his hand. Alone together in this godforsaken swamp in the middle of nowhere, away from the house and the rest of the civilized world, Susie considers it time to finally stop wavering and by hook or by crook speak her piece. Taking his hand she rallies the courage to say what has been gnawing at her for months. Susie gives his fingers a good, firm squeeze and demands Mick's full attention. "Mick Lee, now please listen to me. At late, I've done everything I can think of to make it obvious how I feel about you. And before you interrupt and say you're too old for me, hear me out. I've never met a finer man, and it's not likely one is ever going to come along—at least not one I'm looking for." She relaxes her grip on his hand and gently caresses his fingers. "I love you, Mick. I need you in my life. It's been very hard not saying anything sooner—and excuse me for coming on this bold—but I just have to express myself openly. It's gotten to the point where it wouldn't be right if I didn't." She pauses to swallow hard, takes a deep breath and concludes,

"I sense you feel the same way, but if by some chance you don't, I have to know. And I have to know now, Mick. So, please simply tell me where I stand with you."

Without hesitation, Mick takes Susie in his arms and kisses her. This long, passionate, perfect kiss is the purest thing ever to pass his lips. Though he is uncertain whether it is her charm or the whiskey that has led to this impulsive show of affection, it really doesn't matter. Mick knows he loved her well before this. Right here, right now, he never wants to let her go.

Amazed at this unexpected twist, Mick holds his girl adoringly and strokes her hair. He thinks to himself how wonderful it truly is to be with someone so spectacular. Mick gives her a childish grin, and they both laugh happily—like young school kids unsure what to do next.

With Mick's kiss, Susie's worries have all been put to rest. But her intuition is strong: Something more is troubling him than her unexpected arrival to this foreboding place. Gently, she asks, "What are you doing here, Mick? Why aren't you with your appointment? Weren't you meeting with someone tonight?"

"Well, Susie," Mick says, "this was supposed to be my appointment. But it looks as though it's going to be a no-show for my guest." Mick takes just a moment to stare back into the darkness. "I'm guessing he probably never did exist—except maybe of my own creation. And now I admit that I couldn't tell you why I was so driven to come back here. Just had to finally prove to myself . . ."

Gazing back at Susie, he continues, "It's shocking how toxins from a corn mash can make you see all kinds of bizarre things. Seems that just a few sips of shine from a backwoods distillery can warp a man's rationality such that he conjures his inner demons—palpable enough to render him harm." He smiles wistfully. "But all it takes to show him the truth is the heart of a good woman."

Susie smiles back and adds, "Amen, reverend. That's what true love is all about, isn't it?"

"Yes, my darling, it is. That's the way it will always be. By no means shall I ever grant you cause to imagine differently. I pledge you that."

Susie gives Mick a playful wink and asks, "Would you mind if we went home? We can talk more of it there—all night in front of the fireplace if you prefer. It's freezing out here. And, frankly, my feet are soaked."

"Yes, let's go home," Mick says. "A comfortable fire and a hot cup of tea sound absolutely wonderful. I can't think of anything I'd rather do, or anyone I'd rather be with."

He knows that, once the final effects of the brew have worn off, some kind of explanation for the evening will be warranted. "I have a few stories to share that will better clarify this evening's mystery. But honestly, I'm still sifting through the details for myself. I'll start by telling what I know is true and then try to take it from there." Mick pats his hand lightly on his left breast

pocket. "I also have a small, tattered rag to show you. It was a gift from my mother to my grandfather. But I'm afraid you'll have to bear my step a little," he says, stumbling slightly. "I did have a swig of my grandfather's private recipe, and it seems to disagree with my equilibrium."

As he holds her guiding hand in his, Susie tells him, "I'll keep you steady from here on, reverend. Don't you worry about that. And I do look forward to hearing your stories—every single one of them."

From the perplexed expression on Mick's face, Susie wonders whether he is trying to remember something important. "Is there more troubling you Mick?" she inquires.

"There is something I need to know. It's been on the back of my mind the entire night, and I just can't shake it."

"What is that?" Susie asks with all interest.

"Remind me . . . was 'Mrs. Susie Lee, the good reverend's wife' the name you find most becoming, or am I mistaken?" Tears fill her eyes as Mick wraps her in his warm Mackintosh. Another kiss is shared, and together the two disappear into the night, arm in arm, forever as one.

* * *

Out of sight, in the darkness atop the train trestle, are two men in attendance—guardian angels of sorts—the same companions who, a short time earlier, safely escorted Susie to Mick's side. Even though neither man is a stranger to Mick Lee, they deliberately remained unobserved to those below them. These specters knew of the impending danger and stayed in wait to furnish protection if required.

"Your grandson is going to be fine now, John. No more worries about that," says one of the men, breaching the silence between them. "As a matter of fact, I believe they are both going to be so much more than fine."

With a quick glance at his cohort, John nods and remarks, "They do look happy together, don't they, Luther?" He beams with pride. "My grandson—he's one hell of a man." Luther, his body eternally free of all illness and odd twitches, respectfully tips his hat. "So were you, John. So were you."

John asks, "Tell me, Luther, what happened to Beelz? Where'd that bastard go? Last I saw he was hiding in the fire, ready to jump Mick from behind. When Beelz reached out and grabbed his foot, I was going to rush down there and break that murderous demon in two . . . until you stopped me." Puzzled, John inquires, "Why'd ya do that, Luther? Why did you interfere? You know something I don't?"

Luther cocks his head toward the scene below and explains. "Take a look at the base of the brushwood

fire, down in the fusty mud. You can see the footprints of Mick and Susie—where they stood and where they kissed. But if you look closely you'll also see the remains of the evil one's arm, malformed into cold, gray ash precisely where it grabbed the good reverend's foot."

"How's that possible?" asks John. "It's been my experience devils don't normally up and turn into ash."

"Allow me to make plain something you already know, John," Luther says. "Love is the one thing that is of heaven as well as this earth. That's why the Devil can never reign over it, and love will eradicate his soulless carcass every time he wages battle against it. It was their true love for each other that destroyed him. Even the Beast is no match for the affection of Susie's touch, and when they both placed their hands on Mick, her heart inadvertently disintegrated Beelz's very being. And all that remains on the ground is an unrecognizable heap of dust."

"I'm nobody's fool, Luther," John said, shaking his head. "I know well enough his accursed spirit still exist somewhere. Will Beelz ever find his way back here—from wherever he is now?"

"Definitely not any time so soon it should trouble you," Luther replies. "That burden is behind us. I'm expecting smooth sailing from here on for Mick and Susie. Their future is looking as grand as a fresh jar of shine glistening in the moonlight. But seriously, John," Luther persists, "I've got something that must be said, and I want you to listen carefully."

"We've known each other for quite a spell, Luther." John bows his head in regard. "I'm probably already one step ahead of you on this. Go ahead and speak your piece. I'll take no offense by it."

"All right, John. I'll start by stating the obvious. Susie is a caring but strong woman. She clearly possesses many of your better qualities. When need be, she'll see Mick through the bad as well as the good."

"She does have gumption," John affirms.

Luther takes John by the sleeve. "And with that I'm serving you notice. As of this moment, you are officially relieved of duty, sir. Mick doesn't need us looking after him any longer. Susie's got it from here. It's her job now." Before his judgment can be questioned, Luther continues, "That's the way it has to be. From here on out, Mick shall appreciate safe haven under her aegis. You've paid your dues."

"Yeah, I'm good with that. All this excitement is wearing hard on me." John shakes his head, trying to clear it, and remarks, "I can't remember ever feeling this tuckered out."

Luther puts forward a steady hand and offers a welcomed invitation. "Let me help fetch you home, John. I know the way." Before they disappear into the night, they enjoy a last look around at what used to be their old stomping grounds.

"You're coming home, too, aren't you, Luther?"

"No, I still have work to do here, but I'll see you to old Saint Peter's gate. There you'll be replenished." He then pledges, "And I will peek in on the kids once in a while for you—just to put your soul at rest."

"You're a true friend, Luther." Weary-headed and dog-tired, John notes an observation he made earlier. "Did you see the way Susie winked at my grandson? That girl winks like I do. She's up to something. My word, that boy has gotten himself a good one there."

John pauses, his thoughts taking a different turn as he recalls the life he led—all the selfish decisions, the childish pranks, and, of course, the time he spent incarcerated at the state college. "You really think they'll let me in, Luther? On the level, I'm not real convinced."

"All has been forgiven, John. Trust me on this one— your name is in the Book. I suppose it probably isn't written in gold at the top of a page, but nevertheless, it's there," assures Luther. "They'll be expecting you."

With every step taken, their mortal forms fade away bit by bit until both men become fully transparent. John's voice continues to chime until it is but a whisper, resounding on the night's breeze. "I hope those darn Purser brothers aren't going to be anywhere we're going. And if I see anything that even slightly resembles what might be their sister, I'm turning around and going straight to hell. Mark my words, Luther. I swear I will turn around."

THE END

MOSES GETS THE BOOT

A sizzling fastball smacked into the catcher's mitt. "Strike one!" screamed the umpire. Unsettled by the pitcher's accuracy and speed, Number 23 stepped out of the batter's box to compose himself. He didn't want to mess this one up; it was the twelve-and-under league semi-finals and the game was on the line. The batter bent over and grabbed a fistful of dirt. Stalling for a moment's time, he rubbed it thoroughly between his palms. The catcher tossed the ball back to the mound before the last of the soil fell from his hands.

After a warm-up swing the batter returned to the plate. He straightened his helmet and raked his cleats in the pulverized silt, forming an ankle-high cloud of dust. He then took a stance, raised his bat, and waited. The pitcher, hiding the ball behind his glove, received a signal from the catcher. One finger down. A curveball. The pitcher nodded.

The umpire squatted behind the catcher to align his view. To provide a suitable target for the pitcher, the catcher stretched his mitt forward towards home plate. Then the heckling began. "Hey, batter, batter!" the boys on the opposing team chanted. Intense concentration kept any of it from reaching Number 23's brain—he would not be swayed; he was in the zone.

The batter's eyes beamed with anticipation. Holding his bat at the ready, he waited. The pitcher glared at the batter. The batter held his pose. Spit dribbled down the pitcher's chin as he wrapped two fingers over the stitches of the hardball. The chanting reached fever pitch. The pitcher glowered.

"Hurry up and chuck that dang ball, Mick. It's getting late and I'm hungry!" came a demanding plea from the bleachers. It was the boy's grandfather. The chanting stopped and was quickly substituted with snickering from the crowd. The next four pitches walked the batter.

I recall this spectacle in great detail because the boy pitching that day was me. My grandfather's outburst had temporarily cost me my dignity—and the game. And all because of his rumbling stomach. I shouldn't have been caught off-guard by Old Gramps' outburst; he was the curmudgeonly type who just couldn't help himself—especially when my cunning delay tactics were interfering with his dinnertime. Still, to say I was humiliated was an understatement.

This tragedy had no lasting ill impact on my psyche, however. And I can't say that I was ever truly passionate

for the game. At that age many of us boys joined a ball team simply because our friends did. I became the team's pitcher due to my ability to throw straight, and few of the other kids who were there wanted to be front and center during every play. Swinging the bat came easy enough; making contact with the ball proved to be more difficult. Spending a sunny afternoon on the field with my teammates was always fun, but in no way did it compare to an outing with my grandfather. His colorful words of wisdom and crazy antics filled the day. That's why after a few hours of sulking, the incident didn't really bother me much. As I've hinted, baseball is not my first game of choice anyway. I have since learned to value sports that are a tad more adventurous. Personally, I take pleasure in the exhilaration of a chase, the challenge of man against beast, and the heft of a loaded firearm in my hands. Throw in an element of cunning and surprise, you'll find me in Heaven's Paradise.

One such sport I've truly come to love that meets these criteria is coon hunting. I admit it took a minute for my appreciation to fully kick in, but later that year when Grandfather initiated me into the world of hunting the coon, I was hooked. There was a certain romance attached to the idea of venturing out into the night under the glow of the moon, the baying of hounds your only guide. The entire family—including the dog—can partake in this exercise. Boys don't have any physical advantage over girls, and better yet, you sometimes get to shoot something. From the moment the tailgate drops and the dogs are released, you and your canine companions are bonded in complete partnership. In no time at all, a hound's bay will electrify the mood,

announcing its own equivalent to "Play ball!" And while the hunt may last well into the night, it soon becomes apparent this game requires no seventh-inning stretch.

To those unfamiliar with the sport, some of the language used by coon hunting enthusiasts to describe a heady evening's foray might sound a little foreign at first. By applying a measure of common sense, though, you'll soon learn the expressions and acceptable slang used to convey the affair. For instance, "striking a trail" and "trailing" a raccoon happens when the hunters release their dogs at a chosen place to begin the hunt. Without delay and purely by scent detection, the dogs go off in search of a pathway where a raccoon may have passed. Once the hounds discover the route, the next step is for the dogs to ascertain the direction of travel the raccoon was heading—easier said than done, given that the coon's scent goes both ways—coming and going. If the dog opts for the wrong course of travel, he will be leading you away from your quarry instead of toward it. To avoid this from happening it's very helpful to run the young, inexperienced pups amongst tested, reliable hounds. Their mutual instinct of competition and drive will keep playful minds better focused on the hunt.

Another term in the lexicon of the sport of coon hunting is "treeing," used when the dogs have tracked a coon's scent trail to a spot where it has retreated and taken refuge. This can be up a tree, in a hollow log, or any isolated place a coon can hide. A dog that is misleading and habitually declares the raccoon is at the wrong location is typically labeled as a "liar" and cannot be relied upon. Undesirable game, which is anything

other than a raccoon, is considered to be "trash." These expressions colorfully enhance the subsequent story-telling of the coon hunting adventure, and lend credence to the saga as it is being shared.

Anyone wishing to be acknowledged as a bona fide coon hunter, be it as a serious competitor or recreational enthusiast, must master one essential skill: the ability to interpret the individual actions of each hound merely by listening to their bay even while managing an entire pack of dogs. From a great distance, a capable ear should be able to identify which dog is working a trail, which is bumping trash, or which is keeping a coon up a tree.

Occasionally the sport is adulterated by uncouth riffraff who believe another fundamental skill for success includes the fine art of beer drinking, thinking it necessary to attempt to master that talent prior to learning anything else. You can usually recognize these suds suckers by the elaborate yarns they spin and the pitiful-looking cur barking tirelessly in the back of their truck. In certain dubious circles you'll find many a hound awarded a suspiciously astounding eulogy when the beers are opened. Inherently, if you know my grandfather, you have already realized I am talking about him. I love the old man dearly, and don't necessarily consider him riffraff, but he has never been much concerned with being a bona fide, legitimate anything. He regards beer drinking and coon hunting as synonymous. Maybe that's why he refers to it as a "Hunting Party," with colossal emphasis on party.

Gramps is regularly challenged by other inebriated braggarts to prove his extraordinary tall tales of battle and conquests. Obviously, they spew similar lies, just not as well. And after throwing back a few too many, they begin to freely suggest contradictory opinions. At some point, the majority of these oral clashes spiral to where hot tempers rage and accusations fly. Before long, fuming red faces get close enough to butt foreheads as they exchange garbled, inexplicit, lip-spraying obscenities. Publicly questioning a man's garnished rendition of his hunting experience is most generally initiated by those who are mad drunk and looking for a fight. These characters construe this challenge more seriously than if a loudmouth bully had dumped a drink over their girlfriend's head and dared them to do something about it. A fella can't overlook anyone insulting his dog as easily as he can some jerk who soaks his sweetheart with beer. Insolence this grievous necessitates a demand for satisfaction which can only be settled by a duel. Choice of weapons: coon dogs. The ensuing duel: as expected, another Nite Hunt.

A traditional Nite Hunt competition is an organized sporting event in which a team consisting of a well-trained hound dog and its human ally is scored on its performance in trailing and treeing coon. Years of dedication and training are needed to best your opponents. By no means should these respected, supervised hunting events be confused with the objectionable activities associated with my grandfather's unsanctioned contests. Rarely is there ever a decisive winner to any of his canine crusades because every one of the human contestants is a drunken liar and, more often than not, their dogs cannot be trusted either. These

poorly trained mutts often strike on the first scent that tickles their nose, not taking into account if it's a bobcat, possum, deer, or skunk. Even if you are present to witness the affair, you'll still walk away with little more than half the truth.

When a coon has been located, the sportsmen decide if the prey will be harvested. Hunting with my grandfather has taught me that harvesting prey isn't always a simple task, and frequently it's more trouble than it's worth. At least these intoxicated buffoons realize they're not sober enough to carry a loaded gun during these barroom-generated disputes as regards to whose dog reigns supreme. So once the decision has been made, some unfortunate fool must climb the tree and throw the ornery rascal down to the hounds. Casting down coon (also known as "flinging coon") is usually executed by the drunkest bumpkin in the group. This accomplice almost always has a nickname. Some of the more memorable handles that come to mind include the monikers: Stumpy, Two-Fingers, Chew Toy, Fang Bait, and Stupid. Even though his partners get him hammered for free, the job does have its obvious drawbacks. In short, it's not good to be this schmuck.

After the coon has successfully been treed, Grandpa and his pals surmise the trick is not to rush right in. Finish your beer, he says. Give the mongrels a chance to work up their dander. Make them want the coon bad enough to snap at the air and fight for it. When dogs get that ecstatic, they will attack absolutely anything that falls from the tree, be it man or beast. This is my grandfather's favorite part of the hunt. My favorite part is watching Grandfather climb after the raccoon.

Be informed, even with a large army behind you, it's not very clever to do this. But if the imbibed liquid courage and motivation still compel you, never try it by yourself. Somebody needs to keep a spotlight on the coon and watch for it to move. On occasion, a brave soul, scooting out on a limb and inching himself towards his bounty, has glanced up to find the critter coming back his way with an alarming attitude. Believe me, until we sprout wings and learn to fly, letting go of the branch to wrestle a squalling thirty-pound cyclone with teeth is not an option. When you have a pack of bloodthirsty dogs below awaiting the arrival of fresh meat, gravity can be a bitch.

Late December of that year, during the Christmas holiday season, Grandpa and I embarked on my very first coon hunting adventure. Armed with a flashlight and a flask (for Grandpa, of course) we worked his dogs along the river bluffs. He had just bought a huge blue tick named Moses. The hound was publicized for sale in a popular nationwide coon-hunting magazine, and Grandpa purchased the dog—sight unseen—strictly due to the reputation of its pedigree. If you could judge a book by its cover—or an animal by its physique—Moses did appear to have the goods in all the right places. Supposedly, he was a pure-bred from lineage that consistently produces some very impressive Nite Hunt champions. These four-legged athletes are renowned for possessing an aggressive temperament comparable to baseball's notorious Ty Cobb, who was known to turn the ball field into a battlefield, having heart and prowess matching that of the beloved Lou Gehrig, and owning brutally explosive power like the legendary Great

The Notorious Ty Cobb

Bambino, Babe Ruth. But keeping in mind Grandpa's previous dealings with dogs, I, of course, had my doubts.

We set out under the light of a full moon, uncontested by a clear, calm sky. With ease, it naturally lit our way. Not the best conditions for a hunt: Gramps always held that game was much less abundant when the moon was at its brightest. And besides, it felt too cold for coon to be on the ground. Any intelligent animal should have been curled up, nice and warm in its den—or at home lounging in his favorite easy chair by the fireplace with a steaming cup of hot cider and a good book. Obviously, grandfather exercises his own will and wasn't leaving until he saw this behemoth nab a prize coon. Excited as I was, I wasn't so sure, and after traipsing around the

woods with a pack of increasingly agitated hounds and no hint of coon, I was freezing.

It wasn't long before the cold and lack of a trail had quashed any excitement I had left, and I decided that I'd had enough of this dismal evening. Put me on the pitcher's mound with an angry batter and throw all the taunts at me that you want, old man, I thought. Even that would be better than this disappointment. So, I warned Grandpa that, like it or not, I was returning to our truck—and taking the flashlight with me to better find my way. His determination unwavering, he said he would keep hunting alone. As I was leaving, he released the hounds again, fully confident they would eventually strike. "Good luck," I muttered halfheartedly, and abandoned him there, but not before I spied him withdrawing his tarnished flask from the waistband of his dungarees and enjoying several healthy sips of blood-warming distilled refreshment. He sat on a stump and patiently waited, savoring the moment.

As I made my way back to the truck, my conscience gnawed at me. Grandpa's mantra of "No man should ever hunt alone" echoing in my mind. With a sigh, I turned around and decided to follow him from a distance. I wouldn't want anything to happen to the old man—and besides, keeping at a distance meant I wouldn't have to apologize if nothing more were to come of that night's quest.

Just as I felt myself losing all feeling in the tips of my fingers, I finally heard it. Sound travels far at night when the air is still. The dogs were roughly a quarter

mile away, but judging from the speed with which Grandfather replaced his hip flask and jumped up from the stump on which he'd been sitting, I knew they must have had something. Without hesitation, he sprang to his feet and gave chase. Jogging in the dark without a lamp never faltered the elderly man's step. His eyes adjusted quickly to the shadows under the trees as he pursued the pack along a deer trail. For an old man, he was surprisingly agile, and I had a hard time keeping up, even from a distance. The posse circled back my way and was running hot. With noses popping, they forced their prey to seek refuge in an oak. The regal blue tick commanded attention. His bay proclaimed victory to anyone within earshot. My God! Grandpa's finally gotten a righteous dog, I thought. Despite myself, I urged, "Come on, Moses!"

"Get on 'em, boys!" Grandpa shouted with gusto, still moving at the pace of a man half his age.

Grandfather found the mob of canines beneath a large tree. He knew this meant the scoundrel was probably near the top hugging a limb. Problem was, Gramps didn't have the flashlight—I did. Of course I could have revealed myself from my hiding place and offered it to him, but that would have spoiled the fun. Instead, I watched as he scrupulously scanned the upper branches, waiting for the slightest movement—anything that would confirm its presence.

"Now I've got you!" Grandfather growled. For a brief second the moon reflected in the coon's eyes. Its pupils blazed. Though barely able to define its silhouette, even I could see that this was a big one. "Probably a tough old boar, plump and ready for winter," Grandpa muttered gleefully. "Or a fat-bellied sow just right for my cooking pot," he answered himself with obvious satisfaction.

Clearly, nothing was going to deter him from bagging this coon—flashlight or not. Convinced the moon would betray his quarry if it moved, the old man shimmied up the tree. A chill crept up my spine as I watched the hounds leap to chomp and obliterate broken twigs that fell as he climbed to the higher branches. I came closer, wondering whether I should offer help, but then dismissed the thought. This was a matter of pride. Grandpa would want to claim this one for himself. With a gasp, I watched as he reached for a hold, then slipped when a cracked limb gave way under his weight. He was able to secure himself from falling with the debris

by thrusting a frantic bear hug around the oak's trunk. The horde of dogs rioted, abandoning all loyalty. "Steady, you fool," he blurted to himself, "or those mutineers will be fetching your balls next."

The man with unyielding stubbornness paused but a minute before mustering his nerve and continued to stalk the coon. The closer Grandfather got, the better he saw his prize cowering at his approach. Retreating behind a clump of withered leaves, the raccoon must have wedged itself between forks of a branch. With cautious effort, Grandpa scooted out on the limb within inches of the unfortunate wretch. He reached for the varmint and grabbed it at the base of its tail. As if from the lips of God to the ears of Lucifer, Grandpa screamed with damnation, "I cast you down, Coon!"

He actually shouldn't have done that. Just when all was going as planned, I saw that there was a problem. When Grandpa jerked its butt and attempted to fling the creature from its perch, the hefty coon didn't fling and Grandpa was left clutching nothing but a fistful of plucked fur. Utterly clueless as to what had just transpired, he wondered aloud, "Where'd that big bastard go?"

The raccoon had held firm and remained tightly fixed to the branch. On top of that, this one seemed to be plagued with a severe anger management problem and, needless to say, didn't take kindly to such a rude introduction. The deranged devil pounced upon Grandpa's backside and tore deep into the seat of his britches. If Gramps had shrieked any louder, I'm sure

the inhabitants of the nearby cemetery would have woken up and yodeled back.

The sadistic, unforeseen mauling made it next to impossible for Grandpa to stay balanced on the limb, but with all his might he somehow held on. Still screaming soprano from the monster biting at his rear, he bucked like a bee-stung mule and broke free from the fiend's death grip. The coon fell to the next branch down, but it quickly rallied and started back up the tree to do battle with Grandpa for a second time. In an attempt to escape, Grandpa tried to climb even farther out onto the branch. He didn't get far before the Beast from Hell came at him

again. Kicking hysterically at the coon, Gramps shook the limb so hard even the oversized furball had trouble holding on. This put the dogs in a terrible frenzy.

Directly under Grandpa, a mean pack of trouble nipped and yapped anxiously, desperate to devour the first body that hit dirt. Making matters worse, an enraged maniac was sinking its incisors into the left heel of my grandfather's threadbare cowboy boot. The squalling banshee chewed leather and wouldn't let go. Without divine intervention, the coon was destined to dine on toes. Remarkably, Grandpa must have charmed the good graces of some Higher Power, because the cowboy boot pulled loose and slid off his foot. The obese raccoon, still clutching the ejected footwear, instantaneously plunged to the vicious clan below. That's when things got ugly.

With a tremendous bound, Moses surged upward, striving to snatch the exposed assailant in free fall. Gobs of slobber oozed over his lips, creating a web of slime between his open jowls and teeth as he rocketed skyward to intercept the coon. A ferocious snarl avowed the carnivore's intent. Euphoric anticipation of shredding live flesh hideously broadcast in the dog's eyes.

Moses was wholly fixated on killing. But this blind obsession masked an unknown fatal flaw: his apparent near-sightedness. Instead of clenching his canines into the flesh of a coon, he missed the mark, his ascending muzzle getting firmly stuck inside the tube of Gramps' descending boot. And this was not just any boot; concealed within it was a vile, nauseating stench born

of blight and sin—a smell that could bring even a purebred hound to its knees. The rank aroma promptly waged an assault upon the dog's olfactory senses. Moses could not fathom what may have been festering in the bowels of that leather sarcophagus, but he did, in fact, deem it to be pure evil. Poor Moses didn't know what had hit him. When it comes to foul-smelling feet, Grandpa supremely rules.

The panic-stricken dog flailed back to earth. A claustrophobic struggle for breath filled his powerful lungs with a generous snout full of Grandfather-tainted odor-eater foot powder, until the big guy passed out midair. He might have suffocated if the lodged boot hadn't popped off his face, when his body flopped onto the hard, frozen ground. Moses didn't even twitch. Eyes that moments before had burned with cinders of ire now rolled back deep into their sockets and searched for inner tranquility.

All of the other dogs, certain the coon was the cause of this gladiator's downfall, cowered together in their pack. Their frenzied baying turned to pathetic whimpers. Any creature capable of administering such a thorough thrashing so swiftly was incomprehensible. Sensing fear, the coon took quick advantage of the dogs' apprehension and attacked. Their minds boggled and horrified, the hounds bolted back to our vehicle with tails tucked, yelping all the way. Triumphant, the bully unabashedly strutted over to the unconscious blue tick. Then, with a twitch of its backside, the coon pissed on Old Moses and scurried away unchallenged. Adding insult to injury, the Masked Bandit took the procured left boot with him as a memento of his conquest.

Grandpa shelled out a bundle for Moses, expecting a sure winner in return for his money. But sadly, the finest selective breeding doesn't always produce a champ. Regardless of what sire is chosen, the Mighty Casey of the Mudville Nine sometimes really does strike out. When I last saw Moses, Grandpa was chasing him alongside the dirt road where our truck was parked. Plumes of white foot powder billowed from the nostrils of the disorientated hound each time Gramps kicked him in the tail with his remaining boot. Moses flew past me so fast I was practically toppled by the whole hullabaloo. I wouldn't be surprised if he ran all the way to the Gulf of Mexico, miraculously parted the waters, and fled to Cuba seeking asylum in the Caribbean Promised Land before slowing down to gather his wits.

The true whereabouts of Moses will forever be shrouded in mystery. Even now, every time Gramps tells the tale, it has a different ending, depending on which mood takes him—and how much home-made shine he's consumed. My favorite one is this: Determined to make something of himself, for months Moses wandered this land aimlessly—far and near, pondering his fate in fear of what might become of him. Then one mid April night, under the light of the moon, Moses found his way onto a baseball field, just as the crack of the bat sent a flyball deep into the outfield—and right into the jowls of Old Moses. "You're out!" the umpire screeched, as the gathered crowd erupted in cheers. One and all lifted the hound shoulder high and paraded him about. Thereupon, the winning team adopted Moses as their official mascot—taking him on tour to all their games.

It's quite a stretch of the imagination to believe a wayfaring dog could possibly win at baseball—but, all the same, I still like the story well enough to repeat it to anyone who will listen. Whatever the future held for Moses back then, I certainly didn't expect him to attend anymore "Hunting Parties." Rookie or not, how do you make a respectable comeback after a coon pees on your head? It's just not done.

MR. O'LEARY'S COW

Mother had been waiting a lifetime for this moment—for the chance to share her creative genius and earn the kind of honor and respect shared only amongst men. This was her time to shine, her opportunity to exercise her womanly wiles and solve the problem that had been plaguing Dad ever since he determined that he would, no matter what it took, find a way of fitting that muffler onto his beloved Ford pickup truck. Like trying to shove a square peg into a round hole, it seemed there was no solution to Dad's conundrum. Until Mom stepped in. No longer merely the lady of the house, Mom would sweep in and, without breaking a sweat, work her magic, thus forever sealing her status as a tire-iron-wielding, beer-serving goddess. Or so she thought.

My mother was a short, chubby woman with a heart of gold—the type of mom who could almost smother you with her big loving hugs and exuberant smooches. She smelled like homemade buttermilk biscuits dipped in

honey, and could pan-fry the most wonderful chicken. But although her made-from-scratch sugar cookies were hailed as the best in the county, her automotive knowledge was a different story. Truth be told, Momma didn't know the difference between a lug nut and a carburetor.

My father, by contrast, couldn't toast a slice of bread but considered himself nothing less than a first-rate backyard mechanic. Every year he eagerly anticipated the onset of autumn—not for its colorful displays of reds, oranges, and yellows; or for the comforting crackle of a freshly laid fire. Nope. For Dad autumn meant one thing: preparing his vehicles for winter. In all his paternal diligence, he didn't stop with a simple oil change and tune up. He did an entire lube job, sprayed the wheel wells with an undercoat protection, replaced plug wires, changed the radiator fluid, and slapped on a couple coats of wax for good measure. And once he was satisfied the basics were complete, he would then attempt to repair those niggling mechanical faults that had been on the back burner all year.

One such mishap requiring attention was replacing the muffler on his Ford pickup. The muffler had been badly damaged after, according to Dad, a large rock leapt—yes "leapt"—from the pasture as he was checking on the cattle. To be clear: Dad had many virtues, but truth-telling, especially when he was in the wrong, was not one of them. Having accompanied Dad many a time on his daily excursions to tend to his herd, I can attest that it is only by the mercy of God that I am in one piece today. Dad drove that pickup so recklessly, with such careless

abandon, that even the cows, well, cowered in fear when Dad careened onto the field.

His stopgap to the hanging muffler was to truss the exhaust together by wrapping it with baling wire. But when its thunderous rumbling sent the cattle into a full-out stampede, it soon became evident that the battered old farm truck needed more than a temporary mend.

Feeling defeated, Dad nevertheless had to face the facts: he needed to buy a new muffler. No big deal, right? It was for Dad, who took pride in being able to fix anything. So, instead of taking the pickup to our local auto repair shop and leaving it to the experts, Dad opted to order the part from a salvage yard and do the repair himself. Though Mom and I tried to dissuade him, given his propensity to listen half as well as the cat, our efforts were in vain. He assured us he knew what he was doing, and, in the unlikely event that he didn't, he would be a martyr to his motto: "every man should make his own mistakes and deal with them accordingly." Noble as it sounds, this philosophy got Father sued more than once.

The problem began when the new part arrived. I recall finding Dad in the garage, beer in one hand (which, in itself, wasn't unusual), the other hand scratching his head in consternation as he studied the muffler as if it were some rare artifact. Even as I kid, I could tell that there was no way, short of using dynamite and a crowbar, that he was going to get that misshapen muffler on his pickup. The easy solution would have been to return the part and get the correct one, but clearly that would not have been nearly as fun. Instead, Dad greased the exhaust pipe,

pounded it with a mallet, and wiggled and twisted it as though he were wrestling a wild beast. He tried pushing it on with his feet as he hung from the rear bumper. He even tried putting it on backwards. With each successive failed attempt, he'd take a few swigs of Budweiser, shake his head, throw something in frustration, and try again.

Anytime Mother heard another wrench bounce off the wall or a toolbox slide across the floor after being kicked, she'd poke her head cautiously into the garage and announce, "Don't worry honey! I've brought you a fresh brew!" And then, once Dad had settled down with his much-needed refreshment, Mom would offer her assistance, convinced that, given the opportunity, she could unlock the mystery. "It's just like readin' a recipe," she'd say. "As long as you follow the steps, you'll get a delicious pie at the end." Wise words, but Dad never followed a recipe for anything. Nevertheless, after about fourteen cold ones and a thorough lack of new ideas, my father did the unthinkable: he actually asked Mother if she had any thoughts on the matter. Surely the man was either intoxicated or delirious—maybe both.

While Mother watched with rapt attention, Dad walked her around the truck, patiently explaining in great detail every unsuccessful attempt. He seemed very impressed when Mother appeared to understand all of his strategies, nodding her head and grunting at opportune times. His ego sufficiently stroked, he proceeded to give a thirty-minute lecture on the principles of a muffler and the elementary operation of a combustion engine. He figured that was pretty important since my mom had never driven an

automobile before in her life—and he didn't mind
showing off his mechanical knowledge.

At the conclusion of his orientation, Mother clapped
her hands excitedly and announced she had the ideal
solution. By this time Dad must have really been feeling
the effects from St. Louis' King of Beers, because he
didn't even question her. He gibbered like a confused
toddler as Mom led him by the arm and made him get
behind the truck. Then, she squatted Pops down real low
and instructed him to hold the muffler firm in his hands
and grip it tight. Mom aligned it with the exhaust pipe
and, when things appeared to be centered just right, she
ordered Father not to move, under any circumstances.
When he asked her repeatedly what she was doing,
Mother responded cryptically, "Trust me. I have a plan."

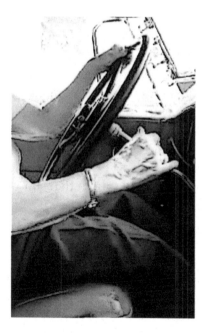

With the passion of a preacher at a Southern Baptist revival, Mom insisted that, come hell or high water, they would overcome this trial and the pickup would be born into a new life. And so, with God on her side, and Dad too inebriated to protest, Mother hopped inside the pickup and fired it up. Dad dutifully stayed exactly where he was told. Then, she shoved the Ford's transmission into reverse and punched the gas.

The expletives that spewed forth from my dad's mouth in the ensuing near-death experience would have made the Devil himself squirm. Lucky for Father, the garage door was partially raised and he darted under it. But the door wasn't high enough for the pickup to clear it. I'm not implying it slowed Mother down any; given this was her first-ever driving experience, she momentarily forgot how to. The top of the cab busted that door into kindling. Dad sprinted across the yard like Olympic gold medalist Jesse Owens as Mom pushed the pedal to the metal, mistaking the accelerator for the brake. She plowed over the clothesline, destroyed the south end of the chicken coop, four-wheeled through their garden, and relocated the birdbath—all while driving in reverse just moments after receiving a verbal driving lesson. When asked after the fact why she hadn't listened to Dad's repeated pleas to "STOP!" Mom could only recall Dad screaming something about the "sun-on-a-beach" somewhere and "mother truckers"; with the muffler firmly fixed to his hand, the old Ford was too loud for her to hear him clearly.

Father predicted that if he jumped on the propane tank and waved his hands like a lunatic, Mother would

definitely have enough common sense to stop. Well, it's clear now that he was not clairvoyant, but apparently he had done some lumberjacking in his day. After Mother rammed the truck into the tank and knocked it off its stand, the darn ol' thing went plummeting down the hill. Watching him, you'd swear Dad was a champion log roller. But even the best lumberjacks fall, though I'm guessing most don't dive face first into a manure pile. The propane tank ended up in the pond, and the gas leaked out of it, poisoning the fish that Dad had stocked it with only a few days previously.

In the end, by process of elimination, Mom did eventually figure out that "the stop pedal," as she called it, "was darn right next to the 'go pedal' the whole time." Would you believe it? The irony of it all is that Dad never did get that muffler to fit. The whole damn thing was an expensive, death-defying waste of time.

To top it all off, when my father tried to file for the damage done to the farm, the insurance company threatened to have him arrested for turning in a false claim. They refused to believe it was possible that a sweet old farmer's wife could do more damage than what Godzilla did to the city of Tokyo. For Dad, there was only one way to fight his case. He decided he would take a trip to the insurance company's home office in Chicago. I firmly suggested that he should not take Mother. With a vulgar proclamation, Dad made it crystal clear that his days of soliciting advice were over. Mother was his secret weapon; he was convinced that those non-believing bureaucrats need only be in Mom's presence to be swayed.

History tells us that many years ago, a large section of the city of Chicago burned to the ground. Legend says the Great Chicago Fire supposedly happened because Mrs. O'Leary's irritable cow kicked over a lantern one evening while it was being milked, and a catastrophic fire ensued. As a result, approximately 300 people died and more than 100,000 residents were left homeless. The city burned for days before the inferno was under control, destroying more than 3 square miles.

With that in mind, Dad ranted on and on to me about Mom and her destructive propensities, as he compared her to that cow. Though he was mumbling incoherently, through his babble I distinguished words to the effect that he was taking Mrs. O'Leary's fat bovine back to Chicago to once again put a fire under some asses. Whether Mom minded being compared to a bovine, I'd never thought to ask; at any rate, given it was her "plan" that got them into this mess in the first place, I don't think she'd dare make a fuss. As with most things, her short-term solution was to pacify dad with fresh baked goods and, of course, beer.

I'm not sure what happened in Illinois—I can only imagine. All I know is when Father returned from the Land of Lincoln, he announced with a smug smile that he had a settlement check for the full amount of the claim. In exchange, Mother had to sign a legal agreement stating she would never go back to the Windy City again. And from what I can gather, Chicago was more than pleased to seal that deal.

With the money provided from the settlement, we had the pond drained, refilled, and restocked with fish. We had a new garage door hung, and a beautiful south addition built onto the chicken coop. The truck's been fixed—this time by bona fide mechanics—with a correctly sized muffler clamped firmly in place. The propane tank, birdbath, and clothesline are back where they belong, but the yield of ripe produce unharvested from the garden was ruined.

Lesser men might have forsaken their wives for such calamity, but in the end, I think that Dad saw it was worth it, and rather than be angry, he was proud of Mom's aptitude at proving him right. With the help of his spouse, a simple farmer in the form of my father demonstrated the measure of his honest character before a multitude of big shots, corporate lawyers, bean counters, and pencil pushers. Attesting to Dad's integrity, Mom had successfully performed her magic, making everyone in attendance a woeful, true believer. And I suppose that made Dad feel like he was the king of the world—or at least husband to one hell of an incredible cow.

WITH SILVER BELLS
AND COCKLE SHELLS – AND LITTLE
KITTENS ALL IN A ROW

(A parody on the Nursery Rhyme: "Mary, Mary, Quite Contrary")

"If you want to grow something, girls, you have to put it in the ground. Why, y'all can make anything flourish if you do it right. It's easy once you try." With childlike zeal, my mother demonstrated by placing one of the bedding plants into a shallow hole Dad had prepared, and evenly patted it upright into place, while my daughters Jade and Ruby eagerly watched the show unfold. Jade, the oldest, was five at the time, and Ruby, three.

To continue her lesson on proper gardening, Mother explained, "You should strive to be earnest maids and water your garden every day because that makes it happy, happy, happy. And if you're blessed, with a touch of luck and a spoonful of magic, your efforts will be rewarded." With a firm nod of her head she further acknowledged, "This is my foolproof prescription for success."

Ever since I can remember, the moment the first spring robin would set foot upon our yard, my mom and dad

would practically trip over themselves to get outside and start planting. For a time even our dear old dog would get involved, although all he tried to sow were more bones. Even now that my siblings and I are grown and have children of our own, Mom and Dad still get a thrill out of playing in the dirt. Fruits, flowers, vegetables, herbs, peppers—whatever gets planted—it makes no difference to them. With one exception: grapes. Mom has never allowed Dad to grow grapes.

My dad would have a thriving vineyard by now if Mom had let him, but she never has. And for good reason: no doubt the harvest would be a temptation too strong to resist, and Dad would squander every spare moment perfecting the fine art of winemaking. Then, of course, he'd certainly want to celebrate by offering a toast—to each cow in the pasture, one bovine at a time. I don't know how hard it is to make decent wine, but I expect it all has the same effect if you drink enough of it, and that would be great for Pops! But even though Mom does her best to keep a tight rein on what gets planted and where, Dad, being the resourceful man that he is, regularly attempts to circumvent her imposed restrictions. Who knows . . . one of his sly attempts might actually get past Mom someday. Dad is nothing if not persistent.

When I was just a lad, Mom tried hard to initiate me into the secret rites of gardening; and now, when I visit with my own children, she is eager to impart her knowledge of the subject on to them. On this particular visit, my daughters became inquisitive as to what she and my father were doing, curiously watching as their grandfather crawled on his knees and repeatedly

scooped out equal amounts of finely tilled soil with a hand spade. My mother followed close behind, dropping in tiny bedding plants while cautiously packing the spindly roots under mounds of dirt. Always the first to encourage the kids to learn new things, Mom attempted to simplify what she was doing, alluding to their favorite nursery rhyme in the hopes that my girls would instantly grasp her meaning and share her passion for planting.

If I'd have been there that morning, I would have offered my mother some free advice: unless you intend to watch their every move for the rest of the day, always be clear in presenting the facts to my kids. Nursery rhymes are good for entertainment but are not intended to impart life skills. Sending kids off unsupervised and less than fully informed could very well result in global destruction. At least, that's how it is with my girls.

My daughters weren't searching for the secrets to life. Most certainly, they were only hoping to have some fun and impress their grandparents with their newfound gardening ability. Dad truly enjoys his time in the garden, so it was only natural that they became interested in what he was doing. Mother could have easily discouraged them by simply expounding on how much work was involved; that would have been enough to terrify any kid back into the house, to the relative safety of an afternoon spent playing with dolls and drawing pictures. Instead, having made the whole process sound as though they were planting some incredibly delightful enchanted sprites in Fairy Tale Land, my mother naturally piqued the girls' curiosity to the point that they wanted a turn at it.

So, Mother gaily provided the girls with their own tray of small tomato plants and told them to go find a spot somewhere by the barn and start a patch there—well away from her precious garden. She affirmed to them soberly, "Nobody but Old Pa digs in this garden, because if they do, they're probably gettin' a whippin'." This prompted a wide-eyed reaction from the girls, because they'd heard tales about Old Pa's spankings. "Now, on your way and leave us be for a spell," she said, waving them away with a flick of her hand.

Jade frowned. Clearly she'd been thinking Mother was going to help them get their garden started. To bolster her granddaughter, Mom smiled and softly added, "Sugar, we've got our share of work to do here, and I'm sure y'all do fine. Go have fun!" Mom promised to check on their progress after a bit, but she apparently lost track of time—while also forgetting how wild the imagination of young children can be.

Sometime later, when Mother was taking a break, she observed Jade struggling to turn on the water spigot, wrestling the faucet with great effort. She watched bemusedly as the handle yielded to Jade's determined hand. Seemingly satisfied with the flow of water, my daughter stretched the garden hose across the gravel driveway toward the back of the barn. Busy as a bee, Jade then came back around and gave the twisted hose a few added tugs, further extending it until Ruby was heard shouting, "Okay! That's enough!"

When Mom asked if they had finished with the plants, she was shocked to hear Jade say that she and Ruby had

agreed that they no longer wanted to grow tomatoes and had thrown the plants in the grass "for the geese to eat." Staring at the garden hose, Mom wondered—with a sinking feeling—what mischief my children had been stirring up. Suddenly a dull pain throbbed deep in her belly as she envisioned a number of predicaments that might have occurred—none of them good. With the slightest quiver in her voice, she inquired, "Child, please enlighten me. If the geese ate your tomato plants, what's the water for?"

"For making happy, happy kitties," Jade replied matter-of-factly.

A cold sweat beaded across Mother's forehead. Near panic-stricken by Jade's response, Mom's breathing quickly became so labored it caused her loose-fitting dental work to slip out of place. With every exaggerated breath, a symphony of high-pitched whistling noises blasted from the gaps between her dislodged teeth. Once Mother was able to steady herself, she asked, "Darlin', where are the kittens?"

With a great big grin, Jade blurted, "Me and Ruby put the kitties in our garden."

Believe it or not, for a portly woman, Mother can hold her own in a foot race. In a dash to get to the bottom of the mystery, she nearly lost her yard slippers as she tracked the water hose across the driveway. And the sight she met defied belief: behind the barn Mom found eight newly born bantam kittens buried up to their necks in dirt, each in their own shallow hole, begging for

God's sweet mercy. Ruby was laughing like a loon and having a ball as she held the water nozzle and sprayed their heads with a cascading shower.

Carefully, Mother rescued each of the pitiful creatures from their muddy graves and took them into the kitchen. One by one, she gently cleaned and dried their wet, filthy fur. Jade, who is usually a polite, affectionate child, became tremendously upset. She thought they had followed the directions as prescribed. And now here was my mother picking the babies out of the ground before they were full grown. Watching her grandma, Jade put her fisted hands on her hips and huffed in anguish, "Old Pa would spank you if you did that to his garden. Heck, I wanna grow more kitties instead of your ol' goose-eaten tomatoes!"

Before Mother's pleasant disposition was further tested, Dad quickly stepped in, trying to educate his granddaughter on where kittens actually came from, describing the process in such vivid, graphic detail that even a veterinarian would squirm in embarrassment. The only things lacking from his elaborate descriptions were flash cards and poster illustrations. But, mercifully, Father's interpretation exceeded the limits of a five-year-old girl's understanding. She'd stopped listening after the first line: "When a daddy kitten mates with a mommy kitten..." It was all too much.

Needless to say, his enlightenment of the birds and the bees scared Jade half to death, and she ran screaming from the room. When I arrived soon after that to retrieve my kids, Mom explained why one of my daughters was sulking and the other, hiding. I wasn't too confident about what to do or say to them, but I was certain somewhere between Mother's merry, animated rendition of life and Father's horror stories there must exist a perfect explanation. I knew I had better think of something fast before Ruby started inquiring about what was wrong with her sis.

In the spirit of the day, I thought I could possibly explain sexual intercourse and the birth of kittens in a style more befitting a young child: by relating an anecdote that was like planting a garden—but not a garden of living, breathing creatures. I found Jade hiding behind the banister of the back porch and persuaded her to take my hand and join me so that I might have a talk with her. We strolled around the yard, as I searched the recesses of my mind for words of wisdom. Doing

my best to set the mood, I tried to imitate the smooth style of Harper Lee's beloved character Atticus Finch. So, I lowered my voice and softly attempted to capture his fatherly persona. I then orated my fundamental perception of the "Seasons of Life" with all the wit of a barnyard poet. My depiction went something like this:

A time to till and sow the earth is the spring season of birth.
Then summer arrives and what has been sown
will mature till it is grown.
With autumn comes a harvest festival, a time to reap and eat.
And lastly, tis a season for winter's eternal sleep.
From birth to death, toil to rest, each of us shall abide.
There is a time to gather stones and a time to cast them aside.
We love, as it is our fate to go forth and procreate;
for we are told to be fruitful and multiply.
This you will better understand why
after hearing your own baby's first cry.
In this precious life, we all have an end —we all have a start;
and be assured, you are forever dear in our Father's heart.

More than a little pleased with my improvised prologue, I was about to continue when, by chance, I glanced down and saw Jade staring up at me like I was the brainless scarecrow from the land of Oz. From her expression, it was plain to see the poor child had absolutely no idea what I was gibbering on about. Her innocence had me feeling so completely befuddled, I half expected to be joined at any minute by a tin man and cowardly lion. All I could do was ogle back at her with an apologetic look stuck on my face. Clearly, my attempt had failed, and her bemused reaction rendered me utterly speechless. With all my self-acclaimed

brilliance, I wasn't explaining the biological conundrum of life any better than my parents had.

Truth be known, I ended up telling her to just forget about it and go help Pops grow some grapes—but not to tell Grandma that I'd told her so. I didn't intend to be contrary about proper child rearing, but, good Lord, I didn't know what else to say. Perhaps imbibing some of the fruit's sweet nectar might have made the words come more easily, in a language a child would understand. For now, I surmised, maybe filling my girls' sweet heads with images of magic garden sprites in a Fairy Tale Land was for the best—with the clear understanding that they are to ask before they attempt to plant anything again. Undeniably, I still need suitable advice on the subject. So, if you've got anything practical to add, please, do share. Aside from pretty maids, or little kittens all in a row, tell me, how does your garden grow?

MOTHER'S TINY DANCER

If I wind the key
prima ballerina will dance for me.
Open the music box—watch her turn;
bitsy danseuse would you please?
White doll's dress, pearls and lace
girl so lovely poised in place.
Twirl to the melody waiting to play
a favored chime in my mother's day.
She loved your song, one so dear,
I remember her singing—oh so clear.
Delight my heart, you do appease.
Yes, pretty girl
I'll turn the key.

FROM THE AUTHOR

I do not profess to be a writer, but I do enjoy telling a good yarn when I can con someone into listening. And I've discovered "storytelling and writing" are two completely different crafts. Who would of thunk it; right? Being a successful author requires talent, and lots of it. Being a storyteller takes nothing more than a couple of cold beers and a fabricated lie to spin. Admittedly, I'm pretty fair at the beer drinking and lying. But when putting pen to paper, trying to get the words exactly right proved to be a god-awful torment.

With saying that, I'm somewhat embarrassed to divulge, I do not have the ability to review my own written stories—all the way through from beginning to end. The truth is I am cursed by a reading disorder. Oh sure, I can fumble through a short paragraph before I lose the printed letters on the page, but what fun is that?

Yeah, that slight handicap is partly the reason why I'm merely a teller of tales and not a writer. I'll not expound on the technicalities of why my reading capability sucks,

but I do confess it would be nice if I could at least read my own stuff, more than just a few sentences at a time. With the help of two very patient editors, I did actually write these stories myself—but they took several years to accomplish.

Now that I've thoroughly revealed my most inconvenient imperfection, hopefully you can appreciate me for who I am and overlook what I am not. First of all I am pleased to announce that I am an ordained minister—a responsibility that I take very seriously. I assist the homeless by feeding them, and when possible, helping them find employment. I am successful at owning and operating my own business. Even though I'm retired from the Department of Corrections, I still enjoy the company of other people. When I was a professional kennel master, I assisted law enforcement agencies in search and rescue operations. On occasion, I am hired to photograph concerts and sporting events. I travel around these United States every year and love visiting our National Parks. Sometimes I eat too much, laugh too loud, and when I can, I sleep too late in the day. Simply put, don't let obstacles keep you from your pursuit of happiness. Get out there and conquer your world with the talents you've been blessed with!